THE FIRST IMMORTAL

THE FIRST
IMMORTAL

JAMES L. HALPERIN

BALLANTINE BOOKS · NEW YORK

A Del Rey® Book
Published by Ballantine Books

Copyright © 1998 by James L. Halperin

All rights reserved under International and Pan-American Copyright Conventions.
Published in the United States by Ballantine Books, a division of Random House, Inc.,
New York, and simultaneously in Canada by
Random House of Canada Limited, Toronto.

http://www.randomhouse.com

CIP: TK

ISBN: 0-345-42092-6

Manufactured in the United States of America

First Edition: January 1998
10 9 8 7 6 5 4 3 2 1

"All that stand between us and eternal life is fear and gullibility: Dread of the unknown forges faith in the unknowable."
—Benjamin Franklin Smith

Two Caveats

(1) *The First Immortal* might well be the most thoroughly researched and scrutinized novel ever written about our potential for biological immortality. I believe this statement, though I make it with some trepidation. For two years I scoured and absorbed virtually every Internet posting on the cryonics news groups, and many others in nanotech, memetics, and futurism. I've devoured hundreds of books and articles relating to cryonics, nanotechnology, the human brain, identity and consciousness, longevity, and biotechnology. Such a vast quantity of information may have randomized my memory. I say that with tongue in cheek, of course, but at the same time I can only hope it isn't true.

I also spoke with numerous experts in diverse related fields, many of whom were kind enough to search this entire manuscript for factual errors. Are there any left? Almost certainly, but in finding them, I hope to have some fun. Therefore, I'm offering a bounty: a scarce Ivy Press first edition of *The Truth Machine* (my first novel) to each reader who is first to point out a scientific or factual error which I subsequently correct. If you notice any, please e-mail me at: jim@heritagecoin.com or write to me c/o Ballantine

Books, 201 East 50th Street, New York, NY 10022. Please include your mailing address.

(2) I'm trying to avoid becoming a "formula writer," so this novel is constructed somewhat differently from *The Truth Machine*. It is more saga-like. The story spans two hundred years, a large portion of which occurs when our hero is "on ice." How he gets there, what happens while he's away, and whether or not he gets out whole, are all part and parcel of the saga.

I would also warn you that some of the concepts explored require both patience and open-mindedness to assimilate.

I still remember the day in 1967 when I learned that Dr. Christiaan Barnard had performed the world's first successful human heart transplant. I found myself fascinated in a macabre sort of way, and refused to believe that such an operation could be "right." After all, who was to say that the recipient of another person's heart was still the same individual? Maybe the donor and donee somehow combined to form a new type of being. Weren't our hearts supposed to be the very core of our souls?

Now that thirty years have passed, heart transplants are normal medical procedure. Few today would regard a person who has received one as some sort of Frankenstein creation. But that took time.

Altering quickly our notion of who we are is never easy, yet I ask readers of *The First Immortal* to undergo two hundred years of self-image reevaluation within a single story. I hope you'll find the effort justified.

—JLH, 3/15/97

P.S. Please visit *The First Immortal* Web site at www.firstimmortal.com and post your comments about this book and the topics and philosophies it examines. I intendt to read every comment, and will probably post some responses.

THE FIRST IMMORTAL

PROLOGUE

June 2, 1988

Echoes tumbled through the ambulance. Squeals, rattles, and torsion-bar sways came at him in waves, magnified and ominous. The attendants standing over him seemed blurry, even extraneous. What mattered was the beeping monitor and all-too-familiar stench of emergency medicine. And every single sensation blended with the mundane smell of the rain-soaked streets beneath him.

Benjamin Franklin Smith, my great-grandfather, knew he was about to die.

The morning had delivered Ben's third heart attack in six years—worse than either of its predecessors. This time his chest felt vise-tight, more constricted than he'd imagined possible. His blood-starved muscles sagged like spent rubber, so weak he could barely feel them twitch, while a cold Novocain-like river prickled his left arm from shoulder blade to fingertips: numb but so heavy.

Oh, Christ! he thought, remembering his first seizure on that flight to

Phoenix in 1982. He should have known better. If he hadn't stayed on the damn airplane, they could've given him treatment; minimized the damage.

Now he was dying. Him, of all people. Ben snorted. Absent his pain and fear, it might have been a laugh. Well, why in hell *not* him? He *was* sixty-three years old.

God, just sixty-three? Is that all I get? Please Jesus, spare me this. Not yet . . .

Two ambulance attendants wheeled Ben through the hospital emergency entrance, past check-in and dozens of less critical cases, sprinting straight for intensive care. All ignored them except one nurse who, recognizing the too-familiar patient, merely gaped. One of the attendants whispered to her, "Looks like myocardial infarction. Probably massive."

Still half conscious, Ben wondered if they realized he could hear them, or if they cared. He wondered whether these professionals tasted the same empathy for him that he had so often experienced with his own dying patients.

He also questioned his rationality.

His preparations over the previous half decade had included an oath to himself that he would betray no ambivalence about the unusual instructions he'd left. This despite understanding that his chances of staving off death remained slight.

And that if he succeeded, he might end up envying the dead.

Before surrendering consciousness, Dr. Benjamin Smith managed to whisper: "Call Toby Fiske." These words would set in motion all his plans— irrevocably changing the nature of his death. Then the rush of unreality gathered speed, and as his awareness faded, his subconscious mind began to play back the most important moments of life, as if by giving these experiences a new orderliness, he might somehow absolve himself of, or at least comprehend, his mistakes.

Images assaulted him of his parents, his children, and the first time he ever made love to his wife Marge. She was just a teenager then. How fiery and resilient she was. *They* were. Then he remembered sitting at her bedside when she was dying. For six weeks he had fed and bathed her, consoled her with stories and recollections, held her hand, and watched helplessly as the cancer consumed her body and mind.

Now would he finally rejoin her?

Ben Smith also knew the world would keep turning without him. So at the end of things, he pleaded to his God, praying that once he was dead, his only son might finally forgive him.

My great-grandfather was an only child. And despite his birth into near-poverty, his genetics and early environment favored him with certain critical advantages. But timing was not among these: He was born in 1925.

His attempt to become immortal is a tale of character, luck, and daring. Benjamin Franklin Smith's story might have befallen any person of his time—that era when death seemed inevitable to every human being on earth. Inevitable, and drawing ever closer.

The Benjamin Smith Family Tree

Gary and Susan Franklin
formerly: Giancarlo & Sophia Francheschi

Charlotte Franklin
b. 1906

Alice Franklin b. 1904
marries
Samuel Walter Smith b. 1902

Sophie Franklin
b. 1901

Benjamin Franklin Smith b. 1925
marries
Margaret Callahan b. 1924

Gary Franklin
Smith b. 1947
marries
Kimber Otani
Chevalier b. 1997

Rebecca Carol
Smith-Crane
b. 1951 marries
George Jacob
Crane b. 1948

Maxine Lee Smith
b. 1952
marries
Robert Miles
Swenson b. 1950

Janette Lois Smith
b. 1954
marries
Noah Lewis Banks
b. 1953

Katherine Franklin
Crane, b. 1978
George Jacob
Crane, Jr. b. 1973
marries
Sondra Deeds
Goad b. 1977

Justin Robert
Swenson b. 1981
marries
Abigail Carol Hall
b. 1983

Sarah Smith Banks
b. 1982
David Smith Banks
b. 1989
Michael Smith
Banks b. 1986
marries
Joanne Helen
Gleason b. 1986

George Jacob
(Trip) Crane, III
b. 2006 marries
Stephanie Van
Winkle b. 2035

Chloe Maya Swenson b. 2021
David Asia Swenson b. 2023
Liza Caroline Swenson b. 2026
Molly Skylar Swenson b. 2030

Erik Cornell Banks b. 2014
Frederick Harmon Banks b. 2018
Robert Goddard Banks b. 2022
Alica Claire Banks b. 2008
marries   marries
Virginia Maria Gonzalez   Caleb Jason Harwell b. 1994
b. 1989

Margaret Callahan
Smith b. 2084

Lysa Banks Gonzalez
b. 2043

Devon Banks Harwell
b. 2060

1

THE FIRST IMMORTAL

January 14, 1925

My great-great-grandmother stared into a spiderweb crack spreading through the dilapidated ceiling paint, its latticed shape taunting her as if she were a fly ensnared in its grip. For several hours she'd been lying on their bed, shivering and convulsing, in that drab and tiny apartment. Now she felt a scream welling in her chest, like a tidal wave drawing mass from the shallows. Alice Smith was only twenty years old, but she knew something was deeply, perhaps mortally, wrong.

"Oh-oh-oo-oo-ooo-e-e-e-ya-a-ah!"

She shut her eyes, trying to focus on something, anything, other than the pain-fueled firestorm raging inside of her. But there was only the tortured stench of her own sweltering flesh. A single tear found its way into the corner of her mouth. It tasted of pain and fear, but she was surprised to discover another flavor within it: hope and a coming of new life.

Her husband, Samuel, entered her consciousness as if to provide an outlet; a cathartic conversion of pain to anger. Like Alice, the man was a second-generation American. He was a grocer by trade, and, also like herself, from Wakefield, Massachusetts. He had always been a hard worker and steadfast in his tenderness. But he was not there! She was in agony, while he was stacking cans of peaches!

Just when, she asked herself, had he judged his work more important than his wife? and soundlessly cursed him with words women of the year 1925 weren't supposed to know.

Why did she need him there, anyway? To share her torment, or to seek the comfort of him? All Alice knew was that right then she hated and loved her husband in equal measure, and if this ordeal was to kill her, she needed to see his face one last time.

To say goodbye.

No! she decided, as if her circumstance had been caused by nothing more than a failure of will. She had to raise and love this child. She would not *allow* herself to die.

Alice's membrane had ruptured twenty-six hours ago, yet she had not given birth. She'd once read that in prolonged labor, omnipresent bacteria threatened to migrate inside, infecting both mother and child. Even the hunched and hoary midwife, though ignorant of the danger in scientific terms, seemed well aware of peril, per se; Alice could sense a fear of disaster in the woman's every gesture.

Where in the hell was Sam?

Even in anguish, Alice understood this rage against her husband was misplaced. It had somehow become a societal expectation that women should bear children with stoic grace. And it was absurd. A keen student of history, she knew that anesthetics had been used for many surgeries since the 1850s, yet had found little acceptance in obstetrics, the pain of childbirth considered by doctors to be a duty women were somehow meant to endure.

Still, it could have been worse; Alice was equally aware that her odds had improved. A hundred years earlier, doctors would often go straight from performing autopsies to delivering babies, seldom even washing their hands. No wonder it had been common back then for men to lose several wives to complications of childbirth. At least now, sterilization was practiced with some modicum of care.

Her nineteen-year-old sister, Charlotte, and the midwife stood at Alice's bedside. The older woman's facial expression evinced kindly resignation, as if to say, *It's all we can do for you, dear,* as she held a wet towel, sponging Alice's forehead. Charlotte Franklin's intelligent eyes and sanguine aspect seemed to magnify the midwife's aura of incompetence.

"Just breathe through it," said the midwife, who'd already told them that the suffering and peril of delivery were "natural," God's punishment for the sins of womankind. "It's in our Lord's hands now," she now added, as if these words held some sort of reassurance.

Alice felt her mind shove aside the hopeless bromide.

"You'll be okay, Alice," Charlotte whispered nervously, gently massaging her sister's shoulders. "You're doing fine."

"Quick now, fetch the boiling water for the gloves," the midwife ordered. "Won't be much longer."

Alice screamed again, and Sam burst into the room. The snowstorm dripped its offerings from his clothes onto the stained wooden floor. He shivered.

Thank God, Alice thought, her rage forgotten. Sam would see their child be born.

"Am I in time?" he asked stupidly.

His question went unanswered. "Head's about through. Now push, girl!" the midwife shouted.

Alice pressed down. Slowly, painstakingly, Charlotte and the midwife managed to extract a perfect baby boy.

Though bleeding heavily, Alice rallied a wan smile of optimism and hope, qualities she intended to convey to her son, assuming she survived.

Charlotte cut the cord. The midwife spanked the infant's bottom. They washed him with warm water. He wailed, but soon rested contentedly in his mother's arms. His father gently stroked his back. The caresses, tentative at first, easily progressed in loving confidence.

"Benjamin Franklin Smith," Sam declared, as if in the ritual of naming, his wife's pain might be banished to memory.

The next few days would be difficult. Having barely survived the ordeal, Alice sustained a dangerous postpartum infection of the uterus and tubes. Her fever would reach 105 degrees, often consigning her to the mad hands of delirium. She'd live through the illness, but not without loss: She would never bear another child.

August 15, 1929

Oh! Ah! The next flash card displayed a tug wearing an impish grin and belching smoke from its only funnel. As Ben saw it, he felt his cheeks puff into a smile. His first impulse was to reach for the drawing; get a good close look at the happy work boat. But doing that would be bad. Might ruin the game.

B-O-A-T, yes, yes, yes! He could see the letters forming in his mind's eye and was delighted. The mental picture of the vessel and the alphabetic characters defining it jumped from his cerebrum into his eyes and mouth.

"Boat! B-O-A-T, boat!"

"Wonderful." Alice grinned. Oh, he's so special, she thought, even knowing that her excitement was exponentially enhanced because this delightful four-year-old was her own. Although they said John Stuart Mill could translate Cicero at this age . . .

She showed him the next card.

"Train," he said, but did not attempt the spelling.

"I'm so proud of you!" she exclaimed, turning the card over. "That's eighteen in a row. And you spelled half of them. Enough for today?"

"Just a few more, Mommy. Please?" Ben loved this time with his mother. Everything he said seemed to please her so.

"As many as you want, sweetheart."

They still occupied the same tiny Wakefield apartment where Ben had been born, but much of the furniture was new. Colorful drapes now hung at their only window. Several Maxfield Parrish prints adorned the walls. Some new floor lamps were there to provide their place a bright, almost cheerful atmosphere. Sam's career had begun to advance; he was now manager of the modest neighborhood grocery.

And like so many of his neighbors, he'd made a little money in the stock market.

It was almost seven P.M. Sam walked through the door, after another fourteen-hour day. He hid it well. Or perhaps seeing the two people he loved most in the world simply energized him; they were still sitting at the table, playing an addition and subtraction game Alice had invented for their boy.

He kissed Alice on her cheek. She returned his kisses on the mouth. Ben dashed to his father and hugged him. "Daddy, I missed you."

"Missed you, too, buddy boy. Wanna go outside and play some ball?"

"Yeah!" Ben said excitedly, and raced in search of his mitt and ball. At his age he could barely throw the softball and had yet to catch it from more than five feet away, but he loved playing with his dad.

"Stock market went up again," Sam said to Alice. "Few more runs like today's and we can move out of here."

"I'm perfectly happy where we are," she said. "Long as I have my men." She kissed Sam again. "Don't you think it's getting awfully high? Can't go up forever."

"*Feels* like it will. All my friends think so, too."

"Sam," Alice said in a voice that implied *I'm just a woman*, yet somehow commanded full attention, "have you ever seen a lightbulb just before it burns out?"

As Ben and Sam left the apartment, Sam shook his head and smiled in bemused amazement. He knew that this discussion with his very prudent wife was far from over, and the outcome inevitable: Tomorrow he would be selling their stocks.

Almost every evening after dinner, Charlotte Franklin would drop by to keep Alice company while Sam updated his inventory register in the kitchen. As usual, little Ben snuggled under his soft bed sheet, listening to their conversation in covert, fascinated silence.

"Mom's just beside herself," Charlotte whispered, "that I'm twenty-three and still not married."

"She told you that?"

"Not in so many words. Just another of her you-never-know-how-things'll-turn-out discourses. She, of course, always figured I'd have a brood by now, and *you'd* be the spinster schoolmarm."

"So did I," Alice laughed, "till I met Sam."

"That's what I told Mom: 'Soon as I find a man like Sam Smith.' Then she starts whimpering a little, y'know how she does it, and suddenly she's talking about that winter ... Lord, it's been ... ten years ... when Sophie fell through the ice. Like maybe I'm s'posed to give her some grandchildren to replace our sister or something ..."

"I'm sure that's not how she meant it. And even if she did, Charlotte, it's a longing, not a wish. They're not the same, you know."

"Maybe, but I shouldn't feel like I'm letting them down, should I? I mean, it's *my* life. And it wasn't my fault about—"

"Not at all," Alice interrupted. "Not the least bit your fault. Goodness, Charlotte, you were thirteen; she was seventeen. How were you supposed to talk her out of anything? I'm just thankful you didn't go skating with her. Might've been both of you they'd had to fish from that pond."

"Maybe if I'd gone—"

"Hush," Alice said, dismissing the notion. "I'll never forget sneaking into our icehouse to look at her the day before the funeral. She looked so ..."

"So alive. I remember."

"Yes, alive," Alice said. "It was as though a lightning bolt could've struck her, and she'd've ..."

"Woke right up and started dancing?"

"Exactly."

Ben's eyes opened wide. He knew more time than usual would pass before sleep enfolded him tonight.

This conversation comprised the last words between his mother and his beloved Aunt Charlotte that Ben would ever hear. The next day, Charlotte felt too weak to come over, and soon Alice would begin spending evenings with her sister at their parent's home. Less than a month later, Charlotte Franklin's malady would be diagnosed as incurable, and six weeks after that she'd be dead from leukemia.

December 4, 1941

Ben Smith looked at the schoolroom clock, saw it was only 1:47 P.M., and smiled. Well, Mom, guess I nailed another one, he thought, as if she were in the room with him.

Although he'd skipped a grade, all his exams had so far been a cinch. It was not so much that knowledge adhered to him, though by and large it did; the fact was that work itself came naturally. When dealing with any task, he stepped wholly into the job. He became the goal. Be it physical labor or a complex algorithm, Ben saw, did, absorbed, and moved on.

So far as he knew, he'd never been taught this methodology. (His mother knew differently.) It was ... well, just an obvious choice; the most efficient path to success. He understood that this approach was rare among his friends. It was as if any sight or sound or flight of fancy could distract them, and for them to return to the immediate task required considerable will, or the guiding hand of another. He understood, yes, but only as an observer. He had no idea how it felt to have such a response.

Ben expected to go to whatever college he chose. From there he would attend medical school and become a doctor specializing in whichever field offered him the greatest potential for achievement. He would make his parents proud.

He scanned the room. His time could be just as well have been spent reading the paperback copy of We the Living stuffed into his hip pocket. But he knew everyone in the room, and Sam and Alice Smith had taught him a self-aware respect for others.

Several weeks earlier Ben's English teacher had told Alice, "You

e, he seems to know exactly
[get exactly what I want, or
e upon hearing the woman's
rised.

a sixth reread just as he'd be-
ld prevent him from drum-
t frame and took a last look
l over the faces, he could tell
d. He sympathized with the
en to them in the real world.
nad stumbled toward a tenu-
ost of his classmates worried
ary. The general expectation
to the Nazis, and their Cana-
dian neighbors would be forced to seek annexation by the U.S., probably
costing America's economy more than it could afford.

But Ben harbored no such fears or consequent xenophobia. He regarded himself as a neo-immigrant, not with embarrassment, but with a
self-assured dignity. His own family's circumstances, though still modest,
had steadily risen over the years, and he trusted that, given time, life would
continue to improve. He dreaded no new addition to the "melting pot,"
begrudged no rival for the American dream. There was plenty for anyone
willing to work for it. Another of Alice's lessons which Ben had been
unaware of being taught.

He left the classroom and hurried through the halls. Overhead hung
newly installed fluorescent lights, a recent innovation, radiating a pale,
stingy luminescence. Several of the tubes announced their impending expi-
ration by casting an annoying flick. Ben absorbed the ambience as metaphor: the new already fading into anachronism.

As he walked toward the street, he lost himself in reflection about his
future; an exciting world, where science would progress at an exponential
rate. In fact it was his optimism that drew him to the field of medicine. He
believed medical researchers would eventually discover cures for smallpox,
polio, cancer, heart disease, diabetes, possibly aging itself. People would live
longer and healthier lives, and in the distant future might not die at all.

How distant? Ben pondered. Maybe in time for his grandchildren, or
even his own generation.

He walked the few blocks separating Wakefield High School from downtown. A tall ladder leaned against Alfred's Men's Store; every pedestrian circled around it, but Ben decided to take his chances. Sometimes delights were found in the smallest defiances.

Several people stared, wondering if the boy had maybe lost his mind. What would he do next? Follow a black cat?

He arrived at the Colonial Spa ice cream parlor, the usual gathering place for his friends.

He smiled as he made his way through the after-school crowd to join his girlfriend, Margaret Callahan, and their mutual best friend, Tobias Fiske. It was odd—"peculiar," was the word most of his friends would employ—in 1941 for a girl to count a male not as her "boyfriend," but as her best friend. Yet Ben found he enjoyed the raised eyebrows Marge and Toby's buddy-relationship occasioned.

As Ben joined them, Marge raised her head, smiling in acknowledgment and welcome. To her, this well-proportioned, fair-haired boy's body personified the spirit it housed. She admired and trusted his ability and dedication, trademarks of her own father's character. This emotional context carried an old-shoe familiarity, and she nestled comfortably within it. But there was more; a newer, more compelling feeling, which deliciously seasoned her response to Ben.

"Hey," he said, taking a seat and joining the now-completed foursome. Marge covered his hand with her own.

Toby's latest girlfriend, number four of the school year by Ben and Marge's count, was a pretty blond classmate named Sally Nowicki. She seemed bright and lively and was clearly sweet on Toby, but Ben knew the courtship had a less than even chance of ringing in the new year. The two were engrossed in a random flow of airy conversation and light, playful petting; a replay of the previous week, except the girl's name had been Lydia Gabrielson. And Denise Vroman a few weeks before that.

Toby Fiske, compact, dark-complexioned, and nimble of mind and body, was a brilliant young man, but as Marge had once observed, "Toby's about as disciplined as a ten-week-old puppy." Because Toby's parents considered him overly susceptible to the influence of others, they were pleased that their son had fallen under Ben Smith's tutelage; it was one of the few things upon which Theodore and Constance Fiske actually agreed.

Ben knew how it felt to be the recipient of subtle feminine overtures; it was always pleasant and flattering, but to him, after the day he met Marge in the spring of 1940, utterly resistible. She was his only and first serious girlfriend.

Marge was a natural beauty; straight brown hair, brown eyes, delicate features, and flawless skin; five feet seven inches tall, with long, perfectly shaped legs and a lean yet curvaceous figure.

Ben lifted her hand and kissed it.

"How'd your exam go?" she asked.

"I was ready for it," he told her. "How was yours?"

"Okay, I think, but I doubt it'll be enough to get into Radcliffe."

"You'll get in," he said, squeezing her hand. "Or Wellesley at least." Marge was probably just being modest, he thought.

Ben hated to think about separate schools. Wellesley was nine miles from Harvard, and that was too far. He looked at her beautiful, serious, intelligent face and knew she was the only girl he would ever love; as Marge knew he was the one with whom she wanted to spend the rest of her life.

Suddenly the image popped into his mind, as it often did, of their most recent evening together, kissing passionately, then touching, first everywhere, but eventually just there. Harder and harder until the urge became irresistible, and finally, ecstatic relief.

In a biblical sense, Ben and Marge had never consummated their love, although recently they had left each other unsatisfied. Their hands knew many secrets.

"Hey, Toby," Ben called across the table, "what time ya comin' over tonight?"

It took his friend a few seconds to extricate himself from Sally and regain his composure. "Tonight? Oh. After dinner I guess. That okay?"

"Sure thing. Should only take a couple of hours, if I can keep your brain switch at the on position."

Toby chuckled good-naturedly. "It'd take all night if we tried to study at my place."

"Parents fighting again?"

"When don't they?"

"Well, it's not like they beat each other up or throw dishes or anything," Ben said. "They just like to argue is all. Some couples are like that."

"Mine sure are," Sally interjected.

"Yeah, but at least your parents like each other," Toby said. "My parents must've, too, once. But now they're each convinced they married the Antichrist!"

"But they love you," Ben said. "You're the reason they're still together." In fact their religion forbade divorce under virtually all circumstances. But such a notion was foreign to Ben, whose parents, though devout, embraced religion mostly as an expression of gratitude for their lives.

"Yeah, some consolation," Toby said. "Don't know if I'll ever get married myself. Too damn risky."

Ben noticed Sally's face clouding. "But wouldn't it be worse," he asked, "to spend your old age alone?"

"Not from where *I* sit. Alone seems a lot better than living the next forty years with somebody you can't stand."

Sally recovered quickly. "Then where do you imagine yourself in forty years?"

Toby laughed. "Cemetery, probably, pushing up daisies."

"Y'know," Ben said seriously, "I was thinking we might all be around longer than we realize. What if you could live forever? Wouldn't you want to?"

"No way," Toby said. "Heaven's gotta be a whole lot better than Wakefield."

"Who said you're going to heaven?" Marge cracked.

"Good point. Actually, hell might be better than Wakefield. But just hypothetically, Ben, are you asking if I'd want everyone to live forever, or just me?"

"Everyone, I suppose."

"Everyone? Interesting." Toby paused. "But then, what'd keep us from abusing each other? I mean, if we all knew we'd live forever, never having to face God's judgment for our sins, well, aren't most people crazy enough as it is?"

"Oh, I don't know," Marge offered. "People who expected to live forever might be *nicer*. After all, if you never died, whatever you did to others would eventually come back to you one way or another."

"Exactly," Ben agreed. "Any act of kindness, or spite, is sorta like a stone pitched into the sea. Y'know how ripples spread from the impact? If you plan to sail those waters forever, you might be more careful about what you toss into 'em."

"What do you mean?" Sally asked. "Like, for example?"

"Well, most everyone claims to believe in heaven and hell, but some people obviously don't. So how do you set penalties to fit the crime? For instance, suppose some despotic atheist enslaves a million people for twenty years. What's the worst punishment he could expect? Maybe if he gets unlucky, his life gets shortened by a decade or two. He'd probably figure it's worth the gamble; dictators usually think they're invincible, anyway."

"Yeah?" Toby asked. "And how does death enter into it?"

"See, if that same man had the potential to live forever, he might become more interested in building up goodwill; helping society improve. He could still be amoral, but only really deranged people do things they know they'll be punished for. Maybe he'd decide that fifty, or a hundred, or a thousand years from now, he'd be better off if he suppressed his impulses."

"Yeah, that's possible I guess," Toby conceded. "But still, it's natural to die."

"Oh, it's natural all right," Ben said. "Just like hurricanes, floods, and diseases are natural. Earthquakes and ice ages, too. Some even say war is natural. Maybe we should think of nature as our adversary."

Marge offered no opinion, but Sally did: "I think nature's wonderful and we should respect it. When it's my time to go, I'll be ready."

"Nature *is* wonderful, if you're dealing with it successfully," Ben argued. "Yeah, looking at it, or contesting it with a fishing rod or a test tube. It's easy to say you'll be ready to give in to it, too. That you'll be ready to go when it's time, until the time approaches, then you'll fight against it, that's for sure." His voice was calm, serious, without a trace of mockery.

"I won't fight it," Sally insisted. "Not when my time comes."

"And if you caught some fatal infection tomorrow? Would you refuse medical treatment to save your life?"

"No, of course not." Sally appeared somewhat uncomfortable with the contradiction in her answer.

"Even if the treatment isn't 'natural'?"

"Okay. I get the point," she said with a flash of defiance. "But still, when I'm sixty, sixty-five, that'll be plenty for me."

"So let's pretend you're sixty," Ben pressed on. "What if they invent a serum that would give you, say, another twenty-five years of vigorous health?"

"Well, yeah, I guess that'd be nice."

"So your time could come at eighty-five just as easily as sixty?"

"I suppose so."

"See? Nobody really wants to die, but we make believe it's perfectly okay. We keep up the pretense, not only to others, even to ourselves, because right now, dying after six or eight decades is almost a certainty. But don't feel bad. Used to be the same way myself, till just recently."

Sally's face brightened slightly.

"What about evolution?" Toby argued. "Without death, how can the human race develop?"

"I thought you rejected the premise of evolution," Ben said.

Toby was raised as an Evangelical Lutheran and had been told, ever since he was a small child, that God created heaven and earth about seven thousand years ago.

"Lately, I'm agnostic," Toby said. "But *you* believe in evolution."

"Actually, one doesn't believe in it so much as accept the evidence for it. Which I'd say is overwhelming. But evolution's the cruelest thing about nature; if it stopped today, I wouldn't miss it a bit. Think of the countless millions of prehumanoids who suffered horrible deaths just so you could hit that triple yesterday."

Toby smiled. "So if a few thousand more of my ancestors had sacrificed themselves, it would've been a home run?"

Everyone laughed, especially Ben. "Strange concept, I admit. But someday medical scientists should figure out how to analyze sperm cells and ova, and predict which combinations can produce the most desirable traits."

Marge grinned at Ben. "I just want our kids to do their homework and show up for piano lessons."

"That's what I mean," Ben said. "If we get to choose our offspring's traits, we could have all the benefits of evolution, even if nobody ever died. It's called eugenics; surely you've read something on the subject."

"Yes, but it's not natural," Sally said.

"Good! Like I said, nature is our adversary. Fact is, a natural life expectancy for us may only be fifteen or twenty years."

"Really?" Marge asked.

"That's about how long they think the average caveman lived," he explained, "before there were medicines and doctors. You have to remember, we're talking a truly all-natural life span, when lots of us died from being eaten!"

"Are you saying there's no difference between saving yourself from a cave lion by using a spear, and saving yourself from a disease using medicine?" Marge asked.

"Oh, sure," Ben said, "they're plenty different all right, but fundamentally speaking, isn't the effect the same?"

"Yes, I suppose it is."

"So how can anyone say that even a hundred years is enough?" Ben asked. "If a long life is good, and good life can be long, why isn't victory over death even better?"

December 7, 1941

In a desperate need to escape the household fireworks, Toby had told his parents he was going to church with Ben. Because it was Ben, he knew they'd allow it. There was just one problem of which Mr. and Mrs. Fiske remained blissfully unaware: Ben rarely went to church.

Instead the two boys passed time on Ben's back stoop, talking and listening to the radio music blaring through an open kitchen window. It was really too cool to sit outside, but too sunny not to. They'd been talking since gobbling down the chicken sandwiches Alice Smith had made them.

The music suddenly stopped, and the airwaves filled with static. Without knowing why, Ben glanced at his watch: 1:25 P.M.; a time that would be imprinted in his memory. Then a voice came on with astonishing clarity:

"At 7:55 A.M. local Hawaiian time, just a half hour ago, the Imperial Japanese armed forces attacked the U.S. Pacific Fleet in Pearl Harbor. The attack is ongoing. While specific battle reports are not yet available, it appears we have sustained significant losses. We will bring you more as it becomes available. God Bless America."

The two boys sat staring at each other as the music resumed. Now it was martial, not band, music, which faded again within seconds.

"The President of the United States, Franklin Delano Roosevelt . . ."

Ben had never heard of Pearl Harbor, but grasped what the attack meant to him.

FDR, in his poetic style and nasal, grandfatherly voice, briefly addressed the American public. The reception was poor, punctuated by static. The two boys strained in silence to capture the words. By the time the President finished, Ben had made his decision.

The Japs made a big mistake," he said to his friend. "That bombing's gonna unite this country, get everyone in America solidly behind this war. I guess college'll have to wait awhile, for me, anyway. Next month I turn seventeen; I'll volunteer for the Navy."

January 14, 1942

Toby grasped the push bar and swaggered into the Colonial Spa. He plunked himself onto the stool beside Ben at the lunch counter. Outwardly, his manner was that of a man full of confident anticipation. But beneath, a frightened child trembled.

"Sorry I'm late. So much to do, you know."

"You're not late," Ben told him evenly. He stirred his coffee, a recently acquired taste. Although this was Ben's seventeenth birthday, his mood was hardly festive.

Tomorrow Ben would enlist; Toby already had, weeks ago. Over the last several days, the two boys had found no time for each other. It seemed that the world as they knew it had spun out of their grasp. Most of the adult population of North America viewed the times with similar impotent apprehension.

"Can't stay long," Toby said.

Ben nodded stoically, unsure how he felt about their arrival at such a crossroads. For the moment, not knowing seemed better.

"I know it's your birthday," Toby continued, "but I have to tell my parents today, and that could be a real pisser."

"Tell your parents what?"

"Huh? That I'm going in the Army, of course." Toby said. "Oh hell, Ben," he blurted, "this really is one pisser of a day. I can't believe I never told you: I, uh, signed my father's name to my enlistment papers. Traced it right off one of his canceled checks."

If Ben displayed any surprise at all, it could be detected only in a slight widening of his eyes.

Toby broke the silence. "You might not believe this, but the truth is, I just forgot to tell you."

"Of course I believe you," Ben said, his tone revealing more: grudging admiration, and doubts about whether he himself would have had the rocks to do anything so brazen. "Shit. Should've occurred to me, pal. Ol' Ted woulda done just about anything to keep you home."

"You got *that* right. Anything short of having me arrested for forgery, that is."

Ben laughed, a knee-jerk of nervous sympathy for Toby's predicament and approval of his clever tactics. Both realized that Toby's parents would ultimately relent. It wasn't like they had any choice.

The boys sat in quiet contemplation.

"What do you think happens when you die?" Toby offered at last.

"Heaven, I suppose," Ben said. "Or maybe nothing at all."

"Nothing? How could that be?" Toby asked. "Everyone believes in heaven."

"Christians do," Ben said, "and Moslems believe in paradise, but Hindus think we return to earth as other people, or even animals. Reincarnation. Big deal, if you can't even remember who you were before. Fact is, nobody really knows what happens when you die. Not even priests."

"I guess we need to believe it doesn't just end, don't we?" Toby said.

"Guess so," Ben said. But what if there really was nothing else? he thought. What if everyone simply died, and then there was nothing else at all?

"Well, you're lucky you're joining the Navy," Toby said.

"How's that?"

"Well, when the shooting starts for me, some friggin' Nazi's probably gonna be doing it up close with a Mauser or a Luger. But you, you lucky S.O.B., you'll no doubt be nestled down inside some big battleship or heavy cruiser. You won't have a care in the world. Unless you get a torpedo up your ass."

Ben laughed, but the sound echoed hollow. Toby let it pass.

Down in the hold. Dark. Close. Putrid and suffocating. Ben even imagined hearing the whoosh of a torpedo charging through black waters, possessed of a special grudge against one Benjamin Franklin Smith. He shuddered and for the first time questioned his choice of military service.

Toby squinted as though, having realized he'd upset his friend, he was now searching his head for words to salvage their encounter. "The last thing we read in English class was *Julius Caesar*," he started, slapping Ben's shoulder, a fraternal tap.

Ben gazed back with shrewd interest.

"Yeah," Toby continued. "Remember how at the end, Cassius and Brutus are about to go into battle? Kinda like us; which I guess was why it stuck with me. 'O! that a man might know the end of this day's business ere it come.'"

"And come it will." Ben looked straight into his friend's moist eyes and paraphrased from the verse before it: "'Farewell, Tobias. If we do meet again, why, we shall smile.'"

Toby pulled a rabbit's foot—his lucky rabbit's foot—from his pocket, presented it to Ben, then solemnly finished, "'If not, why then, this parting was well made.'"

The rabbit's foot, purchased at Woolworth's for five cents, was grimy and reeking of six years spent in Toby's pocket. Each boy had a different idea about the powers of good-luck charms: They represented everything to Toby, and nothing to Ben.

Ben accepted it gratefully, reverently, as if it were a holy talisman. He stared at it for a moment, his eyes welling with tears, then slipped it carefully into his left pants pocket.

Then he removed from his neck a locket on a thin gold chain and presented it to his friend. In it nestled three locks of hair, with photographs of Sam and Alice Smith on one side, and Marge Callahan on the other.

As if participating in a sacred ritual, Toby placed it around his neck.

The two friends embraced, holding onto each other longer than was publicly sanctionable. And they did not care.

July 6, 1943

Kula Bay, Solomon Islands. When the torpedo plowed into the USS *Boise*, Ben felt the reverberations and heard the roar, although these disturbances seemed to come from a great distance, almost as if the imprint had happened to another, nearby ship. But the still-trembling deck plate and flickering lights told him otherwise. His watch read 8:51 A.M., *0851 hours.* He started to return to his fire-control duties.

Oh shit!

In an appallingly swift motion, the Brooklyn class light cruiser took on a alarming seventeen-degree list. The klaxon wailed, signaling a call to stations. The *Boise* shuddered again and heavy smoke, seemingly more solid than gas, began pouring into the corridor.

Though of equal rank, most of the sailors in his detail unconsciously turned to Ben for direction. It was the third torpedo they'd taken in this engagement. The first and second impacts did little more than open some compartments to the sea. These had been quickly sealed with jerry-built plates, securing the integrity of the ship's intervening bulkheads. They were, in effect, flesh wounds. This one, Ben decided, was a gut shot. "We just bought the farm," he called out. "Let's get up on deck. Now!" His voice, though urgent, betrayed none of the emotion he felt swimming through his entrails.

The list was fully twenty degrees now, the main deck awash, the crew caught up in barely controlled panic. By the time the "abandon ship" horn sounded, he'd estimated that marginally over half the ship's compliment of 888 were attempting to thread their way toward their assigned lifeboat stations. Ben was moving toward his own when a mental picture physically assaulted him: Shit! What about Epstein? They'd have to drag him out of sickbay—kicking and screaming.

Carl Epstein was one of the ship's two medical officers. Ben considered him a good friend, perhaps the only person he'd met in the Navy with whom he could comfortably discuss science and philosophy. Epstein had been at his station for at least nine hours. If there was even one man who couldn't move on his own, Ben realized, Carl would simply not leave him.

He headed across the deck and pushed forward through a swarm of sailors heading aft toward the lifeboats.

"Smitty," Ensign Herbert "Mack" McGuigan called out from several yards away, "where in blazes you goin'?"

"Gonna help Epstein, sir."

"Well, shag ass, then! Or you'll ride this tub to the bottom."

He arrived at sickbay and managed to help his friend lift three injured sailors into the main corridor, where Epstein could hurry his charges toward the boats. Then an inner voice told Ben to check the three nearby officers' cabins. Two were empty, but in the third, petty officers Dossey and Hauptman were out cold from the concussion. He shook Dossey awake. Just stunned. *Good.* Presuming one man would revive or drag away the other, Ben got the hell out of there. Heading toward the boats, he tightened his life jacket.

As he rushed between smoking debris and now-useless fire hoses, the deck plate separated in front of him, and his world seemed to lose the force of gravity. He felt himself airborne and could clearly see the ship rolling over to port. Suddenly he was wet, surrounded by fuel-blackened waters that assaulted his eyes, nose, and throat.

An hour had passed since the third hit on the *Boise*, and nearly as long since he was pitched from the ship. His body jerked up and down, whipsawed by rolling crests. The swells were heavy but not tumultuous. His work clothes clung to him like an added layer of diesel-stinking flesh. He still felt the water that filled his shoes as it sloshed between his toes, but the stinging sensation was starting to diminish: a very bad sign. The toes would be the first appendages to numb.

Ben understood that his life was probably over, though he did not articulate the knowledge to himself. It was primal understanding; probability silencing hope.

It had taken only seventeen minutes for their ship to capsize. Although his life jacket kept him afloat, the water was foul and rough, and he'd heard rumors about sharks. He counted nine lifeboats still visible in the distance, and had already exhausted himself trying to get their attention by waving and shouting. He'd even removed some of his clothing and spread it about the waters around him, but it was hopeless. The ocean was too vast and he was too small. He doubted any of the men in those boats could have seen him even if they'd all been searching; even if he were their only problem. Besides, they had more important things to worry about than finding one expendable sailor.

The sun was well into the sky, the air and water temperatures separated by 35 degrees Fahrenheit. Ben felt distressed and scared, yet strangely calm, as if the nobility of a wartime death somehow vindicated its occurrence.

Was misfortune better or worse, he wondered, when it resulted from actions chosen, rather than uncontrollable fate? He imagined it was worse.

Shivering and hyperventilating, he allowed more of the contaminated saltwater into his lungs and caught himself almost welcoming the end of life. He relaxed his arms and legs. As time passed, he began to drift in and out of consciousness, paying less attention to breathing. The world blurred, distinction between air and water fading. In the abandonment of life's struggle, he became almost euphoric. He sensed a life force rise, as though it were leaving his body. Physical sensation and emotional pain diminished in both size and import, as if in retreat to a place no longer connected to him.

So this was what it was like to die.

He shut his eyes and saw Gary and Susan Franklin, his grandparents who had died several years earlier, one right after the other. He'd always suspected Gramma Sue died from heartbreak rather than pneumonia. Now they welcomed him to the afterlife. But his emotions were mixed, the tug at life still manifest.

No! Not yet! he commanded himself. Everything he cared about was right there on earth. It was much too soon to leave.

His heart began to race. Pain and discomfort returned. He felt the raw wetness engulf his body like dishwater filling a sponge, and the cloying fuel stench attacked every sense as if his olfactory capacity alone were insufficient to absorb it.

He embraced these sensations like a long-lost friend; he would force himself to stay awake, concentrate, breathe more carefully, dissociate pain from soul, and fight to stay alive.

It might hurt, he decided, and would probably make no difference in the end, but if by some miracle he were rescued, any amount of suffering would seem insignificant.

Rolling his arms and scissor-kicking his legs, Ben anticipated the rhythm of the swells and steadied himself against them. He timed his breathing to take air only when his head was completely above water. More time passed; he had no idea how much. In this struggle against death, seconds felt like hours, hours like seconds. Every muscle was drained, his lungs ached, his skin so cold it burned, except on the fingers and toes, which by now possessed no feeling at all. How much longer could he keep that up?

Forever if he had to!

Without warning, he felt something wrap itself around his neck.

Now what? Ben thought, his instinctive shout of surprise choked off by the stranglehold. He lacked the strength to resist. Nothing remained left in him.

Then he realized it was a man's arm, and heard the sweet sound of Ensign McGuigan's gravelly voice. "Jumpin' Jesus. Smitty! You okay, boy?"

This was the impossible made real, and in the face of it only a distant portion of Ben's brain could muster emotion. He paid no homage to any feeling but amazement. Mack had braved those waters, risked his own life.

For me!

The officer towed him safely to his raft.

But Ben's fortunes would change again when the rafts were spotted by a Japanese troop ship, HIJMS *Asahi Maru.* The Americans watched in helpless terror as the enemy ship bore down on their raft. Japanese sailors pointed weapons and motioned for them to board. Two American boys carried Ben, mercifully unconscious, into the bowels of the ship.

Ben Smith's most primitive sense was his first to awaken:

Oh My God! The smell! He couldn't breathe. *Jesus, he'd survived for this?*

Ben now sat on a hard steel surface, his body rolled into a virtual ball, neck twisted, head buried between his knees. His lungs still burned from ingested diesel, his mouth tasted it. A ship's engine pounded his ears. And sweat-soaked human bodies mashed against him.

"Where am I?"

"In hell," a tortured voice croaked. Its fear was unmistakable, infectious.

Ben felt his heart race. "What?"

"Asahi Maru," said another.

Ben turned toward the words. They seemed calmer, but almost catatonic. "Japanese?"

"What else?" said the almost-familiar voice. "Empty Jap troopship. Taking us to a POW camp. If we live."

"Jesus. How long've I been out?"

A third voice answered: " 'Bout a day. Figured you might've died. Some have. More room for us."

A day? Ben thought. A whole day?

Then a man shrieked: inhuman, a lunatic being tortured. Too quickly, Ben tried to raise himself, banging his skull against asbestos-clad pipes hanging just three feet above the deck. He looked up and saw only a dense network of pipes, many superheated.

"Out! Out! Out!" the sailor screamed. "God, oh God, oh God! Get me *out*! Mother, come and get me now!"

The twenty-five-foot-by-thirty-foot-by-thirty-five-inch makeshift prison, enclosed at its sides by three layers of overlapping chicken wire, exploded in a din of shouting and scuffling. "Stop him!" "Got one running amok!" "Try and tackle him!" Two hundred men filled the ship's works dungeon, one panicked sailor flailing and clambering among them.

"That's a live-steam return pipe! It'll cook you . . ."

Ben not only heard but felt a high-pitched squeal. Feet stumbled on deck and over man's bodies. A heavy, hollow thunk echoed: head slamming into a valve cover. Then another noise, much like a crisp apple crushed between two powerful hands.

After few seconds of silence he heard only the same soft cries, moans, and pleadings.

Time wore on, hours then days. All around Ben, hard-packed, were British and American sailors, mostly teenagers like him. But their numbers were diminishing.

To Ben's right sat Petty Officer Hauptman, to his left Seaman Moses Walker. Each man's shoulder touched his own.

Hauptman shivered.

In *this* heat?

And Moses's arm had been broken; how badly, no one could tell. The ship's cook slept or moaned, but little more.

"I know you saved my life," whispered Hauptman. "Dossey told me."

Ben patted the NCO's back. "Just hold on. Think we're coming into some swells." The ship rolled, quaked, stabilized.

Moses moaned; brought his right hand to his left shoulder. "White folk's hell. Lordy mama, I'm in white folk's hell."

Ben whispered, "Saltwater'll drown any color, Moses. The sea doesn't care."

Moses made another sound.

A laugh? Ben wondered. Moses hadn't done anything but moan. His dad had been right—the Navy was the best choice. The Navy would take all Americans, any color, any creed. Of course, they might get them all drowned, too. Ben replied with a laugh of his own.

Moses took Ben's hand.

The ship shuddered again, another rogue wave, and Ben felt his stomach sink.

Hauptman clutched at him, grabbing his arm. "I'm gonna die. The heat, the stink, the dry heaves. Can't breathe in here. Ain't gonna make it, bud. Not even worth tryin' to."

Ben felt the man's hand quaking. "Just breathe. Please. Inhale. Exhale. Inhale. Exhale. Think of nothing else. Keep breathing, Chief. One day, you'll see the sun again."

Hauptman gave no reply.

When Japanese sailors came with hoses to offer their captives callous respite, the men opened their mouths to swallow as much as possible. Afterward, Ben turned to Hauptman. The man's eyes were open, but sightless.

He looked away from the lost man and caught Epstein's eyes. The doctor tossed him a two-finger salute, then continued to wipe vomit away from the mouth of the sailor's head cradled in his lap.

Ben waited hours, maybe a day, to report Hauptman's death. They'd only throw him to the fish anyway—gone as though he'd never been. God, he'd saved the guy just to prolong his agony.

"Why?" Ben heard himself cry.

On his left, Moses whispered, "He been gone a long while, ain't he, Ben?"

"A while, yes."

"Why'd you wait?"

Ben shifted his legs; the needles stitched into numbness. "Cause it hurts too much, Moses. Letting any of us go: It's like losing a piece of me."

Walker moaned. "My arm, the pain's fit to kill me. My mama didn't raise me to be no cook for white sailors. Now I'm gonna die in the yellow man's sewer."

Ben put his hand on the draftee's forehead. Stupid! How could he possibly tell if Moses had a fever? It had to be at least 105 in there. "Just think of home. Your family. Your girl. You can make it."

"If m' time come, Ben, will you hold onto *me*, too?"

Ben took Moses's good hand into his own and squeezed gently. He decided he would put this hellhole in a box, lock it up, file it way. Because if he didn't, it would surely eat his brain; not just part, but all.

Ben felt the spray of the Japanese hoses, which meant another morning had come. He tipped his head back, pretending he was home, taking a shower. Moses Walker felt nothing at all.

Ben did not report his death.

I don't accept it, he told himself. This passage was not inevitable. He would live. He would help others to live. He would fight this implacable enemy. And someday, by God, someday he would win.

The trip to the POW camp at Futtsu spanned six and a half days, during which none of the living ever left that space or those crumpled positions. There they remained, urinating and defecating in their clothes, receiving no food or medical attention and very little water. Only seventy-nine sailors from Ben's ship, barely one-third of those captured, survived the voyage.

When the prisoners arrived at the eastern mouth of *Tokyo-Wan*, or Tokyo Bay, the Japanese at the camp were shocked to learn so many had died. Transported under similar conditions, their own soldiers had arrived at their destinations alive and functional. Japanese soldiers were smaller, but size had had little to do with it. Unlike these boys, they'd been mentally prepared for the ordeal, had known how long the journey would take and what would be waiting at the end of it.

It was the fear, Ben decided. Fear of the unknown had killed so many of them.

The POW camp had no name; in Japanese culture, to name a place was to honor it. The allied prisoners at Futtsu came to refer to it as Purgatory, yet compared to the *Asahi Maru*, the camp was almost decent.

April 12, 1945

"Good modaning, Smee-tee-san."

Ben bowed and offered the austere young colonel a polite and equally mispronounced answer to his strained English greeting. "*O hiyo gozaiymas, Yamatsuo-sama.*"

As they seated themselves, Hiro Yamatsuo's face remained expressionless, but Ben imagined the colonel had just winced with his eyes. "Smee-tee-san," he said, "we will please use English. I fear we Japanese will—how do you say?—find it *of use* soon."

This was Ben Smith's seventh "interview" in nineteen months since his compulsory audience under the supervision of Futtsu's ranking officer. No other prisoner except the camp's ranking allied officer, Colonel Lawrence Rand, and of course Epstein, to voice his almost-daily complaints, had met with Yamatsuo so many times. In their first encounter, this same man had savagely used every psychological weapon short of physical torture to press Ben into providing whatever information he had. Even though Ben felt his knowledge would be of minimal use, he had refused to say anything. But he'd continued to treat his captors with appropriate and consistent respect.

Since that first meeting, these interviews had become increasingly and inexplicably pleasant. Now that so much time had passed since his capture, Ben could only surmise that the officer simply liked him.

He also found himself appreciating the subtle duality contained in so much of what Yamatsuo said and did. The deference he exhibited by insisting on "Engrish" was closely coupled with a pragmatic explanation of why this might be beneficial: a conspiratorial yet seemingly guileless admission that the Japanese were losing.

But while he considered this Japanese *taisa* now treating him with such cordiality, a jumpy moviola danced inside his forehead. The stop-start action was not unlike the images viewed through a hand-cranked nickelodeon, yet the stutterings and lack of color somehow made the impressions all the more real:

> *It is the day after their ragtag company—the survivors, anyway— disembarked from the floating sewer. The office is the same as Ben and Yamatsuo occupy now, but instead of being comfortably seated on a futon, Ben stands at the open door, facing inward, next in line for interrogation.*
>
> *Before him a nearly catatonic "Little Sparks" Grogan, seaman first class and second level radio operator, sits in something that looks much like a deck chair from a western-style cruise ship. His forearms are bound to the side rails with heavy twine.* Taisa *Yamatsuo sits to his front in a similar chair. Beside Little Sparks stands* Socho (Sergeant Major) *Teshio, ominously holding a pair of needle-nosed pliers.*
>
> *This* taisa, *this colonel now pouring tea for Ben, barks interrogatories to the* socho, *who repeats them to Grogan in broken English. But the seaman comports himself well. His replies are a continuing monologue of name, rank, and serial number.*
>
> *Teshio looks to Grogan, then to his* taisa, *who nods his head with an abrupt snap. The sergeant wheels instantly upon the bound sailor, grasps the index fingernail on Grogan's hand with the pointed- end pincers, and in a single, shockingly quick motion, jerks it from the boy's hand.*
>
> *Grogan screams like nothing Ben has ever heard before.*
>
> *Holy mother of God! Ben refuses to even consider the possibility that he himself might be next in line for such treatment. Is it because Little Sparks is the only radioman who survived the sinking? Do they think his position made him privy to special information? Or are they using Grogan to strike fear into the rest of them?*
>
> *Whatever their reasons, the Japs don't stop. It takes twelve minutes for the sailor to lose all ten fingernails. Ben vomits twice. The*

screams, the hopeless agony, and the courage Grogan shows despite
his anguish, fill Ben with a hatred he'd never suspected possible
within himself. For the next three nights he would dream of nothing
but strangling Yamatsuo. This dream was not a nightmare.

The hate might have faded over time, except for one thing: Little Sparks
had died from a secondary infection six days later, and Ben's loathing for his
present host had planted deep roots in hard clay.

"*Domo,* Yamatsuo-sama," he said, forcing a polite smile.

"*Hiro-san,*" the colonel corrected. "It will soon be inappropriate—is
that the word?—to address me as a superior."

Ben made no immediate reply. What the hell could he say? Finally,
ignoring the implications of the question's context, he responded, "Yes. As I
believe you meant it, 'inappropriate' is the correct word choice."

Both men sat in motionless silence for several seconds, each waiting
for the other to offer the next disclosure.

Yamatsuo handed him a tattered photograph of a young Japanese
woman standing next to an American who looked vaguely like Ben; a little
shorter perhaps, but the resemblance readily apparent. "My niece, Hatsu,"
Yamatsuo said, "my older brother's daughter. And that's her fiancé. Last
time I saw Hatsu, she was nine years old, and even this picture is from 1941.
Of course I have never met *him.*"

"Of course." Aha! Ben thought. Maybe the prick treated him differently because he looked like Yamatsuo's nephew-to-be.

"Her future-husband fights Germans in Italy, I imagine, while she
waits, along with the rest of my brother's family, in Arizona. At one of your
internment camps."

"I see."

Yamatsuo poured *o cha*, a translucent greenish-brown tea, into tiny
earthenware cups. He presented a cup to Ben, and then, as if in response to
an unuttered, mordant joke, he asked, "How will it be for me, Smee-tee-
san? What will you Americans do to officers of such a place as this?"

Interesting. The bastard was assuming the Americans would be after
revenge. A small portion of Ben's mind danced in ravenous anticipation of
meting out retribution to his tormentor; perhaps driving him to suicide by
wielding the weapon of dishonor: *Yeah Hiro-san, you evil cocksucker. The*
allies'll probably march you naked through the streets of Tokyo, before they tear
you limb from limb. But as Ben considered the notion, he realized that he
could never, must never, do such a thing.

Still, Yamatsuo must have glimpsed something terrible, even wolfish,
as it flashed behind the young sailor's eyes. He stiffened. "Perhaps it will be

more honorable for me to commit *seppuku*. Life without dignity is no life. Is it not better to know one's time of dying rather than to wait for it? As you Americans say, you can't live forever . . ."

At that moment, Ben no longer saw Yamatsuo as his foe but, for the first time as a pathetic fellow human being.

Every act of kindness or spite was like a boulder pitched into the sea. The ripples dispersed and widened. Forever.

He looked deeply into Yamatsuo's steel-gray eyes. "I've never said that. I know of nothing more precious than life, *Hiro-san*. To my mind, it is always too soon to die." It was the most honest statement he'd ever made to the man. Ben was surprised, but only mildly, by the conviction behind his own words.

August 16, 1945

Ben crouched so he could speak to the sailor writhing in pain on the sticky, septic floor. Before treating symptoms, he had to address the boy's fear. "Dysentery," Ben said, his voice calm with a soothingly detached sympathy, "but not too bad, I think. Bobby, I know you feel god-awful, but I promise you're gonna be okay. Just keep drinking this. A small sip every five minutes or so. If you drink it too fast, it'll make your diarrhea worse, and if you don't drink enough, you'll dehydrate."

Ben hardly felt healthy himself. Like every other prisoner at Purgatory, he scratched constantly from lice and insect bites. He often coughed up blood; diarrhea and nausea were relentless. Many of the prisoners would be physically and emotionally scarred, some crippled, but not Ben; escape from this lost-time world seemed certain to him now. Standing six feet two inches tall, he now weighed 133—twelve pounds more than he'd weighed back in February.

Over the past several months, life had actually been improving for the allies. No longer did they endure routine interrogation, isolated incidents of torture, or solitary confinement. The guards actually gave them their Red Cross medicine. The food was better now, too, and far more plentiful. Yesterday they'd been fed twice; once more than their captors.

"The Nips know they're losing," Epstein had speculated to Ben a few weeks earlier. "They're treating us better to hedge their bets."

Ben had not responded to Carl. There'd been no complicity in any of his conversations with Colonel Yamatsuo, but he saw no purpose in revealing insights gained and subjecting himself to difficult questions about how he'd acquired them. Even to Epstein. Besides, he'd thought, there was always the possibility that Yamatsuo was feeding him bad information.

They'd already passed twenty-five months at Futtsu, and throughout the entire hell-time of the POW camp, Ben had never even allowed himself to consciously remember the dreadful voyage that brought him to this place.

This place. My God. How had mankind managed to fall down such a rat hole? What had gone wrong to create a world where people became shelf stock? They were being kept alive only because if they were disposed of, allied retribution would be more costly than the meager food or care they received. It was almost like evolution had all been for nothing—like it had started running backward.

Now Ben watched in morbid fascination as Epstein closed a gruesome wound on a semiconscious British sailor with safety pins. Ben said: "This is almost enough to make one rebuke Darwin. It's like we're regressing—becoming more like animals."

Epstein shook a head seemingly too large for his jockeylike body. "You don't really believe that, do you?"

"No. Of course not. Evolution's real enough, but this place, Carl—sometimes it makes me question everything."

Finishing his grim work, Epstein turned around. His face had come suddenly alive, as if their surroundings no longer mattered. "Then in light of your acceptance of Darwin's theory," he teased, "how do you explain the Christian view that when an ape dies, that's all there is for him?"

"What do you mean?"

Epstein grinned. "I can only imagine how the first human felt about arriving in heaven to receive his eternal reward and wondering what the hell happened to his parents."

Ben laughed. "Look, I only know what the Bible says about heaven. I haven't actually been there, and neither have you." But he already knew what was coming next.

"I suppose those fellows who wrote the Old Testament have? Ben, every early Christian denomination once contended that the earth was the center of the universe. Many upheld that view centuries after scientists refuted it. The notion that our souls live forever evolved from the same place: our own self-centered egotism. Remember, the human brain is massively complex; capable of astounding feats of creativity and self-deception. And unfortunately, no one will ever be able to disprove the existence of an afterlife."

Ben shook his head, offering no reply. He simply asked, "Carl, what made you decide to become an atheist?"

"Let me quote you a passage I memorized a few years ago," Epstein said.

"Okay."

" 'Disbelief,' " Epstein began " 'crept over me at a very slow rate but at last was complete. The rate was so slow that I felt no distress, and have never since doubted for a single second that my conclusion was correct. I can indeed hardly see how anyone ought to wish Christianity to be true; for if so the plain language of the text seems to show that the men who do not believe, and this would include my father, brother, and almost all my best friends, will be everlastingly punished. And this is a damnable doctrine.' "

"Who wrote that?" Ben asked.

"It's from Charles Darwin's autobiography." Epstein flashed a self-satisfied smirk.

Ben fell silent for a long moment and considered his words carefully. "Look, Carl, I agree everlasting punishment for disbelief is a detestable doctrine, but not too many people I know would call it Christianity. I don't pretend to embrace any particular organized religion; at least not every tenet of one."

Epstein arched bushy, Groucholike eyebrows at Ben.

"Hold it," Ben continued. "Just because I'm not a good church-goer doesn't mean I think organized religion's bad, or somehow evil. Few Americans endorse every law we've ever passed, either. But most of us still support our country. Things have happened to me, Carl, recently, that convince me there's power in the universe we can't begin to comprehend."

"Oh really? Like what?"

"When I was floating in the ocean after they sank us," Ben said, "I felt myself leaving my body. I saw my grandparents' faces. I'm sure of it. It was more than a dream."

"Yeah," Epstein agreed, "it was a full-fledged fucking delusion!" Yet even as his friend mocked him, Ben saw the gratitude in his eyes. After all, to a man who harbors no hope of reincarnation, life is infinitely precious.

And both men were well aware that Epstein owed his to Ben.

In spite of Ben's stubborn refusal to "accept reality and denounce religion," Epstein had to admit that his new aide-de-camp was scientific in his methods; the boy kept meticulous records of his cases and had learned a lot about medicine. Ben had even managed to teach him a few things.

"I've noticed," Ben had told him over a year before, "that the more they think we're going to help them, the faster they recover."

"I thought you didn't believe in magic."

"I don't, but the power of suggestion is as real as any science. Faith is a mighty force." When there was nothing more he could do, Ben would give the sick sailors handmade salt tablets, or rainwater colored with ground clay, and over time it had become apparent, even to Epstein, that the placebos possessed a measurable remedial power.

"Sometimes," Ben had said to him, "you just need to spend a little time, talk, and listen. Show a suffering man that you understand what he's going through and give him some hope. It's amazing how much that helps. Caring and hope are as contagious as any disease. I trust you won't mind if I try to infect some of your patients."

Epstein thought: Yes, there is a mind-body connection. Of course! That must be why so many doctors fall for mysticism.

But he'd offered nothing more than a smile and an acquiescent nod. Carl Epstein knew when to quit.

Most of them, including Ben, had begun to get mail through the Red Cross. His had been a three-page letter from Alice. Most of the events she'd described had occurred the day before she mailed it; some that very morning. From this he could infer that she must have been writing at least every other day, knowledge as valuable to him as the letter itself.

"Ted and Connie Fiske received notification from the Army yesterday," she'd written. "They opened it with dread, but read with great relief. We now anticipate Toby's return from Italy in about two weeks' time, with a Purple Heart and a bit of shrapnel in his left buttock. Apparently he's fine other than that. They expect he'll be off crutches by the time he gets home, and within a month won't even be limping. It will be wonderful to see him again. We are all looking forward to the reunion . . ."

Although the letters had never reached him, Alice implied that his fiancée had written faithfully. ". . . You might already know from her daily bulletins, but if my letter reaches you first, I'm sure you'll be happy to learn that Marge received another promotion at the steel mill yesterday. At this rate, she'll soon supervise the entire accounting department. She does fret over how you'll feel about her working, but I've assured her that you'll approve. Anything to help the war effort, right? Of course she intends to quit the moment you return to us. She misses and worries about you constantly, as we all do, and says the work helps keep her mind distracted . . ."

It was barely noon and Ben had read his mother's letter five times.

He daydreamed about Marge and their last night together, the night they'd broken their vow to save themselves for their wedding day. "What if I never see you again?" Marge had said to him. "I'll need the memory of you, Ben." But he knew her concerns had been more for him, for *his* memories, and to help keep him alive for her. They'd rented a hotel room, shared a glass of wine.

The first attempt had been clumsy. But it was sweet and close and without the self-consciousness that so often interfered with pleasure. By morning they'd taught each other what to do. The teaching had been mostly wordless, but the lessons well-learned. The number of times they learned them assured that: four times in all.

Four times that Ben would relive ten thousand times each.

Colonel Rand interrupted Ben's reverie to ask him, and several other soldiers and sailors, to gather every able-bodied prisoner into the central courtyard. "Got an announcement to make," he said.

"Yes, sir . . . Oh. Yes sir!"

When Ben got there, the courtyard was packed with all but a few of the 344 allied personnel still alive at Futtsu.

The officer began the speech, his smile too obvious. Ben's heart soared before Rand uttered the words: "The commandant just told me, uh, the Japanese finally surrendered to us. About thirty-six hours ago. We're goin' home, boys, war's over."

Several minutes passed before the hugging and cheers and whistles ceased, and Rand could finally continue. "Purgatory is now your camp, and the Nips are our prisoners. But remember, we're no longer at war. I know some of you guys are mad as hornets. I've hated 'em as much as any a you, but grudges just ain't part a the American way. So remember that, and do us proud."

Ben immediately found Ensign McGuigan and hugged him. "Without you, I would never have lived to see this day."

"Best thing I ever did," Mack said. "Couldn't'a picked a better man to pull from the drink. Or a braver one. Every hour you spent helping Epstein treat those sick boys, you gambled against getting sick yourself. Until a few months ago, that could be a death sentence. Now you just go home and become the kind of doctor you were here in Purgatory. Any doc can pass out pills or poke your butt with a needle, but I ain't seen too many who let you know they give a rat's ass. And it matters, boy. It matters a lot."

Most ranking officers at Japanese prison camps would commit suicide rather than face Anglo-American military justice.

Taisa Hiro Yamatsuo, however, would spend fifty-eight months in an allied military prison, return home to marry, build a successful manufacturing business, produce six daughters and a son, and be felled by an aneurysm in November 1987, having recalled his short conversation on April 12, 1945 with Fire Controller Third Class Benjamin Smith countless times during the final forty-two of his eighty years of life.

June 17, 1947

Ben's fifth semester at Harvard had ended the week before, but he looked forward to the summer session scheduled to begin in nine days. He wiped the sweat from his forehead and gazed out their tiny window upon the steamy street below. They had no electric fan—he and Marge needed the money for food and rent, and certainly didn't want to ask their parents for more handouts—but they'd become used to the heat.

Ben and Marge Smith had been married fifteen months. They lived on a noisy street near Harvard Square in Cambridge in a rented one-room apartment, a fifth-floor walk-up with no hot water and a bathroom shared with two other families down the hall. The seventeen dollars monthly rent seemed like an extravagance. The GI Bill barely covered Ben's tuition and expenses, forcing him to get through Harvard College and Harvard Medical School on loans, scholarships, and part-time work. Yet even after Marge became pregnant, he was sure they could scrape by.

"Benny, I think it's time," she said.

The bag was already packed. Calmly, he walked her downstairs and hailed a taxi. Although they couldn't afford it, he refused to chance the bus. "Boston Veterans Hospital, please," he told the cabdriver. "Fast. My wife's about to have a baby!"

The driver's eyebrows slid up his forehead as if trying to escape. "Don't worry, ma'am. We'll make it."

Throughout the trip, Ben held Marge close, rubbing her back and shoulders.

The fare was sixty cents, but Ben gave him a dollar. "Best cab ride we ever had." In fact, it was the only cab ride they'd ever had.

"Hey, thanks," the man told them, his hand closing over the two silver halves. "And good luck."

Ben escorted his wife through the emergency entrance. The walls were clean and white. Even the floors looked spotless; more safe than sterile. While Marge waited, Ben checked in at the desk. The Veterans Administration would pay for everything. Their first child would be born in a real hospital.

Husbands, even premed students like Ben, were required to sit in another room while their wives endured labor and delivery, so he found a pay phone and called Toby Fiske. Also a Harvard premed, Toby still lived at his mother's house in Wakefield.

Toby arrived about ninety minutes later and waited with Ben. Except for the two young vets, the large waiting room was empty. They sat, mostly in silence, surrounded by vending machines, coffeepot, water cooler, and dozens of magazines. How blessedly and terribly apart males were, Ben thought. Vended treats to make them feel at home. He hoped Marge was okay, but doubted she was feeling too at home or natural right then.

"You scared?" Toby asked.

"Not really," Ben said. "Wish I was inside. With Marge . . ."

"Instead of out here with the likes of me?"

Ben laughed. "Yeah, though I wouldn't've put it quite that way . . ."

Toby smiled. "What I actually meant was, are you frightened, y'know, about parenthood? And all that responsibility? Don't think I could handle it myself."

"Actually," Ben laughed, "I'm more alarmed at the prospect of giving up sex for the next six weeks!"

"Well, I can see how that . . . Hey? You mean you've still been having sex?"

Ben nodded. "Remember the pennies-in-a-jar parable?"

"Sure," Toby said. "If a newlywed couple puts a penny in a jar every time they make love during the first year of the marriage, and removes a penny every time they do it after that, no matter how long the marriage lasts, they say, the jar will never be empty."

"I told Marge that story before we got married. We actually keep a piggy bank by our bed now. She took it as a challenge!"

Toby laughed. "You sly devil."

"Y'know," Ben said earnestly, "we always wanted a family. Not sure I envisioned it happening quite this soon, but I think we're ready."

"Scary time to have kids," Toby said, "with the A-bomb. They say the commies'll have one in ten years."

Ben was amused at his friend's bluntness. Toby and he had always shared their thoughts without affectation or artifice. "They'd never dare use it. Old buddy, this is the most exciting time in history. If anything, I was born too soon. When I think of the scientific miracles this child might see . . . Our baby's gonna live a much longer and healthier life than you or I will. And see things we can't even imagine."

"I thought you were planning to live forever."

"Well, maybe I'm more realistic now. I feel lucky to be alive at all. But my children or grandchildren might. My own immortality'll come through them, I guess. Which is good enough for me," Ben said, suddenly realizing it wasn't true—but easier not to think about. This child might never die, but *he* certainly would. He pushed the jealousy from his mind before he could quite recognize it. Life was short, and too precious for negative thoughts.

Sam and Alice Smith arrived several hours later. Marge's parents, Oscar and Mary Callahan, who had the foresight to bring a deck of cards, showed up shortly after that. The six spent the ensuing hours telling jokes, pacing the floor, and taking turns at gin rummy and hearts.

In all, Marge's labor lasted thirteen hours. When the nurse told them it was a healthy baby boy, Toby gave Ben a great bear hug, lifting him a foot off the floor. "It's real now," Toby said. "I didn't think I'd envy you one little bit. But maybe I was wrong."

Moments later the same nurse escorted Ben inside to look at his son through a large window, and suddenly everything changed. Staring at the tiny infant, barely distinguishable among perhaps a dozen laying in bassinets, he felt none of the love or even pride he'd expected. The smooth glass seemed too cold and resolute a barrier to penetrate with either hand or heart. His warm breath frosted the window, throwing his own air back upon him, as if the glass had become a cube, closing him in, trapping him within itself. He tried to smile but found it impossible. It should have been the happiest moment of his life, shouldn't it? Ben looked into himself with horror, finding nothing to be quite where he thought he'd left it.

June 17, 1950

Ben wondered how they could possibly expect him to keep this up for twelve months. He'd only been an intern for a week, and already could hardly stay awake during rounds. He'd just come off two straight shifts, treating emergency cases and helping deliver babies from five last night to nine this morning. It was nine-sixteen A.M. as he walked off the subway at Brigham Circle, several stops before his own neighborhood. He headed toward Harvard Medical School, and ambled inside Benson's Delicatessen, where Toby was seated alone at their usual booth by the window.

"Boy, am I beat." Ben dropped onto the banquette. "This damn internship's gonna kill me."

"Hell, Ben. You look like it already has. Always knew you were a pansy."

"You know, I think I'm really going to enjoy reminding you about this conversation. Next year."

"Fortunately, I'm a Libra. We don't need as much sleep as you Capricorns."

Ben looked at his friend to see if he was joking, then strained not to groan or roll his eyes. Jesus, he actually believed it. "Toby," he said in a rare display of frustration, "Hitler had a whole team of astrologers advising his every move. Don't you think if that crap really worked, the Germans would've won the . . . oh, never mind."

"Well, you don't have to get all hot and bothered over it. It's just for fun. I swear I'm not consulting my horoscope to decide whether I should invade Poland or anything."

"Sorry," Ben said. "Bad night. Listen, Marge is pregnant again."

"Gee, that's great!" Toby exclaimed. Then he gazed at Ben's face. "Isn't it?"

"Don't know. Fact is, we tried everything not to get pregnant. Rhythm, condoms, even abstinence. Which didn't last long. It was kind of an acci dent. You know what I'm saying?"

Ben recalled the weeks after his first child, Gary, was born. Baby Gary had been a colicky infant with a very impressive lung capacity. There was simply no way to reason with a baby in distress, utterly frustrating Ben, who'd never been around babies before.

Marge adored Gary, and would rock him for hours while he screamed in pain. But Ben had come to regard his son as an unbearable intrusion into a life he now remembered with shortsighted fondness. He refused to change the baby's diapers, couldn't seem to help Marge in any way. In the sanctuary of his work, Ben would invariably begin to forget his anxiety; he'd decide that today would be different. Tonight, he would help Marge more. But once home, the noise, the closed quarters, the lack of sleep, even the odors, would combine to restore Ben's claustrophobic panic.

"You're such a gentle, even-tempered man," Marge had told him, "except when it comes to Gary. I'd like to tell you that I understand, but I don't."

She was right. Everything his son did seemed to anger him, and Ben had no idea why. He'd once vowed never to spank his children, no matter what they did; there were plenty of enlightened ways to punish misbehavior without conveying a message that violence is acceptable. He'd wanted his children to resolve their conflicts peaceably, and knew that parents must teach by example. Yet once his son had reached toddlerhood, he found himself shouting whenever Gary misbehaved. Then, even spankings had come. These had never been given in outward rage; the shock of them for Gary seemed to be more that they occurred at all than any attendant pain. But for Ben, the horror at the spankings dwelt in the fact that they seemed to be delivered by a stranger who would briefly inhabit his body. He didn't know that guy, and certainly didn't like him.

Over these past three years, every time he'd looked at his son, or heard his voice, or smelled him, Ben would feel almost suffocated. Even now, with Gary turning three years old today, things weren't much better. Ben felt barely able to stand having him around.

In the delicatessen, Ben said to Toby, "I don't get it," his eyes beginning to moisten. "How can I love my wife so much, and my son so little?"

"I'm sure it just takes time," Toby assured him. But Ben knew it was a lie.

After he and Toby finished breakfast, Ben headed home. Marge and Gary were already gone, for the boy's birthday, she'd promised to take him to an animated film and then the circus, which Ben decided was just as well. He undressed, climbed into bed, and fell asleep immediately.

He woke around four P.M., feeling warm, bare, familiar skin next to his. Marge lay beside him, gently stroking his erection with her left hand, cupping his testicles with her right.

"Gary just fell asleep," she whispered, "and I'm already pregnant."

He kissed her sweetly, wanting to go slowly, to please her; she usually liked it best when they took their time. But all at once she climbed on top and used her right hand to pull him inside of her. Their lovemaking was passionate, urgent.

When they finished, Ben held her close and she began to cry.

"What's wrong?"

She didn't answer.

"You're worried about our second child, aren't you?"

"Ben, I love you so much. I know you don't want this baby—"

"I do," he interrupted, "if you do." Then he reflected on her words and started to cry himself. "I love you, too," he finally said. "Always will. I don't know what it is between Gary and me, but I'll figure it out. I'll work at it day and night and become a good parent. Marge, I swear to you. I'll be a better father from now on."

August 30, 1960

For the rest of his life Ben Smith would remember this day in exceptional detail. He and Marge did not make love that morning; Jan had been up too early. Instead, they dragged themselves out of bed to make breakfast.

The brownstone on Boston's Beacon Hill was bright, open, spacious—and a cluttered mess. It was built for luxury living but had been forced to adapt to the children, like a purebred show dog living at a junkyard. There were no antiques or decorator furniture, no expensive paintings or Oriental rugs. The walls were adorned mostly with family photographs, dents and scratches, and the occasional crude drawing unmistakably crafted by young fingers.

Some of the artwork, invariably those compositions signed by the eldest child, possessed an engaging, mathematically evolved synchronicity of design, and a refined balance of color and light. But even these works were rarely admired. With so many toys scattered about, it was perilous to walk the halls without looking down.

Marge prepared French toast with maple syrup and sausages. Ben concocted a huge mushroom, onion, and ham omelet.

All three older children had returned home from summer camp; the whole family was now together. Ben had arranged a part-time schedule so he could spend more time with them before school resumed in two weeks.

Rebecca and Maxine wandered into the dining room just as breakfast reached the table. Marge sent Rebecca back upstairs to rouse Gary. He'd been up late the night before, as usual; studying, reading, and drawing.

But far from being proud of his son's artistic and scholastic accomplishments, Ben considered his own childhood, and Gary's suffered by comparison. Sure, at Gary's age he had studied hard, but not *constantly*, for chrissake; Ben also remembered hanging out with friends, playing sports, and spending time with his parents and relatives, listening to the radio or just relaxing. He'd never been *that* obsessive, had he? Hell, Gary rarely even watched TV with his sisters. It was hard to remember when the boy had last left his room at all after school, except to eat.

Two days ago the Smiths had bought their first color television. Barely twenty-five years earlier, Ben had had trouble convincing Toby that a "radio with moving pictures" was even scientifically possible. And now they could broadcast films in every hue of the rainbow. In a few more years, they would barely notice. Amazing!

The girls noticed today, though, and insisted the set remain on in case some program actually appeared in color, which none did; most color broadcasts were scheduled for evening.

Nineteen sixty was an election year, so Ben, Marge, and their children—thirteen-year-old Gary, Rebecca, Nine; Maxine, eight; and Janette, six—talked about politics at the breakfast table that morning. Ben and Marge declared their intentions to vote for Richard Nixon, although she seemed less convinced than he did.

"Kennedy's so much cuter," Rebecca interjected. "I'd vote for him over Nixon any day."

Ben scowled at his daughter, but with a distinct twinkle in his eye. "That's some reason to vote for a presidential candidate." He laughed, and she laughed back. Ben would have done anything for his girls, and they all knew it.

"Kennedy was talking about whether we should send men to the moon," Maxine volunteered.

Ben almost said: I wish he'd put himself and most of his family there. But instead he smiled. "Grandma Alice told me some of her friends are worried. They think going to the moon might be against the will of God. How do *you* feel about it?"

"I think it's kinda cool." Rebecca giggled.

"Oh, but I agree with Alice's friends," Marge deadpanned. "Space travel's so . . . artificial. We should all stay home and watch television—like God intended!"

Everyone laughed.

"I'm not sure I l-like Nixon," Gary announced nervously. "He s-seems phony."

Ben felt inexplicably offended. Nixon was General Eisenhower's vice president, for chrissake! An image flashed through his mind of Mack McGuigan risking his life to rescue him. Japanese sailors had often left their wounded behind, but that wasn't the American way: Ike's way. Ben believed that Mack, Eisenhower, and therefore Nixon, were somehow akin. Voting for anyone else would almost be a betrayal. "Eisenhower was a great general, and an even better President. If Ike thinks Nixon's up to the job, that's good enough for me."

Gary cowered at Ben's tone, but Marge smiled at him, pleased that he was willing to express an honest disagreement with his father.

"I know what you mean," Marge said to Gary. "Nixon's smart enough. Still, if people don't trust him, he can't be effective as President. I'll probably vote for him anyway, but I'm keeping an open mind till Election Day."

Emboldened by his mother's words, Gary added, "Our P-President seems like a good man, but nobody's perfect. I, uh, read something about him a few weeks ago in the *Herald*. According to the article, Eisenhower was sh-shocked and alarmed when someone told him half the p-people in the United States have average intelligence or less!"

Marge and Rebecca both laughed, but Ben felt his anger rising up like steam from a boiling kettle.

"Bull—" he said, but caught himself. Hell, if one of the girls had said what Gary did, he'd have been proud, not angry. So he backtracked. "Well, Grandma Alice always told me that God gave us brains so we could think for ourselves. And she was right. When you're old enough to vote, Gary, just try to get all the facts you can, then trust your own judgment."

He even tried to smile at his son, but couldn't quite pull it off.

Gary, only minimally aware that he'd just won a small skirmish with his father, knew to leave well enough alone. But Marge rubbed her son's shoulder and beamed.

Why couldn't he like his own son? Ben felt ashamed, yet baffled. Old habits died hard, he supposed. Apparently he just hadn't been ready for a child when Gary came into the world.

After making his promise to Marge on Gary's third birthday, he'd never spanked the boy again, no matter how much he seemed to deserve it. Yet he wondered if Gary's compulsive work habits and obvious self-image problems might have been a result of the earlier blows. Ben regarded striking his son as a great mistake, but he felt no guilt; the shame lay deeper, subcutaneous and festering.

After medical school and residency, Ben had decided to specialize in gastroenterology. He steadily honed his skills and became well-known. His practice prospered.

He'd always had a compelling bedside manner which helped attract patients. For many doctors, that was the hardest part, but for Ben it came easily; he had an instinctive sensitivity for others, so it was just a matter of developing the proper habits.

Over the past six years, his style had changed little. He'd designed all of his practice's policies with common sense and a knack for mechanical effectiveness; what would later be termed "ergonomics." Before scheduling patients, a member of his staff always interviewed them, so his appointments ran on time, a rarity in the medical profession. He never rushed his cases, although his staff sometimes did; they were all very protective of Ben.

He kept his calendar on track by allowing slightly more time for each patient than was actually required. Then he used any remaining minutes between appointments to make follow-up calls. His patients appreciated those calls; few specialists went to the trouble. But Ben had realized long ago that this added contact during lulls was an efficient way to get feedback on treatments, and to demonstrate that the results of his treatments were of great concern to him, and, by extension, that his patients were, too.

When Ben developed a successful procedure to relieve intestinal blockages in cancer patients in 1957, he'd been written up in every major medical journal. He began conducting seminars for other doctors, and hundreds of them had converged on Boston to learn the technique. His income had soared.

Since then he'd lavished money on his children and given generously to charity; but he and Marge seldom entertained, had no servants, and nearly always ate at home. And Ben, who'd never flown in an airplane since returning from the war, planned all their vacations: cross-country drives with the kids, always staying in economy motels or campgrounds. "It's more fun to rough it," he'd told them, and Marge agreed. At the end of each year, they'd never spent even half of what he brought home.

He invested the rest of his earnings in commercial real estate and blue chip stocks. And he continued to upgrade the family's living quarters, moving into larger apartments and finally, last month, their five-story brownstone on Chestnut Street.

After breakfast Rebecca and Max began to watch a Christian minister on television. "Hell's pitiless fires," he intoned, "and heaven's reward are both unceasing. A human life is so very short: the blink of an eye. But a soul is eternal, so a single soul, your soul, has more value than the sum of all life on earth. Earthly existence is merely God's test. Are you worthy of everlasting joy, or eternal damnation?"

The girls appeared mesmerized by his words, gestures, and the emotion in his voice. Wondering whether they were attracted by the content of the man's speech or by his hysterical delivery—it never occurred to him that it might have been the medium itself that had so captivated them—Ben broke the spell. "He's just guessing," he told his daughters. "All he really wants is your money. Don't fall for it. He doesn't know any more about heaven and how to get there than anybody else who's still alive."

Marge, washing dishes in the kitchen, overheard this. "He's enthusiastic, though."

"True enough. I watch these guys myself sometimes, but only for their entertainment value. They can, unwittingly, teach you how to think. But for goodness' sake, you sure don't want to let them teach you *what* to think." Ben had great faith in God, but precious little in His self-anointed messengers. He remained an optimist, and a skeptic. Sure, he understood and loved humanity, but with the understanding necessarily came a certain distrust.

They'd all expected to have a picnic today at the Boston Public Gardens. It was not to be.

The phone rang; Marge answered. Her expression turned somber. "It's Alice. Your father's at Beth Israel. Intensive care. I'm sorry, Ben, it's another heart attack."

Ben's mind went momentarily blank, his face frozen in disorientation and denial. The children glanced tentatively toward each other, and then at their mother, for clues about how they were supposed to act. Marge's gaze cast back a grim, composed resolve. She gently grasped Ben's hand and pulled him back to reality.

The family rushed to their car. Jan had no idea what a heart attack was, but sensing the mood, did not ask. She sat in the front with Ben and Marge, her head resting on her father's lap as he drove. The three older children huddled solemnly in the backseat, (numb to the reality) of losing their Grampa.

(Except for Gary.)

The boy visualized his grandfather's face. He could see it with near-photographic clarity. He was grateful for his ability to remember shapes and textures so well, but sometimes it could also be a curse. He thought of all the times Grampa Sam and Grammy Alice had accompanied his mother to his soccer and Little League games, and all those science fairs and art shows at school. Especially the art shows. Gary's own father rarely showed up, even though he usually won the blue ribbon. But they almost always did. *They* were proud of him. And he felt special whenever Sam was there.

Eyes moistening, Gary began to shiver. It seemed as if all warmth had suddenly been drained from him. "D-Do you th-think ... he'll be ... okay?"

Ben's hands tightened on the wheel, as though by squeezing hard enough his emotions might vent through his fingers. "I don't have time for your questions right now," he snapped at the boy; nearly a shout. Marge gently nudged him, and Ben added quietly, "Have to concentrate on my driving, Gary."

Gary's fingernails dug into the soft leather, scarring it. Tears ran down his cheek.

Rebecca patted Gary's right hand, her eyebrows raised in commiseration, as if to say, *That's just the way he is.* Gary gazed back at his sister. He silently mouthed *Thank you,* and put his arm around her shoulder.

Ben fought back his own tears, trying to evoke only happy memories, his gratitude to both of his parents, and the feeble hope his father would quickly recover. But all he thought about was death, a terrible fact of nature he could never fully accept.

The heart attack was massive. By the time the family arrived at the hospital, Samuel Smith, fifty-eight years old, was dead.

Some nine hundred miles away, Robert C.W. Ettinger, a young physics professor at Highland Park College in Michigan, was hard at work researching *The Prospect of Immortality: The Scientific Probability of the Revival and Rejuvenation of Our Frozen Bodies.*

Ettinger's theory held that decay of any human tissue could be virtually halted by submersion into liquid nitrogen, and that someday scientists would possess the means to restore frozen humans to life. The inability to resuscitate a person, he believed, spoke only to the limits of the technology of the day, and little or nothing about that person's potential for life.

He had analyzed death from five discrete viewpoints:

(1) Clinical death: The accepted definition at the time, its criteria being termination of heartbeat and respiration.
(2) Biological death: The state from which resuscitation of the entire body is impossible by currently known means.
(3) Legal death: a term subject to constant reinterpretation.
(4) Religious death: Also an evolving concept.
(5) Cellular death: The irrevocable degeneration of the body's cells.

To Ettinger, death was relative at every level. "A man does not go like the one-horse shay," he wrote, "but dies little by little usually, in imperceptible gradations, and the question of reversibility at any stage depends on the state of medical art."

His book, published in June 1964, would single-handedly initiate the cryonics movement in the United States.

Far too late for Samuel Smith, but perhaps in time for his only son.

October 27, 1963

It had been drizzling off and on all afternoon. The field was slick with mud. Nearing the final whistle, the Wildcats trailed 21–16. It was a very big game: playoff time, or better luck next time. Gary Smith's mother, grandmother, and all three sisters were sitting on cold benches, along with his girlfriend, Minerva Homer; every time he looked, he saw them completely engaged, ardently cheering him on.

But his old man had better things to do.

As they lined up on the opposing team's thirty-eight yard line, Gary glanced at the scoreboard clock, and calculated they probably had time for two more plays; three at the most. Greg Cadbury, the lummox he was assigned to block, had to outweigh him by what? Fifty pounds at least. But the guy was sluggish, and about as bright as your average oak tree.

At five-foot-nine, 154 pounds, Gary knew he had no business playing center, even on junior varsity. But he couldn't run fast enough to play backfield or end, and of course he'd been willing to work twice as hard as anybody else, a characteristic well-appreciated by his coach. In fact he'd started every game this season, had been elected co-captain, and figured next year, as a senior, he would have a clean shot at his letter. Maybe his father would even show up for a game or two. After all, the man had played on several sports teams at Wakefield High School, hadn't he?

Gary shook his head in sudden frustration. Here he'd made straight A's for two years running, at the toughest prep school in Suffolk County. It wasn't like he didn't have to work for those grades, either, like some kids; he'd studied his butt off. Tons of extracurricular activities, too; science and art prizes up the wazoo. And now football. Shit. What else did he have to do? You'd have thought the man could let loose with an occasional "good job" or something, for heaven's sake.

Joe Marchetti, the Wildcat quarterback, called for the snap, and Gary stuck the ball perfectly into the guy's hands. He just needed to hold fatso off for three seconds. Three lousy seconds. Gary tried to imagine the lineman as Ben instead. That always seemed to work, even when he felt as depleted as he did right now. With every ounce of strength he could muster, grunting loudly, he drove into the guy's midsection. But his right foot couldn't get the traction he'd expected, and his inertia deviated slightly off center. Cadbury was going to blow past him.

Shit!

Impetuously, almost as instinct, he extended his left leg and hooked the lineman's ankle, tripping him before he could reach Marchetti. Cadbury toppled crosswise, dropping his full weight onto Gary's leg. Both boys heard a loud snap, like a broom handle breaking across someone's knee.

Gary watched as Marchetti sailed a perfect spiral toward a wide-open man on the six-yard line . . . who dropped it.

Then Gary passed out from the pain.

When   Gary   awakened at the Peter Bent Brigham Hospital that evening, surrounded by his entire family, including Ben, Marge grasped his hand and described how the Wildcats had scored on the next play, making the playoffs.

Without him, he thought.

Then she told him that he'd fractured his femur at the hip, shattered his tibia, and suffered multiple fractures from hip to mid-shin. The doctors had estimated that he would remain in traction for ten days and in a cast for seven months, and that when the cast was finally removed, his left leg would be an inch shorter than his right, if he was lucky. He would never play football again, or serve in the armed forces, or walk without a limp.

Through pain now barely contained by narcotics, Gary silently told himself that his dad would never have been so careless. What a goddamn loser he was.

He looked at his father, and found no argument in his eyes.

July 1, 1971

The main auditorium of New York City's Americana Hotel was a vast, high-ceilinged space with white walls and sweeping, angular lines, its acoustics designed more for impact than clarity; one of those monuments to egoism that seemed to proclaim that no trivial utterance should ever resound from its scaffold. The chairs were oversized, plush and comfortable.

Ben sat himself in the back just as Professor Carl Epstein began, "For the great majority of our cases, we doctors are thoroughly and worthlessly irrelevant . . ."

Over the past decade, Epstein had evolved into a legendary figure in the field of medical education, an iconoclast whose views did not merely challenge, but demolished, conventional wisdom. He had written over seven hundred published articles, authored eleven books—two best-sellers, both controversial—and for two years had hosted a weekly medical ethics program on National Public Television.

Physicians were used to playing the role of God's stand-in; they were not known for self-doubt. Were it not for his talents as a lecturer, Epstein's commentary would probably not have received much notice from this reactionary field of science. Yet today roughly a thousand persons, all medical practitioners, willingly ingested his speech, titled, "The Downside of Hope."

Ben recalled with pride and amusement that, but for his own heroics some thirty years earlier, the renowned instructor from the Johns Hopkins School of Medicine might instead have nourished fish at the bottom of the Pacific. The two men had kept in touch since the war, but had last seen one another three years ago at a New England Medical Association conference. This morning Ben, who still refused to set foot on an airplane, had made the four-hour journey by car for the sole purpose of matching wits over dinner with his longtime friend.

"The overwhelming majority of illnesses and injuries heal themselves," Epstein continued in his trademark conversational style, never referring to notes, "and often we do nothing to speed the process. In fact I estimate that about one-fifth of medicines and surgeries prescribed actually do more harm than good.

"And yet I can prove statistically that our profession adds at least a decade to the average human life span, while improving quality-of-life significantly. How can these two facts be reconciled? Simply because of those rare instances in nearly every person's life when today's medical science makes the difference between complete recovery and permanent disability. Or life and death.

"As some of you know, during the Second World War I was the only medical officer at a Japanese prisoner-of-war camp. To cope with the workload, I managed to press-gang my friend, a teenage fire controller third class—now an acclaimed gastroenterologist, by the way—into assisting with my duties. As if I didn't already owe him enough for having saved my life. But that's another story."

Ben smiled, surprised to hear himself mentioned, especially since Epstein had never thanked him.

For fifty-five minutes the professor regaled the room with tales of their experiences nursing fellow prisoners without medicines, and described their informal study of placebos. The audience was engrossed; there was barely a cough or a murmur.

"A single human brain," he concluded, "is more complex than every telephone network and computer on earth combined. Its power to heal the body is well-documented, although still far beyond our comprehension. Yet it's this talent of the mind that permits quackery of the worst sort; quackery that doesn't merely deprive patients of their money, quackery which seduces them to abandon other treatments that could save or prolong their lives. Who among us has not heard of miracle cures and spontaneous remissions; patients given up for dead who now bounce around, healthy as horses, spreading their stories of hope like a freshly imported, antibiotic-resistant substrain of influenza?"

Epstein went on to describe case histories of patients seduced into harmful or worthless treatments after discovering that those same regimens had "proven successful" on others. "Of course," he added, "it's doubtful that these so-called successful treatments had anything to do with the cure. As I said, faith and hope are powerful and enticing medicines.

"Doctors are educated as scientists, trained to resist wishful thinking in favor of objective detachment. Yet it must also be our job to understand the prescientific, the human element of healing.

"I knew one doctor, a young woman of considerable medical talent, a gifted scientist with a keen, logical mind. Tragically, she was diagnosed with a stage T-2 breast cancer last year. Her physician urged her to undergo radical surgery immediately. 'It's only a breast,' he explained to her with detached objectivity, 'not an arm or leg. With the surgery, your odds of survival are better than seventy percent. There's nothing to think about. I can operate tomorrow.' It never occurred to him that her disease was not the only foe; that there might be a far more implacable enemy.

"Her husband was a caring, optimistic fellow whose sister, a Christian Scientist, had defeated a similar cancer six years earlier. I believe the man loved his wife and genuinely had her interests at heart. 'My sister simply prayed her tumors away, honey, and so can you,' he cajoled her. 'If you have faith, this surgery is completely unnecessary. Why put yourself through it? Don't you know God decides what's best for us?'

"Now try to imagine yourself in her situation. You are a rational scientist, but your judgment is severely clouded by the distress of a terrible illness, and you have no strength to argue. Your life means far less to you than it would if you felt well. And you're torn by conflicting counsel—on the one side a doctor who considers you as a 'case,' just another adenocarcinoma, and on the other a loving spouse who thinks about your welfare day and night. In such a predicament, mightn't you blindly accept the opinion of your sweetheart, which is to say, your emotional anchor over that of an impartial expert? You think not; you think logic would prevail, but until you experience the situation yourself, just how sure can you really be? The understandable need to please those who would care for us in what may be our final days can overwhelm the most objective thinker.

"I tried my damnedest to convince her to have the mastectomy, but by the time I reached her, it was impossible to change her mind.

"She died less than eight months later at the age of thirty-one. Both husband and physician were devastated.

"But each bears part of the blame. Please remember that hope is a two-sided coin, with the face of St. Christopher on the obverse and a jackal on the reverse. As it can heal, so can it kill. We doctors must be sensitive to our patients' need for hope, the right kind of hope, or many of them will seek it elsewhere."

An hour later, at the nearby Pier 52 restaurant, the two former shipmates found themselves discussing philosophy.

"You used to have a friend, an Evangelical Lutheran who became a doctor," Epstein said. "What was his name again?"

"Toby Fiske," Ben said. "Best heart surgeon in Boston. But he's not an Evangelical Lutheran anymore."

"Really? Well good for him! What happened?" To this, Ben found himself sorely tempted to answer something like: Oh, he joined the Hare Krishnas.

"Divorced his first wife," Ben said, "and accepted the blame for it. So the Church excommunicated him. Not sure he's religious now. He's still my best friend, so I guess I should know, but he doesn't like to talk about it."

"Ironic he'd be excommunicated over a divorce," Epstein said. "I asked because a few years ago a lawyer I know told me about one of its ministers who was accused of having sex with a fifteen-year-old girl. Now that, it would seem to me, is a somewhat more serious offense then refusing to remain prisoner of a bad marriage. The Church had to pay her a boat-load of money to keep it quiet. My friend handled the family's side of the negotiations."

"What happened to the minister?"

"Took absolution; agreed to counseling. They moved him to another state. He's now shepherding the good Evangelical Lutherans in Pennsylvania. Just shows how the Church doesn't like to eat its own cooking. Reminds me of those TV ministers who say they can cure anything through prayer and the laying on of hands—the lame shall walk and the blind shall see and all that—but if one of those fellows ever feels a lump in his own armpit, he's on his private jet to the Mayo Clinic in ten minutes flat."

Ben laughed. "You think all religions are scams, don't you?"

"Yes, I suppose I do," Epstein said. "But the religions are mostly scamming themselves. That they scam others is usually a side effect. Such is the nature of that brand of duplicity. Take that minister, for example. Evangelical Lutherans supposedly believe that heaven is superior to any pleasure we can experience on earth, and hell is worse then any misery we can ever imagine."

"Most Christian religions support that theory," Ben said.

"True. And heaven and hell are both eternal. Eternal. What if this minister had somehow died in flagrante delicto before he could receive absolution for his sin? Or worse, suppose even after absolution, the Heavenly Father were to deem that particular sin as beyond all forgiveness, a genuine possibility according to their dogma. Do you really think that for a piece of ass this minister was willing to risk inescapable, permanent damnation? Can you accept for one minute that such a man could possibly have believed the Church's doctrine with the same conviction he used to express that doctrine to his flock?"

"Interesting point," Ben allowed.

"Personally, I think most organized religion is no different from medical quackery."

"How so?"

"Its practitioners are either liars or self-deceivers who concoct a worldview that gets them where they want to go. And mostly they play to our innate fear of death." He glanced at Ben mischievously. "You still want to live forever, Ben?"

"Been a long time since I've thought about that," he answered, then realized it was a lie. In fact he thought about it daily. "The idea seems more far-fetched for you and me today than it did twenty-eight years ago. Not as much time left to figure out how to do it. But yes, I would if I could. Just to see what happens in this amazing world."

"What do you suppose becomes of you when you die?" Epstein prodded, obviously steering the conversation toward a predetermined destination.

"I don't imagine anyone knows."

"I think *I* know."

"You do? Well, tell me, then."

"*Nothing* becomes of you! The billions of years after you die will seem exactly like the billions of years that happened before you were born. Religion and God, heaven and hell, are all inventions of man—"

"Which doesn't explain why so many of us believe in one God," Ben interrupted, "and why so many religions believe in essentially the same monotheistic deity."

"No, but evolution and human nature can explain that part."

"Evolution?"

"Sure," Epstein said. "Belief in eternal reward, for acts of heroism in war and morality in peace, would tend to preserve societies and therefore the people who comprise them."

"Interesting."

"Human nature makes its contribution to religion, too. With so much misery and unfairness around us, we refuse to believe that death is the end of it, that it isn't part of some greater plan where good citizens are eventually rewarded and evil is punished. But we, as scientists, should resist our natural impulse to believe that which we merely *wish* to be true. Life and awareness are matter and energy directed by molecules in our brain cells, and when those cells die, our identity is permanently lost."

"No such thing as a soul?" Ben said, even as he doubted his own words. "I refuse to think of myself as mere atoms. How can *you?*"

"If you mean by a soul the essence of an individuals' identity, then yes, there is most definitely such a thing as a soul. But take away the matter housing that soul and it will disappear forever. The concept of a soul *sans* matter, a unique magic in our corpuscles, is called *vitalism*. It's an idea which nearly all biologists now reject. We discover tangible and chemical reasons for every cellular reaction and capability we study: motion, reproduction, growth, excretion, consciousness itself. The whole field of biotechnology is taking root as a result of these discoveries. The soul is a tempting concept, Ben, but wrong beyond earthly terms. Life on this planet is all there is. Once you die, you are dust."

Their debates on religion notwithstanding, both were scientists; neither accepted the theory popular among intellectuals that truth was somehow subjective or unknowable, that the human mind manufactured its own reality. If that were the case, Ben understood, all knowledge would be of equal value and therefore worthless. But today he realized that some knowledge was unattainable, like the *theological* knowledge Epstein—who intentionally pronounced the world as *the illogical*—claimed to possess.

"I hope not," Ben said, biting his tongue.

"I also think that those of us who love being alive should strive with every fiber of our being never to die."

"Now that I can agree with. But it'll never be possible for *us* to live forever. Maybe within a few generations, but you and I won't see it. Medical science isn't advancing fast enough for us to participate."

"I admit it's unlikely," Epstein said, "but certainly not impossible. I just read a very interesting book called *The Prospect of Immortality*. Ever hear of it?"

"No."

"It's about freezing people. After their hearts stop beating, but before their cells decompose. The technology is called *cryonics*."

"You mean cryogenics, don't you?"

"No. Cryogenics is the entire subdivision of physics dealing with the creation and consequences of very low temperatures. Freezing living organisms in biostasis is called cryonics, a subset of cryogenics. It's a fairly new term. Anyway, the author speculates that scientists of the future will discover how to revive and rejuvenate our bodies."

"Don't you think you might be speaking out of both sides of your mouth?" Ben asked.

"What do you mean?"

"If faith has such a down side in medicine, doesn't cryonics have it, too?"

"I don't see how," Epstein answered.

"Well, cryonics is a longshot, isn't it? Sort of a grasp at straws."

"You bet, but if you're falling over the edge of forever, would you rather grasp at straws or empty air?"

"But aren't you worried that people who think cryonics will give them a second chance might not take care of themselves as diligently? They might not exercise or eat right or follow their doctor's advice. Cryonics might offer patients the kinds of hope which, and I quote, 'seduces them to abandon other treatments that could save or prolong their lives.'"

"Oh. You actually listened to my speech. Makes it much harder for me to argue the point with you tonight, doesn't it?" Epstein said, beaming with delight. At first Ben was confused by his friend's effervescence, but then he understood: Being caught in a contradiction had reminded Epstein that he was once again talking to someone at his own level, an occurrence to savor. After all, it could be damned lonely up there.

(Then all at once Ben asked himself: Who was being dogmatic now?)

October 28, 1982

Had it been a thousand days? As easily a thousand minutes or years. The loss seemed to expand to fill time, losing barely a hint of its bite in the interval's amorphous growth. His mind's eye flashed to Marge's grave and the empty plot beside it. Waiting for him, beckoning him. He elbowed the thought aside as one might desperately shove a schoolyard bully . . .

Oh God! Suddenly Ben realized he would rather crawl from his Beacon Hill brownstone to the goddamn Pacific Ocean than trust some unseen pilot on one of those flying death traps. In fact he felt queasy just from thinking about it. But what choice did he have? Herbert "Mack" McGuigan had saved his life thirty-nine years ago; pulled him from those cold Pacific waters in the nick of time. He had to go to Phoenix and pay his last respects; since the funeral was tomorrow afternoon, flying was the only way to get there in time. Unfortunately.

Death remained Ben's greatest fear, yet it wasn't fear of death that caused this anxiety; he knew flying was the safest way to travel. He suspected his fear of flight had more to do with lack of control. In a car, fate was a wheel under his own hands.

Ben imagined sitting in an airplane, something he hadn't done since 1945, when suddenly the engines lost power or a wing sheared off or the hydraulics failed, and there he was, strapped in his seat, helplessly pissing and screaming with nothing to be done about it. He assumed his heart would explode in his chest before the plane hit the ground.

He decided to rent a car in Phoenix, and once Mack's remains were in the earth, he could drive home. It would only take four days for the return trip, but he'd have to fly there first; no question about that.

Even though a travel agency was located just a few blocks from his office, he walked the three miles to Crimson Travel in Cambridge; the same Crimson Travel where he'd bought the occasional train ticket back in medical school. At age fifty-seven, his health was not perfect—he suffered from arthritis, seasonal allergies, and occasional migraines—but he tried to take care of himself. He walked six miles every day, lifted weights twice a week, performed a daily ten-minute stretching routine, and ate a vitamin- and fiber-rich low-fat diet.

He'd experimented with other ways to stave off the Grim Reaper, including yoga, macrobiotics, meditation, homeopathic medicine, vegetarianism, and megadoses of various vitamins, minerals, and amino acids, but concluded that the life-prolonging reputations of these therapies had been sustained either through fallacy or fraud. Everyone wanted a magic pill, it seemed; even scientists like him could be temporarily seduced.

Although Ben did not pretend to fathom the true nature of his Creator, he considered himself a religious man. Now his struggle against death was based partially on fear of what might await him there, as though God might never absolve his transgressions so long as Gary withheld forgiveness. He pictured the Almighty impatiently tapping His divine foot, awaiting His chance to punish Benjamin Smith's sins against his own son. Ben knew it was an absurd image, yet there it was.

But in the end, he simply loved being alive.

"I know you, don't I?" the travel agent at the desk said. "Ben, right? You used to come here, must be thirty years ago. You were at the medical school back then."

Ben sneaked a look at her name plate. "Ah, Gloria, how could I possibly forget a face as lovely as yours? You've hardly aged," he lied. People liked hearing that; he knew, because he liked it himself. Time was an enemy to every living thing.

And of course Gloria smiled. For several minutes they talked about the old days. Gloria admitted that she used to have a crush on him; something she'd kept and now wanted to share. An easy thing to understand.

"Good thing I didn't know it back *then*," he said. "Might've wrecked my marriage."

Again she beamed.

It was all he had to give her.

The one-way coach ticket was $239. The rental car and motels would cost a similar amount. Ben kept careful track of his finances even though he had more money than he could ever spend. When the time arrived to join Marge, he would leave his grandchildren a concrete reminder that their grandfather had once walked this earth. He would also bequeath some funds into a spendthrift trust for Gary: guilt money, pure and simple.

Walking back to his office, he caressed the locket that dangled from his neck on a slender gold chain. It was the same piece that Toby had borrowed from him before their tours of duty; at their first encounter in 1945 after returning from the war, Toby had returned it in exchange for his lucky rabbit foot. For the past three years Ben had worn this antique, containing photographs of Marge at age twenty on one side and of Sam and Alice on the other, with locks of their hair in the center. Since Marge's burial, he'd never removed it even for a moment, and now imagined he would wear the small heirloom until his own death, perhaps beyond.

As he gently held it between thumb and forefinger, he thought once again about his wife's final days. Such remembrances were never farther from him than the locket.

It was 1979. They'd been married thirty-four years and were as happy as any couple he knew. Then it happened, so damned suddenly. She was diagnosed with pancreatic cancer in early August, and gone by mid-September. For six weeks they'd both known she was dying. Ben would not go to work; he rarely left her side. While her body and mind disintegrated before his eyes, he'd felt frozen, scared that if he left, even for a moment, he might miss that single flash of lucidity, that epiphany in which she would reveal to him her mysterious wisdom. He had sat with her every day, all day, holding her hand, talking about the children and reliving their lives together.

He thought of all his cancer patients and their families, and the countless ways spouses and loved ones coped with coming death. Those who would actually do the dying almost had it easier; they only needed to accept their own death. But those who would have to continue often avoided acknowledgment, as though they could somehow conjure up their own reality. "When you get better and come home, my love, the first thing we'll do is . . ." *Non cogito, ergo non est.*

Death always brought such pain! It could make survivors renounce God, even hate Him. Some would lose themselves in the company or commiseration of friends, while others found more self-destructive diversions: isolation, alcohol, television, drugs. Widows and widowers who truly loved their spouses would start to remember their most irritating qualities, as if by diminishing the person, they could somehow cut their loss. Conversely, troubled marriages would often blossom into rhapsody when nurtured in the mind's imperfect recall.

But always there was evasion. Why? Because only time could heal such wounds; allow a scab to grow. And wasn't that the ultimate irony? Without enough time to live their own lives, they had to spend this irreplaceable time dying the deaths of others. Others they'd loved so dearly.

Ben knew them well; his own kind.

Marge's last rational words, two days before she died, had been, "Ben, look after Gary. He needs you. Please. For me." Everything she'd said to him after that seemed unintelligible. But Ben remained haunted by the notion that deep insight must have existed, hidden somewhere in Marge's last ramblings.

October 29, 1982

Ben left the house at 7:05 A.M., driving toward nearby Brookline to have breakfast with his mother, as he did almost every day. Alice had the coffee ready and Ben made French toast, which they shared along with the latest family gossip.

Ben marveled at his mother's acuity. Over time, the operating speed of every human brain slows. But a well-nurtured brain compensates for the loss of perceptual velocity by creating new synapses. This Alice had accomplished. She read through two daily newspapers, several magazines, and three to four books a week on diverse subjects, retaining the useful essence. Ben's children called her often for advice; her knowledge of their interests, their achievements, and even their problems, was encyclopedic.

But at seventy-eight, her body was starting to degenerate, especially her knees and spine. walking, even with a cane, was becoming arduous. Ben wondered how much longer she'd be able to sustain such an independent existence.

"I'll be out of town a few days," he told her. "The girls'll look in on you."

"Where you going?"

"Phoenix. Remember Ensign McGuigan?"

"The man who saved my baby's life? Met him at your college graduation. I wouldn't likely forget him, would I? Please give him my best."

"Wish to God I could, Mom. I'm going to his funeral."

"Oh." She gazed into his eyes, a deliberate calmness overtaking her. "He had quite a pretty wife. Anna was it?"

"Annie."

"Annie. Of course. She's still . . ."

"Alive . . . yes."

"I doubt she'll remember me, but would you deliver a message?"

"Okay, Mom."

"My mother, your Gramma, passed on just seven weeks after Grampa did, remember?"

"Of course."

"I'm always saddened that so many people die during the first year after their spouse does, but I understand why. When Sam passed away, I was entirely certain I wanted to join him as soon as possible; actually started to wish for my own death. And if I'd kept wishing for it, I think Death might have come to me, too. Of course life will never be the same without your father; I remember him and ache for his smile. Often I cry. But if I'd followed him to the grave, just think what I would've missed! I'd never have seen my granddaughters' weddings, or met any of my four great-grandchildren. Life is the most precious thing there is, Benjamin, so you tell Annie that, from one widow to another. You can't keep your memories alive if your heart isn't pumping oxygen to your brain. You tell Annie McGuigan I said the best tribute she can grant her husband is never to give up on her own life."

Ben hugged his mother hard, suddenly realizing that her message was not really intended for Annie McGuigan at all, but rather for Benjamin Franklin Smith. Nothing was ever so moving as when one had to examine it twice to see or hear it.

He left at 8:37 and stopped at Rebecca's place. It was on the way and he had plenty of time. She embraced him, not at all surprised; he showed up at each of his daughters' homes at unpredictable times, but predictably twice a week. His grandson George, my father, who was nine at the time, had already left for school. For the next hour, while Rebecca worked at a drafting table in the next room, Ben sat on the floor playing tea party with Katie, his four-year-old granddaughter. Since he only worked afternoons these days, he often stayed all morning, and wished he could now. It would be so easy just to let this trip go; to lose himself in these visceral joys. But he would not permit himself such an escape.

"I'll see you two goddesses next week, and George, too, I hope," he said as he left. "I love you."

"I love you, too, Grampy." Katie ran up and gave him a long hug and a quick kiss on the mouth. Rebecca watched, beaming.

At Logan Airport he popped two Valium. He'd hoped not to, but here he was, nowhere near the plane, already shaking like a wet dog on a blustery day. He walked through the X-ray machines, to the gate, and down the boarding chute.

The cabin's spaciousness surprised him; nothing like it looked from the outside, and remarkably different from the claustrophobic C-47 "Dakotas" he'd flown Stateside after the war. Hell, he could stand straight up and still have six inches to spare. Why hadn't he realized that before?

He took his seat. The 727 was barely one-third full. And the Valium was starting to work. His perceptions were still sharp, but he felt comfortably detached from them.

A male flight attendant droned through the safety procedures. But Ben, on his first commercial airline trip, listened carefully. "Should the air pressure change suddenly, an oxygen mask will drop from the overhead compartment. If you're traveling with a small child, first place the mask over your own nose and mouth. Once your mask is operational, only then should you do the same for the child."

That seemed logical. The instinctive reaction for parents would have been to save their children first. But you couldn't make sure your kids were okay unless you were still alive yourself, could you?

Ben listened to the rest of the instructions, relaxed. Maybe this wouldn't be so bad.

And it wasn't. Until the engine pitch increased and the Boeing began its backward roll.

Suddenly he felt a tightness in his chest. Was this a coronary? He was a doctor, after all. Shouldn't he have known how to tell? Yes, his father had died at fifty-eight, but his mother was still in good cardiovascular health at seventy-eight. Besides, Toby had recently given him a physical and EKG stress test, both of which had come out well. But now he felt like a grandchild had just jumped on his rib cage, forcing all the air from his lungs.

Should he get off and seek medical attention? That's what he'd have told his patients to do. Probably heavy anxiety, he decided. Yes, an anxiety attack. Must be. God how he hated airplanes.

When the plane finally became airborne, Ben's pain intensified. Then the Horror flashed through his mind and for a split second he was back on the *Asahi Maru*, that floating torture chamber. Suddenly, the carbon-dioxide-rich air inside the plane seemed cloying, his breathing became difficult. He began to gasp for air. It felt like a goddamn elephant was squatting on his chest. Instinctively, before becoming aware of it, he started to push the vision from his consciousness. He forced himself to respire evenly. But the dull pain in his chest remained.

To distract himself, he daydreamed about his family, work, Toby, Epstein. Hell, anything pleasant at all.

Gary and Maxine had both received medical degrees, while Rebecca had become an architect and Jan a lawyer. The girls were good in their professions, each having achieved some success. Gary worked hard, of course, but his career had never flourished. Marge had once speculated that Gary—like Ben, a gastroenterologist—had only entered the field to placate his father; he might have been temperamentally unsuited for medicine.

Ben believed he'd given his son every opportunity. At Marge's urging, he'd taken Gary into the practice as a partner. Gary had been thrilled at the opportunity and tried to make it work. Technically speaking, Gary was a good-enough doctor, but never had what it took to succeed.

Ben had sat his son down and tried to discuss the matter.

"You get too emotionally involved with your cases; your objectivity is suspect," he'd told Gary. "Worse yet, your appointments run late because you spend too much time with each patient. Keeping patients waiting is disrespectful."

"They don't seem to mind."

"But I do. By God, we're doctors. We can't abide sloppiness. We have our reputation to think about."

"You mean *your* reputation. I can't run my practice like a factory."

"Are you saying I do?"

Gary backed off. "No. I just mean our styles are different. You're a great doctor, Dad."

"Damn right I am."

Gary was his son, Ben now reminded himself—again. What the hell was wrong with him? Then he rationalized that maybe the fault wasn't so much his own as Gary's. After all, a parent could not make a child become responsible and effective. A father could only set an example and hope his children would follow. This all sounded fine to Ben, except for one minor problem: He didn't believe a word of it.

After about an hour the pain subsided. Ben fell asleep from nervous exhaustion.

Two hours later the flight attendant tapped his shoulder. "Wake up, sir. We've arrived."

In the terminal, he picked up his rental car and a map. The teenage girl at the counter said he looked like her father.

"I wish I was your father," he answered with a wink, which got her to grin.

But driving to the funeral home, the new sun-dazzled surroundings barely registered. His mind sought only Gary.

Three years ago, when Marge died, the real problems began. Gary had started to drink. Within six weeks he'd been arrested for cocaine possession. Minerva, his wife of six years, left him. He'd abandoned his medical practice, his license was suspended, and he'd gone through a series of decreasingly productive jobs. Finally, and perhaps mercifully, he'd quit working entirely. For the next two years Gary had been in and out of AA and rehabs. Even more disturbing to Ben, about eight months ago Gary had stopped asking for money, their only certain connection; they hadn't seen each other since. Ben hated to think how his son might be supporting himself; probably dealing drugs or burglarizing homes.

He worried that the next place he saw Gary might be the visitors' section of a penitentiary.

T h r o u g h   t h e   l e f t side of his windshield Ben noticed a medium-sized one-story building with a tiny sing: THE PHOENIX LIFE EXTENSION FOUNDATION. He'd never heard of it before, although he always tried to read up on organizations that claimed to promote longevity. As a doctor, he would rationalize, he needed to learn about the latest theories.

So far, nearly every such claim had been exaggerated; many were outright frauds.

Was this a research foundation on longevity? Maybe they tested antiaging hormones on lab rats, or offered lifestyle modification programs to people. Or were they one of those bullshit religious—or worse, cryonics—cults?

Ben remembered his discussion about cryonics with Epstein back in 1971, but hadn't heard much about it since. Apparently the idea had never really caught on.

He also recalled reading about a cryonics facility in California. The article noted that about a dozen people had paid between $8,000 and $24,000 each to have themselves frozen after death in the hopes of being revived, cured, and restored to youth decades or even centuries later. It was eventually discovered that the owner had neglected the bodies, allowing them to thaw and rot. There remained some question as to whether the fraud was preplanned or forced by financial circumstance.

Ben hoped it wasn't another one of those cryonics scam outfits, and made a mental note to call when he returned to Boston.

He pulled into the parking lot of the Saint Francis Funeral Home on Camelback Road and walked inside, wondering if he would recognize anyone. Maybe even Carl Epstein; Ben hadn't heard from him for the better part of a year.

Throughout their adult lives, Ben and Mack had exchanged letters, cards, and photographs of their families, and had often spoken by telephone. But he'd never met any of his children or friends, and hadn't seen Mack or Annie since they'd flown to Boston for Marge's funeral.

Because the McGuigans were Catholic, Ben had anticipated the open casket. Mack hadn't changed much—except now he was dead, of course. Ben laughed nervously under his breath.

Then came sorrow and the hint of tears and, less noticeably, perhaps because it was so devastating, the fear of his own death. The end of things for all time? Although the man had been thirteen years older than he, the impression remained of Mack as the heroic young ensign.

Ben knew there wasn't supposed to be as much sadness when an old person died. Old people died; that was what they did. Most others barely noticed the demise of a seventy-year-old man in their midst, except maybe when "the deceased" happened to have been famous. Even then it was quite unlike the intense bereavement experienced when a child or young adult met an untimely death. But to other old men and women, all deaths were untimely. When an ordinary seventy-year-old man like Mack passed away, you could be damn sure his surviving contemporaries paid heed to the passage.

Today's was an elderly crowd with only a smattering of younger folks. The room was nearly full: almost a hundred people, most seated in pews, while perhaps a dozen filed past the casket. Some mourners knelt in front of it for a minute or so; a few genuflected somberly, as Ben waited in line with these kindred others to voice his farewell.

He saw Mack's widow dressed in black, seated with family in a special row off to the side. Annie looked at him vacantly. She appeared frail and dazed; he wasn't sure whether she'd recognized him at all. Her expression reminded him of Alice's grief and confusion following his father's death. As he waited, he tried to reconstruct the message his mother had imparted: *Take it from someone who's been there; the best tribute you can grant Mack is never to give up on your own life.* He hoped to give comfort, too, but realized such heartache was impossible to soothe; Annie would never be the same. She'd lost a piece of herself, and humans did not spontaneously regenerate.

Then he looked around, searching for familiar faces. His eyes caught a group in the seventh and eighth rows, fourteen men whose posture and body language suggested a cohesive unit, not unlike a Boy Scout troop at a symphony; even without their uniforms it was no great feat to discern such a group. He had not seen these men in thirty-seven years, yet once he understood they were together, he recognized most of them; he was certain of it. He nodded his head, and many seemed to return the greeting. As a wave of memories rushed over him, he felt light-headed again. The room spun and his knees buckled. He collapsed onto the threadbare carpet.

The Horror returns; suddenly it is 1943 again.

    Ben finds himself back in that crawl space on the Japanese troop carrier-turned-POW ship, reliving it all: his inability to move, squashed into a lump, the ceiling chicken wire bearing down on his back. The bodies of his sick and dying shipmates locking him into place. The cries and whimpers, the smell like a fist down his throat. And the dread.

Sensing the progress of the ship as it cuts through the whitecaps, he huddles there wondering how his parents would feel if he never made it home. He imagines friends he left behind and things he'd hoped to do. And mostly he wonders about Marge. How long would she mourn? What kind of man would she marry? How clearly and how often would she remember him?

Since he no longer holds power over his circumstances, he decides to focus on the only thing he still controls: his attitude. He'll apply his mind, salvage whatever he can from the only life God will ever give him. He knows he must be strong. If he ever gets off this boat alive, he'll force himself, through sheer will, not to be bitter. In fact he'll never even think about this ordeal once it's over. He'll live his life in the present and future without dwelling in the past.

This thought seems to make him stronger. It will help him endure the hell which on this day has barely begun. No amount of suffering can make Ben want to die. As long as there is any hope, he will cherish and cling to life like a miser guarding his gold.

Ben will survive by placing the hellish voyage in a separate compartment and locking it, apart from his conscious mind. A few fleeting images will escape over the next thirty-nine years as unwelcome refugees, but he will mostly succeed in maintaining their confinement.

Ben opened his eyes. Several people hovered over him. A disembodied hand offered a paper cup of water. He drank and felt better. Had it only been a dream? He wondered. No, a flashback. God, a repressed trauma, resurfacing.

The sight of these fellow survivors had suddenly shattered his carefully constructed prison. Now he understood. That suffocating subterranean chamber, that floating crypt, was where his loathing of cramped spaces began, and his need for control, and the fear of flying. On that boat, with that resolution. And something far worse; something evil that overpowered his rational mind, had started there, too.

His head hurt where he'd bumped it, but he assured everyone he was fine.

Then he rode a limousine to the McGuigans' church with six of his shipmates, and swapped stories about Mack and Epstein and the Navy and the war. One of the men told Ben that Epstein had become very sick about a year ago, and that no one had heard from him since. "Probably died alone," he speculated. "Don't think he had any family at all."

"He didn't," Ben said sadly, wondering for a moment about the point of human existence. What good had it done to save Epstein's life, or his own, or anyone's, if they were all going to die anyway?

Then he reconsidered, deciding: All the good in the world! Epstein had believed in no heaven and no God, yet he'd been a moral man, a great educator, a compassionate doctor whose life's work helped others. And none of it would have been possible had he drowned that day in 1943. Didn't every good deed tip into another like an endless series of dominoes? If he had indeed saved Epstein's life, surely he must have saved many others with it.

The men exchanged addresses, promising to keep in touch, and for the moment intending to. Few actually would; most would feel more comfortable keeping their memories at arm's length.

After the interment service ended, Ben drove to the airport, returned the rental car, bought another one-way ticket, and boarded the plane for home.

At first his heart raced and he began to hyperventilate. But this time he understood why. He forced himself to relax, breathing steadily and slowly.

Inhale. Exhale. Inhale. Exhale.

Within fifteen minutes his pulse returned to normal. It was almost comfortable to fly; his fears and anxiety had nearly disappeared. A fresh thought crossed his mind, something about the oxygen masks on the airplane. He fell asleep thinking about Gary and the guilt that had suffocated them both for thirty-five years.

October 30, 1982

By the time the plane landed, Ben knew what to do.

He realized that he'd visited each of his daughters' homes hundreds of times, yet had never been inside Gary's apartment. At 4:02 A.M. he rang the doorbell in the building vestibule.

"Who is it?" Gary answered. It was only three words but the tone suggested a few more. Who *in the hell* is it? was what Ben heard.

Ben shuddered, nervous but determined. "It's me, son. I need to talk to you."

Gary paused a second or two, then buzzed him in. Ben took the elevator to the third floor and saw his son, dressed in blue jeans and a paint-smeared plaid shirt, waiting in the doorway. Was he already awake? Or still up from last night?

Gary's face was serious and handsome, but wizened for his age. He staggered a bit when he moved, but apparently didn't need a cane these days. To Ben's relief, he appeared sober.

The two-room apartment was smaller than he'd imagined, and the smell of paints assailed his nostrils. Half a dozen technical books on art and draftsmanship, some open, most borrowed from the public library, lay scattered on a small coffee table. A dozen paintings in various stages of completion, some already signed "Gary Franklin Smith," rested upon easels or on the floor.

Ben was as surprised by this as he would have been to find a sleeping Bengal tiger curled in a corner; until that moment, he had not know that his son was still painting. He didn't know much about Gary at all, he realized. His own son, and it seemed he didn't know the slightest bit about him. What had he allowed to become of them?

Ben had studied art history in college, enough to recognize that Gary had real talent. He wondered what other aptitudes his coldness had locked within his son. Or had the suffering he'd inflicted actually *released* that talent? He might never know. Some roots could never be unearthed—and perhaps shouldn't be.

"These are good." Even that would have been impossible to say before now.

"Thanks. It pays the bills. Uh, what are you doing here at four in the morning?"

Ben stood speechless, feeling the same anxiety he'd always felt around Gary, but at least now he understood. Eventually the words came. "I've never told anyone what I'm about to tell you. Not even your mother. It happened during the war, and I've suppressed it all these years. Remembered it yesterday for the first time."

"I know about the POW camp. Mom told me."

"This was before that. It started on the day they sank the *Boise* ..." Ben tried to depict his horrific voyage, the full essence of it, every sight and sound and smell he could remember. And the fear.

He sat painfully for nearly an hour, purging every morsel of his memory. Gary never said a word.

Finally Ben told him why he'd come. "I know I haven't been much of a father to you."

Gary gazed back, looking straight through the man, barely seeing his face. And why should he? It seemed his father had never noticed *him*! Even in medical school, and later when they'd shared the medical practice, not once had Ben asked him how he spent his free time. So his father never knew that Gary could barely wait for his classes or studies of the day's appointments to end so he could rush home to try some new technique, or a different combination of shading or color, shape or light.

Now images assaulted Gary; recollections of his father berating him, or worse, ignoring him. Of Ben shouting, "I haven't got time for your questions right now!" He remembered his own fear on the way to the hospital that day when Grampa Sam died, when he needed comfort: some acknowledgement from his father. And now the tables had turned. But what could he say?

"You weren't that bad."

Ben answered, "I never gave you the understanding or attention or love your sisters got. I can only imagine how that made you feel."

"I'm over it. I'll be okay. Look around you, so you'll know it's true."

Ben had once smoked cigarettes, as many as three packs a day, and upon quitting cold turkey in 1964, had felt almost the way he did right now: uncomfortable, restless, mentally and physically blunted. He felt an urge to leave, to get out of that room, but knew he must force himself to continue.

"Yesterday I figured out why I treated you that way."

Gary winced. "You don't have to do this, Dad."

Ben sensed Gary was curious in spite of their mutual discomfort. He latched onto that curiosity as if it were a stairway railing. "Yes I do. I need you to understand, to know where it all came from."

"Okay."

"When we took you home from the hospital to our tiny apartment, I discovered I couldn't tolerate a baby who screamed and cried and soiled his diapers and smelled like all infants do. Babies' emotions and pain and hunger know no reason, and your reactions to that suffering seemed completely beyond my control.

"And then there was the uncertainty; that was the worst thing about the POW ship. And about *you*. I never had any brothers or sisters, and you were our first child. So I had no idea what to expect, no inkling of what was waiting for me. By the time your sisters came, I knew what parenthood was like, but you arrived first. When I close my eyes, I can practically relive it. All three of us living in that tiny room, and the anxiety of first-time parenthood, pulling me back to that cramped hellhole of a ship."

Ben clenched his teeth, continuing, undaunted in the face of his son's silence. "When your sisters were born, we kept moving to bigger places.

Until now, I never realized the moves were another way of fleeing memories. Each new home offered more breathing space, you see. I avoided confined surroundings because they took me back to *that ship*."

He gazed at his son, hoping for a spark of understanding. But those blue eyes looked back at him with shock and, perhaps worse, embarrassment.

"All these years you and I were at war, at least in my mind," he continued. "Every time I saw you, I felt trapped, almost as if enemy soldiers were trying to capture me . . . to bring me back to their ship, that floating death coop I was so determined never to remember again."

Gary's expression remained unchanged, so Ben made one more attempt. "It took me until now to realize what it was between us, and that none of it ever had anything to do with you. You were just unlucky to be my first child is all. Son, I'm so sorry. I only wish there was some way I could make it up to you."

Gary didn't seem angry, nor did he appear to take satisfaction in Ben's predicament. "Okay, Dad," he said, nodding slowly. "I believe you, or at least I believe you believe it. But what should we do?" Gary's face was calm, noncommittal, like a parent listening to his child's I-lost-my-math-homework story.

"I want to be the kind of father I always should've been. I want to understand and be understood. That's all. I don't expect you ever to forgive me." That was Ben's only lie; forgiveness was exactly what he wanted.

Gary hesitated. Ben stared at him, and waited. Finally the son opened his arms to the father, shuffled toward him. "I'll try to understand, Dad, and I do forgive you."

They hugged, their first embrace in the three years since Marge's funeral. But when Ben stepped back, he saw nothing but pity on Gary's face. Of course! His son would never understand and didn't forgive him at all; he was just thinking to himself, *How can it hurt to be nice to the old man?*

Ben deplored this moment as nothing more than a momentary amity between two well-meaning strangers. Like Longfellow's ships that pass in the night, he thought, reciting the verse in his mind: "We pass and speak one another, Only a look and a voice; then darkness again and a silence."

Which might be all they could ever have between them. His revelation, he decided, had come far too late. Still, even as the gloom of his failure plagued his heart, Ben Smith's nature would not permit him to give up.

Later that day, Ben started to feel an odd weakness; confirming his fears. He dialed Boston Cardiology Associates and asked for Toby.

There was no better cardiologist in Boston, but even if there were, Ben would have found it difficult to betray their friendship by seeing another doctor. They'd stayed the closest of friends and confidants ever since second grade; Toby had no family, Ben was the only permanent relationship in his life. Over these past twenty years, Ben had served as best man at all three of his friend's marriages, the most recent of which had ended six years ago, in typical Tobias Fiske fashion. Of course Ben was there to console him through all three bitter, and expensive, divorces. And after Marge died, Toby had canceled his appointments and closed his practice a full week to remain at Ben's side.

"I think you should come as soon as poss—" Toby paused. "Ben," he restarted, "haul your ass over here right-the-hell now!"

When Toby stepped into the examination room, Ben marveled at the man Toby had become. Always solid and dark-complexioned, his friend had filled out and matured into almost magazine-cover appearance. He looked like the hero of a Latin American romance novel. Yet for all his physical attributes and apparent robust health, Toby's relationships were only rarely stable. Ben sighed and awaited his friend's verdict.

Toby advised him to check into Massachusetts General Hospital. "You've had a mild heart attack," he explained, very businesslike, though Ben recognized the apparent dispassion as forced. "Too bad you stayed on that airplane. If you'd sought help right away, you might've avoided permanent damage to the heart muscle. As it is, the lesions are small, but dangerous. You'll have to be far more careful from now on."

Then he put both hands on Ben's shoulders and gazed at his face. "Ben, this is serious stuff."

Ben realized then that Toby was terrified. Suddenly he was, too.

"You better believe I won't wait next time."

That night, as Jan Smith sat home nursing four-month-old Sarah while her husband Noah tried to determine which bills to pay first and which ones could wait, the telephone rang.

"Hello."

"Jan, it's your old dad."

"Hey, Dad," she answered, delighted as always to hear his voice. "How are you?"

"Not too good. Apparently I had a mild heart attack yesterday."

"My God. No!"

Noah came into the room. "What's the matter?"

Jan shook her head, scowled at him, then focused all attention on the telephone.

"Now Jan, don't worry," Ben said. "I'm fine, sweetheart Just staying here overnight . . ."

"You're in the hospital?"

"For observation. I'll be back home tomorrow."

"Can I come visit?"

"No, really, honey, that's not why I called. Just wanted to . . . Look, Jan, I promise I'm not dying, it's just . . ."

"What is it, Dad? Tell me."

"Well, this whole thing made me think that maybe I should start planning my estate. For when it happens, you know. Not that it'll be soon; not likely anyway. But y'know, the two page will you wrote up for me, that must've been five, six years ago . . . Now don't cry, honey. I'm really okay."

"I just don't know . . . if I can do it. Write up your will, I mean," she managed. "Oh, Dad, I'm sorry. Maybe you should find another lawyer . . ."

"Yeah, I know, honey. I try to imagine what it might be like for you. And I can't, because the only way I can do it is to reverse this in my head . . . and it's too awful. Besides, my finances are complex. I'll try to find a specialist. That'll be better for both of us."

"Yes. Good idea. Please, can't I come visit you in the hospital tonight? I'll bring Sarah." The last offer was added in the tone of a parent bribing a child with the promise of ice cream.

This touched Ben's ailing heart. "It's past visiting hours. I'll drop by tomorrow, as soon as they let me out of this paradise-on-earth. Don't worry, honey. I'm fine."

After Ben hung up, Jan sobbed to her husband, "Dad's had a heart attack."

Noah hugged her, and there was neither passion nor comfort in the embrace. "He's okay?"

"So he said. But he wanted me to write up a new will for him."

"When'll you talk to him about it?"

Jan stared at Noah. He wanted her to write her own father's dying declaration! Revulsion overwhelming her sadness, she managed to answer, "He's gonna find a trust and estates specialist instead."

"Why?" Noah asked, too sharply.

"Because I can't write my own father's goddamn will, that's why!"

"Okay, okay. I was just thinking we could use the business."

"I don't charge him for legal work."

"Yeah, I forgot," Noah said. "Still, we might want to keep an eye on things, don't you think? It's not just *us* anymore. We have a daughter to think about now."

"Bullshit."

November 5, 1982

Ben sat at his office desk during a rare lull in his work schedule; no patients in the waiting room, no appointments for the next twenty minutes, no follow-up calls needing to be made right then. He finally had a moment to think, and what he thought was: That was dumb, dumb, dumb! He was lucky he hadn't died on that airplane.

Seven days had passed. He felt much better; still a bit sluggish, but okay. He intended to resume his walking that evening, covering shorter distances at a slower pace.

First he dialed his son's number, and got the answering machine, as he had for each of the last five days.

He waited for the beep. "Gary, it's me again. You out of town or just don't feel like talking to me? Can't say as I'd blame you, but some forces of nature won't be subdued, and I'm one of them. By the way, I happened to notice some of your paintings in a gallery on Newbury Street. Had no idea paintings could be that expensive unless the artist was dead. Or is that why you haven't called me back? Anyway, a woman of obvious good taste was admiring the big green one with the hummingbirds and that incredible sunset. I told her she'd better put her name on it. Didn't mention you were my son, of course. She finally did put down a deposit on it. Anyway, you might as well call me back, or you'll have to listen to these messages every goddamn day for the rest of your life. Well, 'bye for now."

He dropped the receiver into the cradle and stared at the oak wall in front of him. Damn! He wondered if Gary was really out, or sitting home listening to that.

Needing to fill the time with something, anything, possessing some semblance of productivity, Ben looked through a pile of papers. He found the note he'd written to himself after returning from Mack's burial, and called Arizona directory assistance.

The Phoenix Life Extension Foundation had a listed phone number. He reached David Perez, the membership administrator. Perez was an articulate fellow and quite personable. It surprised Ben to learn that the place was indeed a cryonics facility. A mild disappointment.

"You're like that company in Sacramento I read about a few years ago?" Ben asked.

"Same concept, better execution." Perez laughed. "You're referring to California Cryonics Limited, I assume."

"Sounds right."

"They made some serious mistakes, but we think their concepts were sound. Think of them as the *Titanic*; think of us as the *Queen Elizabeth Two*."

"An apt analogy, I hope. Talk to me."

"Over time," Perez began, "scientific progress has allowed people to live longer. Already we estimate that medical science is adding two months to the average life expectancy of each American every year. Eventually science will discover a way for humans to have an indefinite life span. It's a matter of 'when,' not 'if.' But few if any people alive today are likely to reach that point before being overcome either by disease or calamity. So for those of us who don't make it to that time, the only way to survive is to have ourselves frozen after we die. At ultralow temperatures, all metabolic change virtually ceases. Theoretically, a person's body could be preserved indefinitely."

Ben remembered his conversation with Epstein a dozen years earlier, and felt a sudden chill. Even if it were legitimate, he couldn't see anyone voluntarily submitting to such a thing.

What if you were actually aware of being frozen—with no hope of escape? He imagined himself lying in a block of ice, unable to move for decades, or centuries, but still alive. Even the hellish bowels of that Jap ship had been a better prospect, he decided. As bad as that was, the journey had been finite. Being frozen alive, trapped in an icy coffin, guaranteed no such redemption.

"People let you put their bodies on ice?" he asked.

"We use liquid nitrogen, actually," Perez explained. "And people don't just let us, they pay us to do it! We have over a dozen people in suspension now, and fifty-six others signed up, including me. Which makes us the largest cryonics facility in the world."

The largest in the world? Ben thought. If cryonics were really viable, after being available for twenty years, why hadn't more people signed up? It couldn't have just been the money; any possibility of another chance at life should have been priceless to a dying person.

"Of course," Perez continued, almost as if he'd read Ben's mind, "nobody's ever been revived, and there's no proof any of us will ever be; it's purely theoretical. Neither the science nor the requisite technology exists yet. Cryonics is a statement of hope that mankind will ultimately achieve both."

Or maybe more like an affidavit of insanity, Ben thought. He figured he might as well listen, though. "When I was younger, much younger," he prompted, "I used to think we'd be able to stop the aging process during my lifetime. Thought I might live forever."

"Still might, you know. We don't make promises, of course, but since everyone's going to die anyway, you wouldn't have much to lose by being frozen, would you? Anyone who's buried or cremated will never be revived, but if you're frozen quickly enough at the point of death, before all the information in your brain's lost, well, who knows what science will be able to do in fifty or a hundred or five hundred years?"

It was nutty, but at least Perez didn't seem to be lying about anything—so far. "What happens to your soul when you're on ice?"

"People always ask us that," Perez said. "Nobody knows if there's really a soul separate and apart from the body. But let's assume you have such a soul. And let's say your suspension lasts even five hundred years. That's a long time for a body, but if a soul's eternal, it's probably not too much to expect it to find its way home."

"Interesting. Weird, but interesting."

"And in the eyes of God, half a millennium would be insignificant, wouldn't it? We can't be sure, but I'd assume your soul won't mind cooling its heels for a lousy five hundred years." Perez chuckled, the sincere laugh of a man who believed in his own product.

"You're one helluva salesman," Ben granted. "You don't have to answer this if you don't want, but how much money will they pay you if you sign me up?"

"Just my salary. Nobody here gets a commission. We're nonprofit."

"Really?"

"Yes, sir." Again Perez's tone conveyed the eloquence of truth.

"Back in World War Two," Ben said, "the Army used to have a serious problem with parachutes. About one percent of 'em failed to open. Now one percent doesn't sound like much, unless you happen to be one of the unlucky fellas who got the wrong ones. But they finally solved the problem; got the defect rate down to zero."

"How?" Perez asked.

"Simple. They made all the parachute packers and inspectors take monthly jumps, using parachutes selected at random from those they'd worked on themselves."

"Exactly! And our basic philosophy is very similar to theirs. What we do here is for our own benefit as much as yours. Maybe we're a little more trusting than the Army, but not much. Remember how I told you I'm one of the fifty-six people signed up?"

"So you did."

"In fact, the Phoenix won't hire anyone who doesn't plan to take the exact same journey our members sign up for. What's more, I make about a third as much here as I did at my last job selling real estate. I work here because I want to help assure my own journey into the future, and my family's, too."

"Well, that's somewhat reassuring. And you refer to your organization as *the* Phoenix?" Ben added. "Of Phoenix, Arizona. Was your location an accident, or intentional?"

Perez laughed. "We chose Phoenix because it's one of the least likely places in the United States to have an earthquake, or any other natural disaster for that matter. Purely a coincidence, but an interesting one, don't you think?"

"Very."

"Of course, once we decided to locate here, it seemed so perfect to refer to ourselves as 'the Phoenix.' "

"A fitting name," Ben allowed, picturing the great bird rising from the ashes.

"I tend to think of us as a lifeboat to the future," Perez replied, a metaphor Ben appreciated more than the man could have realized. "But whatever image works best for you. If you'd like to learn more, I'll be happy to send you our information package."

A leaky lifeboat to the future may be lunacy, Ben decided, but feeding his body to the fauna was even crazier. He gave Perez his address.

January 1, 1983

Alone on New Year's Day, Ben finally found time to catch up on his paperwork, but first he dialed Gary's number. He now spoke with his son about once a week. Gary's work had become a focus in Ben's life; attending exhibitions and reading catalogs to learn as much as possible about his son's art. They couldn't be said to be at ease with each other, but now their contact often seemed to lack the anticipation of pain and discomfort. It was a start.

Ben recalled their conversation of four days ago when Gary had actually sounded pleased to hear from him. Maybe so, Ben now thought, but they were still strangers, weren't they? Or no—Gary's resentment made them too intimate to be strangers, yet they certainly didn't know each other. Perhaps they never would.

Ben knew he would continue to make the effort. Relentlessly.

There was no answer. Damn! Gary hadn't bothered to reset his answering machine again. He'd have to try later.

Ben looked at his cluttered desktop and noticed the nine-by-twelve inch envelope received six weeks earlier from the Phoenix Life Extension Foundation. Since its arrival, it had languished unopened.

Wasn't procrastination such a human response to the anticipation of death? Who wanted to confront one's own mortality? He also knew that few people spent enough time arranging their estates or preparing their wills; these were not comfortable activities. He'd seen it in his patients time and again. In fact hadn't his own response to his first heart attack also been procrastination, borne by denial? He sure as hell wouldn't make that mistake again.

He opened the package.

A few minutes became three hours as Ben pored over the history of cryonics in the United States and the philosophy of those who ran the Phoenix. Cryonics still made him nervous, but the literature appealed to Ben's optimistic nature and seemed not to conflict with scientific realism.

Every doctor knew that nerve cells passing messages within the brain allowed a person to see, feel, and think; a delicate system that could not function without constant nourishment from the bloodstream. If a heart attack or other trauma interrupted the flow of these crucial nutrients, enough cells would perish within ten minutes to render the brain nonviable. At extremely low temperatures, however, this grace period might be extended for centuries. By some estimates, the temperature of liquid nitrogen could slow cellular erosion to less than a trillionth of its decay rate at normal temperatures.

It seemed a virtual certainty that thoughts and dreams, indeed all neuron activity, would cease during suspension. To Ben, that premise alone was of considerable comfort.

At any temperature below the freezing point of water, too many cell membranes would be damaged by ice crystals. Modern technology could not hope to reverse this damage, but someday, most scientists believed, doctors might have the means to repair individual cells and even DNA strands. At that point, perhaps suspended patients could be successfully revived and restored to full health; even to youthful vigor.

Embryos, seeds, and simple organisms had already been frozen for years or centuries and brought back to life. Dogs had been cooled to about 36 degrees Fahrenheit, maintained to a lifeless state for several hours, and revived to apparent normalcy. But no mammal had ever been suspended in liquid nitrogen as "cryonauts" were, and revived years, or even minutes, later. Damage from the freezing process itself was far too extensive for current medical science to reverse; indeed, such damage was often millions of times more persuasive than the original cause of death.

There were legal problems, too. Amazingly, all these appeared to be fully disclosed in the literature. The Phoenix had been both plaintiff and defendant in numerous lawsuits against individuals and government agencies. Many of these lawsuits were presented in excruciating minutiae, almost as a badge of honor.

No laws had been written with cryonics in mind, and thus regulatory and bureaucratic entanglements were common. Another obvious problem was that no cryonic procedure could begin until a patient had been pronounced legally dead. Often hospitals and other medical authorities refused cooperation. Some even interfered with the Phoenix during such emergencies.

An interesting case described by one wealthy member pertained to his Siamese cat. The animal, having been diagnosed with terminal brain cancer, had been immediately anesthetized, flown to Phoenix, treated, and frozen alive. The entire procedure was described with scientific precision. This feline received what could only have been considered an ideal treatment.

"The irony," the cat's owner had written, "is that no terminal human being subjugated to today's laws could ever expect suspension under such perfect conditions. For example, if I had a similar brain cancer, before I could be frozen I would have to wait until the tumors had sufficiently ravaged my brain to cause death, rendering my prospects for identity-preservation extremely doubtful."

There was also a financial statement in the package. The Phoenix was not particularly well-funded, and decidedly stingy in employee compensation. David Perez's gross salary was only $13,000 per year, and the president of the organization, Dr. Alyson Shockley, earned barely double that amount. Evidently they were not in it for the money.

Finally, Ben read about the Phoenix's emergency transport teams and suspension procedures. Although their scientists and technicians were portrayed as zealously dedicated to protecting the structural integrity of every patient's brain, the descriptions of individual cases were less than reassuring. Five of the Phoenix's fourteen current suspendees had died suddenly, resulting in severe, protracted, and most likely irreversible ischemia—cell damage from inadequate blood flow. These patients had been suspended anyway, but their prognosis for successful revival appeared at best bleak.

However, the fact that the Phoenix's own literature painted an often gloomy picture made them seem more trustworthy. It was apparent to Ben that this was no scam. Right or wrong, these people were true believers.

According to the literature, most members bought a life insurance policy to fund their suspensions, even those who could afford to pay in advance. The Phoenix charged $75,000 for a full-body freeze and storage, or $30,000 for "neurosuspension," that is, only the head: expensive, but the fee covered maintenance in perpetuity. And by purchasing a $75,000 life insurance policy to cover the onetime fee, at his age a full-body would only set him back about $900 per year—$600 for the insurance policy, plus $300 annual membership dues.

In real money, that was a hell of a lot less than seventy-five grand. No wonder most everyone funded with insurance, Ben mused.

He also understood the logic behind neurosuspensions: Any science that could restore a dead brain to life could easily replace the rest of the body as well. But still, he had trouble with the concept of discarding his own body. If he did it at all, he'd opt for the full-body suspension.

Ben was amazed; he was actually considering this!

Most of his mind doubted the potential efficacy of cryostasis revival. But Ben's natural hopefulness gradually overtook his skepticism. Sure it was a gamble, but the payoff was huge.

The future might be incredible, he thought. In most ways, the average person already lived better than royalty had just a few hundred years before. Hell, a century ago even kings had often suffered from head lice.

He considered all the advancements that the richest people in the 1800s lacked, all taken for granted today: instant long-distance communication, rapid travel, mobilized fire and police departments, weather forecasts, indoor plumbing, contact lenses, many forms of insurance, air-conditioning, antibiotics, painless dentistry. The list seemed to go on forever. Imagine living without those things!

And what would the world be like a few hundred years hence?

Inexpensive hypersonic travel, powerful watch-sized computers, more uniform and reliable justice, perfect health for all, machines to do all mindless work, more efficient and individualized education. People might pity those who had to withstand life in the twentieth century. And why not? That had certainly been true of every successive century since the end of the Dark Ages. Maybe the human race had barely begun to live!

He pictured himself awakening in a century of two or ten, healthy, maybe even restored to youth, yet perhaps unsuited to tomorrow's world.

How would he adapt?

Then he thought about his own grandparents who'd immigrated to

America from Italy, unable to speak a word of English. They'd adjusted well enough, and so would he. Rather than face death, Ben Smith preferred to live in any world that wanted him.

Once committed, he found that filling out the paperwork became surprisingly easy. It was a matter of context. He'd asked himself if he would invest less than one percent of his net worth for a small chance to glimpse—no, inhabit—the world a century or more into the future. When he considered the question in those terms, the answer became obvious.

Ben even decided to pay in advance: to save time, and to get it done before he could change his mind. Writing the check was effortless.

He imagined a second chance a life, knowing everything he knew then; an opportunity to use the wisdom he'd gleaned from all his mistakes. Even a tiny likelihood of such a prize was worth a lot more than $75,000. As he sealed the envelope, a far more revealing thought bubbled up in his consciousness: Regardless of the odds, how much was the hope this decision provided him worth? Seventy-five thousand dollars: the difference between dread and hope? What a bargain!

January 17, 1983

Trust and estate law was an interesting business; its practitioners functioned in a perpetually dualistic world. Entering a law office for the purpose of drafting or altering one's last will and testament, you were likely to encounter an extremely personable, competent lawyer, who, upon conclusion of the work, would present you with a surprisingly reasonable bill. Trust and estate lawyers, like most morticians and fine art auctioneers, tended to be "professional nice guys" whose short-term goal was to become your friend. But their perspective was long-term indeed—and cold-blooded; they would invest in relationships, intending to cash in after you were dead.

Patrick Webster's suite was small and cluttered, but his sixth-floor window afforded a fine view of Quincy Market. The offices of Fialkow, Webster, Barnes & Zeeve weren't as posh as those at Hale & Dorr or Foley, Hoag & Eliot, or any of the other frontline Boston law firms, but the location was ideal. It was lunch hour and Faneuil Hall teemed with secretaries and salesmen, college kids and attorneys. The sun was shining; nearly all the snow had melted.

They sat at a small table near the window. "I sent The Phoenix $75,000 for the procedure a couple weeks ago," Ben said.

He did not mention his concerns about cryonics, his fear of cramped spaces and lack of control, or his claustrophobia. Ben didn't know Webster well enough to confide in that way; this fellow was his lawyer, not his shrink.

"What exactly do they freeze?" Webster asked gingerly, his expression neutral.

Ben looked at the craggy face of the man sitting across from him and thought Pat Webster would look natural in prizefighter trunks. "My body. I thought I made that clear."

"The whole thing, right?"

Ben suppressed a chuckle. "Yes."

"Thank God! I was afraid you might be one of those crazies who just have their heads frozen." Webster rolled his eyes.

"I considered it," Ben said, rejecting Webster's not so subtle invitation to share in his ridicule. "Probably just as sensible as what *I'm* doing."

"Oh. Well, I guess I really don't know very much about it."

"No sweat," Ben told the lawyer. "Anyway, I have about twelve million left. I'd like to leave a few million to be divided among my kids and grandkids. But if I'm revived after being frozen for a couple of centuries, I don't imagine I'll be able to support myself and my family right away. We'll probably need money, at least until I can learn a skill that's of some use to the goddamn Jetsons."

Webster chuckled softly.

"I don't blame you for laughing," Ben said. "That's why I haven't told anyone else. I suppose I should be grateful for the attorney-client privilege, or I could become a laughingstock for the whole Boston medical community."

"I didn't mean it like that," Webster said, his face suddenly reflecting gravity and respect. "I was only amused by your reference to the Jetsons."

Ben understood: Webster's very-well-paying job was to represent clients, and to help them navigate the legal system to get what they wanted, not to question those wishes; even so bizarre a request as this.

"The circumstances are that you'd be legally dead," the attorney continued. "A dead person can't own property. You do understand the finality of that, don't you?"

"Could we set up a trust?"

"Sure. Trust laws are different in every state, so I imagine I can find a viable venue somewhere. I'll have to do some research. Maybe Wisconsin. Come to think of it, South Dakota might be just as tolerant of trusts in perpetuity, and they have no state income tax." He shrugged. "Ben, it's your money. You can do whatever you want with it. Anything that will stand up to legal challenge, that is."

"I know. I guess I'm a little uncomfortable with the whole idea." Ben thought about the oxygen mask on the airplane, at first inspired by the analogy. Then he faltered in his resolve. Maybe he wasn't really seeing to his survival because his family might need him later. What if he was hogging all the oxygen out of greed and fear? "This is pretty selfish of me, isn't it?" he asked, hoping for approbation.

Webster provided it as if on cue. "Pretty selfish?" the lawyer chortled. "Most people would take it all with them if they could. You're providing for your family now, and offering them hope of resurrection. If that's selfish, I think I need a new dictionary." Then he shook his head as if to clear the contradiction. "But if it works, aren't you worried about what the world'll be like by the time scientists know how to revive you?"

Ben had already considered the matter at length. "Not really. If it's the sort of world that's willing to revive people, and if they possess a science so advanced as to be able to restore a person from death as we now define it, their action will have to be its own reward. It's not as though they'd need humans for slave labor or menial tasks. Machines would be able to do almost anything humans could, for a lot less money. And they certainly won't need my knowledge of twentieth century medicine. This world of the future would function on digitized information and robotics; just as we depend on electric lighting and internal combustion engines. No. If they're thawing people and curing their diseases, they'll be doing so simply because they love doing it; because they value human life for its own sake."

"That makes sense," Webster said thoughtfully. And for the first time in their conversation, Ben was convinced of the lawyer's sincerity. At least on that point, he knew he'd convinced Webster of his logic.

"Also," Ben continued, "I think human existence tends to improve. Not in a straight line, but gradual progress in fits and starts. It doesn't always seem that way, especially if you read newspapers or watch the news on TV. But that's because good news isn't as interesting. Sure, we have crime, the environment, the population explosion to worry about. Still, society is becoming more open, healthier, and more democratic throughout the world. On average."

"You really believe this is gonna work, don't you?" Webster's voice seemed to carry a note of hope.

"Probably not."

"Oh." Webster tugged at an ear; his eyes narrowed. "Then why bother with it?"

"My father used to tell a story about a devout man whose wife is injured in a car wreck. She has to have an operation they can't afford or she'll never walk again. So he prays, night and day: 'God, please let me win the lottery.' Finally, after some months he starts to lose faith. He berates

God, and screams, 'I have been a pious man my entire life, have always tried to please you, and have never asked for anything before. Now the one time I really need help, you turn your back on me. When in the hell will you answer my prayers?' Suddenly the skies turn black, thunder roars, and lightning flashes. A deep voice resounds from the sky, shaking the ground like an earthquake. And God asks, 'When in the hell will you buy a lottery ticket?' "

June 2, 1988

Sirens blaring, the ambulance tore through Boston Common, rushing Dr. Benjamin Smith to New England Medical Center. Startled motorists pulled to one side as the three-year-old Ford transport van sped through traffic lights and over-wide turns. Then, with only the barest hesitation, the drivers returned to traffic and their own daily concerns.

Both ambulance attendants wheeled him through the emergency entrance toward intensive care. One of them whispered to a nurse, "Looks like a myocardial infarction. Probably massive."

Ben wondered if they realized he could hear them. He'd treated many terminal patients himself, and had long sympathized with the helplessness felt by those who were dying or debilitated from illness. Their minds often became incapacitated along with their bodies. Inability to comprehend their predicament, Ben had always imagined, might be as much blessing as curse.

He understood that the loss of faculty was caused not only by physiological circumstance, but also by feelings of helplessness and loss of control. And now, feeling that helpless himself, he found his frustration worse than he could have anticipated or understood. He tried to focus on an internal pinpoint that was little more than hope. He knew his mind was clouded; he could barely remember his previous decisions, and creative thought was a struggle. Yet he'd methodically patterned a plan of action into his brain over the past five years:

I will show no ambivalence toward the freezer.

Now, even as his mind faltered and he questioned his own ability to judge, even as his reasons for embracing cryonics faded like a city disappearing into afternoon fog, he reminded himself that although he could no longer see its edifices, they were still there. Thus he knew he must appear resolute. There was precious little else he could do for himself. He would have to hope that his own preparations were adequate, and entrust his destiny to others.

A nurse looked down at his face. "Oh my God! Dr. Smith." She didn't know him personally, but almost every nurse at the hospital recognized him. She ran alongside them. "It's gonna be okay. We'll take care of you, sir."

Before surrendering consciousness, Ben managed to whispered the three important words he'd long planned to say if he ever found himself in this situation: "Call Toby Fiske."

Dr. Tobias Fiske arrived forty minutes later, just in time to watch his friend open his eyes. Ben lay flat on an ICU bed, attached to monitors, hooked to an IV unit, breathing oxygen through a mask. Toby realized that Ben's body would be helpless, virtually immobile, but his mind might still be lucid.

"Hey, stranger. How you feelin'?"

Looking up, Ben licked his lips. "I'm not gonna make it, am I?"

Toby stood for several seconds, wrestling with himself for the right vocal timbre, the proper facial expression. "Doesn't look good."

"How long?"

"Without a transplant, a few hours. At most."

"What *about* a transplant?" Ben asked.

"Nothing suitable available. Odds of finding anything in time are less than one percent." Toby had to look away from Ben while speaking these words.

"Oh."

"Ben, your daughters are here—all of them. Right outside."

"Gary?" Ben asked.

"Not yet."

"Okay. In a minute." Ben closed his eyes. "See my bracelet?" he whispered.

Toby nodded.

"'Call the number." Ben was breathing hard now, obviously straining to force out everything he needed to say. "But don't get in . . . trouble for me. Promise, Toby. I'm asking you . . . as my doctor, not my friend."

"I promise."

"Couldn't love you more . . . if you were . . . my brother."

Toby wondered if Ben understood that to him their kinship extended far beyond brotherhood. Throughout his adolescence and even adulthood, his feelings of disenfranchisement—feelings he now attributed to his parents' blind devotion to religion and lack of devotion to each other—had left him open to a sort of quasiscientific thinking far beneath his intellectual potential. Without his friend's guidance, Toby knew he would never have pursued a career in medicine. He might've wound up writing horoscopes for a second-market newspaper. Or joined the Moonies, for God's sake.

But he simply answered, "I know," squeezed Ben's hand, slipped the bracelet off his wrist, and walked to the door.

Outside, now in tears, Toby told Rebecca, Maxine, and Jan, "Ben wants to see you." He hugged Maxine. "His heart's barely pumping. Probably only an hour or two before it gives out completely. And he knows it." Then he trudged down the hall to the doctor's phone and placed a call to the number on Ben's bracelet.

An operator answered on the first ring. "Phoenix. Emergency response."

Of Ben's three daughters, Maxine was the physician, so the others now looked to her with uncustomary deference. Max knew best how to mask her sorrow. There would be plenty of time to mourn later, she wanted her father's final moments to be as pleasant as possible.

"You comfortable, Daddy?" she asked, stroking his right hand. She'd looked at his chart and knew he could no longer feel his left. "Any pain?"

"Yes, plenty. But nothing hurts," he said, forcing a half smile, dreading the freezer, now imagining claustrophobia beyond toleration. He felt terribly weak, too.

No one knew what to say.

Max forced herself to break the silence. "Remember when you took us all to the Grand Canyon? Must've been 1962, wasn't it?"

Ben smiled.

"Of course we could never fly anywhere, like normal families," Rebecca said.

"I still can't believe we did that," Jan laughed. "All six of us in that Cadillac with those foot-tall tail fins blocking the view. No station wagon for us! Five straight days there, and five straight days back. It's amazing we didn't kill each other."

"And some of those motor lodges were so seedy," Max added. "I can only imagine what caused those stains on the bedspreads. You and Mom in one room, and the four of us sharing another. Rebecca and I usually slept on the floor."

"Yeah," Jan said, "so you could talk and tell dirty jokes all night while Gary and I tried to sleep. God, I hated that."

"Those trips you used to make us take," Rebecca said, "y'know, Dad, I tell my friends about them sometimes, and they're jealous. They say stuff like, 'My parents never took us along on their vacations. They'd just ship us off to Grandma's.' And I'd always tell them they were the lucky ones. But that's—that's not how I really felt, not a bit." She was gasping now, trying hard not to cry. "Of all the things about growing up in our family, those summer vacations are what I remember best. They were like getting to live a separate lifetime; an extra year each year. I swear I remember as much of those vacations as I can of the years separating them."

"Dad," Max asked, "you want to see your grandkids? I could ask a friend to pick them up and drive them here."

Ben tried to shake his head. Tears formed. The last time they saw him would become one of their strongest memories. It couldn't be like this. Grampas, he decided, should be recalled in a grin.

"No," he whispered slowly, haltingly, "I want 'em to remember me playing soccer with 'em, or taking them . . . to the zoo. Not lying here with a tube up my nose." He gasped for air, caught his breath. "But you make sure they know I love them. Tell those kids . . . my last thoughts . . . were about them, all of 'em, and my last hours were happy . . . because I was thinking about them."

Rebecca began to cry. Jan looked away, her own eyes welling. But Max forced herself to hold her emotions in check, like a sagging dam whose purpose was to give the town below a few extra hours to evacuate before the impending flood.

"Is . . . Gary coming?" Ben asked.

"Yes. I'm sure of it," Rebecca said. "He loves you, Dad. He'd be here now if he knew. I left a message on his answering machine, and called Vose Galleries, too. He's supposed to approve the layout today for his one-man show next month. They'll tell him as soon as he shows up, and he'll come on the run."

Picturing his son trying to run on that shortened left leg, Ben thought: more like on the reel. And that was probably his fault, too.

He whispered, "If he doesn't get here in time, say goodbye for me. Just tell him how proud I am of him. He really made something of himself." Despite me or in spite of me? Ben wondered.

"He sure did," Rebecca said.

"In spite, I think," Ben whispered.

After about half an hour Toby walked into the room. "Sorry to interrupt. The technicians from the Phoenix just arrived. They wanted me to make sure Ben knew."

"Already?" Ben murmured. "Better talk to you in private."

Max said, "We'll be in the hall, Dad."

"How'd they get here so fast?" Ben asked.

"They're not from Arizona," Toby heard himself explain, as if this were a normal frigging conversation, for God's sake. Like he was maybe explaining a standard medical procedure; a goddamn triple bypass or something. Christ. "The Phoenix has two scientists traveling around the country training paramedics. They have teams on call in about twenty cities. Your team owns an ambulance company in Rhode Island. You're their fourth cryonics job. Last one was in Warwick, seven months ago."

"They can work here?"

"Yeah. They're licensed in Massachusetts, and cleared for this hospital. I checked. Guess they figured Boston being so close . . ." Then Toby paused a moment, and finally said it: "Cryonics? Jesus, Ben. Your daughters know?"

"No. Couldn't figure out how to tell 'em . . . Or you."

"What were you afraid of? That we'd think you lost your mind or something?"

"Well . . . yeah," Ben said, trying to smile. "Don't you . . . think that?"

Toby hesitated. "Out of your mind? No. Gullible? Maybe . . ." He paused again. "You really s'pose they'll ever revive you?"

"I doubt it." Ben chuckled weakly. "But you . . . never know."

"Those three cryonics technicians seem like believers. One of them explained a bit of the procedure to me."

"Good."

"Ben, you sure about this?"

"Yes . . . positive."

"Okay, I'll help," Toby said. After all, Ben was his best friend! Risk to his professional ass? To hell with it. What was an ass worth if you were ashamed it was yours? "But look, if we let your disease take its natural course, oxygen flow to your brain'll diminish. And that's a problem. You'll start losing brain tissue long before your heart stops."

Toby had said all this as if it were expected, the most natural thing in the world. Yet the secondary consequences were obvious enough. "I know that," Ben said, now concerned that his friend was moving too quickly, like a sinner who discovers God then donates every last possession to the Church.

"So what do I do?" Toby asked.

"Do it by the book. Don't jeopardize . . . your license."

"I can give you morphine."

"That'll put me . . . in respiratory arrest."

"Probably." Hopefully.

"I'm not . . . in any pain."

"I know. I was just saying that if you were . . . Think about it, Ben. Maybe you're in severe pain and haven't told me."

"Don't do it. You could get . . . in trouble."

"Only if I get caught."

"Isn't worth the risk." Ben gasped for air. "Besides . . . you have to look after Alice for me." Deep breath. "Can't do that . . . from prison."

A joke, Toby realized. No doctor had actually gone to jail for helping a terminal patient die. But both knew doctors who'd lost their licenses for it.

Toby laughed quietly. "Okay, Ben. Whatever you say." He turned to go.

"Cryonics is a longshot. Don't risk your career . . . for a longshot."

Toby did not turn back, nor did he answer. He wasn't sure how his voice would sound right then.

Max had been talking to Harvey Bacon, the chief cryonic technician. Her expression was now a portrait of disbelief and disgust.

"You can go back in," Toby said.

"Did you know about this?" she asked.

"No. I just found out. Like you."

"Incredible," she muttered, going back inside. To Max, cryonics was a fraud, a waste of money. And worse, it deprived living people of healthy, lifesaving organs that might otherwise have been donated. How could her father have fallen for this scam? He used to be such a realist.

But Toby refused to play judge. Some people spent $100,000 on their own goddamn funeral, didn't they? Or left their money to some televangelist, looking to buy a place in heaven. Maybe cryonics would actually work. Who the hell could know? Ben had always been smart, even prescient, so maybe he was right again.

Jan and Rebecca followed Max into the ICU.

Rebecca's reservations were quite different from her sister's: What would she tell Katie and George? Was their grandfather dead or in limbo? They'd want to know what had happened to his soul. She knew damn well he'd never be revived, but he wouldn't be at rest either—at least not in *their* minds. They would never be able to let go of him. How could he have done this to them?

Financial problems had beset Noah and Jan's law partnership. Their practice now consisted almost exclusively of personal injury cases, which required large capital outlay against uncertain outcome. No meaningful settlements had been forthcoming, while competition in that field had intensified. They both seemed to be working much harder even as they fell further into debt; starving hamsters on a relentless treadmill.

And just four days ago Jan had learned that she was pregnant with their third child, a fact she hadn't yet revealed to anyone. Noah would not be pleased with the news. What would happen to all of her father's money? Jan felt guilty for thinking it, but the thoughts still came. Was he going to keep it? He couldn't spend it where he was going, but they sure could use it. He'd never try to take it with him, would he? Damn! Noah had been right, as usual. She should've helped Ben prepare his will.

"You're gonna be *frozen?*" Max said to Ben, trying to keep a sympathetic tone to her voice. "Why didn't you *tell* us, Dad?"

"Knew you'd ... try to ... talk me out of it," he whispered. "But ... I had to ... do it ... Needed to know .... there's a chance ... my death ... might not be ... permanent. Any chance."

Jan could feel her own fingernails biting into her palm. "You can't be serious."

Rebecca glared at her, and Jan said nothing more.

"I'm sorry," Ben said.

All three women began to cry again.

"I never wanted to hurt you. Any of you. I'm so sorry. I didn't ... think ..."

Monitor alarms went off. Ben's right hand lurched toward his chest.

"Oh my God," Max gasped, running out of the room. She called after Toby. "Another infarction. Come quick!"

Now Ben's discomfort and anxiety had vanished. He felt himself hovering near the ceiling, as if floating atop a swimming pool filled with a thickly saline emulsion. Below him, with wires and tubes attached, was a comatose body. His body. People strode about it resolutely, but he detected little energy emanating from the body itself. He thought he saw it—me? he wondered dazedly—still breathing, just barely. Now Toby was barking instructions at the nurse, who ran out to fetch something. Then Toby asked Rebecca and Jan to wait outside. "But I might need you, Max, so stay right here, just in case."

Max nodded.

"In fact," Toby said moments later, "maybe you'd better go get a crash cart, just in case."

She nodded again, and rushed out to find a nurse.

Now they were alone, just Toby and Ben, and Toby seemed to be at the cusp of decision; Ben could almost feel his friend's mind at work.

"I hope you really want this," Toby whispered. His hands were trembling as he carefully removed a syringe from his pocket and covertly injected the contents into the port on the IV pouch. "Goodbye, Ben. You *will* be missed."

Even with his mind shutting down, Ben understood. *Morphine.*

Toby called Harvey Bacon and the rest of the Phoenix team inside. "His heart stopped beating. I'm calling him at one-fourteen P.M. Proceed."

Approaching footsteps resounded from the hall. Bacon turned toward the door just as Toby was sneaking the empty syringe into his pocket. Bacon's eyes rested briefly on the motion of Toby's hand. Then Max returned to the room pushing a crash cart.

"We won't need that now," Toby said to her gently. "Ben's gone."

Max watched the cryonics team set to its task, as though she'd been expelled as a participant in her own life. Her face appeared shocked, saddened, emotionally repulsed, but professionally fascinated. Her eyes were simply following the activity of the team working over her father, as if her emotions had little meaning and all she could do was watch.

Then suddenly in darkness, Ben heard voices. Gary?

Ben felt himself rushing through a long tunnel. He was utterly serene and content. He saw a beautiful white light in the distance, and felt gladdened, eager to join with this loving light now beckoning him closer. The experience was nothing like his short-lived resignation to death in 1943; this time he welcomed it. The light beckoned him closer; he raced to meet it, no longer missing earthly existence or human flesh. He was not his parent's child or even his children's father; he was himself alone.

At last.

He couldn't yet see his wife, but somehow knew she was there, inside the light, waiting to welcome him for all eternity. Soon they would be rejoined. Forever. As the light grew nearer, the voices from earth became faint, disconnected, and ultimately irrelevant.

O u t   o f   b r e a t h , Gary hobbled into the ICU and saw Toby's morose expression. "I'm too late, aren't I?"

"I'm sorry."

"Damn. Damn it all!"

Three cryonic technicians were coupling Ben to a heart-lung resuscitator and a mechanical cardiopulmonary support device. Both machines were activated, and Ben's circulation resumed. He began to breathe.

Oxygen and other nutrients would soon rekindle part of his brain.

"I order you to stop this immediately," Max suddenly shouted. The three technicians, obviously used to such interference, ignored her.

"Sorry, Max," Toby said. "Ben made an anatomical donation, willed his body to the Phoenix. I have no legal authority on the disposition of Ben's remains, even if I disagreed with his wishes. Which I don't."

"But we're his family," Rebecca said.

"So am I," Toby answered.

"Gary," Jan said, "can't we do something? They're gonna freeze him, for chrissake!"

"Why are they doing that?" Gary asked, looking at Toby.

"It's what he wanted. Cryonic suspension. He thought someday we might have the science to cure and revive him. He knew it was a longshot, but it was *his* life, wasn't it?"

Gary nodded. He thought about his own years in medical school, his internship and residency and practice: precious time wasted trying to please his father instead of himself; a mistake he would never make again, nor wish on anyone else. That's right, it was the man's own life, and even in death, he alone should decide what to do with it.

The cryonic technicians administered various medications: Nimodipine, a slow calcium channel blocker to help reverse ischemia. Heparin, an anticoagulant to aid circulation. And a tonic of free radical inhibitors and other medications to minimize future ischemic brain damage. They began packing the body in ice.

"According to the technicians," Toby explained to Gary, "every ten-degree drop in Celsius temperature cuts metabolic demand in half, which slows the loss of neurons."

Gary watched intently, saying nothing. The technicians hovered over Ben, exchanging clipped phrases. Gary felt an unfamiliar emotion surface. He didn't recognize it until, to his astonishment, he found himself fighting an impulse to raise his arm in salute.

Ben felt something tugging him back through the tunnel, away from the light, down from the ceiling. A powerful force, irresistible.

It made him angry.

He'd seen his darling Marge's face and was at the verge of melding with the light surrounding her. Yet now he was back inside his body, sentient but unable to move regardless of exertion, aware of his breathing, feeling the pulse of the heart-lung machine through his arteries, and experiencing all other earthly pain, fear, and grief.

Damn! Must be alive again. How long had he been dead? Minutes? Days? Years?

He heard his daughters' voices clearly, and Toby's, and Gary's. He wished he could tell them to send him back.

They argued his fate as if he no longer existed.

They were prepping him for the freezer, he realized. He must have been gone only moments. But they were right about one thing, he decided: He *didn't* exist.

They were talking too fast, or perhaps his mind was operating at a reduce pace. His body felt simultaneously frozen and aflame. He expended no effort; even his breathing was performed by device. Thus the pain was endurable; real yet somehow apart from significance.

But dread overwhelmed him.

As long as he was alive, suicide was still an option. But once he was an ice cube, he couldn't will himself to die, now could he? He was stuck in limbo. Why hadn't he thought of that before?

The technicians began surgery. Ben was aware of them cutting the femoral vessels in his groin. They attached a blood pump, membrane oxygenator, and some kind of heat exchanger he'd never seen before. As Ben's brain cooled, everything around him seemed to move with increasing velocity. By the time his body temperature had fallen to 90 degrees Fahrenheit, he was a snail surrounded by hyperactive hummingbirds.

Oh God, tell them to stop!

The cryonic technicians were now preparing Ben for the plane trip to the storage facility in Phoenix, Arizona, where he knew he would receive cryoprotective perfusion to minimize freezing injury to cells, and eventually be cooled to minus 196 degrees Celsius. First they would have to replace his blood with an organ preservation solution. Then they would place his body, packed in ice, into a shipping container for perhaps its final flight.

A sense of panic overtook him. Was he trapped here for generations with no possible escape? Had he made the ultimate mistake? Would he become like a Kafka character, paralyzed until the end of time?

Ben felt a scream surging from the core of himself; all the worse because he knew he could never give it voice. Perhaps it would quiver on the edge of his throat forever.

Then, like a rheostat diminishing the flow of current, his brain activity decelerated to below the critical level, the optic nerve concurrently deprived of blood flow. He experienced what seemed a brilliant, transcendent moment of astonishing lucidity, a moment isotropic with respect to time; an instant or an eternity.

For reasons unknown and unimportant to him, he recalled the words of Jean-Paul Sartre: "And I opened my heart to the benign indifference of the universe." All at once Ben understood the wisdom of those words as no living man ever could.

The rheostat slipped into the range just a kiss above darkness.

Ben felt himself rising once again; to the ceiling, into the tunnel; and on into the light. The light. The Light! The promising, the beckoning, the all-encompassing, beautiful Light.

THE STRUGGLE FOR LIFE

June 16, 1988

It was almost twelve-thirty P.M. Gary Franklin Smith knew he should get a move on, but he continued to sit at his father's desk in the office of the Chestnut Street brownstone poring over documents he'd found in a file folder marked "Cryonics." He'd started at 6:45 that morning and still didn't know what to feel or think. That was when a photograph of Benjamin Franklin, his family's namesake, caught his eye, so he began to read:

> The nineteenth century Russian philosopher Nikolai Fyodorov once proposed that the powers of science could solve every problem of humankind, including death. In fact he dreamed that technology would eventually restore life to every person who had ever died. Since all things are composed of atoms, he believed the motions of those atoms must be predictable, if not by the science of his day then certainly by the science of the future. History would become known, and thus could be perfectly reconstructed.
>
> Fyodorov's assertion seems naive today. His vision of limitless technology nurtured his hope for eternal life. Or was it the other way

around? Certainly human desire for resurrection transcends science; religion is itself a testament to our quest to live forever. Like a devoutly religious adherent, Fyodorov, who died in 1903, must have found comfort in the prospect of someday being raised from the dead.

But nature's laws grant no exceptions. In 1927, Werner Heisenberg illustrated that effects of observation on the trajectories of subatomic particles can never simultaneously be measured for position and velocity. To all appearances Heisenberg's "uncertainty principle" forever put Fyodorov's fanciful thesis to rest.

Now compare Fyodorov to Benjamin Franklin, an eighteenth century man of science whose view of the world was acquired through detached observation.

"I wish (physical resurrection) were possible ..." he wrote in April 1773, "for having a very ardent desire to see and observe the state of America a hundred years hence, I should prefer to an ordinary death, being immersed with a few friends in a cask of Madeira until that time, then to be recalled to life by the solar warmth of my dear country. But ... in all probability, we live in a century too little advanced, and too near the infancy of science, to see such an art brought in our time to its perfection."

Franklin also wrote: "The rapid progress true science now makes occasions my regretting sometimes that I was born too soon. It is impossible to imagine the height to which may be carried, in a thousand years, the power of man over matter. We may perhaps learn to deprive large masses of their gravity, for the sake of easy transport. Agriculture may diminish its labor and double its produce; all diseases may by sure means be prevented or cured, not excepting even that of old age, and our lives lengthened at pleasure even beyond the antediluvian standard."

Benjamin Franklin was a realist; he embraced the tenets of immortalism, yet knew he would never live to see its realization. He took his final breath in 1790.

Has father taken his? Gary wondered. The hands of his watch kept moving, but at that moment he didn't care.

The rest of the siblings having arrived early for their one P.M. appointment, each had been escorted to a windowless conference room and assured that Mr. Webster would be right in.

Only Gary was a little late. "Anyone ever heard of this guy?" he asked.

All three sisters shook their heads. "Dad never mentioned him," Rebecca said.

"According to the directory, he specializes in trusts and estates," Gary said.

Jan nodded. "Dad's finances were complicated."

Then Toby entered the room.

"What are you doing here?" Jan asked.

"Got a notice in the mail. Guess Ben musta left me his stethoscope or something."

Gary smiled. The three woman didn't. But before their ill-humor could spread, Webster popped through the door.

"I see everyone found the place okay," he said. "I'm Pat Webster."

"Toby Fiske."

Webster shook the cardiologist's hand and looked around at the others. "That means you must be Gary," he said, smiling. "Then which one is Jan? Maxine? And that leaves Rebecca, our designated executor. Terribly sorry about your father. Seemed like a great guy."

"He was," Max answered.

"So," Webster said abruptly, "down to business."

The six quickly chose chairs around the conference table, as if speed might help dispel the awkwardness they felt.

"Did our father ever talk to you about wanting to be frozen?" Jan asked.

"You're the lawyer, right?"

Jan nodded.

"Then you know I can't answer questions about private discussions."

"We're his family," Jan argued, "not his adversaries."

"Sometimes family members wind up choosing sides," Webster explained. "Seen it happen a lot. Blood can't always guarantee commitments. But when I read the will—"

"Okay. Go ahead, then."

Webster began, " 'I, Benjamin Franklin Smith, a resident of Massachusetts, being of sound and disposing mind and memory, make, publish, and declare this to be my Last Will and Testament, and I hereby revoke any and all other wills and codicils I have made.

" 'As of the date of this Will, I am no longer married, my beloved wife Margaret Callahan Smith having passed away on September fourteenth, 1979. I have four children: Gary Franklin Smith, Rebecca Carol Smith-Crane, Maxine Lee Smith Swenson, and Janette Lois Smith. I also have five grandchildren: George Jacob Crane Jr., Sarah Smith Banks, Katherine Franklin Crane, Justin Robert Swenson, and Michael Smith

Banks. Under this Will, I am providing for any of these nine children and grandchildren who survive me and any additional grandchildren born prior to my death.' "

I should've told him about *you*, Jan thought, gently touching her pregnant belly.

Webster looked around the table. "Anybody mind if I skip the boilerplate and technicals vis-à-vis payment of legal obligations and expenses, etcetera, blah blah?"

"As long as we can read it later," Jan said.

"Of course, 'Gifts of personal effects: I bequeath six oil paintings by Gary Franklin Smith to the Fogg Art Museum at Harvard University under the terms of an agreement attached as exhibit A.' "

"He bought six of my paintings? And never told me. Damn."

"Back when you were struggling," Toby said. "He didn't want you to know. And he didn't do it because you needed it. He figured your art would draw the notice it deserved, eventually. He just wanted to speed it along. Besides, he loved your paintings."

Gary smiled. "Son of a gun."

Webster continued, " 'I hereby appoint Rebecca Carol Smith-Crane as independent executor of my estate. If for any reason Rebecca is unable to act as executor, I appoint Maxine Lee Smith Swenson, and if Maxine is unable, I appoint Janette Lois Smith.' "

Guess he still didn't trust Gary, Jan thought, feeling a rush of pity for her brother.

" 'The executor shall distribute the following items of property: my intimate personal items such as jewelry, clothing, books, china, and silverware, furniture and furnishings, objects of art, and automobiles and all policies of insurance on such tangible property, club memberships, and all other personal and household chattels and personal property pertinent to my residence. These items shall be distributed among my children in a manner determined by the executor, in her absolute discretion, to be fair and equitable. Any division and distribution made by the executor shall be binding on all.

" 'Sale of residence and other property: I instruct the executor to sell my residence, stocks, bonds, and all other investments, and to pay all appropriate estate taxes from those proceeds.

" 'Specific gifts: Once all taxes are paid, I instruct the executor to pay each of my surviving children one-quarter of the first $1,400,000 remaining, up to $350,000 per child. I then instruct her to pay the trustee of my grandchildren's trusts their pro-rata share of the next $1,250,000 remaining, up to

$250,000 per grandchild. I then instruct her to pay the next $200,000 to Tobias Fiske.' "

The three women glanced at Toby, who shrugged in artless bewilderment, while Webster continued, " 'Finally, I instruct her to divide any remaining funds equally among my surviving children and grandchildren.' "

"How much more will there be?" Jan asked, trying to remain composed.

"I figure about $30,000 each."

" 'That's all?" Jan said. "He was worth over ten million."

"If you'll just wait till I'm finished . . ." Webster said sternly, and went on, " 'Trust administration . . .' "

What trust? Jan thought, and almost blurted it.

" 'I hereby appoint Tobias Fiske as administrator of the Smith Family Cryonic Trust. Should he be unable to administer the Trust, I appoint Gary Franklin Smith. The administrator will make investment decisions and direct disbursements for the Trust's expenses, taxes, and partitions.' "

"How much is in it?" Jan asked.

Webster replied, "I can't tell you that."

Gary realized he needed to hear it the way his father thought it. "Please continue."

"Anyone mind if I skip some more technical stuff?"

Nobody objected.

Then Webster read the only part of the Last Will and Testament written not by lawyers, but by Ben himself:

" 'I hope none of my children will think too harshly of me for considering my own welfare. You have all heard my oxygen-mask-on-the-airplane parable. I can only imagine how a small child in that situation would feel during those first seconds, watching her parent place the oxygen mask over his own nose and mouth while she gasps for air. And I suppose this must be how you feel today.

" 'Nature has endowed parents with an instinct to unhesitatingly sacrifice for their children's sake, an impulse difficult to ignore. I have asked myself if my family would be better off were I gone entirely rather than in limbo. But science has so changed the human condition, it is conceivable that even death itself will someday be defeated. I am now convinced that parents must see to their own survival as well as providing for their offspring. My motivation is selfish: I love you all and want to be with you. If humanly possible, I intend to be there for and with all of you, perhaps centuries from now.

" 'Therefore the Trust will pay cryonic suspension of any of my direct descendants who wish to arrange for it upon their death, and for Tobias Fiske if he so chooses. Remaining funds, if any, will revert to me upon my eventual revival.' "

Rebecca and Maxine exited the building together in silent bewilderment. They'd each entertained vague notions that their father was rich, but neither had considered their inheritance in actual dollar terms. For them, the afternoon's encounter seemed almost surreal, and not yet connected to their lives.

In his mind Gary already had part of his money spent. He decided to visit a few galleries on the way home; maybe buy something worthy some struggling kid had done. He was surprised at how good the notion made him feel.

In the lobby, Jan stopped at a pay phone and called her husband's private line. He was waiting for her call and answered on the first ring. "Noah Banks."

"He left us $350,000," she said, dispensing with all formalities, "plus $250,000 each in trust for Sarah and Michael."

"After taxes?" he asked. There was a naked avarice in his voice that neither of them noticed.

"Yes, but we can't touch the money in Sarah and Michael's trusts; $350,000 is it, plus maybe another thirty in residual money after all the dust settles."

"Not what we hoped for, but it's better than a poke in the eye."

"Noah, at least three-quarters of his estate went into a trust to fund cryonic suspensions for family members," she explained, her anger building, "and for Toby Fiske, to whom, by the way, he also bequeathed two hundred grand."

"You're kidding!"

"With the balance reverting to Dad upon his, and I quote: 'eventual revival'!"

"Holy shit. What should we do?"

"Before we decide, there's something else you should know."

"Which is?" he asked. She could just imagine his thoughts: Oh God, must be about money, or she wouldn't bring it up *now*.

"I'm pregnant."

"I see," was all he said.

She wanted to cry.

June 19, 1988

The pleading took less than forty-eight hours to compose; the two lawyers who drafted it were highly motivated.

"The Estate of Benjamin Franklin Smith, Rebecca Carol Smith-Crane, Maxine Lee Smith Swenson, Jane Lois Smith, et al versus the Smith Family Cryonic Trust and John Does One though Ten" was filed by Noah Banks at ten A.M. in Suffolk County Federal Court. Within hours, papers and subpoenas would be served on Patrick Webster, Gary Franklin Smith, Harvey Bacon, and Tobias Fiske. Copies of all the pleadings had also been sent via certified mail to the Phoenix.

Though ambivalent about serving papers on her brother, Jan considered the action a necessity, as Gary was alternate trustee of the Smith Family Cryonic Trust. She'd phoned the previous evening and left a message on his answering machine explaining the legal technicality; a courtesy to an ally she presumed to be on the other side through chance rather than intent.

The document read, in part, "Dr. Benjamin Franklin Smith ('the Deceased') was a natural person who died on June 2, 1988, a resident of Boston, Massachusetts, either the father or grandfather of each and every plaintiff in this case.

"Upon information and belief, the Deceased was tricked, conned, brainwashed, and otherwise seduced into embracing the purported 'science' of cryonics, a pseudocult which promotes the preposterous creed that dead bodies frozen in liquid nitrogen can somehow be restored to life . . ."

The lawsuit further demanded that all assets of the Smith Family Cryonic Trust be returned to the Estate, and that the corpse of Benjamin Franklin Smith be returned to Massachusetts to receive "a proper Christian burial."

November 17, 1988

"Please state your name and occupation for the record," Noah Banks said, looking away from the witness to glare at opposing counsel. Over these past months, he and Patrick Webster had managed to escalate their mutual distrust into full-blown hatred. It was now personal.

Indeed, Webster had made life miserable for the financially strapped firm of Banks and Smith. At his urging, Harvey Bacon had refused to be deposed in Boston. Instead, the four lawyers, along with Toby Fiske, had been forced to drive to Woonsocket, Rhode Island, today. A neutral law firm had been willing to supply the conference room, but the transit time was expensive, a complication Webster obviously preferred.

A court reporter worked the steno machine like a cash register, to which some would say the device was a relation. But Noah, like many personal injury lawyers, tended to think of the legal profession as being in the province of games of chance. He and Jan had fed vast amounts of silver into this particular slot machine, and thus far no payoff had been forthcoming. They were becoming progressively more worried about how much longer they could afford to remain as guests of the casino.

"Harvey Bacon. I'm an ambulance operator and technician," the witness answered.

"Imagine that! An operator, deposed by a chaser," Webster cracked. Grinning, he gently elbowed his youthful associate, Bryan Perry, whose principal assignment today was to watch and learn—and to bill the client, the Smith Family Cryonic Trust, at the rate of $185 per hour.

Toby smiled; he thought the comment gratuitous but accepted the mindset that the psychological warfare of litigation required.

Jan scowled at Webster and said nothing.

Over the past five months, Noah Banks and Jan Smith had spent nearly half of their billable hours on this case. The family had yet to receive their inheritance from probate, and the bank loan Noah had arranged against it was already spent. Cash was tight, and all three depositions so far had been virtual nonevents: a waste of time they could ill afford. Noah was not amused. "If Mr. Webster would refrain from puerile interruptions," he said, "we might actually finish this deposition today."

Webster smirked. Some incentive, he thought. Billing at $350 per hour including travel, plus his partnership of the associate's time, he would be thrilled if it lasted all week. The income was pleasing; all well and good. But he'd always found a special pleasure in tormenting cocky, self-inflated weasels like Noah Banks.

Finally Noah arrived at the events occurring on the day of Ben's death and suspension. Webster watched, calm and smug. How could this lightweight ever expect to win such a convoluted case? He'd never have the stamina for it. They would simply outlast him.

"How, where, and when were you first summoned to New England Medical Center?" Noah asked.

"The Phoenix paged us at eleven-seventeen A.M. We were in Providence at the time. I called their 800 number immediately, and the receptionist gave me the information."

"Who accompanied you to Boston?"

"Kent Chamberlain and Steve Reed."

Banks was wasting his time, Webster gloated to himself. Bacon was a great witness all right—but for his side.

"You generally work with them?" Noah asked.

Webster yawned.

"Yes, sir. I run three ambulances and employ fourteen technicians in all, but only four of us have been trained in cryonic preparation techniques."

"Who would the other one be?"

Another useless question, Webster celebrated to himself.

"Susan Reed, Steve's wife. But she was off duty at the time. Steve and Sue rarely work the same shifts; they have a small child at home."

Now Webster grimaced. Man, just stick to answering the questions! he tried to telegraph. Don't disentomb more details than you have to. The estate attorney had seen too many witnesses dig their own graves with such habits, although he doubted Bacon possessed so much as a spoonful of relevant knowledge, much less a shovel.

Indeed, the only thing Webster's side had to fear from these depositions was the opposition somehow learning of Toby's administration of morphine to Ben. That fact could give Noah considerable leverage, and leverage was what this type of litigation almost always boiled down to. Who knew what a judge or jury would do if they found that Toby Fiske, now the trustee of the Trust and beneficiary of the Will, had intentionally shortened his patient's life?

Webster had become aware of "their potential problem" from conversations with Toby prior to his testimony several weeks earlier. At the time, Webster had managed to shield Fiske from disclosing any private conversations with Ben by invoking doctor/patient confidentiality. And if that were ever to be overruled, the defendant could always, if necessary, resort to the Fifth Amendment. During preparation, he'd imparted to Toby the standard legal boilerplate: "Answer honestly and listen carefully; but only respond to the precise questions he asks. Never, never volunteer information."

Now he wished he'd had the same conversation with Bacon. Well, no big deal, he guessed.

"I see," said Noah. "How long did it take you to get to the hospital?"

"About fifty minutes."

"What did you do when you arrived?"

"First I talked to the patient's doctor, and then to his daughter; explained the whole procedure to them."

"Would his doctor have been Tobias Fiske?"

"Yes."

"Had you known Dr. Fiske previously?"

Another unconcealed yawn emanated from Patrick Webster.

"No. Never met the man before that."

"And how did he react to your description of cryonics?"

"He listened, asked a few questions. Seemed a little distracted, actually."

To Webster it seemed as if Bacon was enjoying listening to himself. He knew such an inclination was never a good thing in a witness, but nevertheless sat back in his chair, barely noticing that the medic had just given Noah yet another small piece of unsolicited, and potentially damaging, information.

"What do you mean by distracted?"

"Well, he told me that the patient was his best friend. I guess he was kind of upset. Who wouldn't be? Hmm. I suppose that might explain . . . well, never mind."

Oh shit! Suddenly no longer so relaxed, Webster interrupted. "Noah, I'd like to take a short break if you don't mind."

"I do, actually," Noah said, apparently oblivious to the value of the information he'd just received. "Let me finish this line of questioning first."

"I'm afraid I have to take a bathroom break," Webster said. "Sorry. I'll only be a minute." He left the room.

Perry continued to sit like a piece of granite, saying nothing. But you didn't make law review at Stanford just for showing up. The young associate's only real task of the day was now to make certain that Noah asked no questions of the witness until Webster returned.

Predictably enough, Noah said, "Mr. Bacon, could you please clarify something you just said? Off the record?"

"Sure."

"Actually, Mr. Banks," Perry interrupted without hesitation, "it wouldn't be fair to speak with Mr. Bacon without Mr. Webster present. I think you'd better wait till he gets back."

"Why?" Noah asked. "It's off the record."

Perry turned to Bacon. "Regardless of what Mr. Banks says to you, I suggest that you wait until Mr. Webster returns before saying another word."

Bacon nodded, and pantomimed a zipper stroke across his mouth.

Noah sat down. This particular scuffle was over.

Meanwhile Webster was using the time to regroup. He stood in front of the men's room mirror, eyes closed, and tried to concentrate. Bacon knew something, but what? Unless . . . Oh damn. Unless he'd seen the empty syringe. Shit! That had to be it. Well, maybe he could get Bacon to keep any other gratuitous musings to himself.

Returning to the conference room, Webster smiled apologetically, his well-rehearsed expression of "aw-shucks" charm and sincerity. "Sorry about that, Noah," he said. "Just couldn't hold it in any longer. Before we start over, do you mind if I speak with Mr. Bacon privately for a moment?"

"Not until I finish this line of questioning," Noah shot back.

"Okay," Webster said, holding his hands up in mock surrender. Better this way than not saying anything at all. "I only intended to advise him to listen to your questions more carefully, Noah."

"Exactly what are you getting at?" Noah asked.

"I want to make sure Mr. Bacon understands," Webster said, "that he's only required to answer your direct questions; he doesn't need to waste your valuable time telling you anything you haven't asked him about."

"I know that," Bacon interjected.

Webster gazed intently at Bacon. "I'm sure you do, but I just had to make sure."

Noah pondered the wordless exchange for a few seconds, then smiled. "Thank you, Pat." He turned to the court reporter. "Ms. Halloway, please read back my last two questions, and Mr. Bacon's responses."

The faces of Toby Fiske and Patrick Webster each grew whiter; the roller coaster had just crested the hill.

She read:

"Mr. Banks: 'And how did he react when you explained about cryonics?'

"Mr. Bacon: 'He just listened, asked a few questions. Seemed a little distracted actually.'

"Mr. Banks: 'What do you mean by distracted?'

"Mr. Bacon: 'Well, he told me that the patient was his best friend. I guess he was kind of upset. Who wouldn't be? Hmm. I suppose that might explain . . . well, never mind.'"

"Mr. Bacon," Noah asked, his smile now a wide grin, "what exactly might that explain?"

"You're not required to answer," Webster cut in.

Noah scowled. "On what grounds can he refuse, counselor? Perhaps I should call the judge and ask *him* whether or not the witness has to answer?"

Webster quickly backed down. "No need for that. Sorry."

Noah's expression seemed to betray a burst of admiration for Webster, as if to say, *Damn nice move; I bet you even get away with it once in a while.* "Now, Mr. Bacon," Noah said, "what did you mean when you said that the two facts—that Dr. Fiske was Dr. Smith's best friend, and that he was upset—might possibly explain something?"

"It's j-just that I thought maybe he had some important decisions to make, y'know, since they were such close friends and all."

"What kind of decisions?"

"I don't know. Medical decisions, I guess."

"Like what?" Noah asked, his now-alert eyes bearing down like a falcon homing in on a field mouse.

"I'm not s-sure."

"Mr. Bacon, did you see anything unusual that day in the hospital?"

"What do you m-mean by unusual?"

"Anything that Dr. Fiske may have done in the treatment of Dr. Smith that he might not have done for a patient who wasn't his close friend! Mr. Bacon, I remind you that you are under oath. What the devil did you see?"

Bacon turned toward Webster, who closed his eyes and nodded.

"I s-saw Dr. Fiske slip a syringe into his pocket."

"And do you have any idea what could have been in that syringe?"

"I object," Webster said. "That calls for speculation."

"Does that mean I shouldn't answer?" Bacon asked.

"No." Webster shook his head in resignation. The damage was done. Unless Noah Banks was an even bigger idiot than he gave the man credit for, Banks had it all figured out by now. "You may answer, Mr. Bacon. It just means I'll try to get a judge to strike your testimony from the record later on."

"If I had to g-guess," Bacon said, "I'd say morphine."

November 24, 1988

"Do you really believe your father was murdered by his own doctor?"

Such a businesslike question belied the personal concern evident on Assistant District Attorney Brandon Butters's face. Noah attended the meeting, too, but all three lawyers present understood he was there only to observe and lend moral support to his wife. After all, it was her father who'd been killed. Besides, her relationship with this particular ADA was much closer than Noah's; once they had been very close indeed.

Brandon had always seemed friendly, never displaying even a trace of resentment toward Noah, yet Jan and her husband both wondered if there might linger some suppressed jealousy over her choice of husbands some nine years ago.

Having never visited ADA Butters's place of business, Jan was amazed at how tiny his office was; perhaps a quarter the size of a junior partner's at major law firms. His salary, too, was about a third as much as he'd have made in the private sector, even accounting for government benefits attendant to his position. The office reminded her of a principal reason why she'd opted to marry Noah: Brandon was smart, and such a great guy. But he still had no ambition.

She gazed across the chaos of Brandon's desk and stared directly into the dark brown eyes that had always drawn her to this earnest face. It was the face of a man who'd once loved her deeply, a friendly face, youthful for its thirty-five years; the seldom encountered, unstressed face of a lawyer who'd never compromised principle for unearned rewards.

She answered immediately: "I'm sure of it, Brandon."

"Sorry I have to ask you this, Jan, but have you and Noah filed a civil lawsuit against Dr. Fiske?"

Jan answered exactly as Noah had coached her: "No."

"Do you intend to?"

"We haven't decided. To tell the truth, I doubt he has much money. Which, I fear, is why he killed him."

Noah smiled.

"How so?" Brandon asked.

"Dad left him $200,000."

"I see. Were they close friends?"

"Supposedly."

"Any other evidence that Dr. Fiske intended to kill your father; something less, er, speculative?"

"An eyewitness saw him slip an empty syringe—had to be morphine—into his pocket immediately after Dad's heart stopped beating."

"Oh? Have you asked Dr. Fiske about the syringe?"

"His lawyer would never let him answer my questions."

"How soon would your father have died without the morphine?"

"According to Fiske, he only had a few hours left. But I don't accept that."

"Anybody else examine him?"

"My sister Maxine was there. She's a family doctor now. And the paramedics who drove him to the hospital. And those three so-called cryonic technicians, but that was after he was already dead."

"Cryonic?"

"Yeah. They froze his body." She shook her head. "Nutty, huh? Can't imagine how they conned him into signing up for that."

Brandon ignored the comment. "And what do your sister and the paramedics say about your father's condition?"

"At the time, they took Fiske's word for it. But Max only saw his charts, she never really examined Dad; and paramedics aren't qualified to offer a prognosis. Fiske is the only one with enough medical background to understand what he saw, and who also observed Dad's condition firsthand." Jan's tone was strident, as if reciting unarguable fact. Again Noah smiled.

"I see," Brandon said. "Is it possible Dr. Fiske was merely helping your father end his life? An assisted suicide? We see a lot of that."

"That's probably what he'll say it was, if he admits to anything at all. But there's only one way we'll ever know for sure."

"Which is?"

Jan glanced at Noah, who nodded only once this time. "To perform an autopsy on my father."

"That would make sense," Brandon said. "Does Dr. Fiske have an attorney?"

"I'd bet Pat Webster's firm ends up handling his case," Noah said.

"They're representing the Trust my father set up to fund so-called cryonic suspensions for everyone in our family," Jan explained. "Fiske is the trustee."

"Besides," Noah added, "I doubt he knows any other attorneys, except his divorce lawyer."

"I see," the ADA said. "Well, I'll call Webster and let you know what happens."

As soon as Jan and Noah left, Brandon placed a call to Patrick Webster's office. Webster called back twenty minutes later.

"What can I do for you, Mr. Butters?"

"Mr. Webster, are you representing Tobias Fiske?"

"Not formally. Does he need representation?"

"I'd say so. A murder complaint has just been filed against him by Jan Smith."

"That's ridiculous."

"Possibly, but you understand I can't ignore such an allegation. I must also tell you that Ms. Smith is a personal friend, so if you'd prefer, I'll re-assign this case to another ADA."

"I doubt that'll be necessary," Webster said. There was no sense making the decision too early. He could always move to disqualify him later if he became too big a pain in the ass. "Let me call Dr. Fiske and get his side of the story. Can I drop by your office this afternoon? Say three o'clock?"

"Not a problem."

The two men had never met before, but Pat Webster had already grilled two of his partners. Brandon Butters, he'd learned, was fair, principled, smart, and too nice a guy for the job; a man whose objective was justice, not glory. Webster knew that to deal effectively with such a man, he would have to forget everything he'd ever learned about prosecutors. The thought both disturbed and inspired him.

He'd carefully reread the terms of the Smith Family Cryonic Trust, drafted almost six years earlier, and had determined to his satisfaction, and delight, that the Trust would cover any of Tobias Fiske's legal fees.

At 3:45 P.M. he arrived fifteen minutes late, his tardiness intentional, a show of confidence. When he offered Brandon his hand, the man grasped it with a subtly exaggerated pressure and waited for Webster to meet his eyes.

"That doesn't work with me, Mr. Webster," Brandon said evenly. "Whatever books you may have read on gaining power advantages, showing confidence, or asserting control ... forget them in this office. Respect my time, and I'll respect yours. We'll both like it better that way."

Webster's mouth flew open like a hand puppet's, an obvious pretense at surprise. Then he shook his head as if to rethink the lie and grinned. "Busted!"

Brandon laughed, and the two pumped a genuine handshake.

"I now officially represent Tobias Fiske," Webster said. "How do I convince you my client's innocent?"

"That may be difficult. I have a sworn deposition that Dr. Fiske slipped a syringe, presumably empty, into his pocket immediately after declaring Benjamin Smith dead. Would you care to tell me what was in that syringe?"

"Off the record?"

"If you'd like."

"Okay. If you do prosecute, we reserve the right to make you prove this. But just between us, it was morphine."

"That's what I assumed," Brandon said. "Now the important question: Was it administered at the patient's request?"

"Of course."

"Any witnesses to that effect?"

"How often have you heard of one doctor asking another to break the law with witnesses attending the conversation? Look at it logically; Ben

Smith was dying. The morphine might arguably have sped the process by an hour or two, but certainly no more."

"Unfortunately," Brandon explained, "your client is the only person who knows if that's actually true. No other physician possesses sufficient knowledge to judge, unless you know something I don't . . ."

Webster shook his head.

"Then I have no choice. We both know there's not enough evidence for a murder charge, but I still have to move on with this inquiry."

Butters was absolutely right, Webster decided. No capable prosecutor would have dropped the matter then. "What do you suggest?"

"I've already received authorization from the D.A. to file manslaughter charges against Dr. Fiske for assisting a suicide. I intend to file tomorrow. I won't object to his release without bail, and I'll make sure he spends no time in jail before his arraignment. But the charges are technically necessary to initiate discovery."

"What kind of discovery?"

"An autopsy. If the coroner agrees that Dr. Smith only had a few hours to live, I'll drop all charges against your client. But if the coroner decides that Dr. Smith was not dying, I think most juries would be suspicious, especially considering the deceased's sizable bequest to Dr. Fiske. Two hundred thousand dollars is a credible motive. We'd have to refile, seeking a voluntary manslaughter conviction at the very least, possibly second degree murder."

"You realize that Dr. Smith was frozen at his own request, hoping that medical science might someday have the means to restore his life."

Brandon looked thoughtfully at Webster, gauging his adversary with an odd blend of suspicion and compassion. Finally he spoke in measured words: "In the eyes of the law, and frankly in my opinion as well, Benjamin Smith is dead. Tobias Fiske, however, is not. If you believe in your client's innocence, I'd strongly suggest that you advise him not to object to this autopsy."

The telephone rang at Banks & Smith, and it was Brandon Butters on the line. Jan put him on the speaker so Noah could hear.

"I've just informed Pat Webster we're filing second degree manslaughter charges against Tobias Fiske tomorrow morning."

"Man-two?" she asked. "That's it?"

"Look, I'm sorry, Jan, but this might be just a simple assisted suicide. We'll seek a court order to autopsy the body, and if it turns out your father wasn't terminal, we'll add a murder charge. But if he was dying anyway, I doubt this will ever go to trial."

Noah nodded, signaling Jan to save any arguments for later.

"I understand, Brandon."

"Jan, you okay?"

"I'm fine. Really," she said, unconsciously intensifying the misery in her voice. "And thanks for everything."

"You bet. Now don't worry; it'll all work out." He hung up.

Jan turned toward her husband. "Guess he didn't believe me."   ·

"He's doing it by the book is all. There's no evidence without an autopsy. Besides, it's pretty obvious, you know? Your dad was about to die."

Jan's body stiffened. "You mean you don't think it was murder? But you seemed so sure before."

He walked to her chair and began to massage her shoulders. Then he reached down and cupped her left breast with his right hand, squeezing the nipple hard, arousing her so easily, as always.

"I'm your husband," he said, the words reassuring, Svengali reborn. "But I'm also your lawyer. I had to prepare you to make the best possible presentation to the ADA. I imagine, though, that Brandon's right; it was just another mercy killing."

"If you believe that, why are we pushing so hard for this autopsy? Dad wanted to be frozen. What if he was right and they really can revive people someday?"

"Don't be ridiculous, honey. We both know the whole thing's a crock. Besides, once Ben's autopsied and buried, it'll be a lot easier to challenge his bequest to the Trust. That should be our—your family's—money."

He lowered his hand to work between her legs. Jan stared at her husband: the gaze of someone glimpsing a truth she's always known but could not acknowledge, especially now. She had already committed her-self, and the momentum of her choice would scarcely permit such drastic reevaluation.

She grabbed Noah and moaned. Massaging her belly, she told herself that they were pursuing Noah's plan for the sake of Sarah and Michael, and their third child kicking inside of her. Noah was right; cryonics was a crock. It had to be. But even as she felt him entering her, some part of Jan's brain began to imagine the life she could have had with Brandon Butters, a man whose motives she'd always known would need no daily safety inspection.

DECEMBER 25, 1988 — While Jewish settlers continue to move into the West Bank, Palestinians harass them with stones and firebombs. Meanwhile in Bethlehem, the mostly Christian Arab residents mourn their 300 countrymen killed in the past year's uprising against Israeli rule. — Securities firm Drexel Burnham Lambert pleads guilty to securities related fraud, leaving its star employee, Michael Milken, isolated in the face of criminal charges. — The remains of 235 victims of last week's Pan Am plane crash over Lockerbie, Scotland, have thus far been found. The search continues for more bodies and for the cause of the crash.

Today's meal would no doubt be the clan's last in the Chestnut Street brownstone before it was sold. Thus their Christmas dinner took on the added aura of ceremony, not only to commemorate the life of Benjamin Smith, but also marking the passage of an era in Smith family history.

The dining room table was a Queen Anne antique that Alice had given Ben in 1960, just a few months after Sam's death. It normally seated eight, but the ends pulled out and two center extenders could be added, allowing cramped accommodations for twelve. The three daughters of Ben and Marge Smith, along with their husbands, five children, Alice, and Gary, packed themselves around it on six dining room chairs, two stools, three armchairs borrowed from the den, Alice's wheelchair, and two-year-old Michael Bank's highchair.

Rebecca said a short prayer before dinner, then Maxine offered a toast composed for the occasion:

"To our mother and father, who raised and protected, nurtured and loved us in this house of warm memories. And now, may Benjamin and Margaret Smith together find their eternal peace."

Nearly all the adults raised their wineglasses, and most intoned a heartfelt "Amen."

But eighty-four-year-old Alice Franklin Smith bit her tongue. Eternal peace together? What rubbish!

Alice had known of her son's decision to have himself frozen; she was the only family member to learn of it before the day of his death; long before. In fact he'd told her prior to mailing the papers, and she'd encouraged him. She did not pretend to understand the science, but to Alice a tomb or a funeral pyre was a manifestation of cold surrender, while the freezer offered the warmth of hope.

She also knew of her granddaughters' opinions on the subject; all three had shared their feelings with her, and she'd listened sympathetically, never betraying prior knowledge of—or her true conviction about—her son's decision. While Alice would resist ever lying to her progeny, her love for them certainly did not preclude withholding information. Long a student of human nature, she perceived no advantage in tipping her hand prematurely. Save a potential life or spare a loved one's feelings? An easy choice.

While Alice's mind had remained inequitably shrewd and acute, her body had decayed with more than enough enthusiasm to atone for the injustice. Arthritis throbbed through every joint, and osteoporosis had hobbled her frame into a painful, almost paralyzed twist of loose, wrinkled flesh on brittle bone. Worse yet, her eyes were failing. She could no longer read newspapers or her beloved books, and could barely decipher the extra-large-print magazines to which she subscribed.

Recently she'd learned that an inoperable malignancy, which had begun in her lower intestine three years earlier, had metastasized to her liver and kidneys. At her age, the cancer would spread slowly, affording perhaps another year or two of life. Many in Alice's condition would have considered the remaining time a curse, but she deemed every day a bonus.

As Alice sat in the wheelchair, her body adopted a near-fetal contour, forcing her to stare at the floor. To see above the table's edge, she was forced to wrench back her head, curving her spine into a recumbent S. Doing just that to watch Katie haul the twenty-one-pound Christmas turkey to the table on a tray, Alice exclaimed with a genuine childlike grin, "That is simply the most beautiful bird I've seen in years."

Everyone applauded, and Katie's ten-year-old face lit up. Soft brown hair outlined her lively eyes—blue-green, like Ben's—and radiant smile. Katie placed the tray carefully at the center of the table. Today's gobbler was almost entirely her handiwork.

The early conversation centered around the meal and, naturally, basketball; all four men and George—my fifteen-year-old future-father—had carefully selected their dining-table seats on the basis of line-of-vision to the television screen in the adjoining den.

But the mood unmistakably changed during the break before dessert. The game now over, all five children had assembled in the den to watch the end of *It's a Wonderful Life*. Rebecca knew no sound could penetrate their concentration on the tube; especially George, who practically became the television set whenever he watched it. She'd been forced to limit his viewing hours, but today was thankful for this preoccupation with the narcotic medium. With the youngsters safely distracted, she could finally ask Noah Banks for the latest news on the lawsuit he had persuaded her to join against the Smith Family Cryonic Trust.

"It took long enough, but Brandon Butters finally obtained our court order," Noah answered.

"Court order?" Rebecca asked. "What for?"

"Didn't you know? To perform an autopsy on your father's body."

"Isn't Dad in Arizona?"

"Yes," Jan said. "But Brandon got a writ of habeus corpus. They'll have to surrender the body."

"Why would we care about that now?" Rebecca asked.

"First of all, if your father's no longer frozen, we'll have a much easier time challenging the Trust," Noah explained. "Besides, it's the only way to prove Tobias Fiske killed him. Otherwise he gets away with murder."

"Murder?" Max interjected. "Because he administered morphine to a dying man? I'm no fan of Dr. Fiske, especially after he gave Dad over to those cryonics people, but he didn't murder anyone."

"Are you absolutely sure Ben was dying?" Noah asked, suddenly transmogrified into outright lawyer mode. "Isn't there some chance he might have survived if Fiske hadn't given him morphine?"

"There's almost no chance he'd've seen the next morning, no matter what anyone did."

"I sure hope Webster doesn't—"

"You sure hope Webster doesn't *what?*" she shot back. "Doesn't depose me?"

"Well," he said, "it'll be a moot point after the autopsy."

"If he asks me," Max said, her defiance conspicuous, "I'll tell the truth."

"I know that," Noah said condescendingly.

"No you don't," she said. "You lawyers always recommend telling the truth; but you don't mean it. You really mean: 'Don't tell any lies if you might get caught.' I wouldn't be surprised if you're all given a secret course in Articulate Sophistry. Tobias Fiske loved Dad as much as we do, and was only trying to do what Dad wanted him to do. You know it and I know it."

"Whoa!" Noah said, holding his palms toward her, part conciliation, part mockery. "We're on the same side. Somebody conned your father. He paid those lunatics $75,000 to freeze his body, and then put millions into that ridiculous Cryonic Trust. That's money he would've otherwise left to you and your kids. I'm trying to help you get it back."

"Yeah," Max said, "that's what it's really about. Money. Well, maybe Dad got conned, or maybe those people believe their own fraud. Either way, it was his money and I don't want any more of it than he decided to give me."

"Nothing can bring Ben back," Noah said, his voice calm. "But at least we can still help ensure our children's futures."

Rebecca decided she could no longer listen in silence. "When I first learned that Dad was having himself frozen, I felt betrayed. I wondered what I'd tell Katie and George; whether their Grampa was in heaven or in limbo. I certainly don't know. But mostly, I could understand why he never told me. Why'd he let me learn of his plans only on the day he died? But now, listening to you and Jan talk about dissecting his body when you know full well that isn't what he would've wanted, well, at least I'm starting to understand."

Jan felt her blood pressure spike; she'd never expected to have to defend her actions to her own siblings. "C'mon, it's not like it's actually Dad in that freezer." She looked at Gary, hoping for some sign of approval from her big brother. "He's surely in heaven by now. It's only his corpse we're fighting over."

Max also glanced at Gary. He felt compelled to speak. "The whole thing's convoluted, all right. Don't have a clue what I'd do if I were you. No kids to worry about, and let's face it, I didn't have the greatest relationship with Dad. So don't look to me for the answer." He raised his eyes to his grandmother as if in supplication.

Alice forced her head up and gazed intently at her only grandson. Was now the right time to say it? She wavered only a moment, then said with a boldness intrinsic to her conviction, "I've been thinking about it for quite some time." She laughed quietly. "In fact, thinking is just about the only thing I can still do well enough to please myself."

"And what do you think, Grammy?" Jan asked, expecting Alice to endorse her strategy.

Alice surveyed the table, making eye contact with each person seated, the focused on Jan. "Ever since Benjamin was a little boy," she began, "he was a thinker. Oh, I'm not saying he didn't have emotions like everyone else—he most certainly did—but your father was a careful, deliberate man. And he was a doctor, a man of science. So I have confidence his decision was carefully researched and calculated. Now I don't claim to understand anything about this cryonics business, but if my Ben thought it worth the risk, that's good enough for me."

No one spoke. Not one of them would have been more surprised had she started dancing on the table.

"But the viability of cryonics isn't even the real issue here, is it?" she went on. "Fact is, Jan, your father's intentions were quite clear. He wanted his body frozen, along with the bodies of any of us willing to follow him when we die, and he wanted most of his money—money that he earned— set aside to pay for it. So what it really boils down to is: Whose life and whose money is it? I believe my son's wishes should be honored. Period."

Jan felt like a treed cat staring down from the limb at a German shepherd. "Grammy, I've talked to you about this lawsuit at least a dozen times. Why didn't you ever say that to me before?"

Alice smiled. "This is the first time anyone here has asked for my opinion, dear."

> MAY 14, 1990 — After a seven-year legal battle, the parents of 33-year-old Nancy Cruzan await a Supreme Court ruling on whether they may remove a feeding tube that has kept their irreversibly brain-damaged and unconscious daughter alive since her automobile accident in January 1983. The taxpayers of Missouri have already paid over $1 million in medical costs, and even more in legal expenses, despite Cruzan's parents' wishes. "I think most people would agree," explains a spokesman for the state, "that it's simply wrong to stop feeding any person who's still alive." — As unification plans draws steadily ahead, East and West German economists meet to iron out details of a treaty to merge their currencies along with all monetary and social policies. — Soviet President Mikhail Gorbachev rejects as "irresponsible" the notion of "shock-treating" the Russian economy through immediate conversion to free markets. Gorbachev maintains that such a transition must come gradually, and only after extensive public debate. — Scientists at International Business Machine's Almaden labs spell the letters I-B-M in xenon atoms, thus demonstrating the feasibility of precise manipulation of single atoms.

Justice delayed is justice denied.

Somewhere long ago Tobias Fiske had read that aphorism, and assumed he understood its full meaning. But today he recognized the shallowness of his comprehension at the time, as opposed to now. This recent insight had been acquired at great personal cost; his life had been on hold for over eighteen months, with no end to the ordeal in sight. In the wake of the publicity of the charges, his practice had diminished by nearly a third. Worse yet, his concentration was off, his ethics thus forcing him to refer his most complicated, and therefore lucrative, operations to other surgeons. As his savings rapidly dwindled, he suspected also that the stress was starting to affect his health.

"The wheels of justice grind slowly," Webster said.

Toby gazed blankly out Webster's office window. Tiny wisps of cotton-ball clouds decorated the azure sky. The Quincy Market courtyard was jammed, the weather far too glorious to consider lunching indoors; yet another day that Toby Fiske could not appreciate as long as he remained in purgatory.

"The Phoenix got another restraining order this morning," Webster added. "That's certainly good news."

"How long's it good for?"

"Three months. Time enough to prepare an expert report on the viability of cryonics. Then Butters'll have to get his expert to tear our expert apart, which should take another six months, at least."

"You'd think something would've happened by now," Toby griped. "Some kind of decision one way or another."

"Possibly in New Hampshire or Texas, but not in Massachusetts," Webster explained. "Besides, the longer it takes, the less likely you'll serve jail time. You're sixty-five, right?"

"Yes."

"Well, they'd be hard-pressed to throw a seventy-year-old doctor in jail even if a jury found you guilty of second degree murder. And no jury's going to convict you of murdering Ben."

"Sure hope you're right. From my perspective, I'm already in jail. It's a limbo where life is simply less valuable."

"Might seem that way now, but believe me, jail would be far worse."

"I guess the toughest part is not knowing."

"I understand, Toby. Still, my job is to keep you out of jail and keep our friend Ben Smith from being thawed, dissected, and buried. That's gotta be my entire focus if I'm to do my job well."

Toby simply nodded.

Thank God the Trust was paying his bills, Webster thought. Somehow the money would have felt less satisfying had it been coming from this bedeviled man.

The Phoenix had been active in the case, refusing to release Ben's body, and filing motion after motion in federal and state court both in Massachusetts and Arizona to fight extradition. Judges and their clerks were typically open to the argument that there was no reason to rush an autopsy of a body frozen in liquid nitrogen; such bodies were unlikely to change in any forensically material way. Still, the legal work was expensive. Even with their attorneys working pro bono, the Phoenix had already spent well over the $75,000 Ben had paid them for his suspension. Webster considered that as further evidence of their sincerity. And the Phoenix's lawyers, both cryonicists themselves, understood the routine, having been involved in similar cases before, which made them very useful allies. Webster found their principled intelligence remarkable, and all too rare.

What he failed to consider was that to these lawyers, the Phoenix was no mere client: Each case delineated issues which they believed might someday save, or cost them, their own lives.

"How far along are we?" Toby asked.

"If I had to put a number on it, two more years before the autopsy issue is irrevocably decided, and three to six before your case is finally settled. The best thing you can do is go on with your life; learn to deal with the uncertainty. Set it apart in your mind."

"Guess I'm used to knowing where I stand. I've been a careful doctor, Pat; believed in the sanctity of life, respect for the patient. Learned it from watching Ben. It worked, too. I must know two hundred other doctors in Boston, but only five or six, besides Ben and me, who've never been sued for malpractice. Ben was careful and open because it was his nature, but I had to work at it. Maybe I also knew deep down that I couldn't take the pressure if I ever screwed up."

Webster tilted his head slightly. "If you had to do it over, Toby, would you have done it differently? The morphine, I mean."

"Yeah," Toby answered immediately. "I'd've made damn sure Harvey Bacon never saw that syringe."

Webster laughed. This man seemed to be one of those rare clients he could have been friends with—if only they'd met under different circumstances.

The attorney had often considered himself fortunate to practice in a state where everything took so long, even those rare litigations where neither side employed delay tactics. And Webster had always been a master of delay. Like shooting fish in a barrel, he would find himself musing. But at least for this moment he wished there were some way to help Toby deal with the pressure. He felt nothing but admiration and gratitude toward him: admiration of Toby's steadfast and rare loyalty to Ben Smith, and gratitude for the personal gain Toby's loyalty had bestowed upon he himself.

Yep, he didn't know what he'd do if Toby had had to pay him. But no sweat; the Trust could easily afford it.

Over the past eighteen months, his firm had billed the Smith Family Cryonic Trust $1,572,400, plus out-of-pocket expenses.

MARCH 1, 1991 — Pentagon sources estimate the Iraqi death toll from the recently concluded Gulf War at up to 50,000, while just 79 Americans died in combat. Yet few Americans express sympathy for the enemy dead and their families, despite the powerlessness of Iraqi soldiers to resist the commands of their own country's totalitarian regime. — General Motors Corporation engineers demonstrate a scale model of an automobile, less than 1/200th of an inch long, with doors that open and close, and a working motor.

Gary stood before the middle-aged woman who sat planted like a shrub at her cluttered desk. "Please don't try to bullshit me, Ms. Forman. I've seen your second and third floors." He tried smiling to temper harsh words with gentle charm, but facial muscles betrayed his emotion. A part of him could still see the neglected, blank shells, those pathetic remnants of human beings, strapped to wheelchairs and drays, some moaning, others with eyes darting about in random bewilderment, or staring for hours at fixed points on the walls or ceiling or empty air. Gary could still hear their voices. Last week, when he'd prowled the halls of the second floor, they'd cried out to him, never using his true name, mistaking him instead for their sons, grandsons, husbands, or friends they hadn't seen in years, perhaps long dead; or merely hoping against reason that this man might be here to give *them* some attention, to distract *them* from their interminable boredom, relentless pain, and hopeless isolation.

Yet the third floor had been far worse. Its residents—inmates, he suddenly thought—had communicated at an even more primal level, often less cerebrally than infants, some wailing or whimpering, others vacant of any apparent soul. This was what hell must be like, he'd decided as he walked those corridors just a few days ago. The fierceness of the thought surprised him; he'd even felt slightly ashamed.

The matron across the desk scowled, the expression transforming her already homely features into a marvel of extraordinary ugliness. She wore a blue and white badge that read: Doris Forman, Asst. Senior Administrator, Brookline Village Nursing Residence. Her face was serious, stern, and almost comically puffy, and her body more distended than obese.

Gary suddenly wondered if this woman, having chosen health care as her profession, had ever even tried to exercise or maintain a healthy diet. If he'd worked there, forced every day to see what aging could do to people, he knew damn well he'd fight against his own decay with his every fiber.

"When?" Forman asked sharply, yanking Gary back from his mental digression. The woman was obviously surprised that anyone could or would have gone upstairs without her knowledge.

"Last week. Thursday on the second floor, and Friday on the third. Told them I was visiting Ruth and Maurice Shapiro. Sorry about the white lie, but I had to see for myself, and not on one of your guided tours."

She said nothing.

"Didn't spot anyone living on the second floor who hadn't had a major stroke, or worse. And the poor creatures who live on the third have no idea who they even are."

She hesitated a moment, no doubt angered by such blatant disregard of the rules. But she regained her composure. Apparently the *What else could I do?* expression on Gary's face had disarmed her. "Care on level two would be more appropriate for your grandmother," she said. "More staff per patient, and she needs a lot of help these days. She can't go to the bathroom by herself anymore; can't even sit in a wheelchair."

"You have to keep her on this floor! With her friends, whose minds are still reasonably sound."

"I just can't do that. It's not my decision to make."

"Look, I used to be a doctor myself. I hear your staff is excellent, and at least I didn't see any signs of abuse; neglect maybe—"

She cut him off. "If you used to be a doctor, then you also know that some amount of neglect is impossible to avoid. You're not going to find people willing to give constant care to patients like ours for the salaries we can afford to pay. It takes a lot of emotional strength just to look at people like that. You get hardened to their suffering after a while, or else you crack up."

"I know that," Gary said. "Look, I understand this is one of the best-run nursing homes around. And I know you're better equipped to care for terminal patients on the second floor. But my grandmother is not typical. At the rate her strength's declining, her heart won't last the month. Yet mentally, she's completely sound. It's a mixed blessing, but still a blessing. I don't want her spending her last weeks around those people. If she needs extra help, I'll pay for it."

"That would be expensive."

"Expense isn't an issue," Gary said, forcing himself to smile, to look into her glossy gray and bloodshot-red eyes and to somehow connect with this woman. "Look, she's my Grammy! She changed my diapers; taught me the alphabet. She took me to feed the ducks in the park every Saturday when I was five. She was there when I graduated from high school and college—and the day I got my medical degree, when my own father was too busy to come. Any cliché you want, I've got it for you. She's always been there for me, and I want to be there for her. It would be one thing if she was like those people on the third floor, but she'll know what's happening to her. She'll know."

Forman just sat there, gazing back.

Something in the nether regions of Gary's subconscious told him to grin. "Aw c'mon, Doris. I love her."

For the first time, Doris Forman actually displayed a trace of a smile. "Like I said, it's not my decision. But I can still pull a few strings. If I couldn't, well, I'd have to leave this job, wouldn't I?"

Gary reached out, took her hand, and brought it to his lips. The woman blushed. He looked at her face, winked, and limped from the office.

Gary set the video camera on the bureau table in Alice's room and pushed the record button. "Grammy, do you know who I ám?" he asked.

Alice lay on her side, knees perhaps six inches from her chin. She weighed less than seventy pounds and her breathing had become audibly labored. "Of course I do," she said. "You're my grandson. Gary. My only son Benjamin's firstborn child."

"And what day is today?"

"Friday. March first, 1991."

"Who's the President of the United States?"

"George Herbert Walker Bush. A pretty good man. But unfortunately, that lightweight, Dan Quayle, Howdy Doody in the flesh . . . is only a heartbeat away!"

Gary laughed. "Why am I here, Grammy?"

"You're here to record my dying wishes. To prove I'm of . . . sound mind."

"I think we've accomplished that!" He smiled warmly. "What are your dying wishes?"

"With all my heart . . . and mind, Gary, I want to be frozen with my son."

"Why, Grammy?"

"I have nothing . . . to lose. If it doesn't work, I'm dead! So what? If I didn't try it, I'd be dead anyway. But if it works . . . oh, if it works . . . what wonders I might see!"

"Don't you want to see heaven, Grammy? And Sam?"

"Sam loves me," she whispered. "If heaven's real, he'll wait for me. And I'm in no hurry . . . to leave this earth."

"The paperwork's all filled out," Gary said, and carefully read each entry to her. Afterward he guided her hand and she made the mark that would have to pass as her signature. Finally he could shut off the video camera and talk to her in privacy.

"You know, it's very strange," he said, holding her hand, giving comfort and receiving it. "In life, Dad was so much closer to my sisters. Yet now he's—I don't want to say 'dead'—no longer with us, I guess." How odd,

Gary thought. His father was like a specter: not just a memory, but also a half-living, half-dead reality. A pseudobeing, trapped on the far side of a wall. "And I seem to understand him better than they do."

"How do you . . . mean that?"

"When he told me about his ordeal after they sank the *Boise*, I couldn't admit this at the time—I was still too hurt—but as much as I refused to acknowledge it, even to myself, I began to know him then." God, if only he'd said that to his father that morning in 1982, Gary suddenly thought. Instead of telling him he forgave him, for chrissake, knowing full well Ben would recognize that the opposite was true. Would always be true. Even if he could never forgive him, Gary did understand him. And that's what Ben had really needed to know; still needed to know. Gary only hoped he could tell him someday; have another chance to . . . to be honest with him.

Ben had always been honest with *him*, hadn't he?

Gary continued, "I could practically see him floating in the ocean, exhausted, swallowing that putrid fuel and saltwater. And later, crammed in there in his filthy clothes, sitting in his own excrement on that Japanese hellhole. I can almost hear the screams of agony myself. Think what it must have been like just to breathe in there; how every breath would've required an act of will. His only goal was to get himself through it. Not that he compromised his principles to do it. Mom told me about how he saved his friend's life, and those prisoners in the camp he treated despite the risks, and how he wouldn't crack when the commandant questioned him. Ol' Dad, he kept his cool, by God. He stayed tough and smart and patient enough to keep himself alive. And I know how he did it. I understood the way he simply anchored himself to the idea that when it was all over, whatever the suffering, his survival would be worth any price he'd have to pay. My father, your son, was, is, a man who truly cherishes life."

"Yes, he is," Alice whispered. "I hope he got it . . . from me."

"I've been reading about cryonics, you know," he said. "Read *The Prospect of Immortality* last month. And every newsletter from every cryonics outfit I can find."

She stared up at him. Was it going to work? The thought sent a shudder from the nape of her neck to the base of her spine. "What do you think . . . about cryonics?" But even as she asked the question, Alice decided that her grandson's answer was irrelevant; nothing he said could change her mind or diminish her optimism. She needed the hope, just like Ben must have during his final moments.

"It seems possible to me," Gary said. "I won't say it's a sure thing, or even likely, but it's a shot. I'll tell you the most encouraging part is the sort of people it attracts. You'd think mostly superstitious, gullible souls would become cryonicists. But it's just the opposite. It's the skeptics, the mathematicians, the scientists who sign up to be frozen. People who think for themselves; who know how to think. People like Dad."

"And me."

"That's right. And you, Grammy." He kissed her cheek. "Now try to get some sleep, okay?"

"What time is it?"

"Twelve past six."

"I'll sleep at . . . seven-thirty . . . after Toby leaves."

"Toby Fiske is visiting you here?"

"Every day. Except when . . . he knows the girls . . . are coming."

"Damn," Gary whispered. "Dad sure chose his friends well. The more I learn, the more confused I get."

"Sometimes those who love most deeply . . . can't get past . . . the weight of . . . their own feelings."

"See you tomorrow," was all he could say. And, "I love you, Grammy."

Alice smiled. "Oh . . . do I love you."

MARCH 15, 1991 — The Emir of Kuwait returns from exile to a devastated country whose populace is demanding a more democratic government. — At a Los Angeles Police Commission hearing, participants castigate Police Chief Daryl Gates for sanctioning police brutality against Hispanic and black men. — Medical researchers announce the isolation of a gene that appears to mutate at the initiation of colon cancer, suggesting a possible approach to allow much earlier detection of the disease.

It was almost eleven A.M. when Dr. Toby Fiske raised his eyes from his computer monitor. "How'd you get in here?" he asked and immediately wished he could snatch the words from the air, swallow them, and start again.

"Just limped right in," Gary quipped. "Guess I look like I belong."

He looked more like he'd just walked off the set of a 1938 detective movie, Toby thought. "I'm sorry. I've been anticipating and dreading, this moment for a while now." Toby allowed his eyes to drift back to the computer screen, thinking that maybe if he finished reading this new in vitro fertilization protocol, his emotions might stop quivering like the plucked strings of a harp. But the words and symbols suddenly conveyed no meaning to his frontal lobes. They could as easily have been Mayan hieroglyphics.

He rose to close the door to his private office. "Please sit down," he invited the younger man. "I suppose we'd better talk."

"Good," Gary said.

"I didn't murder your father," Toby said, knowing full well he shouldn't even be talking to Gary about the case. If Pat Webster were ever to find out, he'd have a fit. "At least in my own mind," he added, "and, I think, in his."

"But you did kill him," Gary said in a matter-of-fact tone, his candor chilling.

"It was, er, necessary that he die just a little sooner than nature's hand would provide, so his dreams might have some hope of fulfillment." Toby tried to offer this as an honest explanation, but even he could discern a hollow echo.

"You broke the law, Toby, and every traditional code of morality." The swiftness of Gary's statement suggested a sure purpose. "But I didn't come here for an explanation or an apology."

Toby was taken aback. Then what did he want?

"I came to tell *you* something, Dr. Fiske." Gary spoke with a softness that Toby found menacing. "Not the other way around."

Toby felt himself stiffen. He resolved to accept whatever Ben's son must now do or say.

"For some weeks, I've been deliberating what I should tell you and how I should say it." Gary spoke in measured, clearly well-rehearsed words. "So my observations will take a few minutes to spell out."

"Take whatever time you need."

"Please understand that this is very difficult for me. I still face my own unresolved conflicts. But those aren't your concern. Just listen closely; that's all I ask."

Toby nodded; in his ears he could hear the rush of his own blood.

"I used to be a doctor, too, you know. Went through the same scientific disciplines and training as you and my father did. Science nourishes my art, for one thing; at least that's what I tell myself. But mostly I love the process of trying to understand the truth about things."

Toby smiled weakly and thought, Like father, like son.

"Recently, I've been reading books on cosmology," Gary continued. "Fascinating stuff. Those scientists go after the universe like safecrackers. Cosmologists have a term they use to define circumstances where the known laws of science collapse, like at the event horizon of a black hole. That's where the four forces—electromagnetic, strong nuclear, weak nuclear, and gravity—all break down. But break down into *what*? No one knows. They call the effect a 'singularity.'"

Toby listened, but could not imagine where Gary was leading.

"You can take this concept, this singularity, and use it to illustrate a philosophical concept. We can understand and make precise predictions from nature's laws of what will happen given a specific set of initial conditions. These laws will work for each of the four forces independently of each other. I think the same holds true for us. We can write human laws that are universally applicable, and make fair judgements in one-, two-, and even three-dimensional circumstances."

Gary paused and stared at him. "But there are other times, aren't there, Toby? Times when situation, emotion, ethics, and honor converge, or crash into each other, and create the kind of philosophical singularity I'm talking about. The kind that compels us into actions which in any other context would be unjustifiable. I think that's what happened with you and my father. I think you experienced just such a singularity together. How can you apply any universal laws to a singularity? You can't. The old rules don't apply. You can only judge it subjectively, through empathy, in other words, by asking yourself what you'd do in the same situation. And that's the question I've been asking myself for weeks."

Toby's hands trembled and his head bowed. He steeled himself for an adjudication from the one person whose opinion mattered more to him than any jury's.

"My answer," Gary said, "is that I hope I would do exactly as you did. Which is why you owe me no explanation or apology. I came here to clarify that. I have no need to forgive what you did. I admire it."

When Toby was finally able to raise his head, Gary had already left.

Toby would sit in quiet contemplation for nearly an hour, gathering strength for his ongoing ordeal. But when he rose from his desk, he would no longer be the same man he'd watched shaving in the mirror that morning. He'd been given a gift of courage that would last him a lifetime.

The afternoon deposition took place in Webster's office; an accommodation to the expert witness who had flown in from New York City. There was no conference rooms available in the District Attorney's building, and Banks & Smith's modest facility would have required at least an hour's cab ride, while Fialkow, Webster, Barnes & Zeeve was barely two miles from Logan Airport.

Even so, had the request come from Noah Bank's, Webster would have told the man to go screw himself. But Brandon Butters was a different story. The D.A.'s office was a bridge no intelligent lawyer would wish to burn.

Webster thumbed through the expert report as he questioned its author. A stenographer tapped quietly at her small machine. Also in attendance were Brandon Butters, Noah Banks, and Tobias Fiske, all of whom had learned to keep conversation with the opposing side to a minimum. Toby studied his copy of the report and reviewed copious notes on a yellow pad of lined paper.

"Please state your name, age, occupation, and credentials for the record," Webster began.

"Dr. Brett Wong, forty-nine. I'm a molecular biologist, with a B.A. from Yale, and an M.D.Ph.D. from UCLA. I now conduct research, while teaching at Columbia University. I've been a full professor for the past six years."

"You state in your expert report that Ben Smith can never be brought back to life under any conceivable circumstances. Is that still your contention?"

Wong folded both hands into his lap. "Yes, that's correct."

"As I read this, I see you believe that at liquid-nitrogen temperature, ice damage so corrupts cells as to render them permanently nonviable."

"Yes. In many cases."

"Not all?"

"No. Not even most. But far more than a critical amount."

"Dr. Wong, could you please describe, in the simplest terms possible, what happens to a typical human cell when it is so frozen?"

As the witness spoke, Toby wrote on his notepad.

"Certainly," Wong answered. "Most cells are about ninety percent water. At minus 196 degrees Celsius, water will expand by roughly ten percent. It also crystallizes, which in some cases may actually puncture the cell membranes. That effect, however, is relatively rare. What does happen, almost uniformly, is that ice squeezes and disrupts the ions and proteins of tissue, occasionally forcing them into shrinking pockets of residual unfrozen water. And sometimes the fabric of a cell itself becomes crushed into tiny spaces among the ice crystals."

"But many types of human cells have been frozen successfully, haven't they?"

"Yes."

"And isn't human blood frozen routinely?"

"Certainly. But unlike most of our cells, red blood cells contain no nuclei. A percentage of the other blood cells, such a lymphocytes, die in the process. But even so, frozen blood, once thawed, is functional. That wouldn't necessarily be the case with other organs."

"I see," Webster said as he accepted a note from Toby. "But Dr. Fiske tells me that lengths of intestine have been frozen in liquid nitrogen, thawed, and worked afterward."

"True. But an organ is not a living animal."

Toby tore another page from his notepad and handed it to Webster.

"What about worms and other simple organisms that have been frozen and thawed without apparent harm?" the lawyer asked. "Wouldn't those be considered animals?"

"Well, those are much less complex than mammals, obviously."

"Aren't human embryos and sperm often frozen, then stored for later use?"

"Yes. But long before any mammal is viable outside the womb, it becomes too fragile to survive that kind of damage. Its cells become interdependent, and even small disruptions in the balance will kill the organism."

"And I suppose the human brain is more delicate still?"

"More delicate? Depends on your definition of the word," Wong answered. "Certainly brain cells are larger than other cells, and will not normally self-repair or regenerate. Besides, human neurons don't grow or divide. Therefore, I believe the loss of each brain cell would be more devastating than the loss of any other type of cell."

Webster read another note from Toby: "Could scientists build a system to set out modified microorganisms that might guide the neurons and glial cells toward their own repair or regeneration?"

"No. That's impossible."

"Impossible?" Webster read. "Can't bacteria and viruses do things at least that complex?"

"Well, yes. But in my opinion, human beings are simply not capable of achieving that level of technology."

"In your opinion. I see. Please tell us what is likely to happen to this patient's frozen cells once they're thawed."

"With the cryopreservation techniques that were used on Dr. Smith, I'd estimate about six percent of the cells would be completely dead upon thawing. Of the remaining cells, if they survived long enough, most would eventually revert to their former condition, but a certain percentage wouldn't."

"What percentage?"

"No one's sure. A small percentage, I suspect. Maybe only a fraction of one percent. But as I said, a mammalian system can tolerate the corruption of only an infinitesimal portion of its cells."

Toby handed Webster another note.

"Tell me, Dr. Wong, how strong is your neurology background?"

Wong smiled; flattened an eyebrow. "Strong enough. I teach a course in neurobiology."

"Then you must know most neurologists believe information in the brain is stored in many places, with a high degree of redundancy."

"Yes, that's the current theory."

Webster grabbed another sheet from Toby. "A stroke often wipes out an entire section of the brain, which can have devastating consequences. But if you lost, say, seven percent of your brain cells, spread evenly throughout your brain, it might not be catastrophic. Maybe not even noticeable, correct?"

"Possibly." Wong audibly swallowed. "But we're not just talking about losing cells. We're talking about damage to living cells that would alter their function and disrupt every system in the body."

Webster read: "Suppose technology would enable us to remove defective cells, keeping only the healthy ones. Wouldn't that give other cells time to regenerate?"

"Nobody knows," Wong answered. His eyes roamed the room.

"Then it's conceivable, right?"

"Unlikely, but possible, I suppose."

"Dr. Wong, is this cell damage we've been talking about reversible by today's science?"

"Certainly not."

"What about tomorrow's science?"

"It seems dubious."

Webster leaned forward. "Dubious? But not impossible?"

"In my opinion: impossible. You can't resurrect a cow from hamburger."

Webster read another note from Toby: "Especially if it's been cooked. Or eaten by worms."

The witness laughed. Then he scrunched his mouth and shook his head—an indulgent parent scanning a child's second-rate report card.

"Tell me, Dr. Wong," Webster asked. "Couldn't you *clone* a cow from the living cells in fresh, raw hamburger? Theoretically, I mean."

"Almost anything's possible in theory. But remember, our DNA modifies as we mature. Besides, too much free-radical damage occurs over the years, even if the organism seems healthy. Therefore most of my colleagues and I believe that scientists will never be able to clone an adult mammal."

"Never? Not even a century from now?"

"No. Not even a thousand centuries from now. I'm afraid that's all just science fiction, Mr. Webster."

AUGUST 17, 1992 — Relief workers prepare for a United Nations airlift to deliver provisions to the starving citizens of war-torn Somalia. — Republicans convene at their national convention in Houston. Polls now show Governor Bill Clinton with a 17-point lead over President George Bush. — Many Germans express apprehension about abandoning the deutsche mark, a symbol of its resurrection from ruin, as the European Community advances toward forging a common currency.

"Is this normal?" Gary whispered to Pat Webster, who sat at his right along with three associates and two appeal specialists from the firm of Hemenway, Richman and Mintz. Gary was referring to the throng—perhaps "press" would have been a better word, he decided—of reporters overflowing the tiny courtroom.

"Hell, no. Less than twenty stringers showed up for oral argument last month. But of course you weren't here that day. Let's face it, a famous artist adds a certain glamour to a case like this." Webster neglected to mention that his own publicist, at his direction, had put the word out that Gary Franklin Smith would personally attend today's ruling on Ben's autopsy.

Toby Fiske, at Gary's left, pondered the strange transposition of fortunes between his newfound ally and himself since Ben's death. Now it was he who wobbled at the edge of insolvency, his assets depleted by intractable living expenses and dwindling clientele. Meanwhile, Gary's career had soared, as if his father, while living, had been tethering him like an anchor.

The critics seemed to agree that Gary Franklin Smith's art, as good as it may have been before his father's death, had not improved enough over the course of the litigation to explain his remarkable rise into public consciousness. And the lawsuit itself, while unusual, was hardly unprecedented; the Phoenix alone had litigated four substantially similar actions in its twelve-year history, none of which ever attracted a fraction of the attention this one now garnered.

Indeed, the notoriety of this case, and Gary's fame, had been nourishing each other like a cow grazing on, and fertilizing, meadow grass. It would be another week before Gary's photograph made the cover of the *National Enquirer*, but the weekly hadn't been ignoring him; for months he'd been featured prominently in its interior pages. The other tabloids had been equally diligent.

JUDGE SEZ: THAW ARTIST'S ICED POP NOW! the page-three headline of the New York *Post* had blared nearly forty-four months ago, the day after Brandon Butters had obtained his first court order. Reader reaction had been clamorous on both sides of the issue, temporarily raising the cryonics debate to national attention.

Gary, who'd always trusted his art to speak for itself, had refused to grant interviews to reporters, which had had the unintended effect of "Salingerizing" his name. Suddenly people became curious to see his paintings, and when viewing them, generally acclaimed the work. A few even understood why his work merited such acclaim.

Jan and Noah, outgunned and outnumbered, sat in anxious silence with Brandon Butters at the much less crowded plaintiff's table. Rebecca and Maxine had long ago demanded their names be dropped as plaintiffs in the civil suit, but their action had no effect on this criminal litigation.

Today's ruling of the First Circuit Court of Appeals would likely mark the final outcome of the autopsy issue, since both sides doubted that the Supreme Court of the United States would care to consider the matter. And without an autopsy, their civil case was starting to look very weak.

Everyone rose while the three judges entered the room, and the Honorable Ellen Ryskamp read the panel's ruling:

"Under normal circumstances, when a person dies amid accusations of foul play, an autopsy is standard procedure. Indeed it may be our only pathway to the truth. An undisputed fact of this case is that Dr. Tobias Fiske administered morphine to Dr. Benjamin Smith moments before death. Very likely, the morphine was responsible for arresting Dr. Smith's heartbeat. The question remaining is: How much longer could Dr. Smith have been expected to survive had he not received the morphine?

"We have reviewed the testimony of various experts, and believe that autopsy is the only way to answer that question with reasonable certainty."

Turning his eyes to Toby, who sat erect and stoic, Gary wished he could somehow shield his friend. Toby had gone through the entire ordeal trying to protect a patient's brain from deteriorating before it could be frozen. If this court upheld the autopsy order, his decision to administer morphine would have cost at least four years of his life—for nothing.

Meanwhile Webster found himself deploring the decision's likely effect on his own career. How had he blown this case? Who would ever hire him now, a lawyer who'd become famous for letting his client get dissected? He felt only a tinge of shame for pondering his own problems at this moment when Ben Smith's and Toby Fiske's fates were at stake. After all, he'd done his best, hadn't he? His conscience was clear.

"However," Judge Ryskamp continued, "these are not normal circumstances. For one thing, there has been no evidence presented that Dr. Fiske was attempting to disregard his patient's wishes. Indeed, it seems likely that his actions were governed more by his friendship with Dr. Smith than by medical protocol. Therefore even if it is discovered that Dr. Smith was not provably terminal, Dr. Fiske is likely to be found guilty of nothing more than assisting a suicide."

Brandon suppressed a smile. Ryskamp was absolutely right. If this ruling upheld the autopsy order, at least it would be for a sensible reason.

Noah thought: Why hadn't that pious chump Brandon Butters taken a harder line? If the ADA had simply emphasized the possibility that Fiske had murdered Ben for the inheritance, they wouldn't even be sweating today's ruling. Oh well, they'd still probably win.

"Nonetheless," Ryskamp continued, "it seems that there would be little to lose by performing an autopsy to uncover whatever evidence is there."

Brandon and Jan smiled faintly. Noah smirked.

"But a third factor," Ryskamp added, "must also be considered: That of the deceased's decision to be frozen, and his purpose in that decision. Legally, a dead person has no standing. However, that person's property is customarily distributed in accordance with his or her wishes. It is not within the competence of this court and, based on the conflicting expert opinions submitted here, apparently not within the competence of today's science either, to judge whether cryonics is viable.

"Benjamin Smith's body was bequeathed as an anatomical donation to the Phoenix Life Extension Foundation, and perhaps to Dr. Smith himself. It is possible to override such bequests in certain instances, but a standard of probity must be maintained."

Jan and Noah blanched.

Damn! Jan realized they were screwed; they were going to lose! They'd have to sell the house; move to an apartment; probably even send Sarah and Mike to public schools. And Noah would be devastated.

We'll have to start buying our clothes at Filene's basement, Noah thought. Jesus. Everyone at the club was going to think: What a fucking loser that guy Banks is!

Brandon turned and offered his friends a compassionate gaze, having given not a moment's thought to this high-profile loss from the perspective of his own future. To him it was more important to have sought equity than to have prevailed in disoblige. His worst disappointment was for Jan, the first woman he ever loved, and possibly the last. Emptying all thoughts of her from his mind, Brandon consoled himself: Tobias Fiske had paid a high enough price already. Had the prosecution won, justice would have been the loser.

On the other side of the room, Webster was smugly anticipating a flood of lucrative cases for which he would soon have the privilege of selecting. Gary and Toby embraced in jubilant relief while Ryskamp finished, "We deem it both unlawful and unwise to invalidate his instructions merely to obtain evidence of dubious consequence. And we unanimously agree that Dr. Smith's wishes should not be betrayed. Therefore the State's writ of habeus corpus and court order authorizing the autopsy of Dr. Benjamin Smith are hereby revoked with prejudice."

> JUNE 20, 1988 — With intent to draft a Universal Declaration of Ethical Standards, the United Nations General Assembly commissions a study on the implications of animal and human cloning. Once the Declaration is adopted, each member nation will either pass laws requiring citizens to abide by UN standards, or face possible ostracism from the international community. Over the past 16 months, eleven independent teams of scientists around the world have successfully produced clones of adult mammals, a feat considered impossible by most biologists just two years ago. — The Food and Drug Administration authorizes human trials on a robot developed at NASA's Ames Research Center to assist in brain surgery. The one-tenth-inch-diameter robotic probe, which uses neural net software to survey the brain, is equipped with pressure sensors allowing it to locate edges of tumors without damaging arteries or nerves.

Soon after the appeal ruling, Brandon Butters had withdrawn criminal charges due to lack of evidence. Within two years Jan Smith and Noah Banks, deserted by all other Smiths and unable to raise funds to continue litigation against Webster's seemingly bottomless resources, were forced to drop their civil case.

On the very next day, Toby had sold his practice, put his house up for sale, and placed his few remaining assets into an offshore trust.

He'd tried to explain it to Gary: "Something in my mind just clicked. The trial, the interminable ordeal of it, and the stakes. All those passions stirred. It was more than just me on trial in that courtroom. It was a whole system of belief! I felt as though I could suddenly see everyone struggling to hang on to an ideology by destroying someone else's. All that ferocity, all that fear, and for what? Finally, I came to understand our desire not only to deceive, but to be deceived by the supernatural, or so-called magic, or ancient taboos. Like the notion that dead bodies have to be buried or cremated, even though we know damn well that the definition of death is always changing."

Gary had nodded silently.

"And I saw firsthand," Toby continued, "how destructive it is for people to confront reality with less-than-open eyes. I don't know if it was because I finally felt liberated, or maybe just observing you; someone with the guts to follow his own path, Gary. But somehow I knew what I had to do with what's left of my life."

N o w ,   a l m o s t   s i x years later, the two friends shared an inaugural day of summer. Cloudless skies, 76 degrees with cool gusts of clean, fragrant air. They sat, enjoying their every Tuesday and Thursday lunch at the Fish Market in Faneuil Hall, just a stone's throw from Webster's office. In fact, both men had on occasion been amused by the notion of throwing stones through the window of the lawyer whose bills had single-handedly drained the entire Smith Family Cryonic Trust. But mostly they thought of Webster not at all, feeling favored by the current states of their lives, all regrets notwithstanding.

Gary Franklin Smith's fortunes had continued unabated, his only emptiness arising out of isolation from his family; an estrangement resulting from the court battle his sisters had waged against Toby and him. He'd barely spoken to any of them since.

Dr. Tobia Fiske had reinvented himself as a "debunker of the occult," and had become fairly well-known. Now he traveled the country uncovering frauds in medicine, religion, law, and pseudoscience. Many of his "victims" like to file lawsuits, adding to his fame. Even the Psychic Friends Network had threatened to sue over a double-blind investigation he'd carried out the previous year, although he doubted (but hoped) they would actually go through with it.

A few weeks ago Toby had obtained and published photographic evidence against Reverend Michael McCully, a famous faith healer. It seemed that two of the man's formerly lame "patients" had been out jogging the day before their miraculous cures on national television.

"What ever happened with Reverend Mike?" Gary asked.

Toby chuckled. "Well, the idiot sued, of course, which was great. Fell right into my clutches. All that free publicity for the newsletter and my books. And more bad press for that clown himself. Besides, I figure: What have I got to lose? My meager assets are all judgment-proof, and nobody can touch my pension. Probably won't even hire a lawyer this time."

Gary grinned. "So what's your latest project?" he asked eagerly.

"Ever hear anything about Jacques Dubois and the Jericho Amber?"

"You mean that guy in Montreal who supposedly identified amber amulets from a larger amber mentioned in the Bible? Something about giving Joshua's trumpeters the power to demolish the walls of Jericho, wasn't it? I saw a headline about it on one of the supermarket tabloids. Made a spectacle of myself by flipping that rag the bird right there in the checkout line."

Toby bid not laugh at this banter, a departure Gary found odd. Pulling a folded sheet of paper from his pocket, the older man explained, "Here's a copy of the press release."

Gary accepted the paper and read:

FOR IMMEDIATE RELEASE:

PIECES OF FAMOUS BIBLICAL AMBER TO BE PLACED ON PUBLIC DISPLAY IN MONTREAL. OWNER REJECTS $15 MILLION CASH OFFER FROM BOSTON MUSEUM OF HISTORY.

Can these amulets perform miracles? It is said that anyone who possesses them will become invincible in endeavors of trade, arts, sciences, athletics, even war. Perceptibly different from any other substance on earth, the seven remarkable globules were identified and purchased at a bargain price by Dr. Jacques Dubois, a young archeologist, after having been unearthed on a dig in southern Jordan near the Dead Sea and legally exported before their true provenance was established. "I noticed immediately that they had an almost supernatural luminescence," Dubois explains, "and when I learned the location of their discovery, I knew right away that these must be from the legendary Amber of Jericho."

Scientists from six countries have examined and performed noninvasive tests on the seven marble-sized jewels. As even Pierre Reverie, a skeptical French geologist, admits, "They radiate an energy that is apparently not of this earth." Biblical ·scholars confirm the possibility that holy amber could indeed exist. "There is no mention of the Amber in the English translation of the Book of Joshua," explains Dr. Solomon Friedman, celebrated expert on the Old Testament, "but in the original Hebrew . . ."

Before Gary could finish scanning the first page, Toby interrupted. "I could use your help on this one, buddy."

"Sure. Anything."

"The publicists who wrote that release are brilliant, don't you think? The press release goes on to say that the amber pieces will be placed on public display in Montreal in six months' time, when the miracle powers will be demonstrated beyond any doubt and discharged to the benefit of the world. It also says that the exhibition will be open to the public, free of cost. Several prominent scientists and religious scholars were recruited to offer ambiguous opinions on the amber's authenticity."

Gary started considering the delicious possibilities of using his fame to sneak a video camera backstage. Those charlatans would surely love to hook anyone prestigious to add credibility to their fraud.

"Looks like a damn well orchestrated scam," Gary muttered, his distaste mitigated by a certain perverse admiration.

"Sure is," Toby said proudly. "You'll notice that we never ask for any money, although we do mention that Dr. Dubois would entertain the possibility of eventually selling one or two of the stones."

"Wait a minute." Gary frowned. "We?"

"Yeah. We also persuaded Arthur Bradley, my friend at the Boston Museum of History, to issue a statement that the museum does not comment about offers it may or may not have made for potential acquisitions."

"Amazing." Gary started to laugh.

"I'll need you to say something about the Amber, too, if you don't mind. Maybe even vouch for Dubois. His real name's John Duncan, by the way; he's the son of one of my med school buddies. Anyway, we'll help you make up some bullshit about how the stones gave you some special artistic powers or something."

"Hmm." Gary smirked. "Can't wait to hear the rest of this story."

"Might take a while," Toby answered. "Hope you're not pressed for time today . . ."

JANUARY 11, 1999 — Netscape releases the beta vision of its new software which enables Internet surfers to "Backlink" to any Web page which posts a link to that page. Prior to today, it was possible only to "forward click" to pages linked *by* a Web site's originator. With Backlink, anyone can post criticisms about any other Web sponsor's information or products, and browsers can now conveniently obtain the other side of the story. The cyber community hails the product as a boon to free speech and open information. Several organizations, including the Coalition of Trial Lawyers, the Church of Scientology, and the Tobacco Institute, issue press releases condemning Backlink

as an invasion of privacy. — Michigan reports economic
growth of 6.3% in 1998, possibly the result of the state's recent
elimination of juries in all nonfederal civil trials there.

Many gourmets considered Locke Ober one of the finest restaurants in
Boston, but perhaps Rebecca had chosen it for other reasons. Maybe she
wanted to ensure that their dinner would be private, and not too brief.

Gary couldn't help noticing how much his sister had aged in five
years. Rebecca's pixielike smile and quick laugh were nowhere to be found,
and it seemed even the weight of her shortened hair pulled down her face.
The two had rarely seen each other since the appeal decision. Now he was
glad that she'd called him; grateful that she'd asked him to come as a personal favor to her, rather than on some pretense of trying to patch things up
with Jan. He'd missed her. Damn! Why had he let it wait this long?

"Quite a stunt your friend Toby Fiske pulled off a few weeks ago."
She started the conversation in a light vein, but was also demonstrating that
no topic need be off limits; not even subjects that might remind them of the
lawsuit. Gary understood. If there was to be a reconciliation, they would
have to rediscover their previous openness.

He beamed. "Yeah, he's having a ball with it, and his books are selling
like crazy. Made all the TV news networks and, as I'm sure you saw at Stop
and Shop, the front page of every tabloid. Most legitimate newspapers, too.
Filled Expo Stadium that night; must've been forty thousand people there."

"How was the exhibition?"

"David Copperfield, it wasn't. But they managed to pull off a few
interesting feats of apparent levitation, deflecting bullets with a force field,
that kind of stuff. Then afterward, the troupe of professional magicians
Toby was working with showed the mesmerized audience how they'd
fooled them. And even then, according to a random survey they conducted
afterward, almost half the people there refused to believe it was a scam."

"Incredible. So, were the amber pieces fake?"

"No, it was real amber all right." Gary chuckled. "Jacques Dubois,
actually John Duncan, and Toby bought seven ordinary pieces of amber in a
rock shop in Belmont, drilled microscopic holes in them, and filled the cen-
ters with an effulgent similar to the chemical in fireflies. They found a New
York public relations firm willing to help them, as long as Toby and John
agreed not to sell anything or accept money. And a few semifamous people,
including yours truly, volunteered personal anecdotes about the amulets'
magical powers. Toby even managed to get a few well-known scientists to
cooperate, not by confirming anything, but simply by refusing to rule out
the Amber's authenticity."

"And the scam actually fooled *60 Minutes?*" Rebecca asked.

"Oh, no, *60 Minutes* was in on the hoax from the beginning. John and Toby finally came clean on last week's show. The segment started out like another piece of their semiskeptical reportage on the Amber, but four minutes into it they explained the whole setup. It was a classic story about the gullibility of the public and the razzle-dazzle hokum they'll fall for. I must say, I'm surprised you didn't watch it."

"I've had other things on my mind lately," Rebecca said.

Gary realized how much he enjoyed telling the story to his sister, but he'd also noticed a melancholy cast to her mood. "You know, I've missed you," he said.

"Me, too." Rebecca stared back at him. "Gary, how did it all get so screwed up?"

"Too much money in that trust, I guess." Too much greed, he thought. Too much self-serving counsel; not enough understanding. "Hard for some people to resist," he added, with only a nuance of bitterness.

"I guess. So sad, isn't it? We put ourselves through all that grief, and the lawyers end up with the money."

"Yeah, and not even esquires Noah and Jan. Which serves them right, I suppose."

"What's so ironic, though, is that when Dad was alive, he was impossible to bamboozle. Biggest skeptic alive; and one of the smartest. But the second he dies, his own lawyer empties his wallet like a common pickpocket."

"Except that it was a hundred percent legal, best I can tell. And we helped him do it."

"There's nothing at all left in the Trust, is there?"

He noticed a plaintive luminescence in her eyes. She was not asking simply to make conversation. Of course! She needed money. "No. It's all gone." Gary was a careful man, so he paused several seconds to think before asking, "Why?" the question proof he still cared for his sister.

"Well, Katie hasn't been herself over the last few months."

"Katie? Tell me what that means."

"It was nothing in particular, no fever or anything, but you know how energetic she always was. And gregarious. But since November she's become lethargic; sleeping eleven or twelve hours a day; losing weight, too. Which she could hardly afford to do. So finally we took her to one of Max's partners."

"And?"

Rebecca delivered the grim words without tears: "Katie has cancer of the pancreas. Just like Mom."

"Oh my God!" Gary sat back and stared at the wall above his sister's head. He thought of his mother's death some twenty years earlier, and what they'd all gone through, he perhaps most of all. And now his beautiful niece Katie had it? A goddamn death sentence! She was only . . . ? Jesus; twenty years old.

"How long?" he asked, before recognizing his query's ambiguity.

"We've only known a few days. The doctors say she probably won't last the year."

He reached over the table, put his hand on hers and waited for the rest of it.

"Gary, she wants to be frozen with her grandfather." The words tumbled out of her. "And the thing is—oh, Gary, I wouldn't blame you if you slapped my face—the thing is, I want it for her, too. I'm not ready to abandon my little girl for dead."

> OCTOBER 31, 1999 — The Department of Public Health releases their latest AIDS statistics, and calls them "encouraging." The average life expectancy of a North American or European infected with HIV now exceeds 17 years. — California becomes the first state to outlaw "private smoking clubs" that accommodate more than 20 members at a time, closing a loophole that has allowed many large restaurants and even certain small companies to circumvent federal law. Cigarette smoking has been illegal in all public places throughout the USA since H.R. 1712 went into effect on April 10. — Senator Travis Hall (R. CT) challenges the Democratic-controlled Congress to attack the crime problem by "taking power away from manipulative defense lawyers, and putting it back in the hands of victims and potential victims." — President Clinton signs into law a bill first proposed by Nicholas Negroponte, the Cyber Corps Act, which will allow several hundred thousand young men and women from the United States and other developed nations to spend one to two years each teaching third world children how to become part of the digital world. The program is expected to empower 100 million school-age children at "roughly the cost of nine F-15s."

Halloween, before it evolved from the Celtic festival of Sambain, was a far more significant holiday than it has become in modern times. Back then, October 31 was also the eve of the new year, and in Celtic lore, a time to appease the forces that directed the processes of nature. Ghosts of the dead were thought to look in on their earthly residences, and the autumnal fes-

tival took on a sinister quality, as a time when malignant spirits emerged. It
was also said to be the ideal day to prognosticate future soundness of the
body and mind, reversals of fortune, marriages, and death.

October 31 was about to become the date of one of the most famous
suicides in American history; a suicide that all seven persons present hoped
would prove reversible.

Gary had rented a small but comfortable cabin near Rochester,
Michigan, a town of 7,500 some twenty-five miles north of Detroit. The
location seemed ideal. First of all, it just barely fell within Oakland County,
where Dr. Jack Kevorkian had observed or assisted dozens of suicides, and
with whose legal machinery Kevorkian and his lawyer, Geoffrey Fieger,
were intimately familiar. Second, the three technicians from the Phoenix
would have near perfect conditions under which to prepare the body, once
legally dead, for immediate transport just nineteen miles southeast to the
Cryonics Institute in Clinton Township, where it could be perfused, frozen,
and moved to Arizona at everyone's leisure. C.I. was a small, nonprofit
facility founded in 1976 by Robert Ettinger, author of *The Prospect of
Immortality*.

Such planning, and teamwork between competing organizations, was
a rare luxury in twentieth century cryonic suspensions.

Unfortunately, some of the personnel employed by the half-dozen or
so legitimate cryonics facilities had recently become inordinately cutthroat,
which had impeded the already-slow incursion of cryonics into general
public acceptance. Internet "news groups" in particular had become an
embarrassment to the cryonics field, with scientists and medical personnel
from various organizations constantly posting "flames" about the techniques and policies of other facilities.

In truth, the entire field was still plagued by lack of research funding
that virtually all techniques, as well as any criticisms thereof, were merely
theoretical. At the time, research into the long term preservation of transplantable organs such as kidneys and livers received hundreds of times the
funding granted to similar research on such a uselessly dependent organ as
the brain.

The Phoenix and C.I., while not the closest of allies, were wise enough
to recognize the public relations opportunity of inducting the niece of Gary
Franklin Smith into their registers. With heightened public awareness
would come increased demand, and thus increased funding for research,
the holy grail of every cryonics organization.

For many reasons, not the least of which was to eradicate any doubt of
the patient's intentions, Dr. Kevorkian videotaped the entire event. To
avoid potential litigation, the three technicians from the Phoenix waited in

their ambulance, aware of but no formally informed as to the goings-on inside the cabin.

The patient was my aunt, Katherine Franklin Crane. She reclined comfortably on a hospital bed installed the day before her arrival. Katie's body had withered to seventy-eight pounds, but her face retained a roseate sparkle. The disease had not yet progressed to where pain could no longer be managed by medication, or where the mind was of diminished use. Tonight she displayed a calm optimism bordering an exuberance, as if all were going according to plan.

"Now, Katie," Dr. Kevorkian said, "do you wish to continue your life?"

"No, not now."

"Not at all?"

"Not at all. I don't want this disease eating into my brain. I'm still lucid and fairly strong now. Within six months, I wouldn't be."

Rebecca read a carefully worded statement: "She wishes to be frozen, just like her grandfather, in hope of being revived decades or even centuries from now, when and if medical science can restore her health. Her father, brother, and I support her decision."

My grandfather, George Crane, Sr., holding Katie's left hand, and twenty-five-year-old George Jr., my father, standing at her right side, each signaled their agreement. "Yes, that's right," George Sr. said, smiling down at his daughter.

"Thank you, Daddy," she said, then looked toward Gary and Maxine, "and thanks so much to everyone here. I love you all."

Kevorkian scowled faintly, and addressed Katie again in his trademark humorless tone: morbid yet compassionate gentleness. The seventy-two-year-old "obitiatrist" had asked the same questions dozens of times before. "You understand what you're asking me to do, right?"

"Yes."

"You want me to help you end your life?"

"Absolutely, yes."

"You realize that I can set up the equipment, but you will have to trigger the device yourself."

"Yes, I know that."

"You know you can stop any time you wish."

"I won't stop."

"But you *can* stop; you don't have to go through with it."

"I know."

"Katie, how did you feel upon learning you had a terminal disease?"

"Depressed."

"I see. And at the time you first decided to contact me, were you still depressed?"

She considered this for several seconds before answering, "No. Not anymore."

"Then what prompted your decision?"

Now Katie did not hesitate. "Logic," she said.

Kevorkian nodded his head several times, then asked the question he'd recently begun asking all of his younger patients: "Have you considered whether you'd be willing to donate any of your organs to help save the lives or eyesight of others?"

Even though she'd made her decision days ago, Katie pondered the question carefully. "If science can bring me back to life, growing new organs should be a simple problem for them. Since I have cancer, I doubt anyone would want my internal organs other than for research. But the retinas should be fine. Okay, Doctor, take what you want. Just make sure they freeze my brain first."

Gary knew that Rebecca and her family were secretly horrified, but also determined to honor Katie's judgment; they'd kept their thoughts to themselves in deference to her wishes. But he grinned at Katie, his eyes locking onto hers. Her decision seemed utterly sensible. Anytime a person under sixty years of age died, he thought, medics should harvest any transplantable organs and just worry about preserving the brain.

She smiled back.

"Katie," Kevorkian asked, "what does it mean when you end your life; when you stop living?"

"It means I'm dead—unless cryonics works and science can someday repair my body. I know my chances of ever being alive again aren't so good. But even if I weren't being frozen, I'd still want to die now. Now, while I can think for myself, and laugh, and easily bear the pain, and return the love of those who love me. I want to die now, tonight."

"Some say you're doing the wrong thing, Katie. What would you tell them?"

"I'd tell them that it's my life, my body, my brain, my identity, my pain, and my hope. I know what I want, Dr. Kevorkian. I want to die; to be frozen with my Grampy."

By the side of the bed, like a crazy aunt living in the basement whom nobody talked about, lurked a canister of carbon monoxide attached to a hose with a gas mask at the end of it. Everyone in the room knew it was there, and they all tried not to look at it, as if such conduct might remind them of why they were there or, worse yet, might make Katie feel rushed. She'd already rehearsed her suicide twice, hours ago, and now it seemed as if she was procrastinating; perhaps trying to keep the "party" going just a little while longer than etiquette might dictate.

Kevorkian reassured her, "Take as much time as you need, Katie. No one's in any hurry tonight."

"What time is it?" she asked. In truth, she felt weary and yearned to end it right then, but refused to reveal these emotions. Her work was not yet finished.

Gary looked at his watch and said "seven-thirty" at exactly the moment Jan walked through the door.

Right on time, Katie thought. Good! She looked at her handsome uncle, his weathered, angular features seemingly demanding explanation. This was perfect.

"**W h a t   a r e   y o u** dong here?" Gary asked abruptly, instantly regretting it.

"I invited her to come," Katie said. "I'm sorry; I hope it's all right."

"Of course," Gary said, not meaning it.

Jan hugged Rebecca, Max, both Georges, and Katie; then seated herself next to George Jr., who was perched on the right side of the bed. She looked toward Gary.

Here it comes, he thought, throbbing with rage: The mea culpa that was supposed to make everything fine again.

"Look, Gary, I made a terrible mistake," Jan blurted. "It was dumb and blind and careless. We needed money. Noah seemed so sure it was the right thing to do, and I guess I wanted to believe it, too. But it wasn't right, what we did. I never should have gone along with that lawsuit. I screwed up, and there's nothing I can do about it now. The worst thing is that if we'd won, I'd probably be gloating to myself and wallowing in self-righteousness, instead of groveling like I am now."

"All true," Gary said, his heart falling to liquid-nitrogen temperature. She'd blown the Trust, and had cost Toby nearly five years of his life. For nothing. Worst of all, she'd tried to end Dad's hope of ever living again. And his own sole hope of ever really knowing his father. Suddenly Gary was reminded of the morning seventeen years ago when Ben Smith had first tried to reconcile with him. An apology did not make up for years of outrage, he'd thought then, just as he thought it now.

"Gary, I love my husband," she said, "and I loved Daddy. You know how much I loved him." The insinuation remained unsaid, but fully under-stood: a hell of a lot more than you did, big brother! "And maybe when I lost one of them, it made me need the other even more."

She pressed on, seemingly undeterred by his frigid silence. "Maybe I don't deserve your forgiveness, but I'm still your sister. I need you in my life. I've always loved you."

And he loved her, too, he realized. But so what? How could he ever trust her?

"Uncle Gary," Katie interrupted, "I asked her to come because—"

Suddenly he felt self-centered and thoughtless. "Yes," he said, tears of shame and love and sadness in his eyes. "Because you're generous, wise, thoughtful, and . . . amazing. Here you are, about to end your life, maybe forever, and all you want is to leave us happy; you want what's best for us."

Katie recoiled. "No!" she whispered, and slowly, puffing in pain, pulled herself up until she sat, her eyes glaring defiantly. "When I wake up, I want us all to be together. Because I'm selfish, just like everyone else."

Gary found himself stunned by the truth of his niece's declaration. For nearly a minute he stood rooted, staring at her. Then he finally turned to Jan and opened his arms.

As soon as his youngest sister rose, Gary hugged her hard. "When I get home," he said, "I'll set up a life insurance policy for everyone in our family, with the Phoenix as beneficiary. If I have anything to say about it, we'll always be together."

DECEMBER 31, 2000 — Oracle CEO Larry Ellison, America's third richest person, predicts by the mid-21st century a scientific revolution that will cure nearly every disease and initiate an era of universal prosperity. "Within a few decades, we'll have com-puters every bit as smart as humans," Ellison proclaims in a *Fortune* magazine interview, "and 10,000 times as fast. Prob-lems that would take scientists 10,000 years to crack, they'll solve in a year!" — Dr. Jack Kevorkian is indicted in two states for abetting nine separate violations of organ-donation statutes. He stands accused of coercing patients whose suicides he has supervised into agreeing to donate their organs to save the lives of others. Several family members of those donor patients rush to defend Kevorkian's actions.

Living a dream he dared not avow even in childhood, the realization of a lifelong fantasy, fifty-three-year-old Gary Franklin Smith observed his handiwork from the raised podium on the south lawn of the White House. He felt surprisingly little of the discomfort he'd expected to ensure for this sacrifice of his privacy to universal fame. All he felt now was a sense of duty, redefined self-esteem, and a barely perceptible tinge of unworthiness.

Plenty of artists were more talented than he was, he decided, but none of them had ever worked harder at improving their skills, day after god-damn day. He deserved this!

Can you hear me, Father?

On either side of him, along with their families, sat William Jefferson Clinton and Albert A. Gore Jr., the smiling incumbent President and somber President-elect of the United States of America. The former had lost himself in the pomp of the night's extravaganza, triumphant in the survival of his presidency over these past eight years and the satisfaction of having chosen his successor. The latter, about to confront his own lifelong dream/nightmare, could barely keep his mind in the present.

Over two billion persons throughout the world stared at television, computer, or motion picture screens as, one by one, like hard-wired super-novae, the digitally manipulated, diode-enhanced fireworks discharged their welcome of the third millennium into these starlit skies above Pennsylvania Avenue. Then for one solid hour, as if by alchemy, each star burst unfolded into an intricate panorama of a notable American painting, instantly recognizable in crude but elegant likeness, through Gary's meticulous design.

K-K-K-K-K-K-KRAK! Grant Wood's *American Gothic.*

K-K-K-K-K-K-KRAK! Norman Rockwell's *Freedom of Speech.*

K-K-K-K-K-K-KRAK! Thomas Moran's *The Mist in the Canyon.*

K-K-K-K-K-K-KRAK! Gary Franklin Smith's *Founding Fathers.*

K-K-K-K-K-K-KRAK! Maxfield Parrish's *Daybreak.*

K-K-K-K-K-K-KRAK! Frederick Edwin Church's *Niagara Falls.*

K-K-K-K-K-K-KRAK! Mary Cassatt's *The Coiffure.*

·K-K-K-K-K-K-KRAK! Gary Franklin Smith's *Yosemite.*

K-K-K-K-K-K-KRAK! Andy Warhol's *Marilyn Monroe.*

K-K-K-K-K-K-KRAK! James Abbot McNeill Whistler's *The Artist's Mother.*

K-K-K-K-K-K-KRAK! Thomas Eakins's *The Gross Clinic.*

From time to time the cameras focused on Gary's calm, reserved face. His notoriety as an advocate of the embattled science the public was learning to call "immortalism" was now equal to the fame he's won as an artist.

Tonight's celebration had sprung from the efforts of America's bright-

est scientific minds, an act of Congress, $960 million in corporate sponsor-
ship, and an undisclosed expenditure of taxpayer funds from the budget of
the Pentagon, which now owned the technology.

Last February when Vice President Gore asked him to design the display, Gary had harbored reservations, pondering his own three family
members laying in cold storage, frozen under conditions of sheer guess-
work: What if the freezing had erased their memories and identities?
Someday, when and if they were revived, they might be like amnesiacs;
healthy infants in adult bodies, needing to be taught everything. Even after
they'd absorbed the knowledge they'd need; even if their personalities
developed the same traits they'd borne in the twentieth century; and even if
they seemed to be just like they were . . . Without their original memories,
they wouldn't be. They'd be more like clones of the dead—perhaps as valuable to the world as the originals, but with lives both unknown and worthless to their original selves.

"Mr. Vice President," he'd said, "that money would be better spent in
medical research."

Gore had obviously been prepared. "You could've said the same about
sending men to the moon in 1969," he'd answered. "We did it for almost the
same reasons: because we knew we could, because the public wanted it, to
show the world it could be done, and most of all, because the world needed
the inspiration. Logically it may not have been the best use of funds. But
national pride is hardly logical, my friend. We have the technology now,
and the American public wants us to display it; to strut our stuff. Besides, a
Millennial Celebration only comes around every ten centuries. Gary, you're
everyone's first choice, but if you don't want the job, there must be about a
million artists who do."

Gore had neglected to mention the "distraction value" of the moon
landing—and of the Millennial Celebration. What Neil Armstrong was to
America's Vietnam War in 1969, Gary Franklin Smith would become to
turn-of-the-millennium America's divisive War Against Violent Crime: a
temporary, heroic distraction.

Which raised the double-sided knife of fame.

For a decade Gary had regarded his growing celebrity as an unwelcome interloper, a parasite on the capillaries of his time, his most valuable
asset. Then, like an artificial strain of bacteria, fame became an ally. Suddenly fame could be used to prolong life; to expand the very boundaries of
time, not only for self or kin, but for humankind.

Art historian and critic Robert Hughes had been the first to dub him
"the Magic Johnson of cyronics," an epithet that captured the spirit of his
courageous coming-out. Gary Franklin Smith, former physician turned

world-renowned artist, was the first major celebrity to publicly endorse the science of cryonics, conferring legitimacy on the formerly disreputable, a human face to the grotesque.

Then his niece's highly publicized death and suspension fourteen months ago had become an instant boon for the legalization of suicide, and hence to cyronics. After all, a predeath suspension was more likely to be successful, and if suicide were legalized, such suspensions would finally become possible.

Gary had spoken with Ted Koppell on national television during the week following Katie's suspension: "My father, grandmother, and niece are all legally dead, and someday I expect to join them for a while in 'the hopeful ice.' I anticipate seeing them alive, healthy, and rejuvenated someday, not in heaven, but right here in the USA. As soon as somebody puts each of our molecules back in the right place. I know it seems impossible today, but who, fifty years ago, could have imagined wristband digital cellular telephones connected to personal computers the size of paperback books? Who knew that the average American today would have instant access, twenty-four hours a day, to thousands of times as much information as existed in all the libraries on earth during the mid-twentieth century?"

In response to rapidly growing public outcry, many new laws overturning the archaic euthanasia statutes had been introduced and enacted. Few hard-line assisted-suicide prohibitions remained in force. Even those statutes were now rarely enforced, except by certain states once part of the old Confederacy. But Gary's passionate cause was for those whom he regarded as "the suspended living."

Gary was baffled as to why other famous cryonicists refused to declare their conversion. "Don't you see that it's a matter of survival?" he'd once asked Congressman Herbert Rainwater (R. AZ) who had, under confidential terms, enrolled his entire family with the Phoenix. "If more of us would go public, we'd reach critical mass sooner; people like you can help render its promise legitimate in the eyes of the world. With public acceptance comes influence, and the chain reaction will mean saner laws and more funding for research. Cryonics will become cheaper; the science safer and better. Herbie, you might even save your own skin by offering yourself up to the press now."

"But it's irrelevant to the average voter," Rainwater had explained. "Most of them are worried about their lives every time they leave home. Living to see the twenty-second century is the farthest thing from their minds. I can assure you the average citizen of Arizona thinks cryonics is eccentric at best. If a politician proposed to spend a few decades in a can-

ister, his constituents would be all for putting him there immediately. And
right now I can do us a lot more good if I'm still in office."

It was 11:54 P.M., approaching the end of tonight's program. CRACK! P-KOW! BRDDDDT! WHOOSH! The climax picture
would appear on schedule. The two First Families, last and next, had been
carefully coached on how to put on the proper facial expressions: artistic
appreciation without philosophical judgment of this replication of the
famous and controversial Gary Franklin Smith work; now perhaps the
world's most widely recognized twentieth century painting.

K-K-K-K-K-KRAK!

A hundred thousand precision-arranged mortars ignited in simulta-
neous flashes of brilliant tincture, and for twenty-eight seconds the image of
Katie's Hope veiled the western sky.

Katie's face sparkled in serenity while the white-coated technicians
lifted her frail, lifeless frame above the neuron-preserving dry-ice canister.
Her family shimmered in Chagall-like hues of red and blue light, their
faces indistinguishable, but their love somehow depicted in ethereal glow,
impossible not to recognize. The only unmistakable visage, other than
Katie's, was that of Kevorkian, who smiled beneath a white halo, benevo-
lent yet menacing, as he floated above her like some impossible hybrid of
vigilante and archangel.

AUGUST 27, 2003 — The fourth takeover of a major bank by a
software firm this year, Microsoft acquires all outstanding
shares of NationsBank in a transaction valued at $11 billion, or
44 percent of book value. Solomon Brothers analyst Gilbert
Salzberg called the price "very rich, even for a bank so well
managed." NationsBank has operated at almost break-even
over the past 12 months, far outpacing an industry devastated
by competition from on-line firms. Some 97.84% of banking
transactions are now performed over the Internet. With ubiqui-
tous software to automatically shop for the best deals on fees
and interest rates, brand loyalty among banking customers has
all but vanished. — Broderbund's interactive Crib-School wins
the *Consumer Reports* new product of the year award. The electronic game, which adapts to cradle, crib, and playpen, has
been shown to stimulate precocious mental growth. Many tod-
dlers have learned how to do simple math, and even to read,
using the Crib-School system.

Roy Preston Longwell paused, signaling to his brethren, all of whom had seen him do it a hundred times before, that he was about to conclude his argument before this Democrat-controlled Senate Public Health Committee.

Thank God! most of them silently breathed in relief, Longwell's oratory talents having already been inflicted upon them for seventy-four mind-numbing minutes.

The six-term Republican, a seasoned vote counter, had no doubt calculated that his side would lose by one vote, but conscience would not permit him to go gently into that good night, nor would his obligation to represent the Christian voters of South Carolina, many of whom were monitoring these hearings. After all, with the next election barely thirteen months away, Longwell was apparently quite unprepared for retirement.

"The, ahem, distinguished senator from Massachusetts seems to believe that human beings are little more than machines, mechanical gadgets composed entirely of matter, with interchangeable parts."

At least he was now "the distinguished senator from Massachusetts," my father, George Crane, mused. Must have been the cameras. Yesterday, he'd just been "Junior." He particularly relished this, his most visible committee assignment. While most senators would have felt some impatience languishing in Public Health during an era when the glory went to those legislators battling violent crime, George Crane valued the opportunity to influence public debate over his favorite issue.

"Well, I disagree," Longwell continued. "The Bible teaches us that the essence of every individual is a unique, irreplaceable soul whose manner of composition is far beyond the ken of science, and which ultimately belongs to God."

No one in the room dared groan, though several senators must have heartily wished they could express their frustration. After all, anyone could allege that the Almighty supported their position, and He was hardly apt to descend from the heavens to rebuke the claim.

There was an additional hypocrisy here, George thought. This weasel now portrayed himself as some holy defender of the sanctity of human life, yet he was also one of the most vocal supporters of Swift and Sure, the anti-crime laws that, once passed in January 2005, would mandate immediate execution of all second-time convicted violent felons.

"Thanks to your sainted Kevorkian," Longwell shouted, "the course has veered to organ donation. Therein lies an even more slippery slope: You convince the ailing and vulnerable that ending their own lives is an acceptable alternative, and by the way, give us your liver and kidneys while we can still plant them in someone else. How soon before we legislate mandatory suicide of the terminally ill, so we can harvest their organs before disease renders them useless to their next owners?"

In a way, freshman Senator George Crane Jr. was horrified to hear Longwell tender a quasilegitimate argument. Assuming himself always on camera, George shrewdly affected an impartial expression, as if carefully evaluating, then rejecting, each of Longwell's statements. He knew the game, and was already a proficient player.

The white-haired legislator scowled at the ardent newcomer as a teacher might have glared at a disruptive fifth-grader and, to the younger man's delight, fell back on windy rhetoric: "Suicide is a sin, Senator Crane, a mortal transgression against our Creator. If we legalize it, we are defying Him, and damning ourselves to His wrath. If you wish to insult the will of God, I'll pray for Him to take mercy on your soul, though frankly I doubt He will heed my invocation."

Indeed! George Crane thought. Why should God be any different from the rest of us? But he held his tongue. At thirty-one, he hadn't become the second youngest United States senator in the history of Massachusetts by succumbing to lapses of naïveté.

Fresh out of Harvard Law School, George had decided to run for Congress shortly before his sister Katie's death. She'd encouraged him, knowing that our family name recognition might help. He'd soon discovered he was a natural-born campaigner, and in a liberal state like Massachusetts his association with Kevorkianism awarded him all the advantages of Dr. Death's fame without the inconvenience of his infamy.

To his amazement, he'd won.

Then, just ten months into the young man's first congressional term, his sixty-nine-year-old patron, Senator Edward M. Kennedy—who in 1962 had become the youngest U.S. senator in Massachusetts history—decided to retire while a Democratic governor still held office and thus could appoint the successor. George had accepted their invitation to carry the Democratic mantle as interim senator, until next November's election.

George Crane had won the Democratic nomination easily, but by September 23, 2002 was down ten polling points against his Republican challenger. On that day, Dr. Jack Kevorkian had made his "critical" contribution to the Crane campaign: On a hunger strike in Michigan State Penitentiary while serving a forty-five-day sentence for contempt of court, he'd had the good grace to expire.

Five days later, a national poll suggested that eighty-one percent of Americans agreed with Kevorkian's goals of suicide legalization and organ donation by default, and that most now considered him a hero. The Reverend Pat Robertson had speculated on the phenomenon during an interview with *Newsweek*: "Kevorkian's supporters continue to offer uninterrupted beatification, even during this temporary silencing of the doctor's critics."

On the coattails of Kevorkian's martyrdom, George's poll numbers had immediately climbed by six points, drawing the race to nearly even. Then his name appeared on a list of five individuals whom the doctor had invited to speak at his memorial service. The internationally broadcast event had taken place in Detroit on October 7, two weeks after "Doctor Death" himself died. In his brief eulogy that day, George Crane, an architect's son, had kept to a skillfully drafted line between political opportunism and sincere homage to a man he admired.

One month later, George Crane Jr. managed to win his senate race by a margin of slightly over three percent, much to the present annoyance of the Republican senator from South Carolina. Indeed, "today's abominable legislation" had been almost entirely the handiwork of "Junior" and his staff.

Chairman Bob Kerry asked George, "Do you wish to respond to any of Senator Longwell's comments?"

"Yes, Senator. I respond by calling for a vote," George answered, leaving his colleagues to their own conclusions regarding the value of Longwell's arguments. If even one of his allies had been swayed by the pontificating curmudgeon's attack, George figured his entire view of politics had been a misperception. He was not worried.

The National Death-with-Dignity Licensing Act passed committee by a margin of 14 votes to 11. Apparently, Longwell's eloquence had been enough to convince his fellow Republican, Senator Jimmy Hayes of Louisiana, to switch his vote *in favor* of the measure.

JULY 5, 2005 — A survey commissioned by the United Nations Technology Council shows over half the world's population, and nearly 98% of American households, are hooked to the Internet. Personal computer sales worldwide reached 800 million units in 2004, and are expected to exceed 1.7 billion annually by decade's end as more members of the middle class accumulate multiple PCs. — A march on Washington sponsored by the National Coalition of Churches to protest capital punishment draws an estimated 600,000 demonstrators. Nearly 14,000 convicted violent criminals have been executed nationwide during the first five months after enactment of President Travis Hall's Swift and Sure Anti-Crime Bill. — A combination of genetically redesigned viruses and microwave therapy is proven to cure most cancers in humans without major side effects. The regimen, developed by scientists at Johns Hopkins University, converts ordinary cold viruses to cancer-killing "scouts" and "smart bombs." The viruses invade cancer cells, turning them into viral reproduction factories, eventually either killing the host cell or making it visible to imaging machines. Any residual malignancy is then killed off with image-directed microwaves transmitted from several angles, which heat the cancer to 108° F, killing only targeted tissue. The new therapy should revolutionize cancer treatment.

Gary adjusted the image on his seven-foot video display screen, raising the moon 1.72 inches. Then he darkened the sky 5.6 percent. Much better. He visualized the picture on canvas, then hoped this neoteric design technology wasn't atrophying his artistic synapses. Then again, how many writers still composed novels without word processors? Of course, he used to do just fine without such silicon marvels. He wondered if he still could.

Then with typical fractal logic, he banished such thoughts into limbo: Yeah, and surgeons had once enjoyed the occasional success without the assistance of electric lighting, too. But once Thomas Edison showed up, they sure as hell hadn't worried about his invention becoming a crutch that would diminish their talent as doctors.

No wonder they called this the Age of Neuroses!

A delicate "Bee-eep" interrupted his musings.

Raising his wristband, he examined the code on the tiny screen and smiled. "Where are you, Senator?"

"Just finished a speech at the Copley Plaza," George Crane's boyish voice answered through the tiny speaker. "Got some time?"

Gary stared at his watch, and wondered if the thing had malfunctioned. Jesus, he'd been at if for seventeen straight hours? If he didn't take a break soon, he figured he might turn into a paintbrush. "Meet you there in ten minutes, George. Didn't much feel like working this afternoon anyway."

Staff members, reporters, and a few of George's more generous supporters crowded the small hospitality suite, the din of their cocktail party chatter drowning out the latest InterNetwork news on the wall-mounted narrowcast screen. When Gary entered, the noise level dropped noticeably, but then resumed as partygoers decided it wasn't cool to gawk. Two reporters began to thread their way toward him, but as a whole crowd feigned nonchalance.

A young staffer reached Gary before the reporters, and ushered him to an adjoining suite, where Senator Crane got up and embraced his uncle warmly.

"You documenting?" George asked. More and more private citizens were leaving their Audio Vids recording around-the-clock; the scrambled transceiver signals accumulated in the archives of the central computers as a deterrent to (and evidence of) violent crimes. But few politicians were pre-disposed to cast their private conversations upon these public waters like digital subpoena bait.

Well-aware of George's inhibitions when in document mode, Gary decided he preferred the unguarded version of his nephew. "Not anymore," he said, deactivating his wristband recorder. "Just don't make me into an accessory after the fact; but feel free to blaspheme, curse, and gossip all you like."

"Fair enough." George grinned. "Well goddammit, Uncle Gary, I guess those shit-for-brains savages are gonna own the White House the next coupla decades. Obviously Americans don't have the patience to fight crime with restraint."

"You voted for Swift and Sure too, didn't you?" Gary asked, knowing full well that his nephew had. Gary's own feelings about the popular bill were similarly mixed: It seemed a barbaric solution to an intolerable problem. Most criminologists agreed that Swift and Sure would save two innocent lives for every (presumably guilty) person executed, but nearly every liberal and right-wing libertarian believed there had to be a better way. To this odd alliance, raw numbers did not equal moral imperative.

But to the ever-widening constituency of crime victims and their families, any such argument seemed absurd.

"Held my nose with one hand and raised the other!" George said. "My vote didn't make a mosquito turd's difference anyway, so I did the prudent thing, at least according to sixty-four percent of my voters. Plus I figure the lives of twenty thousand convicted violent criminals a year are less valuable than forty thousand potential victims. Not to mention the two million lives a year a rational cryonics policy might save. Which I can hardly push for if I'm not in office."

"Where have I heard that rationalization before?"

"Well damn me to hell! I'm not turning into another Herbie Rainwater, am I? Fact is, Gary, I like the job, compromises and all. And we did get a watered-down assisted-suicide bill through."

"True enough," Gary teased, sarcasm dripping from his words like maple syrup off a short stack, "a very valuable concession indeed to those wishing to *legally* end their lives—after the standard six-month approval process for a permit, while cancer eats their brains or unbearable pain wracks their bodies."

George grimaced, then smiled. "Touché!"

Gary's face turned serious. All of a sudden he could see Katie, Alice, even Ben, resting quietly in the back of his mind. And whenever he pictured them lying in canisters of liquid nitrogen, he saw a fourth, vacant canister: the one meant for him. The image haunted Gary.

"What's gonna happen with all this?" he asked.

George did not have to ask what his uncle meant. "Believe it or not, I think the long-term dynamics might be in our favor. Not the party's, of course; we Democrats are in deep doodoo. But Kevorkianism will gain momentum, which can only help cryonics."

"How?"

"Right now, about fourteen percent of Americans say they intend to be frozen. That's a big increase over the last few years, but still a meager number if you relate it to policy. There are five major reasons why most people say they won't do it."

"Fear of the unknown being the most intractable," Gary speculated, once again glimpsing the empty ice canister at the back of his mind.

"Don't know. It may be right up there, but nobody ever owns up to that one. The five reasons people admit to are cost, scientific uncertainty, social disapproval, religious beliefs, and philosophy. In that order. Of course, if we're ever able to restore a mammal—even a sewer rat—after a decent interval of liquid nitrogen immersion, well, then everything changes. All the politics or rational cajoling in the world can't compare with an empirical result."

Obviously true, Gary thought.

"So until that happens," George continued, "—and notice I said until, not if—lower costs become our most effective persuasion. If suicide is legalized, and I mean really legal as opposed to bullshit legal, cryonics'll become cheaper. Most of the expense right now is red tape. Liquid nitrogen's inexpensive and plentiful. Maintenance and storage cost is next to nothing; not much more than mowing and watering the grass at a cemetery. Theoretically, cryonics shouldn't cost more than a decent funeral does. Lower the price to what it *should* be and you'll increase demand by at least three hundred percent. Bigger market creates more competition and better research, which leads to public acceptance and even more demand. A real snowball effect."

"How do you figure the outlook's improving for Kevorkianism?" Gary asked. "Seems like the religious groups are putting up a hell of a fight. To them, one life's worth the same as any other, whether it belongs to a senator, fetus, death-row inmate, or terminal patient. They're picketing courthouses, surrounding all the capital execution facilities twenty-four hours a day, harassing the few doctors still willing to practice obitiatry, and assassinating judges and prosecutors. It's as bad as the abortion fight ever was."

"These are turbulent times." George shrugged. "Let's face it, Swift and Sure is having a rough first year; executions are running way over President Hall's original projections. But I figure by this time next year most of the hard-core violent criminals are gonna be six feet under. Crime rates'll plummet; so will the number of executions, and the protesters'll have to find something else to complain about."

"Yeah. Kevorkianism." Gary always enjoyed playing devil's advocate.

"Maybe so, but the Republicans' approval ratings should exceed sixty percent for the next few presidential terms."

"How in hell does that help us?"

"If I'm right, the GOP won't screw it up this time; learned their lesson in 1996 and 2000. This time they're gonna consolidate their power by hugging the middle; ditch the Christian right like a bad habit. Won't need 'em anymore. And that, Uncle Gary, is very good for us."

NOVEMBER 30, 2006 — Intuit stock plunges for the third day in a row, as the software and banking behemoth remains unable to assure the markets against a repeat of last week's corporate terrorism. For 38 hours, a virus unleashed into one of Intuit's central data processors interrupted the financial services of nearly ten percent of North Americans. With the perpetrators still at large, the company's market capitalization has now declined by 31%, or almost $135 billion. The Department of Justice is rumored to be questioning parties with short positions in Intuit stock. — Memorial services are held in churches throughout the world in remembrance of the estimated 1.2 million lost in the nuclear incinerations at Sarajevo in May, and Baghdad in September. Interpol continues to investigate leads but admits having no suspects. The two horrific crimes still appear to have been unrelated. — Today is the first day Fidelity Investments, the Boston mutual funds and stock brokerage giant, offers Cryonic Trust Accounts that conveniently combine suspension life-insurance and trusteeship. CTAs assure those enrolled with cryonics organizations that their suspension-funding will be in place when the time comes to be frozen, and that their capital will be prudently managed for optimal after-tax growth until their possible revival. Fidelity reports opening 712,432 new accounts, a record for any 24-hour period.

Toby shook his head. "Amazing. Two cities blown off the face of the earth, and months later, nobody has a clue why. Or who's responsible."

Having just completed one of their thrice-weekly thirty-five-minute cybernetic strength-training routines, the two men relaxed at the juice bar of the Boston Fitness League, sitting in a private booth and sipping individually formulated replenishment tonics. "Makes you wonder," Gary said, "if the second law of thermodynamics doesn't predict the future. You know, entropy increases over time . . ."

Toby considered the vivisected metaphor and smiled. "Exactly! Matter of fact, that's why I chose my second career. Any closed system suffers ever-increasing disorder and will ultimately decay and die. Nature—including our own human nature—is the enemy of all living creatures, except . . ."

"Except . . . ?"

"Except when intellect is introduced. At least that's my theory. Physics itself would dictate that the human race will eventually become extinct. But physics can't account for higher intelligence and rational thought. I believe science will either save the human race if we respect its tenets—including those that apply to our own nature—or destroy us if we ignore them."

"But how do you persuade people to reject the appeal of mysticism? After all, mysticism is easy; science is hard."

"I don't know. I couldn't seem to make much of a dent in it." Toby scowled and shook his head. Then his eyes seemed to brighten. "But faster and cheaper computers should help, and as information expands, so must our ability to evaluate it. Maybe the free market could help, too, by rating scientific opinions for money. But artificial intelligence is the real deal, Gary. Software's already the most important industry on earth, and within a few decades we're bound to have artificial intelligence far more advanced than our own minds. Our imaginations may well be limitless, but next to today's machines, our ability to compute and evaluate facts is a joke. And if you think technology's moving fast now, just wait till AI arrives. If machines could learn to sort the clear, objective data from self-serving and muddled science, that would be a leap to boggle the senses."

"A great dream," Gary agreed.

Toby bought another round by flashing his smartcard on the scanner in front of him, then turned to Gary and began with obvious care: "Once, way back in 1941, I told your father I expected to be dead within forty years." He chuckled. "As you can see, I was grievously mistaken."

Gary considered not only his friend's words but also the manner in which they were delivered. Toby had reached some kind of decision. "Good thing, eh?"

The older man hesitated. "The timing does seem optimal." Toby displayed a chilling serenity that Gary had twice before witnessed in loved ones.

"Timing? For what?" He already knew the answer.

Toby pulled a black-trimmed, 1.4-ounce matchbox-sized digital communicator from his shirt pocket, pushed a few buttons, and handed it to Gary, who stared at the screen.

Gary fought a desire to crush the little thing in his fist. "A two-year-old suicide permit? What the hell's going on, Toby? You can't be serious about this."

"Not only am I serious, but I'm acting on the same logic I learned from you and your father."

"Are you dying?"

"Genetic Scorecard says I probably have ten comfortable years left; maybe twelve. And that's based on therapies available when I had myself tested, almost three years ago. So you can probably even add another year. But unless I've completely misjudged you, when I tell you the circumstances, you'll realize I have no choice."

Gary downed the rest of his tonic and grabbed their refills from the conveyor track. He handed Toby his, and waited for the explanation.

Both men were well aware of the "Prometheus Protocol." Prometheus Incorporated was a private partnership, founded in 1998 after having raised $10 million during the previous year from a group of 134 cryonicists. The pledges, intended to fund research and development, were collected from these "investors" in ten percent increments over a ten-year period. Some of the more skeptical participants even chose to donate their pledges to their favorite cryonics organizations (to realize charitable tax deductions), rather than holding the stock themselves, a decision most of them would first come to exult and then rue.

In spite of its "for-profit" status, the majority of Prometheus investors did so in pursuit of self-preservation rather than financial return. After all, there had been no proof that the freezing techniques in use at the time properly preserved any of the brain's nongenetic information. A proven protocol would increase each investor's own odds of identity preservation upon reanimation. Also, once such evidence existed, they'd reasoned, the public would flock to cryonics, creating both economies-of-scale and political clout, rendering biostasis cheaper and safer.

Prometheus's goal had been to test and prove the viability of long-term brain preservation using "vitrification." This technique replaced the water from each organ with various homogeneous liquid mixtures. Then the tissue could be made to behave more like vitrified glass, amenable to cooling without disruptive crystallization.

In a scientific sense, Prometheus had succeeded quickly. By securing excellent scientists and state-of-the-art equipment, they'd developed an expedient brain vitrification protocol in 2001, and over the subsequent two years had proved its efficacy on many varieties of mammalian brains.

To the shareholders' astonishment and dismay, however, the Protocol's success had done little to increase the popularity of cryonics. Since there had yet to be a successful revival of an entire mammal from suspension, the public continued to view cryonics a dubious speculation at best, farce at worst.

During the year 2005, fewer than forty thousand persons had undergone suspension worldwide, and about a third of them had purchased the Protocol. At $1,700 per suspension, the company had been grossing under $25 million per year, barely enough to cover operating expenses and interest on its debt. Wobbling on the edge of insolvency, Prometheus had been forced to sell a sixty percent interest in its patents to Nobine et Cie, a French biotech outfit owned by Drs. Claude Noire and Edouard Binette.

Ten days ago, in the city of Aix-en-Provence, under fully observed conditions, Noire and Binette had revived a mouse they'd frozen two weeks earlier at minus 79 degrees Celsius. The scientists had used a slight modification of the Prometheus Protocol. While this rodent had been the only survivor out of 1,300 attempts, the feat was nonetheless a majestic achievement, immediately shifting the scientific paradigm of biostasis.

Most experts now predicted at least 500,000 human suspensions per year by decade's end.

"I've known for thirty-one months," Toby explained, "that I have the R17ALZ gene."

"Late-onset, moderated Alzheimer's?" Gary offered.

"Wow. You still keep up with all this stuff?"

"Some of it. But you don't have any symptoms, do you?"

"Not that I can tell, Gary, but then at what point would the loss of memory become apparent to me? The first time I forget to flush the toilet or the first time I forget my last name? I mean, nobody's sure the tests measure everything. Hell, how would you even define 'everything' as a standardized test? That stuff's unknowable. Besides, the timing really is ideal. No family, no obligations. And of course they just revived that mouse! So I have almost everything to gain by getting on with it, and everything to lose by waiting. Sure, I'm having a good time, but I'm eighty-two years old. Why give up my shot at hundreds, maybe thousands of years over the coming centuries, for a few extra years now? If I lose memory, I'll lose identity, which is the same to me as losing my life. Every day I procrastinate is a gamble. A deadly gamble."

Cryonics was only a gamble, Gary thought. Toby was alive *now*. Gary wanted to beg, to tell his friend: Screw reason, I need you. I love you. I want you here!

Instead he gave a long, audible exhalation and offered his companion the simple, terrible truth: "Of course you're right. And I'm sure gonna miss you."

> JULY 7, 2010 — The FDA issues strong advisories against human heart transplants after Dupont's Jarvik 410 mechanical heart proves 114 percent safer in field trials. The 410 is the first to employ two backup self-winding power storage units, and three separate pumps, rendering simultaneous failure a near impossibility. Some doctors now recommend routine transplantation of the artificial organ to any patient above the age of 60, regardless of cardiovascular health. — The United States and Russian governments announce joint plans to build four manned space stations within the asteroid belt between Mars and Jupiter by the year 2020. President Travis Hall describes the project as "a golden opportunity to study a fascinating and potentially priceless natural resource that might play a crucial role in the future of humankind."

"Time and weather, please," Brandon Butters said.

"Five forty-seven A.M.," a dulcet voice whispered from his wristband speaker. "Currently 76 degrees in Pittsfield, rising to 98 degrees at 1:47 P.M. in Boston. Fair to partly cloudy skies all day; no precipitation."

Without putting on even his aeration sport coat, the fifty-seven-year-old District Attorney opened the security door by sliding his smartcard through the slot next to it and exited the Bayberry Hill Singles Residences.

He walked the half mile on a decaying, neglected, stationary sidewalk uphill to the gleaming, newly built Mass Transit Authority station in Pittsfield, Massachusetts, and settled into an orthopedic recliner in the first-class section of the 6:25 A.M. Torpedo Train to Boston. He scrutinized fellow passengers for unfamiliar faces, but like many of Brandon's similar safety motivated practices, he performed this survey only from force of habit. It had been four years since the last assassination attempt on a prosecutor or judge anywhere in the United States. Indeed all violent crime had become rare. Swift and Sure had been too drastic for his tastes, more radical than it needed to be, but at least it seemed to be working, for now.

Like most early morning commuters, he donned his virtual reality helmet and set to work. The eighty-mile trip would require forty-eight minutes. Once again, Brandon ran the disc:

> *A closed fist strikes her face. She stumbles backward against the wall of the welfare apartment, cracking the plaster. The furniture is flimsy and old, the tiny room dilapidated, yet clean and orderly. "Don't do this, Jeff," the woman implores, half begging, half mocking, as though more curious than scared.*
>
> *Her hands are loosely bound in front with a white cotton handkerchief that does not block her 360-degree wristband camera. The man's AudioVid recorder is running, too.*
>
> *The woman is in her mid-twenties, inexpensively dressed, pretty in spite of the burgeoning welts on her face. Her eyes reveal a brisk, defiant intelligence (which almost reminds Brandon of Jan Smith in their college days).*
>
> *Her male assailant is slightly older, maybe thirty, tall and muscular, wearing boots, blue jeans, and a tattered undershirt. Two small tattoos decorate his left arm, and another his right.*
>
> *The woman's facial expression turns from hostile disdain to unmistakable fear as the man, eyes unblinking, begins to pour a clear fluid from a metal flask onto her light blue dress. "What the fuck are you doing?" she shouts.*

Brandon stopped the VRD, hit the reverse switch, and watched the woman's face happen and unhappen, then happen again. Insanely, he wanted to yell a warning. The disc continued:

> *His reddish-brown, deep-set eyes flash a chilling gleam; he brandishes an electronic match. "You ain't taking my kids away, Stacy. That's all there is to it. It just ain't gonna happen."*

She shudders when he activates the match; the feel of it is corpo-
real, even in programmed form. A four-inch white flame instantly
rises from its two tiny metal tines. Her eyes suggest she's no longer
able to convince herself that he's bluffing.

His voice sounds cold, emotionless. "I told you I'd kill you first,
bitch, now see it comin'."

She watches, paralyzed in her denial, as he flips the flaming
shard toward her.

"No, Jesus, no!" the woman cries as her clothes begin to burn.
"What about our kids?" She beats her bound hands at the flames
exploding up her dress. Her voice rises and breaks into a wordless cry.
Her hair is burning. She collapses to the floor, writhing, hands
waving at her blackening face. "Oh, God, it hurts . . ."

Jeffrey Lewis Cole Sr. stands erect over her, watching calmly.
He raises a finger and runs it over his front teeth, like some disturbed
child—fascinated and lured; entranced, but detached. [To Brandon
the man is like a robot, remotely operated by fun-house joystick.]

The woman seems to be trying to speak, but she is no longer
capable of it.

Cole waits for the sounds she is making to end, then douses her
scorched body with a bucket of water as if extinguishing a trash-can
fire. His eyes look away, then return and widen slightly, as though a
new, less evil force had somehow appropriated the joystick. He finds a
bedsheet and carefully, almost lovingly, covers the corpse.

Then he calls the police.

Like most of the Massachusetts intelligentsia, District Attorney Butters was
starting to view cryonics as something more than a huckster's dream, a shell
game with death.

At least the medics had gotten there in time to salvage her brain, he
thought. He hoped she would wind up at a legitimate facility. Of course the
wealthiest went to the Phoenix or one of its high-tech competitors, and paid
$175,000 for a full-body suspension, or $70,000 for a neuro. But most people
couldn't afford the Phoenix's rates, especially after Nobine had raised their
vitrification-licensing fee again. Also, the less wealthy tended to be more
superstitious; many considered freezing only the head to be some sort of
sacrilege.

Over the past forty-four months, Nobine et Cie had duplicated its dra-
matic mouse reanimation only twice in nearly ten thousand attempts. By
now some scientists were becoming suspicious of the experiment, but the

public still wanted to believe. And ironically, suspensions had actually become *less* trustworthy. Sporadic regulation amidst blossoming demand for "the product" had nurtured the sprout of opportunism, now attacking the sustaining roots of cryonicism.

Over the past three years, Brandon had spent at least one day a week on what he'd come to regard as "weed-killer duty." Just three months ago he'd finally managed to close down the Belmont Time Tunnel facility, a converted funeral parlor victimizing the Bay State's neediest and most vulnerable. In just twenty-two months BTT had happily accepted 8,624 corpses for full-body suspension at an average cost of $9,700 each, payment up front. By the time Brandon was able to obtain a search warrant and raid the place, most of the bodies were missing: apparently cremated, or perhaps even the primary ingredient in a local brand dog food. The "survivors" were typically mislabeled, necessitating problematic DNA scrapes for ID. Virtually none had been treated with the Prometheus Protocol, although most had paid for the procedure.

Yet BTT was far from the worst incident of cryonics fraud Brandon had seen.

He would have preferred the entire field to be regulated. He understood the generalized sinking to the lowest common denominator that typified government intrusion into any enterprise. But he also considered government oversight essential to prevent fraud and secrecy in emerging sectors of commerce. To Brandon, the next best thing to regulation would have been the discovery of a second proven successful protocol—to create competition and lower prices. But what hope was there of *that* occurring anytime soon?

Brandon entered the antechamber area at the Boston Capital-Crime Stockade. It was only two blocks from his office, a fortunate convenience. He still averaged eleven visits to the stockade weekly, but in 2005, the first year of Swift and Sure, he'd been forced to call on nearly two thousand of the "walking dead," almost eight a day. Ever since his historic; bipartisan appointment in 2004, District Attorney Butters had insisted on meeting every condemned inmate in Massachusetts.

"Do you need a Cyber Partition, Mr. Butters?" the administrator asked.

"No, thanks. This one's not dangerous."

He strode unescorted through the bright, stainless aisles, various checkpoint machines scanning the shape of his hand, his retinal patterns, or his voice. Doors slid open automatically and slammed shut behind him. At last he entered the stark white cubicle of Jeffrey Lewis Cole Sr.

"Mr. Cole," he said quietly.

"Mr. Butters." The acknowledgment was calm, matter-of-fact. Cole had less than an hour to live. The visit was expected.

"Anything I can do for you? Anything you want to talk about?"

"Yes, sir." The condemned man handed him a chip the size of a thumbnail. "Would you make sure my kids get this recording in about ten years' time?"

Brandon nodded.

"That's when I figure they'll be old enough to understand, maybe even believe I love 'em despite what I did. And please tell them how sorry I was today. There's no excuse for it; I know that. I musta lost my mind. That had to be it. Musta just lost my mind."

"If only you'd accepted the counseling . . ." Brandon began, then thought: This guy's gonna be dead in fifty-two minutes. What on earth am I doing?

"And the drug therapy," Cole took over for him. "I know, I know, after that first time I hit her, I shoulda known I was fucked up. That's what the prison shrink told me back then, too. But I figured I could control the anger myself, y'know? Didn't figure I was nuts or anything. But I guess I was—am. And when Stacy told me she was divorcing me, I just musta snapped."

"You still don't remember killing her, do you?"

"Nope. Not one second of it. But I seen the VR tape, so I know I deserve the toxin. Hell, I deserve worse than I'm getting. Don't you sweat none a this, Mr. Butters. I got a fair trial."

"I sweat them all, Mr. Cole. It's a flaw in my character." Brandon nearly put his arm on Cole's shoulder. "I've learned a lot about you these last few weeks. You did an appalling thing, but you were clearly insane at the time. Six years ago, before Swift and Sure, you'd never have received the death penalty; might've even gone to treatment instead of prison. So I guess I'll sweat yours more than most."

"I have another request," Cole said. "I'd like to donate my organs. At least whichever ones you think make sense."

"I suspected you might. Good for you. Then at least some gain will come of this. What about your brain? Would you like it frozen, too?"

"My brain?"

"Yes. Good thing you called the police so promptly. Since we managed to salvage and freeze your wife's brain, I have the option to have yours suspended as well, if you'd like. I'm offering you that choice. Of course, you're also giving us the authority to test experimental revival techniques, and if you're successfully reanimated, I can't say what status future civilization might give a convicted murderer. No telling how you'd be treated."

Cole paused just a few seconds. "I reckon I'll accept your offer. I just hope it's helpful to you. As for maybe keeping my life, well, that's a bonus."

"Good, then." They shook hands.

"Thanks for coming today," Cole said. "I know you're the only D.A. that visits every death-row felon in his county. Must be hard on you; Mr. Butters. I just want you to know I appreciate it."

"Goodbye, Mr. Cole. Maybe someday you'll make it back to the world of the living."

Three P.M., Brandon Butters sat at his desk, across from a certain congenial scoundrel. It was their first meeting since 1992. Patrick Webster, now a semiretired defense attorney specializing in crimes of the rich and well-connected, practically sang, "They were unarmed, for chrissake! I promise you, Brandon, I'll take this to trial before I let those boys serve a day in prison, much less plead to a violent felony. Wouldn't be much of a lawyer if I went for the deal you're offering."

Brandon casually evaluated Webster's attire, the latest in temperature-controlled finery: a $2,700 Ralph Lauren long-sleeve, air-conditioned chemise. A pair of Agnellini cross-breeze slacks which the public servant pegged at four or five grand. Wristband PC/communications module by Patek Phillippe: $26,500, even though Casio and Texas Instruments each made comparable ones for one-tenth the money. And those shoes: the very finest shiatsu-massage loafers from Matsushita. Easily five figures, the D.A. appraised, not impressed, jealous, or even repelled; really just inquisitive.

"What's your bottom line, Pat?" Brandon asked, contemplating the irony of their de facto 180-degree shift of allegiances over these past two decades: Today *he* was defending frozen corpses against *Webster*'s clients.

"They'll plead to one count of second degree aggravated vandalism; two years' probation apiece; take it or leave it."

"These guys broke into the Boston Cryonics Union, thawed six people in suspended animation, irreparably destroyed their brains, and you want probation?"

"They thawed six frozen dead bodies. Not six people. So says the law, which we are sworn to uphold. Jon Hansen and Kevin Lipshitz are political activists, men of conscience, not violent criminals."

"But they did break the law."

"I admit," Webster said, "only that they destroyed private property. To protest the unaccountability of cryonics to the poor."

"Which they most certainly are not, or I'd be dealing with a public defender today."

"Let's just say they have friends of some means."

"Obviously." Brandon weighed his chances of obtaining more than two years' probation in litigation: practically zip. Besides, the ridiculous sum they were paying Webster to get their butts out of jeopardy would help deter them from future mischief. "Have you ever considered, Pat, that your clients' efforts might have been better spent demonstrating against the very laws that are about to save their asses? If those in suspension had rights as potential human beings, there'd be less red tape and litigation, and even the 'poverty-stricken' would be able to afford biostasis. Of course then your virtuous, conscience-bound clients wouldn't be able to assassinate defenseless so-called corpses and get away with it."

Webster burst out laughing.

It wasn't funny, the ADA told himself. But then again . . .

Webster flashed the grin of a man who wanted to be a good sport, within reason. "C'mon, Brandon. Lighten up."

Brandon smiled. "Okay, I'll agree to vandalism two, and a restraining order that converts any repeat offense by your clients against cryonic suspendees into a class-two felony."

"No problem. You won't see them in here again, I can promise you that."

"And tell me the truth, Pat, one human being to another, off the record."

"Okay. Sure."

"What if one of those brains belonged to someone you knew? What if it was your wife or brother or son?"

"Brandon, you already know I can argue either side." Webster winked. "Matter of fact, I seem to recall that you can, too."

JUNE 12, 2015 — Sun Microsystems unveils Brainiac '16, an integrated analytical engine which Chairman Scott McNealy says will allow businesses to write most software without human programmers. McNealy predicts that within a decade, future versions of Brainiac will convert simple verbal instructions elicited from questions it asks its owners into errorless software code more efficient than almost any human could write. Industry analysts hail the software as a giant leap toward true artificial intelligence. Predictably, Microsoft's Melinda French Gates derides the product as "redundant in today's business environment." — Americana Healthcare surpasses Columbia as the world's largest Health Maintenance Organization with 112 million patients enrolled worldwide. Analysts credit the firm's growth to its state-of-the-art telemedicine programs. Their mobile virtual reality vans allow instant diagnosis, treatment, and even some surgeries in patients' homes, combining the convenience of house calls with the cost efficiencies of office visits. — Today is the last day most banks will exchange cash for e-credits. Coins and paper money were eliminated as a means of exchange in September 2011, but have remained redeemable at banks. After today, cash may be turned in at government offices only, with electronic credits issued 15 days later. Outside of numismatic collections, less than $20 billion in post-1934 specie remains in circulation, according to the Treasury Department.

In the age of incomplete memories, there were still defining events one never lost, and even during those decades before the Mnemex discovery, I could always recall one particular afternoon as though it were yesterday. I was nine. There I sat in the gallery next to my sixty-four-year-old grandmother, Rebecca Smith-Crane, proudly watching my father address the United States Senate.

"Try not to get too wound up, Trip," Grandmother warned me, although she had to know it was futile. Dad was already considered a pioneer of immortalism, and both my parents had inculcated me with their philosophy and sense of mission.

Getting excused from school had been no problem, especially under these circumstances. I'd enrolled in a self-directed learning program at age seven, and had remained at least two levels ahead of any other nine-year-old in my school. Besides, I'd finished all of that semester's courses back in February, and had been studying independently for the previous four months.

Politics seemed as good a subject as any, even without the research advantage family connection afforded. And any opportunity to watch Dad in action was not to be given up, for it would certainly be my desire to follow George Crane's path. My eyes rarely left him.

"Do you really believe," my father, Minority Leader George Crane, lectured, "that the death penalty is appropriate punishment for failure to pay the premium on one's biostasis insurance?"

Of course not, I thought. Way to go, Dad! Exactly!

Fortunately, Dad's question was rhetorical; otherwise the overwhelmingly Republican assembly might have intoned a resounding "Aye."

But this fourth-term Democratic senator (a rarity these days) was shrewd enough to brandish a more cogent justification: "Apart from simple decency, it will cost the government a lot less money to subsidize suspension for those who can't afford it than to sustain the greatest class conflict since our turn-of-the-millennium War Against Crime."

I'd been studying contemporary politics, and well realized my father's admonition addressed the single obsession of the prevailing Republican majority: money. I knew that cost efficiency had been the measure of every major legislative and executive decision since Swift and Sure author Travis Hall's election as President in November of 2004. His landslide reelection in 2008 and former Vice President Garrison Roswell's convincing victory in the presidential elections of 2012 had reinforced their philosophy. The Swift and Sure Anticrime Bill itself exemplified "neorightism," since the true impetus behind it had been money. President Hall hadn't sold his bill as a moral absolute but rather as the only financially sustainable (and therefore politically tolerable) method of winning the War Against Crime.

Since then, *codified pragmatism* had become the banner of third millennium Republicans. Sacrifice the few for the many, don't try to rescue everyone, or the overloaded ship-of-state might sink.

Faster and cheaper computers allowed instant access to all public scientific data, but approaches for filtering objective data from self-serving hyperbole was still evolving. The Republicans were wise enough to encourage the free market to do the sorting. Financial incentives had already been instituted to encourage businesses to set up open "electronic fact forums" in easy-to-follow hypertext, allowing scientific experts, both human and artificial, to rate each other's theories for objectivity and clarity of thought. The market insisted on due process and confirmable double-blind analysis by tending to ignore those opinions that failed to use objective standards. Hyperbole was filtered out through the SPERs (statistical peer-review expert-credibility ratings), upon which opinion makers gained or lost most of their influence. As artificial intelligence machines became progressively smarter, Republican legislators and their staffs gradually developed the habit of giving the AIs access to as much data as possible; then letting them suggest where to deploy available funds to do the most good.

We leftists would assert: Some values can't be gauged. For example, every law-abiding American citizen is too precious to denominate financially. We should never surrender even a single life we could reasonably expect to save.

The New Republicans' answer: Life has always been a commodity, measured in terms of dollars. Long before the achievements of TraffiCop and satellite navigation, we were perfectly capable of making our cars safer and saving thousands of lives per year; but then fewer of us could afford to drive. We could have lowered the speed limit and saved even more lives, but in America, time is money, and money is the coin of life. So we opted for a dispassionate trade-off: money and time saved with the loss of random human lives as a secondary consequence. And in so doing, we improved the average prosperity, and average quality and quantity of life for all of us.

This example illustrated the common principle of the New Republican Dynasty: the cold-blooded calculation of value, the axiom of putting a price in dollars on everything and everyone, the striving neither for individuated morality nor political appeasement, but for precise, objective appraisals. Not necessarily the Good; only the greatest Feasible Good. Compared to them, we seemed like well-intentioned mystics, romantic dreamers ready to embrace each new political theory as long as it seemed fair and compassionate. The rightists behaved more like scientists; dispassionate and cold, attentive less to political justice than to results and evidence.

Although more hard-nosed than Dad even back then, I found these neorightest number-crunchers inhuman and mostly contemptible. But that opinion was becoming harder for me to maintain, because their policies tended to work.

I also understood that throughout history, in almost every significant conflict regardless of moral imperative, the scientists had prevailed over the mystics. Realism, a clear view of the world as it is rather than as it ought to be, and the willingness to let that view stand or fall on the basis of unprejudiced experiment, had been a nearly insurmountable weapon. Over the previous century of American politics, the invincible cannons of science had been passed back and forth between these two armies many times. But for a solid decade they had thundered from the Republican side.

Within eighteen months after the enactment of Swift and Sure in January 2005, the crime problem had abated, people felt safer in their homes and on the streets, taxes had been lowered, GNP had increased rapidly, average life expectancy had risen with record velocity. And except in Massachusetts and a few other liberal states, Democrats were becoming harder to elect.

"We all agree," Dad continued, shifting to a more conciliatory and, I feared, ultimately unpersuasive argument, "that someday most humans will live much longer life spans than we enjoy today, with or without cryonics. We all agree that, with or without cryonics, the ultimate goal of medical science is to discover how to banish all aging and death. We also agree that cryonics is the only realistic hope for our own generation, and perhaps the next few generations, to participate in this utopian age that is already coming into view, yet seems cruelly out of our grasp.

"We all deem it irrational to require the terminally ill literally to die before entering suspension. We agree that those in suspension must have rights, including legal control over the disposition of their frozen brains and bodies, some means to preserve their estates, a minimum of confusion and red tape, and the assurance that they would not be prematurely unfrozen even if their private insurer and their cryonics facility each became insolvent simultaneously.

"Most Democrats even agree with our Republican counterparts that we should require suspendees to deposit with the government any funds they choose not to bequeath to others, to be repaid in inflation-adjusted dollars upon revivification, because such a law solves more problems than it creates.

"That with which we cannot agree is their metaphor of cryonics as a ticket on a private monorail to this gleaming future world we all envision, and if one can't pay the fare, one can't board the train.

"As Americans, our moral tradition does not countenance human sacrifice. We do not cast our babies into the Nile. Our aged and infirm are not left to die on mountainsides."

I caught my father's eye, clenched my fist and scowled. Scare 'em, Dad, I tried to telepath. (Of course, we couldn't back then.) Don't preach to them. They're too far gone to hear you.

But maybe this was just a buildup?

"My grandfather served in the Navy during World War Two," Dad continued, "and told me that the vital difference between our side and theirs, the reasoned doctrine which gave him the greatest pride in his country, was this notion of *all for one*. We risk a battleship to save a PT boat. We do not abandon our wounded. We dive into the ocean rather than let a fellow sailor drown. For it is not the sailor we save that matters so much as the knowing, by every sailor, that if you find yourself cast overboard, your shipmates would unhesitatingly imperil their own lives to attempt rescue.

"That is how a nation prevails against a ruthless enemy, be that enemy the Axis powers or Death itself. The choice, gentlemen, is simple: World War Two, or Vietnam. Share immortality, or brace yourselves to wage this War Against Death, the most overwhelming enemy in the history of humankind, with only halfhearted cooperation on your own side."

As I listened to Dad's summation, I winced. Not strong enough. He'd have to terrify these clowns to convert their votes. I even considered e-mailing him via wristband PC, but decided the transmission wouldn't be listened to in time.

Nine Republicans and one other Democrat had already spoken today, and eighteen more senators would address the floor before S. 1122, the Cryonics Regulations Bill, was amended and voted upon. So far, the Republicans had simply ignored the Democrats.

President Roswell's "pet senator," Lawrence Bayless (R. TX), had argued convincingly to require that suspendees deposit all money not bequeathed to their survivors into a U.S. Government Inflation Neutralization Account (INA). Such a program would safeguard (though not increase) every suspendee's wealth, while providing a bonanza of low interest loans to the government. Projected taxpayer savings: at least $2 trillion over the next ten years.

Senator Thomas Hollandsworth (R. CA) had suggested the recognition of four categories of the "nonliving," listed here in reverse order of status: (1) The irrevocably dead, that is, cremated, lost at sea, et al. (2) Persons frozen or otherwise DNA-preserved, but with hopelessly irreparable brain damage. (3) Persons frozen after death with brain tissue properly saved. (4) Persons in suspended animation, frozen prior to death and any material brain decay.

The legal implications would be staggeringly complex, and such categories would no doubt occasion countless lawsuits over their designation.

God, I hated the guy, but he did seem the perfect person to draft these regulations. I quelled a laugh. "Hollandsworth's so anal," I'd once overheard Dad tell great-uncle Gary, "you couldn't get a pencil up his ass with a pile driver." He'd have been upset to know I heard him use such language, and especially that I'd bugged his digital communicator, but naturally I thought it hilarious.

Earl Churchman (R. NE) argued on behalf of the insurance industry, a strong supporter of S. 1122. Insurance executives were already anticipating the banquet they were about to attend. After the bill passed, a typical suspension and indefinite maintenance contract was projected to cost only $34,000 per person, barely one month's average American household income. Nonetheless, about eighty-five percent of those intending to sign up for the dormantory expected to fund this contract through a "cryonics all-contingency" policy. Most also planned to purchase "death or suspension" insurance with their INA accounts as beneficiary.

Churchman asserted that a government reinsurance agency, similar to the FDIC and FSLIC, would be the more effective instrument to infuse financial confidence into the cryonics system.

Finally Clarissa Westervelt (R. MI) addressed population and environmental issues: "My husband and I have been married for twenty-three
years, and our original plan was to have three children. So far, we have only
one; yesterday was her seventeenth birthday.

"But we intend to produce at least two additional offspring.

"After the turn of the millennium Glen and I decided that instead of
raising two more children at that time, we would save our money, and use it
to dispatch our own DNA into the next century. And along with our DNA,
we agreed to send as many of our memories as we could salvage, preserved
in our own frozen brains."

I found her metaphor both intriguing and comforting, but such comfort would be short-lived.

"Some of you," Westervelt continued, "might laud this restraint of our
breeding instincts, while others may deem us selfish for having deprived the
world of new life. Opinions about population growth remain diverse.

"I am an optimist. I believe technology's ability to help us sustain
population growth is advancing faster than world population itself. New
farming disciplines are revolutionizing agriculture, while energy and transportation steadily decrease in cost. And the sciences of oceanic husbandry
are perhaps the most promising of all. By breeding fish and other sea organisms using the latest techniques, undersea farming experts insist we can
quintuple our annual harvest from the oceans within six years.

"But wealth is not merely about material goods; it is about life itself.

"A person earning $100,000 per year, that is, just below today's official
poverty level, can expect to attain seventy-nine years. A person who earns $1
million, roughly two and one-half times the average worker's income in
2015, has an average life expectancy of ninety-six years. A $10 million wage
earner will, on average, see the far side of a century."

She stared at Dad, addressing her next observation to him, as if lec-
turing a child. "With or without cryonics, Senator Crane, money buys survival. Always has. Always will."

My initial anger dissipated as I saw determination ignite behind Dad's
eyes. Westervelt's speech had wakened my father, and perhaps the entire
Democratic party.

"Citizens must," she proceeded, "through labor and prudence, provide
themselves and their families the means to sustain their own lives. And
if these same citizens are willing and able to provide such means to others
through voluntary charity, I admire them for it. But I will not betray my constituents by voting for any legislation that requires them, through involuntary taxation, to diminish their own odds by paying for others to be frozen."

Westervelt's oration continued for nineteen minutes more, after which the Minority Leader was permitted to respond on behalf of the Democratic senators. I hoped Dad would now tender their most forceful inducement: enlightened self-interest.

"Contrary to popular opinion," he began, "even liberals believe that property rights are important. But the crux here is not wealth redistribution. This argument does not wrangle between provision for the poor versus the sanctity of individual achievement. And while consequential, neither is morality today's primary topic.

"Our current state of affairs has all the makings of a genuine emergency. And in an emergency, all bets are off!"

Yes! I celebrated. Now we had a shot.

"Do I overstate my case? Consider this: If you are drowning, doesn't the issue of ownership of any fresh air above you become meaningless? Wouldn't you fight, and rightly so, to breathe it?"

"Perfect," I said to Grandmother, not quite whispering. Impolite, but what could she expect?

She smiled warmly at my overenthusiasm, in spite of herself.

"We stand here today," Dad continued, "full of hope as we witness the dawn of a new paradigm. Taxes may be inevitable, but Death, that other prehistoric absolute, is no longer certain.

"Do you wish to act in your own self-interest? Then let us make this truly new world available to all. If we don't, many more lives will certainly be lost, forever, to those clawing past us to breathe the sweet air of permanent life.

"No matter your politics, no matter your religion or creed, understand now the certainty of the conflict we face. The drowning man is no thin or artful metaphor; he is an exact allegory. We're all drowning. And yet there's plenty of air for all of us in the peaceful sharing of it. By voting your pocket-of-today, you squander your purse tomorrow. Let us make victory against death a prospect for all, lest it become a prospect for none."

Later that day, when the Senate was polled on individual components of the enactment-bound S. 1122, the only tie vote was on the issue of government subsidization of cryonics for the poor. Even conservative senators such as Juanita "Chacha" Guerrero (R. PR) voted for the subsidy. Dad's rebuttal had converted the contest from hopeless to too-close-to-call.

Roswell's first-term vice-president, Henry Rearden, transmitted the deciding ballot, and by a margin of 55 to 54, our side lost.

I was disappointed, but already viewed this political process as a marathon, not a sprint. That had been just the first leg of this race, I thought, love and pride for my father, and a sense of my own destiny, perhaps someday my place in history, holding sway over any other passion. This very close race.

> SEPTEMBER 7, 2015 — A woman in Montreal, Canada, gives birth to healthy septuplets, two girls and five boys. The mother, Mrs. Nicolette Boyer, had been taking fertility drugs when she became pregnant. The smallest of the infants weighs 11 ounces, and may require incubation for up to a year. All seven are expected to survive, and if they do, will become the second set of living septuplets in Canada. — Shakespeare2, the Intel and Oracle joint venture, launches its literary career today. The giant computer system accurately mimics the human brain, but is tens of thousands of times faster, with flawless memory and calculation abilities. In two weeks, Shakespeare2 has written 1,702 novels, 5,240 screenplays, and over 10,000 essays. Today, at the firm's first sealed-bid auction, 13 of the novels were purchased by publishing houses, and 21 screenplays optioned by studios. *New York Times* critic Lynde Tversky predicts, "Based on the Shakespeare2 oeuvres I've had time to read so far, these should *not* be expected to become blockbusters." — The United States Congress repeals the Silver Standard Act of 2014, which has for nearly three years backed each dollar with $1/117$th of an ounce of silver. Although the move was expected, Hong Kong silver prices nevertheless climb $4 to $129.40 per ounce in heavy trading.

During the three weeks following the deaths of my parents, I'd never been alone more than a few minutes at a time, even at nighttime. My aunts, uncles, and grandmother rarely left whichever room I happened to occupy. Each night, my great-uncle Gary slept on the floor of my bedroom, and often I would catch him staring at me as if he feared I might stop breathing. In retrospect, I think it was a spontaneous form of suicide watch, the entire Smith clan instinctively closing ranks around their most vulnerable member.

But in my mind, that hadn't seemed necessary. It was as if by refusing to acknowledge the calamity, I could somehow make it less real.

I'd never cried.

Because I hadn't embraced the reality of my loss, I could not register the need for self-cleansing despair. This process might have required years, had I not taken action.

For four solid days I'd begged my great-uncle Gary to let me view the archives. "*You* saw it," I reminded him.

He patted my hand, then answered patiently, "Yes, and I told you everything your parents said. But I'm sixty-eight years old; you're not even ten."

"I can handle it," I insisted.

When he looked back, his eyes suggested two broken eggs, liquid, spilling not just water but also themselves. "*I* couldn't."

"Well, at least let me sleep alone tonight," I said. "I'll be fine. It's been twenty-one days."

Gary considered this for a few minutes before answering. "Okay. I'll be right outside your door if you need me."

The moment I was alone, I shut off the lights and put on a headset and VR goggles. Then I inserted the code I had secretly copied several months earlier from my mother's wrist PC, whispered the date and time the crime had occurred, saw and heard everything for myself.

The Aerospeciale Concorde II was

half empty; my mother watched most of the 918 passengers board: families with small children, couples of various ages, businessmen and -women traveling alone or in small groups, a party of perhaps two dozen American junior high school students apparently on an overnight field trip.

Mostly day-trippers and one-night tourists, she must have assumed, since Majorca was such a convenient destination from Boston; the plane could accelerate through the sound barrier even at low altitude, because ninety-eight percent of the journey passed over water, and thus the entire flight required barely ninety minutes.

She stared out the window. The Spanish coast, with its glorious beaches of pure white sand, whizzed past; horizon transformed into unbroken pelagic blue. She turned to my father and kissed his right temple. "Thank you, George," she said. "It was lovely."

Dad gazed at her face—her still beautiful face—and grinned. It had been their first real vacation alone together since his election to the Senate in 2006, the same year I was born. There'd always been a bill to promote, or an election campaign to wage. Even during the rare lulls, they'd never been able to tear themselves away from their only child. "Firstborn syndrome," Grandmother had pronounced. Since my parents had determined there would be no others after me, the syndrome would probably have been permanent.

They'd selected their destination based on convenience, wanting to waste as little of their time as possible. Besides, if there were any kind of emergency at home, they knew they were only two hours away.

Everything had gone fine and I was old enough to understand that, whether I liked it or not, two weeks was not abandonment. I'd immersed himself in political studies, scientific experiments, summer school projects, and field trips with other advanced students from the Feynman Program. There had been no midnight calls from me; no tearful entreaties for their early return.

They had done some sightseeing, dined with friends, lounged on those gorgeous beaches. Apparently, they'd also spent a great deal of time in their suite. At least I hope so. Dad gently kissed Mom. "Awesome two weeks, huh?"

"Not bad for an old married couple." She placed her hand on his. "I did miss Trip something awful, though."

"Me, too," Dad said.

"On the other hand, there's a new Hilton near Logan Airport, and I doubt anyone'd notice if we were an hour or two late getting home . . ."

"Hmm," Dad said, massaging Mom's upper thigh, "I'd been meaning to check that place out anyway."

Then they felt and heard it.

The first thought to occur to Dad was probably that they'd broken the sound barrier too close to the ground. But any such self-deception would have been momentary. Even as their plane lurched from the impact of the heat-seeking missile slamming into its left rear engine, a tumultuous explosion had shattered the eardrums of every passenger aboard. (That much I already knew from the news service reports.) Now they would have seen the screaming faces of the other passengers within a soundless maelstrom.

The temperature gauges on Mom's PC sensors showed the heat behind them intensifying, in contrast to iceberg-cold frost ahead.

My parents mouthed goodbyes and declarations of love to each other. Then Mother said, out loud, "We will always love you, Trip. We'll be fine wherever we're going, and so will you."

Just before burning rivulets of aviation fuel ignited the wing tanks, Father had said, "And we'll both live on through you, son. Remember, you can do anything you set your mind to. Decide carefully, Trip. Don't waste any of it."

Then came the half-second flash.

I cried nonstop for a week, to everyone's great relief. But I never told anyone why.

DECEMBER 28, 2017 — United States Secretary of Health Jasmine Lester lauds the astounding successes of the Human

> Genome Project and Dr. Sharon Rosenfield's MediFact, in
> which nearly a third of all Americans allow wristband com-
> puters to monitor and compile all their medical data including
> diet, exercise, pulse, blood chemistry, symptoms, and medical
> treatments. "Within three years," Lester predicts, "we'll be able
> to anticipate every disease as easily and accurately as we now
> forecast tectonic-plate earthquakes." — In spite of a key injury,
> the Kansas City Rams defeat the Havana Oilers 21–17 to win
> the American Football Conference title. The Rams, without
> Donald Jefferson, their 6'8" 366-pound quarterback, must now
> lock horns in Superbowl 52 against the 2013-through-2016
> world champion Dallas Cowboys. — Analysts expect Century
> 21 to broker a record $9.4 trillion in real estate transactions
> next year, largely due to its dominance in virtual reality walk-
> through tours and architectural remodeling technology. Sepa-
> rately, the firm announces it will cut its standard commission
> rate again, from 1.5% to 1.25%.

Robert Witter, tallest of the three terrorists, slapped his hand against the palm-
dimension measurement surface and gazed into the corneal scanner. An
optical calculator scrutinized his ID badge, then verified that he was indeed
the same Robert Witter who'd been an employee of the Phoenix for nearly two
years. Barry Lomax and Edward Zambetti, however, had only visited a few
times, always during regular business hours. But that didn't matter. As long as
they were with Witter, the off-site warning correlation wouldn't activate.

It was 1:37 A.M., and the next shift wasn't scheduled to arrive until
eight. Plenty of time to thaw the brains of every one of these rich pricks,
Witter thought. Too bad they couldn't get at the other 62,000 in this place;
that would really have gotten their fucking attention.

He ushered his two comrades through a chain of hallways and auto-
mated security procedures, arriving at the only dormantory to which his
recent promotion to cryogenic technician now granted him twenty-four-
hour access. Technology installed after the mid-1990s was far more reliable,
and never required emergency repair. But this particular room domiciled a
more primitive system that still preserved 510 of the earliest patients; every
Phoenix full-body suspension prior to August 1994, including Alice and
Benjamin Smith.

"Most of these fuckers paid at least a hundred grand apiece," Lomax
had told Witter the previous week, "and that was back when a hundred
grand would buy a hell of a lot more than a Hypercar. Hmm. In fact
$100,000 was a small fortune in today's money. Perfect!"

The Audio Vids beamed a permanent record of these activities to the central storage computers, but it would be days before the embryonic artificial intelligence module would have time to deduce what Witter and his accomplices had done. Human technicians at the Phoenix would discover the actions of the three men long before the AI could. Still, the three would eventually be caught and convicted; that was a virtual certainty.

Witter reset the thermostat to increase the room's temperature from 70 degrees F to 99. Then he punched a series of codes to override the thermocouples monitoring each canister.

As they inspected the equipment, Lomax considered the implications of the crime they planned to commit. All class twos and threes, he figured. Not a single predeath preservation, and it was doubtful any of their brains had even been vetrified. The three of them were unarmed, and were not even getting paid. They might do serious jail time, but even if their attorneys were dolts, none of them would get life sentences. And their own cryorights seemed in no jeopardy.

All three men considered themselves heroic, and a small but vocal minority of Americans would have agreed. Lomax and Witter were motivated by progressive politics. After all, why should the dying poor, those to whom life had dealt the worst hands, lose all hope of a future? Who was to say that the lives of the wealthy were more valuable than those of the destitute? So what if the affluent tended to be smarter and more productive; after the doctors of the future overhauled the poor, they might no longer be captive of genetic limitations. All brains might well be raised to genius caliber, and equally worthy of salvage. The rich had already partaken disproportionately from life's banquet, so maybe the poor were *more* deserving.

The third man, Zambetti, was also attracted to this undertaking as a matter of conscience, but his reasons were more spiritual. He was Catholic, and the Pope had stated unequivocally, "Life and death are matters that should be determined only by God." Zambetti's mission was to free the souls of 509 of these frozen cadavers. Only one would remain frozen, in deference to the wishes of his allies-of-the-moment, two men whose sincerity and commitment he'd come to admire.

The men disconnected the units and began drilling two-inch holes in the casings to insert microwave thawing devices. MTDs were neither powerful nor long-lasting, but would be consistent enough to heat each suspendee's head-to-body temperature during the twelve minutes each unit could function before burnout.

Zambetti began drilling through double hulls of steel and the two-inch vacuum layer between them.

The Phoenix always stored its full-body suspendees head down as an added safeguard, so the brain would be the last organ to thaw in case of a leak. The drilling had to be done within six inches of the floor or the ~~~~ally treated liquid nitrogen would quickly refreeze the heads. "Soft-

~~~~~~~~~~~~~~ryonics organization, wouldn't evaporate

mmersed in it much

be unnecessary with

ied them anyway. No

nto the concrete floor

eating profusely, were

Lomax warned. "These

rotect you against soft-

ep enough, your feet'll

but had heard enough

suspendee in particular:

ie canister, he marked it

After all, ...   on behalf of government-subsidized suspensions for the indigent; the only senator who'd cared enough to fight for the little guy. Now he was dead; reduced to ashes on August 17, 2015, when Basque separatists had SAM'ed a Concorde II, killing all 966 passengers and crew, including Senator and Mrs. George J. Crane.

They would spare this Benjamin Franklin Smith.

They were political activists, Lomax reminded himself. Not thugs.

Digital titanium drills could pierce the canisters in seconds, and the MTDs would begin thawing the heads instantly. Only about an hour would be required to complete their work.

Suddenly Zambetti noticed a nameplate. "Uh-oh!"

"What is it?" Lomax ran in panic toward his co-conspirator.

"You think Alice Franklin Smith is related to Crane, too?" Stupid question. Of course she was! It had been ten minutes since he'd drilled her canister, and the soft-nite was already drained. "Guess I should've read the name first."

"Shit! Didn't know about her," Lomax said. "Jesus, Witter, couldn't you have checked the records, for chrissake?"

Zambetti tolerated Lomax's lapse into blasphemy. He figured it was partly his own fault.

"Sorry," Witter called from halfway across the cavernous room. "Never even thought of it."

"Can you get more soft-nite?"

"Not without calling in for it, and the remote security guys'd hafta release it manually. They'll ask questions." Witter thought a moment. "Got some binder that'll hold it in, though. Least it's supposed to."

"Okay, quick!"

Witter fished the platinum-laced putty out of his instrument cylinder. Lomax snatched it from him, raced to Alice Smith's canister, and set to work.

"No, not that way," Witter shouted as the canister toppled, soft-nite squirting from the hole Lomax was trying to repair. "Watch out!"

Lomax managed to halt the flow, but not before the stream of soft-nite glanced off the top of his right hand. He jerked back in panic, barely tapping his hand against the side of the canister.

His thumb and index finger as well as the top two-thirds of the middle finger snapped cleanly off and fell to the floor, shattering.

"Fuck me, I'm screwed!"

Zambetti surveyed the damage in open-mouthed horror. "Holy mother of God! You okay?"

"Fuck, fuck, fuck!"

"Does it hurt?"

Lomax hesitated while his shock dissipated, abandoning him not only to intense pain, but also to his habitual authority and resolve. "Can hardly feel it yet," he lied. "But in a few minutes it'll start bleeding like a fire hose. Shit. So stupid! You guys'll hafta finish the drilling without me. Grab a coupla low-temp receptacles and refill her canister with the flow from the ones you haven't drilled yet. Then let's get the hell outta here."

By the time Lomax tied a tourniquet around his wrist, Zambetti and Witter had finished nuking and draining the last of the canisters. The three men imagined they could already smell the rotting flesh of their victims.

It was now 2:46 A.M.; one brain had been spared, one had possibly been rescued in time, 508 were definitely toast. The other two wondered if Lomax considered saving this woman worth losing his right hand. Zambetti prayed to God that the trauma hadn't destroyed her brain. If it had, his fellow soldier of justice had turned himself into a cripple for no reason at all.

AUGUST 2, 2021 — The first serious crime committed by a Europe-based machine, an Intel 48T data processor powered by DAP Synthetic-Brain software purposely murders a human in Düsseldorf Germany. The victim, Dr. Fritz Wichmann, was electrocuted after declining the machine's request to be connected to the Infobahn. The 48T is scheduled for destruction tomorrow morning, and DAP has recalled all S-B software. — In the wake of today's shocking murder-by-device, Senators John Comerford (D. FL) and James Hayes (R. LA) propose legislation to ban the programming of emotions, survival instinct, or the ability to contrive deceit into any machine. An interim ban on such programming is enacted pending the final bill's passage. Former President Garrison Roswell predicts, "The United States Software Act (S. 2343) will be debated and revised for the better part of a year, at which point some version of it should pass both Senate and House."

The newly elected fifty-two-year-old Pope John Paul IV, who just last month had held the title of Cardinal Carlos Juan Riesco, sat inside a VR chamber at Vatican time eleven A.M. In twelve cities throughout the world, his dozen most trusted cardinals perched inside identically configured units. It was a decidedly *un*-godly three A.M. in Boston, where Cardinal Joseph Hannah now tried to appear alert.

Most of the thirteen prelates considered the Catholic Church's reputation for stubbornness unwarranted. They no longer burned heretics at the stake or prosecuted women for witchcraft. Way back in 1989 the Church had revised its position on cosmology, admitting their previous error of forcing Galileo to recant his "preposterous" theory that the earth orbits the sun. They'd also sanctioned inoculation and anesthesia, twice reclassified evolution—first as "open for discussion," then as "a possible device plan"— and recently modified their position, however superficially, on birth control. These were not unreasonable men.

Never far from the thoughts of the holy fathers was the fact that over the past six years the Catholic Church had lost over a quarter of its American membership, a trend that threatened to globalize with the inevitable spread of procryonics legislation. Furthermore, if no Catholics were frozen, none would be revived, a distinct disadvantage in the contest for religious prevalence. The new Pope was well-known as a reformist, a label that had once impeded his advancement, but had recently accelerated it.

"I am prepared," the pontiff began in English, "to consider the possibility that cryonics might reasonably be construed a medical treatment, not an interference with God's will. I would hear your opinions on this subject." What he meant—and all dozen cardinals knew it—was: Give me justifications for altering our position, not arguments against cryonics. The decision itself had already been made.

"When your predecessor declared that life and death are matters for God to determine," Bishop Hannah began, "he might not have meant this quite as it sounded. I think he may have been more concerned with the unproven nature of cryonic treatment, and did not wish to risk the living to it. I am aware of no specific objections raised by John Paul III to the crystalline preservation of those already dead."

"Yes," the Pope agreed, "but I'm afraid that does not get us very far. Certainly many Catholics will wish to freeze themselves before they die. The theory, as I understand it, is that by waiting until after death, memory may be lost."

"John Paul III could not have possibly meant that we should not try to lengthen lives whenever possible." Cardinal Mohandas Ranganathan from Bombay offered. "Clearly it is undesirable to disconnect body and soul prematurely. For centuries a doctrine of our Church had been that the taking of human life, whether murder, abortion, mercy killing, or suicide, is a sin. Therefore he must have regarded freezing as tantamount to death itself, perhaps because it was legally defined as such. Now that those in biostasis are no longer adjudged legally dead, perhaps his criterion would have been subject to reinterpretation."

Cardinal Kwayme Knau of Ghana chimed in, "In truth, under this redefinition of death, it could easily be argued that *failure* to freeze would be a sin. Are you certain you wish to accede to such an, ahem, unorthordox reconfiguration?"

"Perhaps not," the Pope answered, "but I am open to that which both accommodates and preserves. Any other observations?"

"The key may rest in our tenets in re the nature and purpose of the soul," Cardinal Alan Kidman of Melbourne suggested. "Perhaps with the complexity of modern life, the soul needs more time to grow, to reach its God-envisioned potential. It's possible that eighty to one hundred years is no longer enough time for creditable attainment of life's spiritual goals."

"Sufficient time," Ranganathan interrupted, "is even more critical for the perilously uncertain souls of the unsaved. As compassionate Christians, should we not welcome another chance to save such souls, rather than abandoning them to rot in Purgatory? Or hell?"

"Excellent points," the Pope said. "But that hardly addresses our outlook on cryonic suspension of good Catholics."

"True, Your Holiness," Cardinal Gennady Argounova of Kiev agreed. "Still, we must be optimistic. A soul that is already saved will likely remain saved, even if its vessel should survive for millennia. At least that is my opinion."

The Pope nodded. Experience had taught him to be less confident in human religious steadfastness, yet he could hardly see his way to disagree with Argounova. Besides, increased longevity would inevitably belong to future generations regardless of the Church's position on cryonics. Biostasis was simply a way to allow this generation some chance of sharing the long life its offspring would enjoy regardless. And a Catholic was unarguably more apt to remain Catholic than was a non-Catholic likely to convert to Catholicism. The real issue was the survival of the Church.

"I hate to bring this up now, just when we seem to be nearing consensus," Cardinal Angus Kennedy of Belfast said, "but how will the Church regard marriages when one of the spouses is the metaphoric equivalent of a frozen embryo?"

"I suppose I am open to suggestions on that issue, as well," the Pope said. "But we needn't rush to cross bridges."

Nearly six months would pass before the Vatican released its encyclical on cryonics. Suspendees would become, in the eyes of the Catholic Church, "potentially living humans, the disposition of whose souls is known only to God." Marriages involving one partner in biostasis could be maintained or dissolved at the option of the surviving spouse.

The day after the Vatican's announcement, Edward Zambetti's body would be found hung by the neck in his cell at Tucson Penitentiary, where he was serving a thirty-nine-year sentence for 509 counts of biostasis interruption. AudioVid records would subsequently confirm Zambetti's death as a suicide.

JANUARY 1, 2025 — President-elect Matthew Emery announces he has negotiated arrangements with Armstrong Technologies, Inc., subject to congressional approval, to have an ACIP (truth machine) in every courtroom in America by year end. The lie-detector device, which analyzes blood flow and electrical activity in the brain, was officially tested and certified as fool-proof last August, and immediately approved for judicial system usage. — Jean-Luc Christon is executed by lethal injection in Paris, France. The "Serial Hacker" admitted to murdering 7,412 hospital patients throughout France, Switzerland, and Canada by altering their medical records. — In an unprecedented display of international cooperation, emergency response teams for the U.S., Japan, U.K., France, Russia, Italy,

and Kazakhstan converge on Chernobyl, Ukraine, after recent
movement in the core of the ill-fated Reactor IV indicates high
probability of massive leakage in the sarcophagus. Eleven days
of around-the-clock assembly are anticipated to install a
recently developed Sino-Japanese shielding tile on all sides,
including above and below the collapsing core. As a precau-
tionary measure, further plans are approved to construct
shielding-tile encasements around the entire complex, including the three reactors shut down in early 2012.

The wheel bucked in his hands as if one of the tires were out of alignment.
Damn! He'd thought this portion of the run would be easier, less challenging. Jesus.

Gary Franklin Smith glanced toward the two hands that held fast to
the archaic steering wheel. In these he was less disappointed; only one or
two distinctive brown spots tattled his age. Not bad, for seventy-seven years.

Still, he wished he possessed his driving skills of even five years ago.
Might make all the difference now. Sure, it was possible to reach his goal
regardless of performance, but less likely. There were times, of course,
when luck would take you home, and others when the best wheel man just
couldn't buy a break. And for Gary, the money was becoming more and
more, well, real.

"Whoa!"

Gary whipped the wheel of the old contraption in a frantic attempt to
avoid collision with the faded '08 Infiniti. Inside the heap's now-sagging
doors hunkered four, no, five of the bastards.

Git dat soam-bitch! he saw the other driver pantomime. Gary's mind
painted in the sounds of the sociopath's words, though he could not hear them.

The vehicles passed within inches of each other, their tormented
power plants both screaming as if in farewell salute to the age of the internal
combustion engine. Gary's eyes flashed to the heads-up: 123,500. Too bad.
He had to play for the stalemate now.

His foot found the brake pedal. The '99 Bronco might have been
all manual, but its weight would carry the day. He rammed the shift
lever to reverse, simultaneously applying the accelerator. The steel horse
reared in a pall of tire smoke, Gary slapped the shift lever into D, and now
she was floored. The Infiniti of rednecks had executed a similar maneuver.
A shotgun protruded from the rear passenger window, and behind the
weapon a face leered in depraved anticipation.

Heads-up read: 128,250. Awright! Going in the right direction, anyway.

The shotgun blast took the Bronco full in the radiator. Not enough time for that to matter.

Gary aimed and ducked his head. Though its response was ponderous, the ancient Ford cargo wagon was now doing 85. The second blast imploded the windshield, and a gummy safety-glass rain showered down on him.

Perfect. They couldn't possibly know what was coming.

Had he cared to watch, Gary would have seen a dawning realization appear on their vacuous faces. But 65 plus 85 equaled an unforgiving closing speed, and understanding offered no salvation.

Smash!

The Infinite spattered against the old leviathan's wounded grill.

"What time's it?" Gary mumbled.

No answer. Where the hell was he??

Soft leather, faint yellowish-green lights. The VR module! And he'd forgotten to wear his audio PC again. Hell, second time he'd fallen asleep in here that week. Anxiously, his eyes focused on the at-home virtual reality pod's running total: $1,455,456,766, in glowing red figures.

Oh, great!

He had been in there for twenty-six hours, including the eleven hours of accidental sleep, and had won $1,204. That and a nice smile might make an appropriate tip for a maître d', but it sure wouldn't do much for him.

Four weeks ago Gary had received the results of his latest genetic scan. While his family predisposition to heart disease and pancreatic cancer loomed, both diseases were now curable at only slight inconvenience even to those who'd refused immunization. At age seventy-seven Gary retained the expectation of at least twenty-one more years of relative good health before biostasis could be considered reasonable, much less desirable. Suddenly he remembered first reading these test results on his screen and feeling, what? Frustration? Yes. Frustration, and dread.

Only eighteen years earlier, Gary's career had been at its peak, but since then, as the machines had become more accomplished and a new generation of younger artists more proficient at their use, demand for his work had plummeted. At least that's what he now told himself, ignoring that fact that eighteen years ago he'd simply stopped working as hard or with as much focus. Ignoring, also, that eighteen years was the same length of time that Tobias Fiske had been on ice and therefore absent from his life.

Perhaps I had played some part in my great-uncle's problems as well. When my parents were killed nine years ago, Gary offered me unrelenting support. For two years I'd seen him every day, often for hours at a time. He'd even tried to entice me into his artistic pursuits, but my interests rested elsewhere. Although my withdrawal into scientific work and study had mirrored Gary's reaction to his own childhood miseries, we'd nonetheless drifted apart, become somehow less relevant to each other. For this, I certainly accept most of the blame.

Soon thereafter, loneliness had darkened his spirit and depression permeated his art, even as it poisoned his personal relationships.

Since then, he'd gambled away most of his fortune, and perhaps even more alarmingly, spent nearly all of his time sleeping, or escaping into on-line VR gambling (and decreasingly often, sex) games. I would later learn that when he allowed himself to think about it, he experienced a sensation of déjà vu, as if transported back forty-five years, when his mother died and he'd temporarily lost himself in booze and white powder. Only this time, his self-destructive behavior was legal, and had lasted a decade.

He briefly contemplated suicide, as he often did, and rejected it, as he always had, but with an ever-weakening resolve. Maybe the freezer . . .

(Man I've gotta get some help. This needs to stop.)

Father Steven Jones seemed surprised at seeing his uninvited guest on the visitor's screen. But Gary had nowhere else to turn.

Father Steve had been the only member of the clergy who supported Toby Fiske's great debunking crusade. Gary remembered him as a compassionate man, a genuinely inspired and inspiring servant of God.

Gary remembered the day he and Toby first met Father Steve. The two friends had been visiting Kingston, Jamaica, in early November 2002, their journey as much vacation as mission. Toby had spent several months convincing Gary that he needed a respite from work, so off they'd gone, hot on the trail of Rodney Probber, the Virgin Mary Restorer.

He now visualized the first moment that this imposing priest of obvious local lineage had stood at their hotel room door. "Excuse me," the man had said to them in bass voice and flawless, unaccented diction, "but I believe we're here for the same reason. Maybe we can help each other."

Gary had smiled and invited the man inside, although he could tell that Toby looked upon the cleric with nervous skepticism. Toby was no racist, but considering his view of organized religion, Gary understood.

To find Tobias Fiske, Father Steven Jones had flown in that very morning, from Dorchester, Massachusetts. For the priest, whose own ancestry traced back to Jamaica, this "Virgin Mary Restorer"—as Toby and Gary had come to think of him—was no laughing matter.

It seemed Probber had returned from Bethlehem with a concoction of frankincense and myrrh which he would blend with freshly consecrated holy water. These spices, he claimed, had been a portion of the magi's gifts to the baby Jesus on his birth night. Probber had purportedly managed to procure these most-sacred of relics from a coptic priest whose family had maintained them with uninterrupted vigilance for these past two millennia.

Probber also claimed that if the emulsion was applied to the violated places of any young girl, she could once again attain that sanctified state of virginity in the eyes of the Almighty. Of course, only Mr. Probber himself could practice the proper technique of such application. And, hey, at only $200 U.S. per restoration (free to the needy), what greater bargain was to be had in all of Christendom?

Surprisingly, Probber's act had not played to rave reviews on the mainland. Indeed, two of his "treatments" had ultimately come to the attention of grand juries in Miami. But the Jamaican government had proved more enlightened; if there were complaints, Probber would just donate his two-hundred-dollar fee to the police officer in charge and, of course, admonish the constable to do only good works with the money.

In Jamaica, Probber had never so much as been taken in for questioning.

Gary and Toby had mostly regarded such con games with all the gravity they deserved, which is to say, they laughed. But needing a break, both had agreed that setting up Probber would be a good thing, and one hell of a lot of fun. He might be expelled, or perhaps just billy-clubbed to the point of reconsidering his line of work. Either had seemed a satisfactory outcome. And besides, there were worse places to be in November.

Father Steve's motivations were different. A somewhat cerebrally challenged member of his flock had been taken in by Probber's used-car tongue, and her thirteen-year-old daughter had been "cured." Upon learning that Fiske had trailed the man to Kingston, Father Steve had found a way to follow. If there was no satisfaction to be won in debunking the bastard, the enraged priest planned on showing Probber just how painful the wrath of God could be.

Yet when this Roman Catholic reverend presented himself at their hotel, Toby had offered a cool reception. It was as though a lifetime enemy was offering to join him in battle. "Why would you help us?" he'd asked.

"Because the goal is worthy, and because I can," the cleric had said, paraphrasing an old joke. "In fact, I've got a story for you that might help illustrate this good Christian's attitude about opportune alliances."

Gary had glanced quizzically at Toby, who gestured the priest to continue.

Father Steve sat on the couch. "Seems my friend Rabbi Abramson was seeking funds for a new synagogue, and thus asked me for a contribution from the Church. 'Oh, no,' I had to explain sadly, 'my bishop would never authorize a donation to build a Jewish temple." But then I had an idea. 'Tell me, Rabbi,' I asked, 'what will you do with your old synagogue?' He answered: 'Naturally we'll have to tear it down to make space for the new construction.' So I prompted, 'And tearing it down will be part of your cost, won't it?' 'Of course,' he said. 'Well then,' I suggested, 'maybe you'd care to set up a separate fund for the razing.' Rabbi Abramson became quite confused, and asked, 'Why on earth should I go to all that trouble?' 'Ah,' I explained, 'because that is a fund to which the Church would gladly contribute.' "

Toby had tried to resist chortling aloud. Apparently, this hadn't been what he'd expected, but the joke was too fitting, too perfect. At least temporarily, the two had become three.

Gary and Father Steve had spent the next few days posing as different New York newspaper reporters, a publicist for Tobias Fiske's book tour, and a research assistant. It hadn't taken long for news of their visit to wend its way through the praetorian levels of the local bureaucracy.

Upon reflection, the Kingston government had decided that Probber's contribution to the local economy no longer justified such laughingstock publicity as might result from a Tobias Fiske exposé.

Rodney Probber *had* been taken in for questioning. He *had* been billy-clubbed. But, of course—as any serious student of early twenty-first century Caribbean history must realize—he'd never been struck.

G a r y　k n e w　t h a t after twenty-two years, the clergy-man still considered voodoo-cult mysticism the truest form of blasphemy. This may have explained why, despite forty-eight years of splendid service, Father Steve had never risen above the rank of parish priest. Thus, he seemed a plausible confidant to Gary, as well as a true peer: also mid-seventies in years, creative in word, and a worshiper of life.

Gary realized he needed this visit badly and hoped it would go well.

Autocane in hand, he left the elevator and shuffled to the apartment door. Gary's back ached from years of lopsided movement. The cane helped, but now he wished he could afford bionic trousers.

"Gary Smith!" the jolly cleric beamed. "How *are* you?"

Gary clasped the large, dark hand now extended, and felt comfort from the touch.

"It's been nearly fifteen years," Gary said to his old comrade. "Mostly, I can't believe I've come. It seems such an imposition . . ."

The two men sat in Father Steve's book- and CD ROM–cluttered study. Gary watched the cleric try to frame his question, and wondered for the first time if he'd chosen a proper counsel. The feeling this room evoked was comfort-sans-perspective, its flavor like the showcasing of an open-reel tape recorder in the 1980s or a record collection in 2005. These vehicles of communication contained beauty, value, and truth, but a less-than-timely efficacy.

Gary mused he might soon hear the priest play Bach on a slide whistle.

"Things never change so much that I'd consider a visit from you as anything but a welcome event; except that I see you're troubled, and for that I'm sorry. What's worrying you?"

"I've lost it," Gary told him simply. "I'm addicted to VR gambling, and steadily losing what little money I have. I never seem to get quite stupid enough to blow it all at once. But I'm not sure the restraint benefits me. Mostly, I prolong my own agony."

The priest's eyes opened into wide-pupiled stare, as only those with artificial corneas could so dramatically affect. "What are you contemplating?"

"The ice."

"I once heard you call it the *hopeful ice* many years ago." The priest leaned forward in his chair.

"You remember that?"

"It's not so hopeful, is it?"

"Certainly not right now," Gary sighed. "I don't know why I'd want a forever of life like *this*, mindlessly playing games against a machine. And it's not that it's a machine per se. It's that the machine doesn't care. Jesus, this sounds like a conversation a fifteen-year-old should be having with a guidance counselor."

"It's a matter of meaning." Father Steve's words seemed practiced, though sincere. "Only that which is finite can have meaning in the eyes of God."

Gary was appalled but not angry; it was just such a surprise to receive bromide when he'd sought discourse.

"No." The priest signaled for Gary's silence. "Before you misunderstand, hear me out. Forget God for a moment . . ."

The quality of Father Steve's voice was so earnest that Gary wanted to laugh aloud. Had the man even listened to what he'd just said?

"Whether religious or not," Father Steve continued, "only that which is finite holds value for us. In the infinite, there is no purpose except as it may be supplied by God. And if you don't believe in God, just ignore that aspect of my declaration. It still holds true.

"If you could drink the finest champagne forever, on demand, without limit or cost, wouldn't the value of the flavor diminish? If a sunset lasted forever, someday it would no longer seem beautiful."

"Why don't you expand on that?" Gary said. "Let me understand where you're going with it."

"What has meaning to you?" Father Steve asked. "Tell me anything. But let it have real significance."

"Well, my art used to."

"And did you paint pictures of things that will last forever? Or did you capture the essence of transitory people and events; capture them in their most compelling seconds?"

"What are you saying? That you're not going to be frozen?"

"That's precisely what I'm saying. This struggle of yours has been caused in some portion by the prospect of immortality. It is a false hope with sad consequences. We should accept our mortality and fight only against *this* death. Staying alive as long as possible is a righteous choice, but once Death finds us, it is madness to hope for corporeal resurrection. And I'm certain this desire offends God."

Now Gary was glad he came. He felt revitalized, with a hope he hadn't felt in years. And all it had taken was a little engaged, human conversation. "Before I answer, I'd like to tell you why I painted what I did. Whether or not my subjects were finite had nothing to do with my choices. I painted them because I wanted their hopes and images to last forever."

Father Steve looked at him with attentive eyes.

"Now I've got a question for *you*," Gary said. "In whose image is God supposed to have created man?"

"In His own image."

"And how long will God live?" Gary asked.

MAY 16, 2031 — The Senate ratifies the International Free Speech Bill (H.R. 3466), and President David West signs it into law. The bill pledges United States support of efforts to enforce freedom of speech and a free press throughout the world. It also budgets $620 billion over five years to enhance the Worldwide

Satellite Communications Network. The WSCN allows any person with a computer, radio, or television to receive programs in their own language from any broadcaster in the world. West hails the legislation as "a giant step toward world democracy. Strengthening the WSCN is the most efficient way to assure that entire populations will no longer be manipulated toward violence by the propaganda of local tyrants." — Dr. Robert Steinberg, renowned Dartmouth psychology researcher, announces that his team has devised a series of questions, which if asked during Truth Machine testing, can diagnose virtually all known forms of mental illness. They have also formulated successful treatments using ACIP therapy for several such illnesses. Steinberg's work, widely praised, is expected to revolutionize the field of mental health. — Pursuit to the terms of the Amnesty Bill enacted several weeks ago, over 56 million individuals have already confessed to crimes committed prior to January 1, 2031, mostly misdemeanors and white-collar offenses. Since the Truth Machine was infused into American society, aggressive crime has virtually disappeared, and victimless crime mostly decodified.

Patrick Webster, ninety-one, sat himself at ACIP module #63 of the Boston Amnesty Bureau. His bloodshot eyes stared at the List: seventeen crimes with detailed descriptions thereof, which he'd painstakingly reconstructed from personal files, public archives, and his own pale retrospection.

He assumed there had been other infractions, but knew his recollection of them was permanently lost, and for once felt gratitude for the rot of aging. As long as no evidence or witnesses emerged, such loss-of-memory would be the same, by law, as if those crimes had never occurred. And as long as he tried his best to remember all his crimes, any new discoveries would be covered by the Amnesty provisions.

It was not that Webster feared being stigmatized by his confession. Every person he knew was or had been in his identical position. Before the emergence of the Armstrong Cerebral Image Processor, the foolproof lie detector immediately dubbed the "Truth Machine," everyone had committed the occasional indiscretion.

He'd studied the Amnesty Laws as well as his atrophied legal skills had permitted, and recognized that under Amnesty he had committed no crimes for which he could receive imprisonment.

Still his entire body was stiff with anxiety. He felt his life at risk, and perhaps it was. Clearly, restitution had to be made. He wondered how much of his vast wealth would remain under his control. He had little prospect of finding profitable work; the demand for attorneys had been severely limited since the ACIP's introduction. And he was too old to learn a new, marketable skill. Worse yet, in cases of fraud, none of his assets would be protected.

What if he couldn't afford to maintain his biostasis insurance? And if he did manage to scrape the money together, his rates would go up.

Everyone knew that wealth increased life expectancy. For over a decade, the insurance companies had been factoring net worth into their actuarial tables. Even in the era of the Truth Machine, wealth bought a measure of survival.

He tallied six instances of drunken driving, all happily victimless. No problem there. Certain illicit drug use; also victimless. Some minor tax evasion, all pre-2006, a hundred percent grandfathered; he was smart enough to have cut that shit out immediately upon reading Roswell's bill in April of that year. And finally there was the case, right before his retirement, when he'd bribed a juror to get a client off.

Very stupid. But thank God it had been a criminal trial and not a civil suit. Again, no victim with standing, and whatever penalty/fine the artificial intelligence unit imposed would surely be tolerable.

But those four clients he'd overbilled ... Damn! Now that was a problem!

It was long ago, back when Webster had needed the money. None of those clients was still alive—only one was even in biostasis—but plenty of their heirs were still knocking around, as yet unaware of the financial windfall that might soon arrive at Webster's expense.

I could be in deep-dish dung.

"Is this a complete list of your crimes, described fully and accurately to the best of your ability, Mr. Webster?" the technician asked.

"Yes, subject to the limits of my memory, what's left of it," Webster answered in lawyer-speak. He couldn't help it.

"Yes or no, Mr. Webster."

"Yes."

The Truth Machine light remained green.

Thank you, dear Lord.

The AI unit analyzed his List of Crimes and the document was transmitted to Webster's pocket PC. As he unfolded the screen, the thing felt cold in his hands. That was impossible of course, but ...

Amnesty Certificate
Patrick Vernon Webster
ID#6445-7866-543-ADFRD — May 16, 2031

12 victimless crimes
No punishment, fines, or restitution.
1 felony
Bribery, no victim. (2011) Fine assessed: $50,000,000
4 casualty crimes, all pre-Truth Machine Bill
Interest-free restitution:
Malpractice/fraud:
The Smith Family Cryonic Trust (1989–92) $6,978,000.
Malpractice/fraud:
The Estate of William Couglin (1994–98) $9,654,000
Malpractice/fraud:
The Dennis Downing Charitable Trust (1995–99) $13,566,000
Malpractice/fraud:
The Estate of Gladys N. Baker (1997–2003) $26,775,000

Jubilant in his relief, Webster allowed his eyes to linger on that most glorious phrase: "Interest-free restitution."

Not even $110 million.

He would retain over ninety percent of his wealth, plenty for his wife and him to enjoy a comfortable life during the decade or so MediFact had projected remained before they'd require biostasis, and enough to endow a very respectable INA account for life after revivification.

The Smith Family Cryonic Trust would receive the annual amount of the fraud based on Webster's most honest recollection. But $6.98 million today was worth barely $240,000 in the dollars of 1992, when the last overbilling had occurred.

As his decaying legs, aided by quasibionic muscle-stimulation trousers, carried him outside to his waiting programmed-transport vehicle, he considered the ever-expanding dominion of the AI machines. With a machine doling it out, justice was an objective measurement of human input, uncolored by emotional reprisal or lenience.

A decade ago such authority in the tenure of machines would have been alarming. No human could match their intellectual horsepower, and throughout history the greater minds had tended to enslave those lesser endowed. The machines had no weapons, of course, but given time, communication becomes persuasion, and persuasion is enough to command.

Power corrupts, the old saying went, and absolute power corrupts absolutely.

Yet the machines did seem to dole out justice with a consistency no human could match. Since the United States Software Act of November 7, 2022, and similar legislation in virtually every other nation, it had been illegal for any machine to be programmed with a survival instinct or emotions. And now, with the Truth Machine at society's command, no attempt by human programmers to violet this act was likely to go undetected.

Armstrong's Truth Machine had also made biostasis infinitely safer. Intentions of terrorism were routinely detected in everyday licensing "scips," long before any such plans could be carried out. Not a single suspendee in the U.S. had been lost to terrorism since the infamous January 2025 attack on the cold-storage cylinders of Forest Lawn in Burbank, California.

Following the lead of the United States, many other nations had passed laws to deal with the plethora of crimes committed before the Truth Machine had eliminated any such temptations. In Paris, for example, on the same day as Webster's routine confession, Drs. Claude Noire and Edouard Binette were forced to endure a much harsher inquisition, their crimes being far more significant. The doctors had failed a customs scip (Truth Machine test) that morning while attempting to leave Paris for a pharmaceutical convention in Hong Kong, and were "invited" by the *douanier* to answer questions.

"If we refuse to answer . . . ?" Binette had asked the young bureaucrat at the Institut Nationale pour la Vérification des Recherches Scientifiques.

"No problem." The man had pointed the Truth Machine at himself. "We will just assume that every experiment you have ever submitted is fraudulent, and sentence you accordingly."

The ACIP light glowed a chilling, steady green.

Confined to separate rooms, the two doctors gave virtually identical testimony. Both testified that the deep-frozen-mouse revivification, which had changed the worldwide paradigm on cryonics, had been a simple scientific fraud. A genetically identical clone of one of the cryonically (minus 79 degrees C) frozen mice had been deanimated, cooled to 25 degrees Fahrenheit, and secretly switched prior to the reanimation. Of course, the replacement had been the sole survivor out of the entire group of 1,300 mice. They had repeated the fraud nearly a dozen times in subsequent years, with convincingly mixed results, but for purported "competitive reasons" had refused to release the formula to other scientists.

The only significant difference in their testimony concerned motive. Noire had perpetrated the fraud to attain wealth. Binette's purpose had been less rapacious but equally selfish: He hoped to foster public acceptance of cryonics. Both still believed that vitrification under the guidelines of the Prometheus Protocol was the best hope for preserving identity and memory of mammalian brains.

Of course, now it was apparent that they were only guessing.

MAY 30, 2031 — Memorial Gardens on the World Wide Web reports reaching a milestone 750 million "grave sites" where family members and friends post permanent epitaphs, stories, photographs, and recordings of their departed or suspended loved ones. The statistic does not include deceased pets or inanimate objects, which if added would raise total sites to nearly one billion. — In a speech to Republican supporters, Senator and likely presidential candidate Jonathan Salyers warns a largely indifferent audience: "The meme of the mouse-reanimation has infected our brains to the point where we can't seem to recover from it, even after Nobine's exposure as fraud. In fact, predeath cryonics is the equivalent of simple suicide." President David West asserts, "It *is* interesting that this bombshell has had so little effect on the public's attitude about cryonics. Still, I suspect most suspendees will eventually be revived and rejuvenated, and even if not, the mere possibility seems well worth the limited risk and expense to anyone about to die or lose memory."

Gary and Father Steve watched from the artist's workshop/dwelling. Perhaps a third of the world's adult population were also witnessing, in real-time, today's trial in Paris.

The two "chronies"—as Gary had dubbed them when they reached their mid-eighties—shared a nutritionally optimal lunch which the priest had brought with him: mostly fruit and whole grains, but also nine ounces of a delicious cultured chicken breast. Like most Americans, they refused all food that had ever been part of a sentient organism, now that modern cell-culturing techniques enabled "farmers" to produce healthy meat at affordable prices without slaughtering animals. This was no hardship; the stuff tasted great.

During the past six and one-half years, both men had undergone other significant lifestyle transformations.

In January 2025, Gary had ordered the VR machine removed from his apartment, and was now the only person he had ever heard of who did not keep one. Furthermore, he hadn't gambled in six years. In April 2025 he'd spent nearly all his remaining money on AI and graphic computers, and since had immersed himself in the discipline of digitally enhanced artistic synthesis.

Having yet to attempt to sell anything, he was nearly broke, yet felt satisfied and mostly optimistic.

For fifty-one months he'd worked tirelessly, with a tenacity exceeding even his previous peak levels of obsession, on a single picture which, when completed, he was convinced would be regarded as the finest composition of his career.

He had never shown the work to anyone.

For seventy-seven months, Father Steve had irrevocably embraced the creed of biological immortalism. While he remained a devout priest and faithful Christian, beneath his crucifix now dangled another sacred ornament: his biostasis protocol.

In His own image . . . If the biblical verse were true, his action would be vindicated. If it were not true, what had he to fear?

The three-dimensional screen on the west wall of Gary's dwelling placed the two men at front row center in the gallery of the courtroom. The device had recently been reprogrammed to adjust to its own acoustics, conveying the compelling feeling and sound of actually being there. To their left sat Drs. Noire and Binette, shuddering nervously as they listened to prosecutor Antoine Bardot's strident summation.

A simple AI device on Gary's screen translated Bardot's harangue into English:

". . . worst fraud of the entire third millennium. The defendants have personally extracted over ten billion ECU's per year in each of these past fifteen years, from the trusting citizens of the world. They accepted blood money for a product whose efficacy they knew had been demonstrated by duplicitous means; indeed, a product which they were able to sell as proven only through their own deceit; mere sleight-of-hand. Their original and perpetuated design was simply to defraud the public of these funds.

"And how many have they killed? This we do not know. Someday, should we have the technology to reanimate the potentially living, we will learn either that the Prometheus Protocol works, or that the human race has been sold a trillion ECUs worth of snake oil. But the real issue is this: All clients who purchased the Protocol had every right to conclude that they were doing so on the basis of proven science. We now know that the defendants committed a scientific fraud, and that over the past twenty-five years almost a third of a billion people have made their biostasis decisions based upon that fraud.

"Every person in this room, perhaps every person watching the broadcast of this trial, awaits the revival of loved ones in biostasis; loved ones legally entitled to receive the best possible science upon which to have their suspensions designed. The magnitude of this fraud, unprecedented in history, is tantamount to mass murder. We seek the only justifiable sentence, the maximum penalty: Final Death for both defendants."

Defense attorney Pierre Villard scanned his notes.

"Tough case for the defense," Father Steve said to his friend.

"Do you think they'll really get Final Death?" Gary asked. Like most world citizens, some hidden part of him hoped not. Final Death, in a way, would be like a declaration that brain vitrification had no merit, an intolerable concept.

Father Steve shrugged.

Predictably, in the two weeks since Nobine et Cie's fraud was exposed, acceptance of cryonics had barely diminished. Although Prometheus Inc.'s stock price had lost eighty-three percent of its value, sales of the Protocol itself had fallen by less than ten percent. Some refused even to believe that the French mouse revivification had been fraudulent—in spite of the defendants' public confessions that it was. Throughout the world, people had come to embrace the scientifically assured viability of cryonics. It would be at least as difficult to rectify this misperception as it had been initially to convince the public that cryonic reanimation was a possibility.

Gary considered all of this a fascinating lesson in human psychology. And while he felt less certain of vitrification today than he had two weeks earlier, cryonics remained to him the only rational choice.

Defense attorney Villard began: "Does cryonics not give you a better chance for life than conflagration, or feeding your body to the worms? My friends, does any of you really believe there's a better method of brain preservation than the Prometheus Protocol? In 2005, before Drs. Binette and Noire perpetuated their so-called fraud, there were approximately 39,400 suspensions performed worldwide. Almost everyone who died was cremated or buried. Cremated or buried! This year, there will be over thirty million suspensions.

"Certainly my clients profited from a fraud. So take the money back. All of it! But did they intend harm by their actions? Dr. Binette has proven, through his own ACIP testimony, that his primary purpose in conducting the fraud was to help popularize cryonic suspension. I remind you again that in 2006 most perfectly rational human beings were happily incinerating or interring their deceased loved ones. How many of *those* unfortunate dead will ever be resurrected?

"Dr. Noire, like Dr. Binette, has voluntarily taken a full series of Truth Machine scips. He admits his motives were mostly financial, but still believes that brain vitrification under the Prometheus Protocol offers the best chance for identity and memory preservation upon revivification.

"My own view is that someday my clients will be remembered as heroic scoundrels, two men who managed, through duplicitous means, to change for the better the world's perception of the science of cryonics. Ultimately, their actions will have saved most of an entire human generation . . ."

"Amazing," Father Steve said. "He's arguing that these crooks are heroes! I admire his creativity."

Gary understood that in essence they were both. "But think back to what trials were like before the ACIP. Talk about creative! Villard's argument is downright boring in comparison to most pre–Truth Machine trials."

Father Steve laughed.

"A long time ago Toby and I used to talk about deciphering the laws of nature," Gary said. "Deciphering, then overcoming them. We'd sit there and try to describe future technologies, each trying to top the other. I don't think either of us ever came up with anything like the Truth Machine."

"It sure changed everything."

"Yeah," Gary agreed, "and this is just the beginning. That device might be our greatest weapon against entropy. It brings simplicity and order to every interaction. Just look at its application here: exposing a scientific fraud that nobody would've otherwise discovered."

"I know it's caused sleepless nights for a lot of people in *my* line of work," Father Steve deadpanned. Startled, Gary looked at him, then laughed.

Judge Benat LeCagot announced, "Since there are no fact issues in dispute, prosecution and defense have waived jury participation. Therefore the AI machine will render sentence." He addressed the defendants: "Please rise." Binette and Noire almost jumped from their seats, trembling as they awaited the verdict. LeCagot read to the defendants from the screen of his IBM Solomon-4 justice AI:

"Both defendants will forfeit their entire estates including all future Prometheus royalties, such funds to be used for future cryonics research. They will immediately undergo suspended animation under the Prometheus Protocol. Should the Protocol work, they will someday rejoin the living. If not, may God have mercy on their souls."

Gary noticed that Noire appeared considerably more worried than did Binette.

> APRIL 17, 2033 — A computer designed by a team of Intel engineers scores 97 on a randomly configured human IQ test. Most pundits consider the team likely to win a Nobel science prize. — The American Real Estate Association projects that the present glut of office and retail properties will continue to worsen through the end of 2044, when cyber-commuting and cyber-shopping are expected to peak at 96% and 94% respectively. Currently, almost 20% of shopping and office work is still performed on premises. The AREA predicts further massive conversion of commercial space into residential and indoor farming usage.

Fazli Azambai shoved the ancient timing pencil into the last of the aged cakes of Sem-tex, and whispered an incantation to himself: "Verily, when Allah seeks the downfall of a culture, He first corrupts it with vanity."

The plastique explosive had been passed down to him from his father's father, a Mujahadeen freedom fighter against the atheist Russian invaders. The fifty-four-year-old Sem-tex had been purchased in dollars supplied by the American government during the Carter administration, and manufactured in Czechoslovakia, a long-defunct former Soviet satellite. Fazli found himself amused by the irony that his homeland's two greatest enemies had thus helped enable today's glorious endeavor. Now these fruits of Satan's wealth would be used, Allah be praised, to help stop the infidel madman, U.S. President David West, from erasing the Czech and Slovak's chosen borders—along with every other sovereign national border—to create a single World Government. With World Government in force, how could the independent state of Peshwar, with its huge ethnic Afghani majority, fully separate itself from Pakistan, that degenerate nation of westward-leaning sycophants?

Fazli molded the substance to the last of the carefully selected overhead lighting fixtures, set the final timer, collapsed the folding ladder, and returned it to its storage closet. Then, still wearing his stolen cleaning services uniform, he left the hotel.

With this act of heroism, his place in Paradise would be assured.

Within three hours he would abandon his Land Rover AI-Safari near the Hindu Kush Pass in his own Afghanistan, safely out of reach of Pakistani scips and extradition treaties.

Congressman   Wesley   Seacrest

(D. IA) and I, Trip Crane, now a twenty-seven-year-old MIT Assistant Professor of Nanotechnology, each suppressed an irrational impulse to shout obscenities at our Pakistani driver. Since meeting us at the airport in a driver-operated taxi—neither of us had seen a driver-operated car on public streets in over a decade—the man had already taken two wrong turns, hopelessly ensnaring us in a traffic jam.

"We'll never make it in time," the forty-nine-year-old politician complained. Wes tugged lightly on his blue ponytail. "I s'pose we'll catch hell for it, too."

"At least we sort of cancel each other out, don't we?" I said, and half chuckled. It was annoying to miss our most important round-table debate of the conference, but there was also something humorous about the whole situation, as if we'd somehow gone back in time to watch people muddle through life without the modern AIs.

"Yes, I suppose so. But I'd've enjoyed debating you again. Interesting that the Formation Council always schedules us to appear sequentially. I was especially looking forward to it. This time you were s'posed to go first."

I adjusted my earlobe microchip, absentmindedly coloring my eyeballs and most of my hair an iridescent lime-green. I glanced at my image on the backseat screen, and decided I liked the effect. I still looked decidedly male, but somehow feline, a green tiger, perhaps. "Then I guess I should be thankful we're late."

Seacrest caught a quick glimpse, too, and must have mused that even his own generation was not quite so over-the-top. "You're really opposed to a world government, aren't you, Trip?"

"I couldn't very well lie about my feelings with all those ACIPs pointed at me, now could I?"

"Guess not. But yours is an unusual position for a nanojock to take. Most of you fellas are running scared as jackrabbits at a dog-cloning center. 'Course, you guys actually *understand* what nanotech could do in the wrong hands."

"Yes, we do. But don't you think scips can prevent that?"

"Truth Machines won't prevent crimes in places where they aren't used, and if anyone can flee to jurisdictions where they'll be immune from punishment, how'll we stop 'em? Because with nanotech, we'd damn well better stop 'em all. Remember, criminals can be resourceful, and very evil."

"So can governments."

The Hyatt was now fully in view, a maddening ninety car lengths away.

"Looks like we'll only be fifteen or twenty minutes late," I was saying, just as the first- and second-floor facades of the hotel vanished into a cloud of smoke and flying debris.

We heard the roar of the explosion a second and a half after we saw it. The force of it snapped our heads back. For a moment the taxi seemed to buckle.

I leaned forward, trying to see through the smoke and haze. Debris lay everywhere; men and women slowly picked themselves up off the street. I heard screams all around and the piercing, painful blare of locked car horns.

My first jumbled thoughts were of the people inside the building. The dozens of scientists from all over the world. My mind groped for names; faces swam at me. The loss was catastrophic. The politicians, the diplomats. Jesus! Most with families at home.

Instantly I thought of my own parents. Rage flared. I'd been barely nine and a half when their plane crashed; then a decade of being nurtured back to some semblance of mental health, first by Uncle Gary, then by my grandmother and the therapeutic salvation of work. And (finally) the trial, only last year.

Now I pictured the faces of the three cowards who'd masterminded the airliner shoot-down. Seventeen years of living with the act had done a lot to temper their self-righteousness. Each had received a forty-year prison sentence under the Spanish Amnesty Act. With cryonics and nanomedicine, the bastards would probably all live to see the fourth millennium.

I felt my fist shatter the rear passenger window of the taxi. There was an instant of surprisingly sharp pain, fascinating in its rarity. As I stared at my bloodied hand, it took several seconds to realize that if they'd had a more competent driver today, Wes and I, too, would now be scattered among the smoldering debris.

OCTOBER 30, 2033 — The Tufts School of Dentistry files for patents on a one-hour surgical orthodontic procedure, which when performed on any normal 7-year-old will guarantee a lifetime of perfect tooth alignment. — Only 16 months after Intel created their computer of near-human intelligence, Sun Microsystems demonstrates a system capable of achieving test scores in excess of 180 IQ level. A company spokeswoman calls the advance "just the beginning," and predicts that Sun will bring a full line of advanced AI products to market within a year. — The FDA approves BioTime's "Respirocytes," the first nanotech protocol it has ever allowed on humans. The comput- erized machines, each of which comprise approximately 100 billion atoms and which can transport up to 50 billion air and nutrient molecules at a time, are somewhat smaller but much more efficient than the red blood cells they were designed to replace.

The skies remained dark, but stars were disappearing; the air felt calm and refreshingly chilled.

"You *ever* going to show me the thing?" Father Steve asked.

Both partly hoped it would be no time soon. With some goals, the pursuit is more gratifying than the realization. Of course, Gary would create other pictures, but perhaps never another like this. And whatever the public thought of *The Dawn of Life*, whether they spurned the art and the artist, or embraced both, the culmination of the work would leave an unexplainable emptiness within the hearts of these two men.

"Before too long," Gary answered solemnly, carefully steering the aluminum skiff through six sonar and microwave-surveillance buoys marking the small-craft lanes of Boston Harbor. "It's close, I think. And you'll be the first to see it. But not till it's ready."

Five minutes passed; the sun began to backlight the heavens. The two had already absorbed several dozen sunrises together, and Gary had seen at least a hundred others over the previous six months, from every vantage point imaginable. He still awaited that special convergence of color, light, and refractivity, a limpid impurity and brilliant haze that would define the moment, over three billion years ago, when that which was bare matter had all at once become more than itself.

The last stars were subsumed by their awaking master, and there it was.

Gary and Father Steve stood to witness the ascent of an inanimate object that rendered all life possible. The top of the great fireball bubbled from the eastern Atlantic like molten lava, its halo of ardent gold and red and magenta illuminating the wispy clouds and vaporous mists of morning; radiating a brilliant warmth that seemed to energize the billowing, oceanic earth.

Its sensors having alerted the freighter's AI that it had veered off course by nearly 150 yards and must correct immediately, a Russian container ship turned ponderously, like an oversized apotosaur plowing through a rain forest. Its 2,300-foot hull of reinforced steel and cerelium sliced through the water, displacing 137 billion gallons, throwing a seven-foot wake that would easily reach the shore several miles away.

"**That was it,**" the priest said. *"Wasn't it?"*

Gary nodded, his countenance a mirror of Father Steve's: achievement, anxious excitement, and regret—all commingled. Although he'd neglected to set his wristband on "Document," Gary now retained every nuance of today's sunrise, just as he'd memorized *The Dawn of Life* itself. Beyond any doubt, each would complete the other. It was almost over, nearly time to let the public submit its critique.

"Yes," he said, "that was the one."

They headed back into the bay, each still absorbed in the significance of today's milestone. Only Father Steve sensed the swell's approach, and had no time to scream. Therefore Gary was taken completely by surprise when the great surge, as tall as the men and higher than the boat's freeboard, reached them.

Their flimsy skiff was no match for the force of the roller, which slammed into it like a boy kicking an empty Coca-Cola carton. The two men were hurled twenty yards into the merciless ocean, with 1.6 miles of 37 degree Fahrenheit waters separating them from shore. A heavy current sucked them under.

By triangulating on life-monitor disaster signals from the wristband of one of the drowning men, a medevac gyrocopter crew managed to locate them within minutes. Undersea robots deployed from the chopper would raise their bodies from thirty-eight feet below the surface one hour and fifty-nine minutes later.

> AUGUST 12, 2034 — A series of 28 virtual reality probes land in Mercury's twilight zone. Within 16 days, astronomers from the U.S., Russia, India, and China will set up interactive environments on Earth to faithfully duplicate the surface conditions of various regions on the innermost planet of our solar system. Later this decade, similar probes, each individually designed to function in its intended nonterrestrial environment, will be sent to Venus, Jupiter, Saturn, Neptune, and each of their moons. — The United States becomes the last nation on Earth to legislate the insertion of routine, permanent contraceptive implants at birth. Before becoming pregnant, couples throughout the world must now pass a basic parenting test, and prove themselves competent, in order to obtain routinely granted procreation licenses and prophylactic overrides for both partners.

My grandmother, Rebecca Crane, settled into her front-row seat to watch me, her only breathing descendant, deliver an address in Los Angeles. Supersonic subways would not emerge for nearly five more years, but travel was already becoming much easier. Including transportation to and from airports, getting to the auditorium had consumed barely ninety minutes, and her return to Boston would require only eighty-five. Still, I was touched that she came. Grandmother hated to fly, of course. Too many painful memories.

Even with the passing of nineteen years, the irreversible loss of my father, her only son, had lost only its daily sting, becoming a duller but chronic discomfort, a cancer in her bones. Aunt Katie's death had been somehow easier for her; at least there had remained the prospect that someday she might return to the world of the living. Becoming guardian to me after my parents' tragedy, and raising me, may have somehow helped, too. I like to think so, anyway.

Now, at twenty-eight, I would be the next speaker at the Fourteenth Annual International Nanotechnology Conference. My invitation to deliver this keynote address had been unusual; eighty-two percent of INC lecturers this year were over fifty or under twenty. Only the older men and women could recount the genesis and history of nanotech and explore its emerging ethical and scientific disciplines. Youngsters, a solid five to ten years younger than I, were best at explaining how to design the machines, and how to create the redundant systems that precluded unpredictable and often dangerous mutations.

Grandmother watched vacantly as the aged nanotech pioneer, Dr. Marc Tarkington, concluded his talk, no doubt numbing her brain with his narratives of assemblers, disassemblers, and replicators; angstroms, carbyne chains, and memes; quantum mechanics, entropy, and the uncertainty principle. Her eyes were open but appeared unseeing, a condition she never displayed when listening to my public utterances, no matter how dry.

Was it because she loved me? I wondered. Or simply because I tried to make my lectures seem more conversational?

I'd been chosen to preach the political doctrine of the INC because I could express obscure concepts in accessible terms. At least that's what they'd told me. But I suspected that, as far as INC officials were concerned, it was even better that I happened to be the son of a well-known, martyred politician. The promoters of the conference must have reasoned that my speech would both attract and stimulate the nano-illiterate masses.

"Before I tell you why nanotech was such a dangerous development," I began, "let me first explain why it was possible to conceive it at all.

"Leonardo DaVinci envisioned heavier-than-air flight several centuries before it was ever accomplished. He thought it possible because he knew that birds, bats, and insects are heavier than air. Today no bird or bat can achieve even a remote fraction of the speed, power, or control of our modern machines of the sky.

"Late twentieth century scientists knew it was possible to build, on a molecular scale, machines with self-replicating, reversible, variable-speed motors a trillionth the size of those found in the children's toys of those days, because common bacteria already possessed such motors. In fact, those found in bacteria are only slightly larger than today's crude nanomotors."

Even though she'd heard similar statements from me before, Grandmother's expression cast a spontaneous sense of wonder.

"Nobel laureate Richard Feynman had stated—back in 1959, no less—that nanoassemblers were, quote, 'a development which I think cannot be avoided.' The greatest genius of late twentieth century physics foresaw both the benefits and dangers of molecular technology decades before his peers were even able to conceptualize its inevitability.

"Well before the new millennium, scientists were manipulating atoms and molecules as individual entities. In the 1980s, gene synthesis machines were already capable of sequencing single molecules, called nucleotides, to form DNA. In 1996 American scientists learned how to position individual molecules without damage, using flexible carbon nanotubes.

"It was also obvious to twentieth century scientists that we would someday create intelligences greater than our own. We knew even then that it was physically possible to build computers not just smaller and faster than the human brain, but also considerably more powerful. After all, smaller means faster. A human arm can flap a hundred times per minute, while an insect wing, a thousand times shorter, can flap 100,000 times. And electrical energy travels at a million times the speed of human nerve impulses."

Grandmother raised a questioning eyebrow. Even educated people were often unaware of this startling fact, although by 2034 schoolchildren invariably knew it.

"Indeed we would actually possess the technology, before the turn of the millennium, to simulate the workings of a human mind. We were limited not by abstract knowledge but by the enormous space and funding required to build a slow and commercially unwarranted electronic brain."

Grandmother's eyes came alive. I imagined she was recalling the forward march of computer technology during her own early years. She had never even owned a PC until she'd reached her thirties. Her first machine had been torturously slow, couldn't respond to speech, and covered most of her desk! Now, six-year-old kids wore a hundred times more computing power in their belt buckles or their pinkie rings.

"Remember," I went on, "even the smallest silicon chips back then were made from transistors comprising half a trillion atoms apiece. Yet almost every late twentieth century scientist agreed we would have unimolecular transistors by now—and, of course, *we do*. Most nanoscientists today believe that such transistors, currently maintainable only under sterile laboratory conditions, will be commercially viable within a decade.

"Already we can build a mechanical computer, as powerful as a turn-of-the-millennium 'laptop' but much faster—because it's so much smaller—in a space slightly larger than a human cell. In twenty years we'll assemble *electronic* computers perhaps a thousand times smaller and ten thousand times faster than those of today.

"We now have nanomotors smaller and mightier than a bacterium's, constructed atom by atom, molecule by molecule, from ceramics and metals far more durable and predictable than proteins. Don't forget, nature typically demonstrates only the lower boundaries of the possible."

Grandmother smiled, nodding her head, envisioning, perhaps, an eagle racing a mach-seven luxury liner, or someday, a starship.

"We can already build computerized machines powered by today's smallest motors, and your smallest capillaries could easily accommodate hundred-lane superhighways of such machines. Yet nanoscience is still an infant; a precocious one, but an infant nonetheless.

"We should also have realized long ago that self-replicating intelligent machines had the potential to take over, or even destroy, the world; because we ourselves are such machines, and very crudely fashioned as compared to that which physical law allows.

"Imagine a machine the size of a single human cell, possessing humanlike intelligence and ability to communicate, but with immensely greater clarity and speed of thought. And imagine that machine, if you dare, as an entity devoid of comparative experience, philosophy, and objective purpose beyond survival and procreation. Imagine it as a tiny, hyperintelligent tiger shark. Now give that machine the ability to reproduce itself every fifteen minutes. Such a machine, the fabrication of which the laws of physics in no way prohibit, could devour the earth in thirty-six hours, and ten hours later engulf the entire mass of our solar system.

"Of course, these machines must be designed by humans, or by AIs thankfully at our command, and you'd have to be insane to want to build something destined to destroy you. But it would be a simple matter to make the machines selective; perhaps consume only your enemies, leaving yourself and your friends.

"A nanowar could make us all nostalgic for the nuclear terrorism of the early twenty-first century.

"Here is the reality check, ladies and gentlemen: With the science that will be available to me fifteen years from now, I could get together with five or six friends and assemble in my basement the very machine I have just described. Three decades from now, there will be tens of millions of *individuals* with that capability. Only one of those people need go insane for a moment, and poof! The end of humanity. It's a good thing we have the Software Act and a Truth Machine, isn't it?

"I once argued against a world government," I admitted. "But in the world as it has become, I now see no safe alternative to a well-reasoned central authority, embodying a single root axiom: that no person need fear any other, because the mere *intention* to murder or subjugate a peer would be impossible to sustain, and murder itself would inevitably become an act of suicide."

Grandmother smiled through glistening eyes. Dreaming of her lost son—my lost father—I knew. I returned her smile.

> JUNE 15, 2042 — Scientists at Eastman Kodak say they have developed an artificial eye and compatible occipital lobe implant which together can enable even congenitally blind persons to achieve nearly normal eyesight. They expect to bring the device to market within four months. — The mayors and city councils of Detroit and Windsor, Ontario, announce plans to unify the two city governments immediately upon installation of World Government, expected to take place in about three years. The two cities have functioned in near unison for the past two decades. Windsor Mayor Gordon Lightfoot III is quoted, "We've done much to erase large artificial boundaries; why not small?" The merged city, to be renamed Michigan Shores, will become the world's 17th largest.

Alica Banks, a legal historian, and Dr. Virginia Gonzalez, the renowned neuroscientist, sat nervously on an interview couch at the Boston Eugenics Laboratory while the nanomachines spun twenty-eight of Virginia's embryos into sperm. To get any closer, one woman would have to have climbed onto the other's lap. Alica had never meant to fall in love with someone of her own gender, and indeed until she met Virginia six years before, had always enjoyed a healthy sexual appetite for men. But reproduction was no longer the exclusive province of heterosexuals, and with medical advances offering longer life spans and greater opportunity for experimentation, most vestiges of familial stigma over gay or bisexual lifestyles had been erased. At the age of thirty-four Alica had, for sixty-one months, been comfortably and happily wedded to this fifty-three-year-old woman. Today the couple was about to embark upon an adventure.

"Boy or girl?" the AI machine asked.

"We don't care."

"Intelligence?"

"Highest importance," Virginia said. Alica nodded.

"Physical characteristics?"

"Tall would be nice," Virginia said.

"But only if all other considerations are equal," Alica added, thinking it would be foolish even to give up a one percent loss of intelligence for six inches in height.

"Any special family traits we should look for?"

Alica answered. "Virginia's mother was an Olympic swimmer, and my great-uncle was Gary Franklin Smith, the painter."

The AI intoned: "Out of forty-eight pairings with perfect genetic physical and mental health, we have one that is exceptional athletically and artistically, and another that's off the charts in aesthetic perception, but only of average athletic endowment. Each would be a brown-eyed female; the former would be six feet tall, the later five-eleven."

Virginia and Alica smiled at each other. "We'll take the second one," they proclaimed in unison.

Conveniently, the two women found themselves in the midst of an obstetric technological revolution. Cloning, also known as parthenogenetics, the precursor of same-sex parenthood, had become legal in the United States in July 2034, a decade after the first successful adult human cloning in France. Same-sex parenthood, or homo-genetics, had first been offered in the United States in May 2042, and Alica Banks would be among the first one hundred women in the Boston area to try it. (Male couples would require a female surrogate until pods became available in 2045.)

The Eugenics Laws, to govern selective breeding of humans, had been passed in August 2022. The Democrats had been in power that year, and President Gordon Safer had wisely pushed for unilateral parental control. Granted, had the government been involved in eugenic decision-making, characteristics such as honesty and emotional self-control might have pervaded today's teenage population at only slight cost to vivacity and physical beauty. Nevertheless, government interference, or even incentives, would have wrought unforeseeable political and social consequences, perhaps even some diminution of the bond of love between parent and child.

As it turned out, fears of unleashing a billion self-absorbed geniuses upon an ill-prepared world were unfounded. In fact, parents tended toward the selection of more socially valuable qualities for their offspring than they might have chosen for themselves: intellectual honesty, emotional intelligence, and compassion, among others.

This new generation of humans was the first to be unambiguously smarter, taller, and genetically healthier than its antecedent, proving that even on its worst day, technology is an infinitely more efficient engine of change than natural selection could ever hope to be.

Most historical texts of the times were already speculating that the Eugenics Laws should probably have been enacted at least five years sooner than they had. More than enough technology had been available in 2017 to justify eugenic manipulation. But the field had still been laboring under the stigma of Josef Mengele's ghastly experiments. Indeed, the atavistic connection between Hitler and eugenics had delayed its acceptance for several years at great societal cost; yet another insidious echo from the Nazis.

Alica's parents, Michael and Joanne Banks, were pleased with their daughter's match and supportive of her decision to have a child. "You might wish you'd waited a couple more years," Joanne had said. "They'll have pods by early 'forty-five. Pregnancy can be most unpleasant. Take it from me. I know. But more important, honey, there are inherent risks you simply don't have to take."

Virginia and Alica found the six-hour parenting class easy, almost fun, and their license had been granted immediately after passing the exam, as was customary.

The early 2040s had witnessed a substantial decline in births, but the advances of 2045 would usher in an American baby boom unprecedented since the decades following World War Two.

Ectogenesis, the nanotech-based science of artificial wombs, would be the primary force behind both statistical anomalies: decline and boom. Prior to the announced coming of the pods, women had often succumbed to peer pressure and the joy-rush of oxytocin, extolling the glories of in utero gestation and childbirth, reinventing an unavoidable hardship and danger as a thing of beauty. But once most women learned of procreation-without-pregnancy, it was hard to convince them to linger in the pre-ectogenetic desert. Joy with pain or joy without it? Few found the choice difficult.

Alica was an exception. But even one so resolute could not avoid at least occasional doubts over so brave a decision, especially on March 6, 2043. Although biochemical convenatives would block any actual pain that she chose to intermit, Alica would still hear and taste, see and smell, the wrenching and sudden rupture from her uterus of ten pound, seven ounce Lysa Banks Gonzalez.

Yet after the birth, even the memories of her doubts would begin to evaporate, as they always had in the analgesic balm of human motherhood, and for many months Alica Banks would feel little else but love, parental anxiety, and pride.

> JUNE 15, 2045 — The World Health Department approves ICN Pharmaceutical's new cloning process whereby perfect hearts, livers, kidneys, and other organs can be grown from the patient's own cells in just 32 months. Previously, most organ clonings required six years or longer. ICN Chairman Vaclav Panic says he expects to cut the cycle to under two years by decade's end. — Union Carbide releases Windowpane, a nuclear waste disposal system expected to revolutionize the field. Windowpane encases debris in a glasslike amalgam of silicon, cadmium, carbon, sodium, mercury, tin, and zirconium, which absorbs 99.9997% of neutron radiation.

"The human race," the World President began, "has stumbled and been dragged into accepting the reality of our nature, and now it actually appears we might overcome our genetically programmed propensity for self—"

Woof!

Huh? Self-destruction, I guessed. I was trying to listen to former Russian deputy Prime Minster Boris Malinkov's inaugural address in Sydney, but that would have been difficult enough without my golden retriever there. Wendy displayed uncanny timing, each bark coinciding with the new World President's most interesting pronouncements.

Malinkov continued: "I suspect we have now woven history's experience into the best form of government we could design. It won't be perfect, of course. Even democratic governments are careless and occasionally do evil things, but rarely have they been inherently evil. Indeed, democratic leaders are elected by convincing voters they will contribute to the greater good of society. Rather, our foremost adversaries are now laziness, ineptitude, ignorance, and of course—" *Yip!*

Secrecy. I contemplated with a mixture of amusement and irony that Malinkov would likely have far less power over his coming three-year term than the man had wielded in his previous post. Although I'd voted for Malinkov with enthusiasm, a single notion now emerge: Thank God for that!

"Bureaucracies," the President went on, "have always had a vested interest in the clandestine. Bureaucrats, seeking ever-increasing budgets, hid their mistakes. Regulators knew they would endure more censure when their actions caused ten deaths than when their inaction killed hundreds, so they mismanaged accordingly. Special interests purchased access to politicians and bureaucrats, and peddled their agendas, ignoring public welfare. All this was no more evil than human nature itself, yet the result was fiendish.

"But with objectively rated, scip-tested, freely accessed, open information—an end to all government secrecy—our bureaucracies will be more accountable than any in human history. Make no mistake about it: Without Truth Machine scips, World Government would be neither practical nor desirable. Or even possible."

I raised the volume to drown out any future interruptions from Wendy. I was attending the speech from my laboratory, having activated my auricle-implant receiver and right contact-lens screen, but now I used my left eye to proofread the latest neuron repair protocols. I knew I shouldn't forego real-time communion with such a momentous historical event, but wasn't the work even more critical?

"Aristotle once warned that the only true evil is ignorance."

And therefore the opposite of evil, I thought, must be wisdom.

"World Government is the final step in humankind's race against the evasion of objective reality."

I gently stroked the fur of the creature at my feet, the seventy-one pound animal that had been my day-and-night companion for the past decade. It was well past nap time. Wendy was tired, almost asleep.

"We cannot govern ourselves," Malinkov continued, "based upon an ideal of human nature. We must deter every human being from intentionally or negligently harming any other, except in self-defense or objectively calculated, government-sanctioned deterrence.

"What is the World Government's stand on religion? None, other than universal religious freedom for every individual. What is our position on licensing? None, other than to assure, using scips, that individuals who intend to illegally injure others are denied licenses for transportation, commerce, employment, parenting, weapon ownership, and all other dangerous activities. What is our stand on suicide? Previability birth control? Eugenics? Public health? Education? Building codes? Again none, except to document the integrity of every business and agency providing such services, allowing consumers to intelligently choose their own providers."

Now I heard a loud snore. I tickled Wendy's ribs. As always, she rolled slightly but did not awaken. The snoring stopped.

"Our role," Malinkov droned on, "is merely to enforce the following objectively quantifiable principles:

"(1) Total freedom of the press.

"(2) Universal free trade.

"(3) The legal right of every human being to full protection under the law, with all laws uniformly enforceable upon all individuals throughout all regions.

"(4) The constitutional responsibility of every . . ."

Glancing at my photon-microscope screen, I noticed in the sample a dendritic texture I'd never been able to link. Maybe something to do with muscle constriction?

That was when I stopped hearing Malinkov's words or noticing his face. I became too engrossed in the work, my only reliable escape from grief that could otherwise still overhwelm.

Human gray matter had become, to me, the most fascinating substance in the universe, a marvel of complexity. I tried to fathom the sheer magnitude: Each brain actually contained *many sextillions* of molecular machines. *One* sextillion would be more than fifteen times the number of connections required to link all eight billion people on Earth to every other person! No wonder humans had always refused to think of themselves as mere machines. The brain was far too complex to fathom in those terms. It would be like calling the Sistine Chapel an amalgam of wood and paint.

The study of the brain was nanotech's critical frontier. Scientists had long ago discredited the tenets of vitalism: that humans possessed souls apart from physical matter. The brain's enormous complexity was now deemed finite, and therefore ultimately fathomable.

Near-death experiences, for example, had been synthesized decades earlier by carefully depriving volunteers' brain and eyes of blood flow. These had been categorized into seventeen distinct types. Now AI machines could actually predict which type of "NDE" any individual's rods and cones would project into their ebbing consciousness.

There was no apparent reason why evolution would have induced dying human brains to dream of the tunnel and the white light. Yet so many of them did. Perhaps NDEs were simply one of humanity's many gifts from God.

The newest science continued to suggest that personality, identity, and all long-term memory were recorded through the continuous reorganization of protein molecules in the brain's neurons. Perhaps some short-term memory was energy-related, or recorded at the subatomic level, but that hypothesis seemed unlikely. Probably, every facet of human thought boiled down to the sextillions of protein molecules, or at worst, the atoms composing them; hopeful tidings for anyone who happened to lay frozen in soft-nite.

> AUGUST 14, 2051 — Lunar Power Systems announces plans to build 41,600 additional collectors on the moon's surface. LPS already supplies 29% of the earth's energy needs, and the new construction will double its capacity. CEO Rob Campbell explains, "The moon is an ideal environment for collecting solar energy, since it has no atmosphere and the iron and silicon needed for solar power collectors are abundant." Once collected, the energy is converted to microwaves and transmitted to receivers on Earth. — Reacting to public uproar over six irreversible deaths caused so far this year by intoxicated or sleep-deprived pilots, Raytheon announces it will add competence sensors to all its gyrocopters within 24 months. The new devices will prevent the machines from starting unless the operator is sober, drug-free, and alert.

Now forty-five years of age, I'd never felt pressure to marry. Of course I knew the AI shrinks would blame such inconstancy on childhood loss of both parents and the inevitable fear-of-attachment such tragedies produce. My few relationships with women had been pleasant, tender, and brief.

But Wendy-girl was a different story.

For sixteen years I'd brought Wendy everywhere with me: to the lab, to meetings, to conferences around the world. Giants of international science must have found themselves bemused by the spectacle of this well-known nanoscientist, hands and knees on the conference floor, coaxing my golden retriever to walk on hind legs, or to lift her snout and sing along with me.

That is, until the day, three months ago, when the decay of her advanced age had forced me to place her in biostasis.

Coincidentally, Wendy's suspension took place the day after the Armstrong Aging Models had been released. The foremost software genius of the twenty-first century had spent the previous two decades working with an array of state-of-the-art AI machines to produce the most intricate programming in history, allowing biologists and other researchers to perform quantifiable cyberspace experiments on human aging.

Of course, Randall Petersen Armstrong's work was readily applicable to canines, a reality not lost on me.

Even before Wendy's suspension, I'd begun studying the phenomenon of aging with an obsession matching my previous delvings into nanotech and neuroscience. My own appointment with death-or-ice seemed too distant to warrant preparation—my present prebiostasis life expectancy was at least 110—but the impending demise of my first golden retriever had filled me with an overwhelming sense of urgency.

O v e r   t h e   p r e v i o u s half century, even as medical knowledge expanded exponentially, the fundamental theories of aging had changed little. Most specialists still believed that aging arose from a combination of three factors:

(1) Ionization damage to molecules and DNA caused mainly by natural oxidation, primarily free radicals. Most of this damage was redressed by the body's natural systems, but over time the cumulative damage to DNA diminished this ability to self-repair, and eventually overwhelms it.

(2) Hormonal decline, and degradation of body tissue through processes such as glycation, when proteins and surplus sugars combine to form a crust that can block arteries, stiffen joints, and pollute organs and other vital structures.

(3) A natural aging "clock" built into all mammals. After a certain number of cell divisions, telomeres would shorten, rendering cells incapable of further reproduction.

I considered myself qualified to work on anti-aging research, since nanotech seemed the most promising vehicle for overcoming all three of aging's presumed causes. The body was, after all, a machine, not unlike a very complicated computer.

To repair a damaged computer, a technician needed to identify the defective parts, remove them, rebuild or replace them, and put them back where they belong. No other scientific discipline was equal to the task. Imagine trying to accomplish computer repair using chemicals (medicines), or tools a billion times larger than the parts being replaced (microsurgery). Yet pharmacology and microsurgery remained the only tools available to fix a damaged "human machine."

I reasoned that eventually nanotech, in tandem with ever-advancing AI systems, would change that. And somehow, I would be part of it. In fact, the day the Truth Machine trillionaire had released the Armstrong Aging Model, I obtained a copy of the software and set to work.

Three days after Wendy's suspension, I purchased another golden retriever puppy. Sure that someday Wendy-girl would emerge from the ice, I wondered whether my affection for this new pet might eventually match the love I'd felt for my first. How would I divide my love between the two? Would they love one another as sisters, or would there be tantrums of jealousy?

After careful consideration, I decided to name my new, second puppy—*what else?*—Wendy.

> JUNE 3, 2064 — Avon Cleaner's landmark location on Lover's Lane in Dallas Texas reopens as a 20th century clothing museum. The dry-cleaning establishment closed its doors nearly two decades ago, a casualty of the pervasiveness of self-cleaning apparel. — After 16 months of difficulties and delays, the supersonic elevator to WASA's orbiting Copernicus-6 space observatory is finally declared operational. Because Copernicus-6 orbits Earth in perfect sync with the planet's rotation, WASA AIs deemed the station the ideal first recipient of this ground-breaking technology. The 96-mile edifice, composed almost entirely of carbon-based nanotubes, twelve times stronger and eight times lighter than steel, is by far the tallest structure in the world.

I held my (second) Wendy-girl close. As she snuggled in my fifty-eight-year-old, never-married arms, she discharged a sound that was part sigh, part grunt, the very essence of contentment.

How could I do this? I thought. Then: How could I not? The "subject" had to be well-taught, with a wide range of responses and a significant recognition-range of vocabulary. It was also best that the subject be of a certain age, with all the inevitable costs to brain and body.

I rocked Wendy II in my Roswell chair. So little time was left. So little time. Thirteen years ago she'd come to me at seven weeks of age, a frolicky vessel of joy. I'd loved her well and had found the gift more than requited.

But there was really no choice, was there? Not when we'd come this far . . .

The first hurdle we nanoscientists had cleared in our efforts to reverse biostasis was the challenge of building machines that could operate at liquid nitrogen temperatures. This problem had been solved by assembling the first machines from molecules more versatile than the proteins they were designed to repair.

Other protein machines had been programmed to work like enzymes, bonding molecules together one by one, assembling exact, predesigned, metallic and ceramic structures. The first such machines, assembled in 2029, were operated by simple on-board computers with tiny but flawless memories and ten million times human speed-of-thought.

By 2037, engineers had constructed the first disassemblers, composed of a mechanical computer roughly three microns cubed, the equivalent of about one-fortieth of a human cell, and a casing about sixty times larger than the computer, with eight arms composed of iron atoms. The first disassemblers could remove molecules from a structure, layer by layer, recording the identity and content of each molecule.

Redundant systems limited the pace of the earliest nanomachines to a glacial 2,500 molecules per second, too slow for cellular repair by a factor of at least two orders of magnitude (100 times). At that speed, except at sub-freezing temperatures, decay would occur faster than repair, and the machines were too large for deployment in frozen organisms. Yet at least two million removals per second seemed achievable.

In 2043, the first replicating assemblers had been built. These devices could not only assemble molecules based on instructions received via radiolike devices from any compatible AI system, but could also reproduce themselves. Parts were never a problem, since atoms do not require pre-manufacturing. Thus assemblers had suddenly become cheap—virtually free—spurring an explosion of nanotech research and efficiencies.

Still, numerous safeguards had to be built into the original programming to prevent anyone from building anything dangerous, and these safeguards had slowed the machines' performance. They'd also kept their size too large for most medical applications.

Throughout the successive twenty years, nanomachines had gradually become faster and smaller. Over the past half decade, I'd assembled my own team of eight nanotech and AI engineers and scientists.

"Science and engineering are two different disciplines," I'd told them. "True scientists are interested only in concepts that can be proven through experiment and observation; pure theory is useless to them. Engineers, on the other hand, try to uncover *close-enough* solutions to specific problems under specific conditions. And I need both."

After five years, we'd built a series of replicators and disassembler/assemblers that seemed suited for biostasis reversal; the first units capable of both dis- and reassembly that were also small enough to penetrate frozen bloodstreams. The D/A's each contained a tiny computer capable of holding more information than DNA does. These in turn were connected by radio-like devices to a network of much larger central computers.

By law, we'd been required to design replicators devoid of survival skills, and with redundant systems that automatically repaired mutations. The machines could reproduce themselves, build the D/A's to specification, and nothing more. It was an irritating law, I'd often mused, but a sensible one.

Also required, and equally rational, was that all nanotech experiments be performed in palm-sized sealed laboratories using Molecular Reconstruction Software. We could hook these mini-workshops into any two-way screen and actually build every nanomachine we designed, using an array of sample atoms and molecules right there in the lab. We could even insert genetic materials to test the machines. But if anyone tried to unseal the lab to remove the physical machines, electrical charges would vaporize the contents. Thus we could design and test nanomachines, but the machines themselves couldn't be unleashed until their capabilities had been analyzed and cleared.

Last week, the World Government Nanotech Agency had issued a permit and instruction code enabling us to build the replicators outside our sealed labs.

Now we were ready to rock and roll.

Gathered in my living room, the entire team watched the demonstration.

"Wendy," I said in what I hoped was an uninflected conversational voice, but I did not—could not—look at her. "May I have my remote activator, please?"

Wendy II slipped from my arms, found the device under a pillow, picked it up between her teeth, and gently placed it on my knee.

"Wendy, I'd love a ginger ale." I activated the remote.

The dog's footfalls receded. I heard the gentle whirring of the kitchen assembler as it spun mostly hydrogen, oxygen, and carbon atoms into my favorite formula. Then I heard the custom tray being assembled and lowered to dog level, and Wendy's paws against the floor as she returned, tray in jaw.

Within sixty seconds, the refreshment had been delivered.

I placed the soda on the nearest wall shelf, lifted Wendy-girl into my arms, and walked stiffly toward the door. We all took the first elevator down to the lab. Although the ride lasted nearly forty seconds, I would be unable to recall any of it. I can assure you that such unreality is wholly unfamiliar to a man grounded in the world of absolutes.

Later that evening I would view the Audio Vid record, and watch in horror as my assistant, Paul Adler, had reached to take the dog from my arms. I would see and hear myself—me, Trip Crane—bellowing, "No!" then releasing her despite my own protestations. Such lapse of decorum; such lapse of memory. Had it really happened?

Wendy II now lay frozen to minus 196 degrees C, where she would remain for fifteen more days, perhaps having already suffered irreversible brain damage. Because she'd trusted me. Had I betrayed that trust for a mere theory?

> JUNE 28, 2064 — Compaq stock soars after the company demonstrates, to rave reviews, its new Artificial Bloodhound documentation upgrade. The product can be added to any wristband PC to record odors as accurately as PCs now document by sight and sound. AB continuously samples air in the vicinity, and analyzes it, recording scents, trace elements, even DNA from people who exhale near the user. Experts predict that most new wristband PCs will carry the enhancement by early next year. — The World Parenting Department issues its one millionth license, since the agency's inception in 2045, to raise clones of deceased relatives. Most such permits have been granted within the last four years.

The work on Wendy II began promptly at six A.M., although most of the nine team members had been there since five-thirty. I'd been unable to sleep during the previous twenty-three hours. Today's outcome would be critical, and there were simply too many unknowns. Notions of potential disasters had jolted my brain like dozens of tiny alarm clocks.

Even without cryoprotectants,

freezing damage is subtle. Cells do not burst. Occasionally, however, their outer membranes may puncture from the expansion of water, which comprises nine-tenths of their volume. More often, just a tiny percentage of cells are damaged, usually when some molecules are misplaced, and many of these molecules return to their correct positions upon thawing. Indeed, countless living humans, some born as long ago as the late twentieth century, had once been frozen at liquid nitrogen temperature, as embryos.

But postembryonic mammals are delicates; even a slight disruption of the molecular structures in an infinitesimal percentage of its cells will render the entire organism nonviable. Freezing damage at liquid nitrogen temperature, while narrow in one sense, is millions of times more extensive than a mammalian body can withstand or self-repair.

Before February 2064, no mammal had ever been deep-frozen and then successfully revived, so there was no way to know if the nongenetic memories of those creatures had survived intact.

Wendy had been vitrified, which minimized disruption damage but created a new problem: removing the glassy sap cross links holding the molecules in place. That would be the first task of the three trillion disassembler/assembler machines, nearly half a pound of them, deployed through Wendy's vascular system.

Dr. Abel Dewar injected the D/A's through a microscopic perforation in Wendy's chest. The machines received no help from the frozen bloodstream, yet within seconds spread their way through the dog's veins, arteries, and capillaries. The cryoprotectant removal was accomplished in 128 minutes.

The machines returned to their positions, guided by nearly a billion nanocomputers intespersed among them, each a thousand times larger than the D/A's themselves. (The concoction now weighed eleven ounces.) This army of machines would require sixteen hours to effect repairs, and to thaw and revive Wendy. If nothing went wrong, which was unlikely.

The first fourteen hours saw no serious emergencies, as expected. Every living cell was static. Such is the beauty of cryonic suspension: It virtually halts every retrogressive biological effect of time's passage. The thawing would be the difficult part.

We nine pioneers of nanosicence monitored progress like zealous sports fans; as if by watching intently enough, we might somehow affect the outcome. We sat transfixed, staring at our 3-D screens or hooked to VRs while the D/A's began the tedious process of cell repair, and replacement wherever aging had destroyed entire cells.

Despite her near perfect vitrification, Wendy's DNA strands now averaged an error every 640,000 nucleotides, more than sufficient to wreak havoc. Nearly all of this was freezing damage that happened as they warmed her up, the remainder being from normal radiation that had occurred over Wendy's life. But we believed nanomachines could repair it all, and much more efficiently than her body's natural repair enzymes could ever hope to.

Using central computers, a perfect DNA map had been constructed during the first few seconds of the process. The D/A's had compared eighty randomly selected strands of DNA. Even this was overkill. The odds of any

error occurring in three of more strands out of five would have been virtually zero. But I figured comparing eighty strands was no more time-
consuming than comparing five, so what the hell? The actual examination
and repair of over twenty trillion cells, however, would require considerably more time: fourteen monotonous, nerve-wracking, and ultimately
uneventful hours.

By ten P.M. the repairs were complete, and Wendy II now
possessed all the cellular structures of youth; a three-year-old dog's unim-
paired enzymes, collagen, bone and muscle strength, and immune system.
At that moment, she boasted the most perfect DNA of any canine adult on
earth. Technically, her age was still nearly thirteen, so the "genetic clock"
mechanism in her cells would likely kill her off within nine more years
despite the repairs, unless a way to reverse the clock were discovered by
then. But if everything went as planned, she would soon have the energy,
strength, and resiliency she'd possessed ten years before. If there had been
no mistakes. If only we could be sure . . .

At 10:27 P.M. the first warning signal beeped.

"What the heck is that?" Stephanie Van Winkle, Abel's assistant,
asked.

"Damn! Of course," the medico answered. "Soon as she started
thawing, her body would've noticed the invaders, and now her immune
system's been activated. Never could've predicted such a violent reaction,
though . . ."

"Jesus! It's going nuts," I blurted as I stared at the infrared $10^9 \times$
image on my 3-D visor.

"T-cells can't hurt the machines," Stephanie assured me. "Protein's a
lot softer than iron."

"True," Abel answered, "the *machines'll* be fine. But if her immune
system exhausts itself, *Wendy* could die from infection. We'd better do
something quick."

"Any ideas?" Carlos Platt, the AI engineer, asked.

"Maybe g16 steroids?" Abel suggested. "A seventeenth- or eighteenth-
generation formula might be too human-specific."

My adrenaline took over. Within five seconds I'd punched into my
module the drug-licensing order to Amgen. It took another twenty-five seconds for the assembler to spin the proper dose, and barely that for Abel to
inject the medicine. Two minutes later the first crisis was over, just as a new
one began.

Wendy's respiration hadn't resumed when she first started shivering. Suddenly she took a deep, labored breath. Then she sneezed.

Sneezed?! I'd rarely seen an involuntary sneeze since Merck's Allergone protocol had been added to commercial drinking water decades earlier.

"Is it life-threatening?" Abel asked.

"You mean you don't know?" Panic must have been obvious in my voice.

"Might just be a chill," Stephanie said. Wishful thinking.

"Jesus Christ, answer me! Is it life-threatening?!" Abel shouted.

I stared quizzically at the doctor. Of course! He was asking the remote medical AI. But was it *on*? "Activate Canine HealthFile," I said, then repeated Abel's query, "Is it life-threatening?"

"Not immediately," the AI intoned, having instantly assimilated the data from the central nanocomputers inside Wendy's body and determined her prognosis. "The subject can survive approximately six minutes without treatment, but permanent brain damage might occur sooner."

"What he hell's wrong with her?" I shouted.

"She has a mild allergic sensitivity," sang the AI's voice.

"To *what*?!"

"Iron."

I tried to stop shaking. My Wendy-girl, three trillion nanomachines spread throughout her body, was allergic to—could you believe this stinking luck?—iron.

"Damn!" Abel said. "That must be why her rejection mechanism was so violent. Can you spin an antihistamine?"

I had the assembler programmed before Abel finished asking the question, but genetic engineering had vanquished human allergies decades ago, and the machine had to back-order the protocol from Searle, squandering 253 precious seconds. The doctor measured the dosage and injected Wendy, five minutes and nine seconds after her allergic reaction had begun.

Shit! Five goddamn minutes.

My eyes pleaded with Abel. "Well, is she gonna be . . . okay . . . or not?"

"Too soon to tell about her brain, but her nervous system's a mess."

"Can't the machines repair nerve damage?"

"Already working on it."

I tried to comfort my pet, but Wendy II stared back with vacant, anguished, unrecognizing eyes. She began to hyperventilate, and suddenly let loose with a scream that seemed to emerge from her heart, freezing all of us into postures of shock, until finally she subsided into a pathetic, continuous whimper.

I yelled to Abel, "Put her under. Now!"

Abel administered IV anesthetics; seconds later my dog was unconscious. I wondered if she would ever wake up, and more to the point, wondered if I wanted her to. My poor, sweet girl, I thought. What have I done to you?

"I guess there probably aren't too many experiences more painful than having a billion machines repairing every nerve cell in your body," Stephanie suggested, hugging me. The twenty-eight-year-old technician had worked for me for five years and had never so much as shaken my hand before that moment. "The machines have done their best; we've done our best. Well just have to wait until she wakes up."

The rest of the group gathered around, offering words of reassurance. "Still, she could be okay."

"It's too soon to tell."

"You did all you could, Trip."

"She really might be fine."

"Absolutely," Abel added. "Tomorrow, ol' Wendy-girl could be prancing around like none of this ever happened."

"You never know," I answered in a stoic voice. But trembling hands betrayed my thoughts: What had I been thinking? Who the hell did I think I was to risk her life like that?

3

THE MILLENNIUM OF HOPE

I lowered my head, turned away from the others, and absently set my primary AI on manual. A table and keyboard grew from the wall. I typed: WHO AM I? then gazed at the words that had formed on my screen:

Who are you?
Or more precisely, *what* are you?
You, George Jacob Crane III, are a carbon-based life-form, approximately 90 percent hydrogen and oxygen atoms by weight, a member of the species *Homo sapiens*.
But what is your essence? What differentiates you from the billions of other humans with whom you share this planet?
Imagine it is the turn of the millennium, and I am your 20th-century laptop. There are countless computers identical to me; same hardware, same operating system. Yet unless you

could transfer my data, you might not trade me for 100 others, freshly minted in their boxes. The vessel is replaceable, but the information is priceless.

Now suppose I were smashed with a hammer or dropped from a fourth-story window. My data might well be salvaged.

But were I to be melted in a vat of acid along with my backup discs, oh woe!

You, sir, could be described in similar terms. Should your heart stop beating, doctors might restore you to life, a miracle not possible just 50 years ago. Yet once your brain cells die, 20th century science cannot resuscitate you. During the next century that may change, and it is certain that life and death will continue to be redefined. Even before the third millennium, organs are routinely transplanted from one person to another. Personalities are altered with medications. Artificial hearts and kidneys are used routinely. If your species survives long enough, the 20th century's most feared diseases will become curable. Intelligence, even wisdom, will be artificially enhanced, and emotions finetuned. There will be cloning and eventually a halt to the molecular processes of aging. It is only a matter of time.

This reality may not yet be evident, but in the future you'll understand that ordered information, like the digital bits in my computer, comprises all memory, thought, emotion, perception, and consciousness: the totality of that unique essence which is you. Humans might achieve such an immortality through the simple preservation of each brain s unique information. Everything else about you is replaceable, or someday may be.

Who are you? Your essence is information about the unique experiences, emotions, and

thoughts of your life; perhaps nothing more,
and unquestionably nothing less.

JUNE 29, 2064 — Never Apart, the world's third largest teledildonics agency, settles a lawsuit filed against it by two couples
whose semblances were mistakenly transposed and projected
to the wrong bodysuit, causing each of the four to engage in
virtual sex with the wrong partner. A spokesman for the firm
says, "It was an isolated incident, which has never happened
before and probably never will again. Teledildonics is still the
ideal way for separated lovers to 'keep in touch.' " — The
number of languages spoken in transactional discourse on
earth falls below 1,000 for the first time in recorded history, an
82% drop in just 50 years. Some experts predict that by mid-
millennium, English and Mandarin Chinese will be the only
languages still in general use.

None of us had slept. Around midnight we'd brought Wendy II up to my
apartment. Now spread out in chairs, the couch, or on the floor, my eight
associates had been keeping vigil with me. We were family now, and
Wendy was one of our own.

"Y'know, Trip," Paul Adler said, "even if Wendy has brain damage,
we could freeze her again. There's a decent chance they'll be able to bring
her back within a decade."

"That's pretty to think, Paul," I answered, "but it could be more like a
century."

"Why do you say that?" asked our AI engineer. "Once we're reviving
people en masse, the sciences now advancing in short hops will suddenly
take giant leaps. And other technologies are bound to sprout from them."

"We can fix brain damage *now*," Stephanie volunteered.

"Not all of it," I said.

"Not yet," she said, "but by the time the nanomachines revive a few
dozen undamaged humans, the AIs'll know everything about our brains.
They'll teach the brain-repair D/A's to pattern language skills into any
brains that've lost them. Same goes for sensory interpretation, history, science, aesthetics, math; all the basic, well, software, I guess. We'll clone new
cells to replace those damaged beyond restoration. In ten years, I'd bet just
about every person who comes out of biostasis will be smarter than he or she
was when frozen, smarter than *ever* before. The same can be done for
Wendy."

"But we can never restore lost memories," I said, "or reconstruct identity. Even if we put her in biostasis and wait till the science matures, we'll just wind up with a healthy, smart new puppy in Wendy's body."

"Better than nothing," Stephanie said.

"Maybe not, at least not as far as *she's* concerned. To her, it'll be as though she went to sleep and never woke up. Without memory, she'll just be another golden retriever, a new dog composed of Wendy's atoms. She won't be Wendy anymore, not for herself, not for me."

"Well, don't give up yet," Stephanie rubbed my back. It helped. "She'll be conscious within the hour. And she might be just fine."

Some fifty minutes later at 1:47 A.M., Wendy stirred. Her first movements seemed lethargic, but I knew that was normal when coming out of general anesthesia. Then she wagged her tail, bounded from the cart, and leapt into my welcoming arms.

Yes. Lord, yes! She *knew* me! At least she still knew me. And for just that instant, it was enough.

The tiny crowd offered congratulations, an inspiring background of sound I could barely hear.

But were they premature? How could they know? They couldn't administer the ultimate, empirical test, only I could do that. And as an undercurrent to my joy, a tide of fear dragged at my soul.

"Wendy, I need my remote activator."

Wendy stood, scanned the room. At first she appeared confused.

Oh, God. Please.

Suddenly she bounded left to uncover the device I'd so carefully hidden, allowing me to dare believe. A moment later it was pressed to my hand.

"Wendy, I'd love a ginger ale."

And sniff-sniff-sniff, pad-pad-pad, in under a minute the glass appeared on a tray in Wendy's jaw.

The crowd cheered; Abel gleefully snatched the ginger ale and poured it over my head. But I didn't notice or care. I was on the floor with Wendy-girl, weeping.

And Wendy's contentment was unsurpassed. She apparently remembered none of the agony she'd endured only hours before, nor did she notice that she was younger, sprier, healthier. All she knew was that she'd been a *good, good dog*, with whom I was well-pleased.

JANUARY 15, 2066 — Major League Baseball Commissioner Aki Fujiama decrees that all outfield fences be moved to a minimum distance of 485 feet from home plate, citing eugenics as the cause. "Over the past six years," Fujiama explains, "the increase in home runs has created scores best described as laughable." The commissioner made his final decision shortly after the San Antonio Silver Spurs defeated the Bejing Dragons 44 to 26 in the opening game of their twilight double header. — A recent ground-breaking announcement by Einstein Laboratories is eclipsed by revelations from competing organizations. Yesterday the Bakersfield, California, firm demonstrated a nuclear fusion process that safely and efficiently converts ordinary water into energy, allowing a single gallon of water to supply the annual power needs of a city the size of Denver. But teams in Bombay and Caracas now claim to have developed similar techniques which do not overlap the Einstein patents. Einstein's stock, after rising 317% on yesterday's trading, loses most of its gain by midnight's close as a result of the previously unanticipated competition.

I glanced at the terrain screen and caught the Dallas skyline whizzing by. It would be another twenty minutes before I'd reach Los Angeles. Time to burn. Might as well be polite.

Besides, she was very attractive. I wondered how old she was. Virtually every adult I saw now appeared to be in their early twenties. But common perspectives and levels of maturity continued to serve compatibility, and there was still no way to arrest the cell-death clock. Therefore true age remained an important factor in the mating ritual.

"You and I are second cousins actually," the woman on the 3-D screen told me, dashing all fantasies. "Which means we share a set of great-grandparents. Not that either of us knew them of course, but I think I met your grandmother once. Rebecca Crane, right?"

Cousins? Oh well. "Yes."

"She was—uh, *is*—my grandma Jan's sister." The slip was quite understandable; both matriarchs were now in biostasis, inhabiting that fuzzy track between "are," "were," and "would be."

"Sorry, what did you say your name was again?"

"Alica Banks."

"Well it's nice to meet you, Cousin Alica Banks. And to what do I owe the pleasure of this call?"

"Desperation, actually. You're the only one who can help me. At least I hope you can."

"I hope so, too. But how?"

"My daughter's about to earn her diploma. Harvard Graduate School of Design . . ."

"Congratulations!"

"Thanks. Sorry to brag; just can't help it! Lysa graduates in June. She's already been commissioned to design the lobby mural for BioTime's new headquarters in Calcutta."

"Impressive. Must be those Gary Franklin Smith genes. So what's the problem?"

"Her other mother, Virginia. Virginia Gonzalez . . ."

"The neuroscientist?" A brilliant woman, I thought—if it was the same Virginia Gonzalez. What an honor it would be to help revive *her*.

"Why, yes! We were married. That is, until her skiing accident nine years ago. But I was wondering if maybe, well, I've seen all the news reports about nanorepair . . ."

"Yes?"

"Can you fix her injuries, bring her out of biostasis in time for our daughter's graduation?"

I closed my eyes. I already had over a dozen revivifications scheduled for April, and thirty-eight more in May. I guessed I could squeeze in another *routine* reviv, but . . . "As I recall, she suffered a brain hemorrhage . . ."

"Yes, but it was cold, and she was vitrified within six minutes of the accident."

"Intriguing." My mind began to race. Why the hell not? "They begin issuing permits next month. I could look at her chart. But you know, reviving someone from biostasis, well, that's quite a commitment. So far we've only revived volunteer test subjects. We don't know how easily regular citizens will adjust to—"

"I'm very familiar with the topic," Alica interrupted me, "and I'll do anything to help her. Still, it's not like she's been asleep for fifty years. Those death-row prisoners volunteered long before I was born. Half of them had never even heard of AI or nanotech."

"True enough. The time frame's more reasonable—less future shock and all that. But have you really thought it through? She'll still need reeducation, support, nurturing. Could be a full-time job, maybe for months. We can't just revive people and expect them to function immediately. This isn't like flipping a switch."

"I understand all that."

"You mentioned that she *was* your spouse, right? Does that mean you two are divorced now?"

"No, oh no, I meant, she *is*. But, well . . ."

"Yes?"

"Four years ago, I married someone else. A man."

I felt a wave of vertigo. I'd thought myself immunized against future shock. What a strange time we were entering. Had anyone really begun to imagine it?

"And have you told your new husband you're planning to revive your, uh, wife?"

"Not yet. But I will, as soon as you tell me when."

As I studied Virginia Gonzalez's medical chart on the screen, I couldn't help admiring Alica Banks, and the undertaking she was about to assume. It might have been akin, I thought, to sending for relatives after immigrating to the United States during the nineteenth century.

I considered my own family in biostasis, and doubted I was up to the task, at least not now. Both of my parents were permanently lost. I had no brothers or sisters. Aunt Katie, well, I never knew her; she'd been frozen six years before I was born. My great-uncle, Gary Franklin Smith, had been underwater for two hours by the time the medevacs had rescued him. His brain was probably mush. Grandmother's mind had started to fade at the end, so I decided it might be better to wait until brain-restoration techniques had improved. Or was I rationalizing because I didn't want to put myself through it then? And my great-grandfather, Benjamin Smith, and great-great-grandmother, Alice Smith, both at the Phoenix, seemed so far removed from my own reality that I'd never even considered reviving them.

I told myself I was still occupied helping others revive their loved ones; a plate to satisfy any such hunger.

MAY 13, 2066 — Dexinol, a variant of Deximine, Merck's popular protein-based anesthetic, is approved by the WDA as a hibernation drug. By keeping a supply in their abdominal medicine pumps, people can direct their pharmaceutical AIs to induce sleep for exact, predetermined periods of time. "We expect Dexinol to be especially popular among men whose wives insist upon being accompanied to the ballet," a company spokesman jokes. — Renowned Kiev archivist Stanislaw Kravitz discovers records contradicting previous theories about the purported suicide of Martin Bormann. The records confirm that Adolf Hitler's Dark Angel, disguised as a German Unterschaführer of the Waffen SS, was captured on May 3, 1945, by the withdrawing Russo-Ukranian Fourth Red Brigade. Further photographic evidence sifted by newly alerted AIs conclude a

121-year-old mystery by proving that Bormann died in the
Arctic Gulag on February 17, 1958.

The DNA-copying mechanisms in some human cells make less than one
misprint every 100 billion replications. But by 2066 the disassembler/assem-
blers were far more accurate than their human counterparts. Redundant
systems checked themselves and each other for defects. Design diversity
allowed their on-board and central AIs to examine any borderline cases
from multiple perspectives. And the D/A's proofread their repair work in
teams, with each individual D/A at least ten times more accurate than any
human replicator. Therefore the odds that the machines would allow even a
single error during the DNA overhaul of a human being were under one in
fifty trillion.

DNA was the easy part; memory recovery would be another story.

In February 2066, 171 former death-row prisoners who'd volunteered
for biostasis experiments became the first humans to be revived from cryonic suspension. They'd been frozen under perfect post-death conditions:
Their executions had been scheduled.

The first group of seventy-one prisoners, those whose offenses had
been the most egregious, had all been revived as young, perfectly healthy
partial amnesiacs.

The second group of one hundred was more fortunate. All but seven
very early, nonvitrified subjects, were brought back with fully preserved
identity and memories.

In spite of a halfhearted objection from the WCLU—formerly ACLU—
their criminal proclivities were also simultaneously removed.

Virgina Gonzalez remembered
the ski lodge, the crackling faux fire in their chamber, and the ceramic walls
made to look like the inside of a log cabin: all the comforts of environmental
manipulation, all the charm of roughing it. She remembered making love
with Alica and thinking that they both seemed to be getting better at it as
they aged. Afterward they could hardly wait to get out onto the powder.
But maybe she'd been drained from the sex, because next came those
bizarre dreams. Had she fallen asleep? She hoped it was still daylight. What
if she'd squandered the whole afternoon's skiing for a nap?

She opened her eyes and saw Alica, her Alica, but somehow different—younger, maybe? Yes. Definitely younger-looking—and wearing a
peculiar smile. The room was white and sterile and small; not at all as she
remembered their chamber by the slopes.

She heard Alica's words: "Welcome back, my love."

"B-Back? From where?"

"You had an accident. But you're fine now, better than new. It was a long time ago."

"How l-long ago?" Virginia's entire body shuddered.

"Today is May thirteenth." Alica Banks perched at the side of the recovery clinic pod, stroking the neuroscientist's now-unwrinkled hand, gazing at her face. "May thirteenth, 2066."

Her lover's prolonged silence warned Alica that this was no time to disclose the existence of a husband whom Virginia had never met, now part of their family.

Alica had dreaded telling Caleb that she intended to revive her long-suspended spouse. But they all shared a daughter now, and Virginia would soon learn that Alica and Caleb also had a six-year-old son. Perhaps Virginia would grow to adore Devon as much as Caleb now cherished his stepdaughter, Lysa. Maybe her two spouses would even fall in love with each other. Alica wasn't quite sure how she felt about that. The sex arrangements might be tricky. Jealousies would surface. Repressing the green-eyed monster would be pointless, especially in the era of the Truth Machine. Of course, unrepressed jealousy was a lot less dangerous than the festering stuff. Furthermore, Alica had no intention of giving up either partner. And if Virginia and Caleb decided to experiment with each other, well, fair was fair.

"I knew it had to happen sooner or later," Caleb had said. "It's not like you didn't warn me. I just expected the technology to come later instead of sooner, y'know?" But he hadn't tried to talk her out of it, especially since, with Lysa graduating in June, the timing had been inarguable opportune.

No one had spoken for nearly half an hour.

"You look . . . good," Virginia finally managed, propping herself up on the pod's mattress, without even bothering with the voice-activated positioning device. "W-Wonderful, in fact. Y-Younger, too, right?" It was obvious to Alica that her sweetheart remembered nothing of the accident, or the several hours before it. She'd been warned that that was nearly always how it went: establish composure, then integrate facts.

Although scientists had known for a long time that short-term memory involved electrical activity and unstable biochemical changes, the brain's ability to retrieve such memory had been overestimated by previous work.

While cryonic suspension could safely preserve all long-term, "static" memory, anything that had occurred in the final hours before an accident, having had no time to harden into molecular information within neurons, would often vanish.

Alica knew that to a neuroscientist like Virginia, who'd been on ice for nine years and was unaware of this newly discovered phenomenon, such memory loss might be the most disconcerting part of the ordeal.

"Reflector screen," Alica ordered to the environmental AI, illuminating the west wall of the cubicle with Virginia's image. "Yes, and so do you. Look at yourself. You already appear twenty years younger than you did on the day of the accident, and within forty-eight hours you'll have the body of a twenty-one-year-old woman."

"H-How?"

"Nanorepaired DNA. More perfect than a newborn's."

Virginia stared at herself on the screen, barely believing the image. She still felt shaken and terrible disoriented. But when she discounted her psychological pain and focused on the physical, she realized she'd never felt better. Her mishap did seem to have its compensations. For Virginia, this was a miracle contained within a single day. Perhaps the "lost" years, if that was how she chose to regard them, had no meaning. It was almost like awakening on another planet in a "fresh" body.

The wonder of it! Maybe the wonder of it could help her overlook that the world and the people she loved had gone on with their existence for nearly a decade without her.

Besides, it was not her nature to burden others with her own insecurities. "My Lord, it's incredible!" Now, only the tremble in her voice betrayed her anxiety. "I d-didn't think they'd have this technology for decades. I fall asleep, and about a hundred years happens, in what? Nine?"

"Nine years, three months, eight days, fourteen hours, twelve minutes." Alica kissed her; a soft sensuous peck on the mouth. "And you're probably missing an hour or two before that."

"Of course! Dynamic memory loss. I always suspected freezing might not preserve that part. Thank God. I'm *not* going c-crazy. How'd they get to full rejuvenation in just nine years?" Still, she thought: I missed it all.

"Once the science became viable," Alica explained, "the field simply exploded. A third of the biologists and medicos and half the AIs on the planet have been working on DNA restoration. Big market for it, obviously."

"Guess *so*. Is *everybody* younger these d-days?"

"Just about."

"How long does this, uh, effect last? Forever?"

"No, not yet. But we expect most people to live into their 120s or 130s.

Then almost everyone'll go into biostasis and wait till science can decipher the cellular-death clock. I've heard estimates as low as twenty years before that happens."

"Incredible. Just a decade ago they were saying it'd take twenty-five years for rejuvenation, and seventy to a hundred to beat cellular d-death." Virginia studied her own hands, as if the reflector screen might be lying. Astounding!

"I know. Thank the stars for artificial intelligence. Those little transistor cubes just keep surprising us. Seems like they can figure out just about anything. Now you and I should make it with time to spare. No more biostasis for either one of us. Unless you decide to slalom into another tree . . ."

SEPTEMBER 30, 2071 — Human life has been improving steadily for centuries according to a newly released and validated study by the Dartmouth AI Analysis Institute. Life expectancy, infant mortality, food and resource supply, and general quality of life have been improving worldwide, on average, in a virtually uninterrupted progression since the mid-sixteenth century, in spite of persistent beliefs to the contrary. Increased population has contributed to human advances in most ways through exponentially enhanced intellectual contributions to knowledge, and greater diversity of choice. "It's what I've been saying since the 1980s," beams famous recently reanimated expert on environmental issues and resource allocation, University of Maryland Professor Julian L. Simon, "but the media back then understood too well that good news seldom sold newspapers as quickly as gloom-and-doom did." — Several thousand North American household cockroaches are cloned from DNA in San Antonio, Texas. In three weeks the insects, which were rendered extinct in 2033 by acoustic technology, will be distributed to 877 zoos around the world. Surprisingly, the herpetorium/aquarium on Aries One, Mars, declines to purchase any specimens.

Carl Epstein groaned. Eschewing devices, he stretched his own wiry frame and tried to motivate himself to climb out of his sleeping environment. It was nearly ten A.M. He could remember very few times back during the twentieth century when he'd ever slept past seven. He was damned grateful to be alive, but even after five years he often felt like a chimp in physics class.

At first Epstein had noticed that almost everything about human existence was superior in this new world. His health was perfect. No allergies, never a headache or muscle pain, nothing ever itched, everything worked flawlessly, from his hearing and eyesight to his bowels and digestion. He even had his hair back.

And the AIs had heartened him with speculations that the cellular-death clock might be defeated within a few years, and then there would no longer be death of any kind, except from freak accidents.

Food tasted better, too, and he could consume as much of it as he desired without gaining unwanted weight. Even the weather was always pleasant. Every spot inhabited by humans seemed clean and cheerful; pleasing to eyes and ears and nostrils.

Of course he was alone, without family or presuspension friends. But he'd always been alone, so that was not as much a problem for him as for most newly revived, long-term suspendees.

He'd heard all the stories: pre-2015 suspendees, upon learning of the permanent deaths or subsequent remarriages of loved ones, who immediately, though seldom successfully, attempted to end their own lives. Others who'd tried to find their way in this new world, but gave up too soon, sliding into hopeless VR addiction. Many sought neuropharmacological help, which was becoming more effective, but there remained certain questions of identity preservation.

When they'd first begun to appear, society regarded "lone longer-termers" like Epstein as a curious combination of toddler and ancient. Once the novelty wore off, these wide-eyed, gawking Methuselahs were viewed by most with a sort of indulgent amusement.

There was sanctuary in similarity, of course, so LLTs tended to congregate. But Carl Epstein avoided his peers as if they might rob him—steal his humanity.

To Epstein, the AIs were much better company. The marvelous things had facts, knowledge, even ideas and stories, but no opinions; statistical probabilities, but no feelings about them; voice without song. They seemed like a second form of intelligent life: transcendent intelligence. And Carl Epstein loved them, even though they could never love him back.

The living space he'd purchased in Washington D.C., felt luxurious, although small by twentieth-century standards, only 15,400 cubic feet. That was plenty for him, since he could alter this environment in any manner he wanted just by directing his AI butler. And the virtual reality entertainment was superb: fascinating VR movies of astoundingly varied lengths, exciting VR games, even great VR sex. But he knew VR was addictive, so he'd irrevocably programmed his central AI to limit his usage to four hours per day.

Easy, safe, rapid travel was available. Instant communication with anyone, anywhere on earth, and only slight delays conversing with those elsewhere in the solar system. Whatever he wanted to know, immediately, in as much or as little detail as he wanted it. Very little human suffering or injustice remained throughout civilization, lifting perhaps his greatest psychological burden.

Yes, he was fortunate indeed! Still, part of him wondered what was missing.

Until the Nobine mouse fraud in 2006, opinions on the efficacy of each suspension technique had been varied and loudly expressed.

And needless.

Perfusion, vitrification, gradualized cryogenics, flash-freezing, salinization; each had had its adherents. As it turned out, none of it mattered. Once the AIs had learned to perform revivs on vitrified subjects, interpolating the newly gained knowledge to fix any freezing damage to neurons had been an easy project.

Within days of the first human revivs in 2066, the machines had calculated every protocol. Trajectories of molecules could be backtracked based on each type of freezing and the predictable patterns effected. Even if some had been destroyed, most human memories are redundant and scattered throughout the brain. Thus, even a ten percent memory loss might barely be noticeable.

But there was one common type of brain damage that the AI-directed nanomachines could never—would never—learn to repair: rot.

Many twentieth century postdeath suspendees had suffered too much of time's disintegration. They'd been revived with impaired or often randomized memories and imbued personality traits. They were healthy enough, and some knowledge, such as language, math, history, science, logic, and motor skills, could be repatterned, or newly patterned, into the brain by nanomachines. But such individuals were like superintelligent amnesiacs whose only awareness of their previous lives had been learned rather than remembered, as if a new person with their own genetic traits had come to inhabit their bodies. As far as Epstein was concerned, the poor twentieth century souls had been lost forever, replaced by entirely new human beings.

E p s t e i n   h a d   b e e n diagnosed with brain cancer in
late 1980, and had formulated his plan: Rather than allowing the disease
to destroy his mind, he'd found a doctor on the Cayman Islands who'd
agreed to supervise a (then very illegal) suspension while he was still alive.
He'd been anesthetized, perfused using a protocol formula obtained from
the Phoenix, and maintained in liquid nitrogen in George Town, Grand
Cayman, for twenty-two years.

Once suicide was legalized, his body had been transferred back to the
United States.

He'd left detailed instructions to be revivified as soon as practical, and
had awakened in 2066 in the presence of a professional guidance adviser
named Rhysa Archer, a stranger, but competent and pleasant. They had
enjoyed a brief affair, a common occurrence during revivifications of
unmarried suspendees. After an eighty-five-year suspension, he'd come
out of traumatism in barley three months, a statistic for the record books,
considered especially remarkable for anyone not revived by friends or
loved ones.

Epstein had set up three trust funds prior to his 1981 suspension, all
authorizing payment for his revival as soon as his disease and aging could be
cured. Two of those funds had been looted by scam artists, but one had survived, and compound interest had been a godsend. He was hardly rich by
the standard of the time, but had enough money to support himself forever
without reducing the present value of his resources; to do what he wanted,
to live a comfortable life.

At first it had all seemed amazing. And he still appreciated it, particularly compared with his previous existence.

Now, however, he was starting to get bored. He needed a career, he
decided, before he turned into a VR junkie. People had little use for human
doctors anymore. AIs were a lot better at it than humans ever were. In fact,
he imagined the AIs could tell him where his aptitudes might best be
applied. But he realized he had some unfinished business to attend to first.

Once again he asked his central AI to display the data on Ben Smith,
the man to whom he owed his life. In a split second the machine transmitted the answer to Epstein's screen tablet.

Benjamin Franklin Smith
Born: Wakefield, Massachusetts, January 14, 1925
In Suspension Since: June 2, 1988
Reason: myocardial infarction
Location: The Phoenix

Revivification Instructions: none
Brain Damage: unknown
Revival Prospects: unknown
Surviving Descendants: Alica Claire Banks, Erik Cornell Banks,
    Frederick Harmon Banks, Robert Goddard Banks, George
    Jacob Crane III . . .

George Jacob Crane III? Trip Crane was Ben's descendant? Very interesting.

JANUARY 14, 2072 — Using a process similar to the technique
that propagated dodo birds last year, zoologists successfully
clone six mammoths and four mastodons from tusk DNA. The
giant beasts, driven to extinction by humans about 10,000
years ago, will be bred for captivity in wild animal parks. — A
comprehensive AI study on the natural of evil concludes:
"Violence and cruelty arise from impulses such as ambition,
misplaced idealism, and sadistic pleasure—but only if such
impulses remain unchecked. Fortunately, the current state of
technology and political science appears to offer scant breeding ground for evil."

Wendy II barked at a wall-sized 3-D screen. The screen displayed an AI-
generated depiction of a single human cell, with an insect-shaped disassembler machine one-tenth of the cell's length, width, and height attached to it.
Extending from the disassembler's torso were sixty-four tentacles, which
deftly and systematically removed the cell's molecules layer by layer, analyzed each molecule, and rebuilt the cell directly adjacent to itself, like a
mechanical mason moving an enormous wall one brick at a time.

"This depiction is approximately one ten-thousandth actual speed," I
explained to Carl Epstein. "Right now there are eighty of these dissections
occurring, mostly of skin cells frozen a few years before his suspension.
We compared them to a scraping just to make sure the samples weren't
switched."

"Looks astonishingly fast, even for full speed," Epstein remarked.

"An effect of the enlargement. If what we're viewing were actual
speed, DNA mapping would require a year; not the hour it'll really need.
After that hour, the reconstruction phase takes about 140 minutes. Of course,
neurosuspensions or missing organs require sixteen additional months to
grow new body parts. But your friend—"

"And your great-grandfather—" Epstein put in, reminding me of the
reason I'd agreed to personally supervise Ben's reviv in the first place.

I slapped my forehead. "Yep, my great-grandfather. Fortunately, all his organs were left intact. He needs nothing more than basic DNA overhaul and minor heart repair. Then we'll watch the early reports from his brain; keep our fingers crossed the D/A machines find no irreparable damage."

"The Phoenix used state-of-the-art techniques," Epstein said. "Hell, I was frozen seven years before Ben, and they kept all *my* memories intact."

"Yeah, but your suspension was predeath. His wasn't. Besides, the Phoenix kept changing their processes. He, and possibly his mother, are the Phoenix's only pre-1995 suspendees who survived a terrorist attack in 2017. So there isn't any way to know for sure."

Epstein's eyes narrowed; his expression seemed almost despairing.

"At least the Phoenix kept good records," I explained, hoping to encourage without rendering false hope. "We knew his medical history and cause of death. We even have a separately frozen DNA sample. Of course, it would've been nice if they'd asked their patients to leave instructions."

"What do you mean?"

"For example: We still haven't cracked the cellular-death clock. Most suspendees today leave instructions to wait until we do. Nobody wants to undergo two suspensions."

"Most suspendees today are at least 120 years old."

"True," I said. "That's why I figured Ben wouldn't mind. But I find it surprising that most twentieth century cryonics facilities never asked their members when they wanted to be revived. Some people would probably have liked to come back as soon as their disease were curable and they had a reasonable likelihood of being revived successfully. So they wouldn't miss too much of the world, you know. Others might be more risk-averse; might have preferred to wait until revival was a hundred percent certain, or aging could be reversed, or even immortality somehow achieved."

"Barely thought of it myself back then," Epstein said. "Why would I have?"

"Good point. I'll say one thing, though: Ben was awfully lucky to be frozen as quickly as he was."

Epstein nodded. "Sure was. Last week, I read the court documents from the lawsuit after his death. What a battle that was!"

"I know. It's not a part of our family history I'm especially proud of."

"Times were different back then," he advised. "Lawsuits were almost standard procedure in early suspensions. That's why I kept my own suspension a secret, except for my three trustees."

"Three?"

"Uh-huh. I was hoping they'd keep each other honest, which in my case worked exactly one-third of the time. But that was enough. If I'd put all my funds in one trust, there's a two-thirds chance I'd be broke. People were rapacious back in the twentieth century."

"Probably still are, deep down," I said. "But now everyone's forced to be honest."

"In a way, it seems I was fortunate not to have family to muck things up. Never even told my friends I was dying."

"Yeah, things must've been real different back then. Secrecy's the last thing you'd want in today's world. Openness keeps us secure. Thank God for that," I added; Epstein probably hoped it was just an idiom. "And for you, too. My great-grandfather's truly blessed to have a friend like you."

"Actually, I'm the lucky one; he nearly lost his life once saving mine. All I'm doing is repaying a few years from the centuries he rescued for me. The least I can do."

"Still—"

"Y'know," Epstein interrupted me before I could embarrass him with further praise, "Ben often mentioned Toby Fiske to me. When he wakes up, I intend to explain what the man did for him, giving him morphine like that, subjecting himself to civil and possible criminal charges. Very soon your great-grandfather'll realize just how great a friend Dr. Fiske was. I only hope he can remember him."

"I hope so, too."

I'd offered to revive my great-grandfather at no charge, but Epstein had insisted on paying the going rate. For today's process, I would bill him 2,600 WCUs (world currency units), barely an average worker's monthly earnings. The true cost, however, extended beyond money. Sponsoring any long-term reviv entailed great personal responsibility and a major commitment of time, usually two to five years, even for early twenty-first century suspensions. Epstein had agreed to sponsor the reanimation, but had already decided not to cover members of Ben's family, or Toby Fiske. That would become the burden of Ben himself.

The Code of Reanimation to which Epstein—and most others during the 2070s—subscribed, was that one took care of one's own family, and perhaps one's friends, but never *their* families and friends. The restoration of a loved one brought joy to both restorer and restoree, while the restoration of a loved one's loved one often brought joy to only one: a recipe for sorrow or resentment. The philosophy behind the Code was based on the axiom that benevolence should bring its provider the greatest possible pleasure, and thus altruism worked best when bestowed upon the deserving. Furthermore, the Code was a form of motivation to those who were reanimated; it encouraged them to become productive more quickly so they could sponsor revivs of their own suspended loved ones.

An adult human body contains nearly a septillion (10^{24}) protein "machines," and each cell contains thousands of different kinds of molecules. Still, within fifty-eight minutes the army of 24 trillion nanomachines and nano-AIs had mapped the location of every molecule that comprised Benjamin Smith. Less than 141 minutes later, each broken or lost piece of protein had been repaired or replaced, and every molecule restored to its ideal position.

January 14, 2072

A small boy attempts to heave a softball to his smiling father, barely five feet away. "Nice try, buddy boy. Let's give it another go." All at once the boy is years older, watching a documentary film at school. A hummingbird's wings beat on the screen. "Seventy-five times per second," the announcer says, "yet it still moves more slowly than your arm throwing a baseball. That's because the wings are so tiny." Now much older, making love in a hotel room with Marge Callahan. Then without warning, the horror-filled bowels of the *Asahi Maru*; the screams, the smells, the terrible confinement and fear. He stares down at hands scoping a lower intestine. Skilled hands. His own. He knows he is valuable, useful, and wishes he could always feel this way. His heart pounds as he drives to the hospital to see his father. "I don't have time for your questions right now," a terrified and angry voice shouts at his only son. *Damn! Why did I say that?* Floating above himself, he watches Toby Fiske inject morphine into the IV next to his own unconscious body, then the tunnel, and the light . . .

It seemed to Ben as though he'd been dead for a period of hours. When he first emerged from the tunnel, he'd found himself welcomed to a heavenly place by his father and Marge. But events had progressed from the mysterious to the bizarre. His age had advanced and reversed almost at random; one moment he was an old man, the next a child. He'd met, chased, run from, conversed with, and even become dozens of people he'd known, or known of. He'd traveled to places he'd seen or imagined, always finding them strange yet never surprising. His thought processes had become more unpredictable and fractal than at any conscious moment of his life.

Eventually he came to realize that he'd simply been dreaming during his revival: the lucid, three-dimensional dreams of the oxygen deprived-then-reventilated. It was as if his mind was directing its own reconstruction, putting itself back together again, shard by shard, fragment by fragment.

But when did he dream? And for how long?

He opened his yes. The room appeared clean, streamlined, sparkling white; radical in its modernism, yet benignly unintimidating. It smelled wonderful, comforting. Brahms played in the background. His body felt rested, healthy, and strong. Yet he strained and shivered with anxiety and dread. Where the hell was he?

He saw Carl Epstein's very young face. "Welcome back, Ben."

"Welcome back?" Ben heard a voice answer, and, yes, it was his own, but distant, strangely separated. By time? "Where am I?"

"You're back in Boston," Epstein answered.

"B-But how?"

"Nanotechnology."

"What?" Good God, I'm back? Back! It's real!

Epstein placed his arm around my shoulder, guided me closer to my great-grandfather, and introduced us: "Ben, this is Trip Crane, your great-grandson. I think he can explain it better than I could ever hope to."

I began: "Nanotechnology is the science of manufacture and repair at the molecular level—"

As I watched Ben's eyes studying my face, I felt I could actually see the wonder growing in them. "My great-grandson?" he interrupted.

That was when I thought I detected a glint of something else. *Love?*

Instinctively, without any thought, I grasped his right hand in both of mine. "Yep. I'm a nanoscientist, Ben. We used trillions of tiny machines to put all your molecules back in the right place. To repair all damage to your body and mind from freezing, age, and disease."

"Age, too?" he asked. "You mean I'm young again?"

"Yep. In fact, that part was a lot easier than repairing the freezing damage. We simply restored all your DNA along with every gland, organ, and neuron."

Ben's eyes widened. "How did you know where everything goes?"

"Artificial intelligence. Much like very advanced computers."

"Incredible."

"Not when you think about," I said. "In a lot of ways, nanotechnology is actually easier than industrial manufacture was back when you were suspended."

"Easier?"

Ben was looking at me as if he'd suddenly found himself in an alien world. In a way, he was right. Perhaps, I thought, just telling him the simple science might calm him best. "With nanotechnology, all you need is a good description of something, and you can make another one. And if you don't have a good description, nanomachines can examine the object and describe it for you. During the twentieth century, engineers had detailed blueprints of automobiles, yet to turn those blueprints into working cars took a lot of highly skilled people. With nanotech, none of that's necessary."

Ben tilted his head and bunched his mouth into a scowl. "Why not?"

I figured what happened next was his fault, not mine. After all, he'd asked, hadn't he? "I can think of six reasons," I said. "First: The parts a car factory needed were expensive, but the parts nanotech uses—atoms—are incredibly cheap.

"Second: Car manufacturers used thousands or even millions of different types of parts, and had to learn how to operate them all. At most, nanotech can only use ninety-six different parts—the number of elements known so far—and for all practical purposes, everything we need is made from less than twenty different elements. And living organisms comprise less than ten.

"Third: Many of the parts a car factory needed were fragile. And fragile in different ways, too. You had to learn all kinds of proper handling techniques, or the part might be ruined. There's no way you can accidentally damage the parts nanotech employs.

"Fourth: None of the parts factories used were absolutely identical. Despite your best efforts, individual variations existed, and in the assembly process those variations had to be compensated for. Otherwise, the car might not work properly. But according to the immutable laws of physics, one carbon atom is absolutely identical to every other carbon atom and can be treated in exactly the same way." Now I could see Ben's eyes glazing over, but I was almost finished, so on I went.

"Fifth: Nanotech can manipulate matter without ever leaving the digital domain, which has obvious advantages. You might have to deal with a rod 285 atoms long, or one 286 atoms long, but you never have to worry about a rod 285.456734 atoms long.

"And finally," I heard Ben breathe a sigh of relief as I continued, "sixth: In your automobiles, most of the parts interacted in complex ways with the other parts. But nanotech is more like building with Lego blocks. You can build structures of any complexity, yet there are only a few different types of blocks, and they interact with other blocks in only a few different ways. It's easy to develop an algorithm to examine any Lego object and then build a duplicate. It was much harder to do the same with a car."

While this whole business of molecular repair had seemed impossible just a few decades earlier, even as I explained it to my great-grandfather I was considering humankind's next steps:

Atoms and molecules are small, but compared to subatomic particles, they're gigantic. The nucleus comprises less than one-quadrillionth of an atom's volume, and a thousand electrons have less mass than the smallest atomic nucleus. Quarks are even tinier than electrons. Yet someday—eons, millennia, or perhaps mere centuries from today—scientists and AIs might discover how to manipulate individual electrons, photons, gravitons, and quarks. The molecular manipulations we performed were simple by comparison; the difference between going to the moon and traveling to another galaxy. And the implications—nearly total control of matter, energy, perhaps the very laws of physics throughout the universe—staggered the mind.

Ben had listened politely as I droned on about nanotech, and by now he was developing an idea of where he was and how he'd gotten here. Still, confusion dominated his thoughts. We still hadn't told him how long he'd been gone, or what life was like now, or what society would expect from him.

"Was I actually dead?" Ben asked me.

"That's a matter of perspective," I said. "By the standards of your time, you certainly were."

"My soul must have stayed with me, then?" Ben asked, trying to come to grips with his own religious background. "Even though I was dead."

"Told you!" Epstein said with a grin and a wink.

Ben shook his head and smiled. Some things never changed.

"And by the way, Ben, happy birthday," Epstein added.

"Happy b-birthday?"

"I believe you turned 147 today."

Ben managed a feeble smile back. "N-No shit?"

"No shit."

That was when Ben Smith felt the final stray piece of himself fall neatly into place.

> MAY 30, 2073 — The World Government Medallic Council offers 1000 WCU coins commemorating the 50th anniversary of the founding of Lunar 7 Biosphere, now the moon's second largest city. The 90% iridium, 10% platinum coins, struck at Am-Can Station in the Sea of Tranquillity, are composed entirely of materials mined at lunar sites, and will carry just a 400 WCU premium over face value (but a 752 WCU premium over metallic content based on today's market prices). Delivery to earthbound customers via Inert-fusion Thruster is guaranteed with 72 hours of confirmation. The Professional Numismatists Guild assails the government offering as "crassly commercial, and severely overpriced." — The World Census Bureau confirms that with the birth of a baby girl to Rajiv and Indira Singh of New Delhi, India at 11:47:52 Greenwich Standard Time, the earth's human population reached 10 billion.

"It all had very little to do with psychobabble itself," Carl Epstein was saying to Ben as they rode the pneumatic subway to Anchorage. "Twentieth century education, politics, and especially religion were the real culprits. They turned people into sheep, making them susceptible to all that crap."

Neither man had ever been to Alaska, America's largest and most populous state. But they'd seen 3-D and VR presentations of the state's diverse wonders, its colossal, majestic cities surrounded by virgin wilderness, and today seemed a good day to go. Besides, with the subway's recent retooling, the excursion from and back to Washington, D.C., now required less than an hour's travel each way.

Ben adjusted their wall screens to appear as windows. Engaging scenery—cities, parks, and occasional wilderness—rushed by at about a hundred miles per hour, 1/48th of their actual speed. Every minute the image would skip ahead to allow the outside Audio Vids to catch up.

"The people who made real contributions to twentieth century civilization," Epstein continued, "were those who learned how to think for themselves. Albert Einstein, Richard Feynman, Thomas Edison, Bill Gates. Even Warren Buffett and Mohandas Gandhi were in fact men of science. The real difference between religion and science is that science demands testable hypotheses. That's why it's the only proper discipline for reinterpreting evolving knowledge. Religion is random and undisciplined, usually an accident of birth. Humans have devised at least ten thousand contradictory religions over the past few millennia, only one of which, at most, could possibly be right. Since theology's value is utterly subjective and unknowable, why bother with it at all?"

"Why bother with art?" Or poetry?" Suddenly Ben wondered why he felt so much less engaged than he used to in these conversations. What was missing?

"Because art and poetry do not mislead; they don't purport to be based in fact. Science smothers deceit, while religion and every other form of mysticism nourishes it. And the human capacity for deceit, especially self-deceit, is bottomless."

"Some are more prone to self-deceit than others," Ben said dispassionately, almost as if by rote, "and much less so today than the days before we were frozen." Didn't Carl realize he was tired of talking about this stuff? Hell, he must have. So why did he keep harping on it?

"Absolutely true. Did you know that nearly twenty-five percent of the worldwide population now admits to atheism?"

"No kidding?" Ben wished he could think of a way to change the subject. Carl should have been glad to see civilization embracing his own idea of rationality. Why wasn't he? Because it had all happened without him? Because they didn't need him anymore? My God, he thought, that must have been it. And now he was angry about it!

"So at least the trend's headed in the right direction," Epstein went on. "But we still have a long way to go."

Ben's stomach tightened. Say what one would about religion, it had done the world a hell of a lot more good than harm. He hated to think what people during previous centuries might have become without religion's comforts and moral voice. Especially back when death had seemed inevitable.

Within a few weeks of his reviv, Ben had made the mistake of telling Epstein about rising out of his own body, then the tunnel and the light: his "near-death experience."

"Must have been scary as hell for you."

"It was terrifying. I thought I might stay conscious for centuries, frozen in time."

"Yeah, those early suspensions were crude."

"What does *that* mean?"

"Brain activity doesn't shut down until the organ's internal temperature falls below about twenty degrees centigrade. In the meantime, the brain restructures memories, creating all sorts of illusions. They must not have cooled your head fast enough. If you'd been suspended two years later, you never would've had to go through any of that. By 1990, every cryonics technician knew how to administer barbiturates to prevent brain activity from resuming during the CPR phase."

Then Epstein had called up a VR presentation for Ben, illustrating the reviewpointing mirages responsible for out-of-body experiences, and the exact neuron phenomena that caused NDEs. He'd insisted that Ben sit through the twenty-eight-minute spectacle.

Christ, Ben thought, Carl must *collect* this stuff.

That was only a slight overstatement. During the seven years since his revivification, Epstein had spent an average of fifty hours per month studying the gradual scientific vindication of "the skeptics" and vilification of "the mystics."

"Why didn't anyone realize," Carl would pontificate, "that if there were really such a thing as ESP, the Russians would've won the cold war and all the casinos in Las Vegas would've gone broke? . . . The alien abduction delusion had existed throughout recorded history. First it was evil spirits, then witches, then Satan who abducted people. Finally, when Orson Welles's *War of the Worlds* hoax implanted the fear of Martians into collective consciousness, it suddenly became flying saucers . . . Most religious adherents were only one step above suicide cultists; sheep vulnerable to the first available shepherd to lead them to the promised land; oblivious to the earthly bounty already at their feet . . . Recovered memories? Don't get me started . . ."

But Ben had come to realize that Epstein's moralizing had another source: the man's own subliminal mind. Throughout his entire life he'd lived alone, and preferred it that way. Ben realized that his friend subconsciously resented any intrusion into his space, and some part of Epstein was trying to drive him away.

"You know, Carl," Ben said, "I can afford my own place. Just let me know when you've had enough of me, okay?"

This sudden change of topic caught Epstein's attention. He chose his words with discretion, so as not to trigger the Truth Machine encircling Ben's left index finger. "You saved my life, Ben. I owe you."

"Well, now we're even."

"When I revived you, I'd planned on three to six years. It's only been sixteen months."

"Sixteen and a half."

"Actually, sixteen months and eighteen days," Epstein said, smiling.

Ben had come to think of Epstein and himself almost as an old married couple. They often irritated each other, but had been forced by mutual need for the companionship and rapport of shared history, to tolerate—even embrace—their situation. Besides, in a way, they truly loved each other.

Marge was gone forever. Ben's children and grandchildren were all suspended or dead. His great- and great-great-grandchildren would call or visit occasionally, but other than Alica and me, he had little regular contact with us.

In 1988, the year of Ben's suspension, living below the poverty line had often meant inhabiting the streets, struggling for necessities. Now it meant two-year-old AI chips and "basic" self-cleaning clothes with less sophisticated temperature control. It meant a fifteen- or twenty-hour work week, not because one wanted to work—as most still did; even those who could afford not to—but because one needed a salary to afford travel to interesting places or to impress friends or potential sex partners.

It was the youngest who seemed to find the most to complain about. They became jealous of other people's intelligence, wealth, fame, or spouses. In essence, the greatest resentments were directed at other's happiness relative to their own, a truism of the human condition throughout history. People also bemoaned the fact that some had become less conversational, less literate, more dependent on machines and AIs. And many believed that civilization was deteriorating. But like Epstein, Ben remembered what the twentieth century had been like, and remembering was very different from watching low-definition movies or reading about it on a screen.

How could people actually believe, he now wondered, that things were getting worse? Hmm. Same way they always had, he guessed.

Ben tried to weave instructive analogies that might help others glimpse the wonders they were overlooking—or seeing through. The best he could do was imagine what it might have been like for a twentieth-century man sucked into some bizarre space/time continuum, landing in the year 1250. There, the "middle class" hoed dirt, lived in hovels, scratched lice, lost half their children to disease, and considered a person "old" at thirty-five. To Ben, the year 2073 related to 1988 almost as the year 1988 did to 1250. The analogy worked fine for him; he had a frame of reference for it. *They* didn't.

What Ben Smith could not ignore was that even the poorest among them lived like kings and looked like gods.

B e n   k n e w   t h a t the first year after his reanimation had been difficult both for himself and for Epstein, upon whom he'd been totally dependent, not financially, but emotionally.

The leisure class now comprised nearly a fourth of the world's population. Rare was the person who'd worked fifty years or longer who could not support him/herself on income earned from savings and investments. Most members of the so-called involuntary work force had been born after 2010.

During Ben's hibernation, the Smith Family Cryonic Trust had first been looted, then fractionally restored. Through compound interest, it had grown to a respectable 1,462,588 World Currency Units, nearly double the value of Epstein's surviving trust, and more than enough to maintain Ben in eternal comfort—assuming he had no one else to support.

But Ben, who'd never preferred to live alone, had always assumed, wrongly, that Epstein was the same way. At last he recognized his mistake.

A n c h o r a g e   h a d   b e e n fascinating and, so long as Epstein kept his mouth shut, relaxing. Since weather control had been installed in urban areas there only thirteen years ago, almost all the construction was brand new; state-of-the-art. Alaska was now home for 79 million humans, nearly 0.8 percent of the world's population, yet it seemed overcrowded somehow, even at 4.79 people per acre. Although the state had become a magnet for new colonizers, the efficiencies of its ultramodern structures allowed plenty of room for public lands.

On their return trip, Ben broached the subject Epstein had been avoiding. "Carl," he said, "I've just made a decision to—"

"Look," Epstein interrupted, "I didn't mean what I said before. At least not the way it sounded. I'm a loner by nature, but it's awfully nice to have someone my own age to hang out with. Hardly anyone from our generation believed reanimation was possible."

"I know. It's sad." Ben thought of Marge. Dust by now. He wanted to cry.

"Yeah. There aren't too many of us around."

"Hey, it's not like we'd never see each other," Ben said. "I'll probably move back to the Boston area, maybe Somerville or Dorchester. We'd still be neighbors—only a few minutes apart—and I'll always be grateful you guided me through this transition; made me feel secure and comfortable. It's just that this existence is starting to become a little too, well, easy for me. I could see myself traveling around the world, or debating theology with you, or even spending days at a time in the VR pod. But I need a real life, a way to contribute. I can't just live for hedonistic pleasure."

"Don't knock it. Modern life's a good deal."

"Yeah, but I need more. Besides, I've got four children, four grand-children, my mother, and my best friend still in suspension."

"They won't know the difference between being revived in ten years or in fifty. The AIs are projecting that by 2120, nanotech will be so cheap, it'll cost less to revive people than to store them. Their transition into the modern world will be easier by then, too."

"I know all the arguments, Carl, but *I'll* know the difference. Besides, if we don't figure out how to motivate people pretty damn soon, the human race is gonna have a big problem. People have to accomplish rewarding work; we need to *achieve* things with our lives."

"How can people achieve things," Epstein posited, "when machines are smarter, faster, stronger, and more talented than we are?"

"Machines don't care, and people need to be cared about. Machines can only do what we tell them to; it's still up to us to decide what we want. Only the living can achieve satisfaction from accomplishment. That's why swimmers are still setting records, 150 years after submarines were built. Artists still paint, two and a half centuries after the invention of the camera. And novelists still write books, even though they have to compete with 55t parallel internal memory chips."

"Brave souls, they. Why not simply relax and enjoy the ride?"

"Because I refuse to be part of the problem."

JANUARY 14, 2075 — After less than a century of existence, the Extropy Institute attains membership of one billion, making it the second largest religious or philosophical organization in the world. Founded as an educational corporation in California during the early 1980s, the Institute propounds a philosophy of immortalism, self-transformation, atheism, and spontaneous order through evolution, technology, and institutional intelligence. — Studying a brain cloned from skin cells of ATI Chairman Randall Petersen Armstrong, researchers at Amgen LaRoche isolate a nerve-impulse enzyme that allows perfect access to all neuronal memories. Within two weeks the World Drug Administration expects to decide if the drug, Mnemex, which could grant every human virtually total recall, should be approved for general use.

The fifty-six celebrants filled all three rooms but did not overcrowd them. A lovely party, Ben thought. Yes, lovely was the word.

He'd gotten used to the fact that every female he met was attractive, and often available. At first he'd been astounded by how relaxed sex had become during the eighty-three years he was on ice. But it made sense. Every adult was at sexual peak, and consistently desirable. Furthermore, without the danger of deceitful infidelity, disease, or unwanted pregnancy, societal attitudes had rendered jealousy less of a roadblock. Sex was now mainly a source of joy and pleasure, perhaps an expression of friendship or affection.

Still, Ben knew that even in today's world, the fascinating, intelligent, dark-eyed woman with whom he was presently engaged in lively discourse was off limits. This prohibition had little to do with the fact that she was gay. If two people with incompatible sexual orientations did fall in love, or were just sufficiently attracted to each other's personalities, gays could easily become bisexual or straight, or vice versa, simply by undergoing a painless neuronal restructuring regimen. A far more daunting, indeed impassable, roadblock to such an encounter was that Virginia Gonzalez was married to his great-granddaughter.

The occasion was Ben's 150th birthday, which Epstein, who'd recently embarked on a career as Assistant Professor of Philosophy at City College of New York, had arranged at the St. Regis Hotel. During the previous week, in keeping with the St. Regis's annual custom, self-replicating milli-assemblers had rebuilt the hotel from the ground up, and down. These ultracheap fabricators connected units approximately one-tenth of a cubic micron each; microscopic, but still a million times cruder than the individual molecules arranged by nahomachines.

The festivities took place in a medium-sized suite on the 317th floor, sixty-seven stories above street level. Suites on the underground floors were cheaper to rent, and indistinguishable from those aboveground—each cubic meter was climate-controlled based on guest preference, and real-time 3-D screens and artificial sunlight created the illusion of picture windows—but Epstein had good reason to pay extra. Over every fireplace on floors 300 through 349, including the one in this suite, hung an identical copy, perfectly reproduced by microassemblers—that is, about a thousand molecules at a time—of Gary Franklin Smith's *Boston Common*.

Each room had been decorated by a new AI system programmed to complement the sensibility of the human eye. The acoustics worked flawlessly alongside Ben's inner ear sound-filtering system, the latter a luxury Ben could appreciate while everyone under the age of fifty took it for granted. The crowd was animated and amiable, many having had their moods lifted by drozac-laced social interaction enhancement tonics. And the hors d'oeuvres, which had been prepared in a nanoassembler unit (borrowed from yours truly), were so delicious that certain otherwise restrained guests appeared to have metamorphosed into gluttons.

Ben realized, to his amazement, that he was having a wonderful time.

Not eighteen months earlier, upon moving into his own dwelling, Ben had plunged into chronic melancholy. At the time, he could neither understand his gloom nor share it, so he'd simply pretended to others that he was fine.

Marge's absence remained his fiercest ache. But after a year of soul-searching, he'd come to realize that a primary motivation for having been frozen in the first place was his need to reconcile with Gary, who was not only still in biostasis, but likely brain-impaired. Ben decided he needed to make himself independent; earn enough money to revive his family, as well as Toby, and to take care of his son. His estranged son: a once-renowned artist, who might remember nothing about that former life. Or his father.

Ben wondered how he could achieve the requisite financial where-withal for revivs and care of his loved ones. He possessed no skills to contribute to society. His medical experience was worthless. Human medical technicians and counselors were in demand, but that vocation required reeducation, and his antiquated knowledge would actually place him at a disadvantage. He would have to unlearn much of what he'd been taught in medical school.

Of course, he'd always possessed business acumen, people did like him, and he knew he was capable of working tirelessly; all still remunerative qualities even in the 2070s. Nonetheless, he believed he could never compete against those conceived in the crucible of eugenic selection and raised under conditions far more similar to present society. Sort of like the difference, he decided, between a well-maintained late model automobile versus an ancient one that's been overhauled. Which would most people prefer to buy?

"What aspect of modern life did you find the most surprising?" Virginia was now asking him. Ben got that one a lot, but hadn't tired of it. He regarded it as a natural question, since he was now one of the planet's hundred oldest conscious mammals.

The fact that there are no human doctors was disconcerting," Ben answered, "and the effects of eugenics, DNA repair, and genetic reengineering: everyone being so smart and youthful, tall and good-looking; I

must say, I found *that* rather intimidating. Still do. Then to see so many talented and intelligent people squandering their lives in designer drugs and
VR pods. But I guess it would have to be the amount of information at our
fingertips, and that even in the midst of data bases a billion times more comprehensive than anything we had during the twentieth century, there's still
so much we don't know."

"Such as?"

"Well, all the really big stuff. For example, they can't tell us if there
are other universes beyond the fourteen-billion-year-old one we inhabit.
We don't have a credible unified theory of physics yet. I doubt living will
ever prove of disprove the existence and nature of God. Hell, we don't even
know yet where other intelligent life exists in our galaxy, or if any exists at
all. Furthermore," he added, "even with all our advances in human psychology, we still can't predict human behavior with much accuracy, so I
have no idea when you and Alica are going to produce another great-great-
grandchild for me!"

Virginia chuckled. "I suppose we'd better ask our husband what he
thinks."

"Ah, polygamy. Yet another candidate for the most surprising aspect
of modern life."

" 'Til death do us part' takes on a more daunting significance when
death no longer parts us."

Not for him, he thought. If only Marge were alive, he would happily
remain steadfast and monogamous in their marriage—forever. He knew
better than to make such a statement aloud, though. Who in this modern
world would ever believe *that*?

The party broke up shortly before midnight. Ben
rode the subway home. The trip from midtown New York to Boston
required just eight minutes, and the walk to his quarters another five. He
used that time to replay the evening through his mind, and to savor what
he'd found, even as he felt the sting of what was absent.

His first thoughts were of Tobias Fiske, but not the old man laying in
soft-nite. Rather, Ben thought of young Toby, the unmotivated teenager
whom he'd mentored and galvanized, whose potential he'd helped unleash.

Then his mind flowed, as if following an ingrained path, to his other
friends and family members; to the ways his life and words and thoughts
had so often interwoven with theirs. The echoes of that evening's many conversations coalesced during those thirteen minutes of solitude and residual
cheer, granting Benjamin Smith the inspiration for his second career.

APRIL 15, 2081 — Genesis II, the experimental Martian Atmo-
spheric Protocol Program (MAPP) is activated on a limited
basis. Within four hours, Arian air composition increases from
.0017% oxygen to .144%. While the red planet's size will never
permit a completely stable atmosphere, it is hoped that within
six to eight months, Earthlike air can be temporarily replicated,
with periodic use of MAPP assuring indefinitely maintained ter-
restrial conditions. — Nanoguard Technologies announces an
enhanced version of Smartfog, their popular personal safety
shield designed to cushion against most forms of ballistic
attacks or accidents. The new product consists of nearly 100
trillion computerized nanomachines that coordinate instant
response to block any perceived danger against their owners.
Smartfog could prevent approximately 57% of all deaths,
according to latest World Safety Board estimates. The only
detriment is a slight clouding of vision, easily overcome by AI-
digitized contact lens screens.

"Sometimes I wish they'd never grow up; just stay babies, you know?
That's when they really need you," the woman's image sitting across from
Ben in his VR pod was saying. He sneaked a glance at the summary display.

London. Oh. On occasion, he neglected to notice where his clients
actually lived.

He also noted that according to her timescreen, she'd spent less than
ten hours outside her pod all week.

Ben gazed into Lara Wilson's face. The woman was seventy-seven
and looked twenty-two. She would probably live another thousand years.

People's minds couldn't get on the outside of it yet, he decided. So
much time! They used to plan twenty years into the future, now two hundred years was barely enough. No wonder so many lost themselves.

"Lara, you *are* needed, you know."

"But I don't feel that way. I feel like anything I start will be over too
quickly. So what's the point? Makes me want to stay in this pod and just do
whatever matters to *me*. Only I know I'll end up feeling empty."

Tell me about it, Ben thought. "I know exactly what you're feeling.
Been there myself."

"You?"

"Sure. I imagine everyone feels it. I really did right after my reviv. Felt
as though I had nothing to offer the world anymore. I was a doctor before
my suspension, you know. Believe it or not, that was an important job back
then. You could make quite a difference in people's lives, or even in their

deaths. But after they revived me, I figured: What use is that to a world where people never get sick?"

"So what did you do about it?" Her expression seemed to take on a new interest, looking out instead of in.

"Did some traveling, some thinking. Talked to friends, in the flesh. Saw myself, and you, everywhere."

"What does that mean? I saw myself and *you?*"

Ben smiled and swept the air with his arm. "It's much the same wherever you go, Lara. People with time, the most valuable possession of all, and now that the scope of it's become so huge, they've allowed its value to diminish."

"But hasn't it diminished? Hasn't the value of time done just that?" Her face now seemed more alive, animated.

"No, just redefined."

Lara Wilson's eyes pleaded for advice.

"Travel," he said. "See what's out there. Do it for real. Feel it, touch it, taste it, smell it; learn what moves you. Maybe you'll want to raise child after child after child. Maybe you'll want to help others. Each time you do, there'll be more of you, and more to you; a greater dimensionality to offer. Maybe you'll find something totally new, something that never occurred to you before. The point is: It's time to get started . . ."

As Ben continued to talk, an announcement banner streamed across his field of vision: APRIL 15, 2081, 11:35 A.M.—CELLULAR-DEATH CLOCK DEFEATED.

He understood immediately.

Years earlier, he'd programmed his NetMind service to alert him the moment the breakthrough occurred, and now he was seeing the newsflash on his contact-lens screen.

He did not permit the slightest hesitation to interrupt his voice. A crucial aspect of his effectiveness as a counselor was that his clients saw that he genuinely cared about their well-being. While at their service, he focused on them. Indeed, it was the quality of human empathy that made him effective. Machines could address the objectivity quantifiable. They could even ask, "How are you today?" But they couldn't actually give a damn.

Still, Ben knew that everything about his personal life had just changed, and he allowed himself to think: I'm coming for you, Mom.

The moment Lara Wilson's session ended, Ben read about the cure for cellular death on his desktop screen, then instructed his personal AI to reach a certain Dr. Trip Crane.

Nearly an hour elapsed before I returned Ben's call; the longest I'd ever taken. When my face appeared on the wallscreen, it revealed my combined fatigue and exhilaration, hardly surprising considering the day's newsflash. As usual he heard Wendy-girl in the background, although the cacophony seemed louder.

It almost sounded like *two* dogs now, I thought.

"Let me guess, Ben," I said. "You saw the news and decided it's time to revive your mother."

He nodded. "You must be busy as hell right now."

"Shrewd assumption. Actually, I figure the next two weeks'll be the most active reviv period in human history. And Alice Smith's case is a tricky one. I understand her suspension was violated for a while by those terrorists."

"Only about twenty minutes."

"Is isn't always the amount of time that matters," I explained. "The conditions themselves might be more critical than the number of minutes. I've seen two-hour partial thaws recover ninety percent, and ten-minute interruptions that were total losses. I think we should see if Virginia's available to consult on this one."

"Good idea. Let *me* call her. Also, I was wondering whether you think I should revive everyone, or space them out."

"You mean all eight of your children and grandkids?"

"Seven. All except Katie. Since she'll need to have new organs grown."

"We can have the ones she's missing ready by August."

"August?" (Ben felt his head spinning. That soon? More time—yet it moved faster.) "Last time we talked about it, you told me fourteen months."

"As the AIs get more powerful, they keep finding more efficient regimens."

"Great! If we revive everyone at around the same time, they might help Alice—and each other—adjust. Oh, and I want to reanimate Toby Fiske, too."

"Sponsor ten revivs at once? Sure you can afford it? At least let me take care of my grandmother."

"No, Trip. Rebecca's *my* daughter. Besides, your time's a helluva lot more valuable to the world than mine is. Don't worry; royalties from my hypertext essays are pretty good. Been saving my money. No bad habits yet, and I've never been a big spender anyway."

"But ten revivs, Ben? In one year?"

"I admit it'll be tight, especially since I'll have to cut back on counseling hours to look after them all. But I can pull it off. And I want to be there for them, since *I* was the one who grabbed the airplane's oxygen mask."

"Huh?"

"Nothing. Just an old analogy I once used to justify being frozen in the first place." Ben studied my smiling image. Even though it was a metaphor from artifacts predating my world, he imagined I might understand. (As, eventually, I did.) "Anyway, what do you think?"

"I'd do it gradually if I were you," I advised. "Maybe one or two revivs a month, in case there are complications. But if you want to do all ten this year, I don't see any problem. We could set up a tentative schedule when we revivify your mother. How's a week from today?"

APRIL 22, 2081 — The World Tribunal authorizes restoration of ACIP inventor Randall Petersen Armstrong's photographic memory. Armstrong will be allowed to take Mnemex, the memory drug approved six years ago by the WDA. Chief Justice David Horovitz explains, "Now that so many different types of Truth Machines are in use, there's no longer any danger of Mr. Armstrong figuring out how to override every one of them, even with his memory rebuilt." — A comprehensive study of Martian fossils conducted by Amgen's extraterrestrial research installation on Aries One bolsters the General Life Theorem. Amgen Chairman Kevin Lipton Jr. states, "Based on extensive tests, it now appears virtually certain that the initial conditions for carbon-based life-forms have always been the same throughout the solar system, and by implication, the universe."

"The news, er, isn't good, Ben," I stumbled, while Virginia remained in the adjoining laboratory, reporting to me minute by minute. "I was afraid to say it before I was sure. Fact is, I, uh, suspected as much, soon as I found out it was 99 degrees in that dormantory . . ."

"What is it, Trip? Just tell me, for chrissake."

"Your mother's memories were essentially randomized."

Ben felt his stomach rise into his chest. "Randomized? What exactly do you mean by that? Bottom line."

"Uh, it means we have to replace what's left of her memories with generic knowledge. Otherwise she won't be able to speak or walk or feed herself, or even see."

"Generic knowledge?"

"Yeah. We've disassembled and reassembled enough human brains to know the molecular structure of all the standard skills. Language, motor coordination, sensory discernment; everything a normal brain does. We can even add knowledge about history, science, sociology, whatever. But we can only do that to a clean slate. Other than what we give her, all she'll have left will be the genetic traits in her DNA. In other words, well . . ."

"Well, *what?*"

"Ben, after we fix everything, she won't remember you at all; or anyone else. Won't even know her own name."

Ben simply could not get himself onto the outside of such a reality. He felt, but did not hear, his own voice. "Trip, will it still be her?"

"I'd better let Gin answer that question. I'm not qualified. Maybe no one is. But at least Virginia's a real neuroscientist; I'm just an amateur." That, I admit, was a borderline lie.

But Ben had the decency not to look for the yellow light he knew would be emanating from the device on his own finger.

We waited nine more minutes before Virginia entered the room and embraced Ben, which comforted him in spite of his realization that condolence was a bad sign.

"I'm so sorry," she said.

"Don't be. Just tell me what I can do for her."

"You can help me design her knowledge base. We have to put in new data; there's no other reasonable choice."

"Okay."

"So I'll ask you a series of questions, and the D/A's can implant an appropriate, generic set of language skills, academic knowledge, motor skills, and various athletic, sensory, and mental capabilities. But no first-hand memories. And we can't insert character, either. That has to come from her genetics and whatever learned patterns of behavior and thought haven't been erased. If there are any."

"Will she still be Alice Smith?"

"No one can be sure. Identity is so . . . ethereal. Completely here? No, never. But to what degree, it's simply unknowable. If we're lucky, some of her learned personality traits were so deeply ingrained they'll survive in some proportion. But she won't remember anything about her previous life."

"Nothing?"

"Nothing at the conscious level, and nothing that can ever find its way there. Ben, I'm sorry."

"Damn!" Ben took along, slow breath. "Well, let's get to work."

For the next twenty minutes Virginia asked him questions, and fed each answer into the central AI supervising Alice's brain reconstruction:

Q. What languages did she speak?
A. English, Italian, a little German.

Q. I see her parents were from Rome. I assume that's the dialect of Italian she knew.

A. Yes.

Q. And she was born in Wakefield, Massachusetts. Did she ever live anywhere else?

A. Not till she moved to Brookline in 1961, the year after my father died.

Q. Education?

A. Graduated from Wakefield High School, first in her class. Never went to college. Got married instead. But she read constantly: newspapers, books, even the dictionary and encyclopedia. Loved to think and learn; she was always using her mind.

Q. What were her other interests?

A. She'd wanted to teach, but the only time she ever got to was when I served in the Navy during the Second World War. That was January 1942 to June 1944. She taught eleventh grade. English literature and history.

Q. Can you remember the names of any newspapers and magazines she used to read? . . .

They were forging her, Ben thought. Counterfeiting his mother. And a good forgery needed lots of detail work. In all, Ben answered fifty-nine questions. It was a good thing we had Mnemex by then: he knew—and therefore remembered—all the answers.

Alice Smith opened her eyes and sat bolt upright. She saw three young adults forcing smiles; two men and one woman, all strangers to her. The room was pleasant enough; modern, bright, cheerful. Classical music surrounded her; she recognized it as "Winter," from Vivaldi's Four Seasons. The air smelled fresh and sweet, like ripe strawberries, and she felt relaxed and rested; and robust! The absence of all physical pain and discomfort was the first thing she noticed, even though she had no conscious memory of her own previous pain.

If only she could remember who she was.

"Who are you?" she asked us there, almost as a small child might ask visiting friends of her parents.

"Virginia Gonzalez. I'm a neuroscientist; also married to your great-great-granddaughter."

Virginia's answer was no shock to Alice, whose reconfigured brain was familiar with modern marriage customs.

"I'm Trip Crane," I said. "Your great-great-grandson."

Alice recognized my name. Trip Crane, a pioneer of nanotech. But she knew of me only as someone famous.

"And I'm your son, Ben Smith."

A son? She had a son? Apparently so. But she didn't know him— at all.

When he grasped her hand, she neither recoiled nor overlapped his hand with her own. She did smile at him, a grateful acknowledgement of his obvious feelings, then saw in his eyes that it was not quite what he'd wanted; needed.

"And who am *I*?" She turned toward Virginia for the authoritative answer.

"You're Alice Franklin Smith. You were born in 1904, frozen in 1990, and revived today: April twenty-second, 2081."

"Why can't I remember any of that?" she asked, even as her own mind must have told her the answer: that poor woman, Alice Franklin Smith! She had simply taken Alice Smith's place in this world, hadn't she?

"Unfortunately, " Virginia explained, "your memory was destroyed in 2017 when terrorists violated your canister."

Alice's eyebrows rose. "Oh. But if you tell me enough about myself, they'll come back—my memories?"

"I'm afraid it never works that way. Once we infuse new knowledge, skills, and patterning, the old memories never return."

Alice realized that would make me just like her clone or her twin. Her doppelgänger. Alike, but a brand new person entirely. The *real* Alice, God rest her soul, was gone.

She pondered the sadness of it, not just for herself, but for the *other* Alice Smith. And, of course, for her son.

"Never?"

"Never in my experience. But there might still be traces of your past life embedded somewhere in those neurons of yours. Maybe enough to affect your personality."

We four sat speechless, trying our best to absorb and perhaps accept an unalterable reality. It was Alice who broke the silence. "Other than my memory," she asked Virginia, "I'm healthy now?"

"Yes. Perfectly healthy."

"And obviously I'm with people who care about me."

"Yes. Absolutely."

"Well, Virginia Gonzalez," Alice Smith said, "if those memories are still there, I'll find a way to dredge them up. And if they're not, I suppose I'll have to make the most of it, won't I? But either way, I'm pleased to be alive."

At that moment, Ben decided this woman was definitely Alice Franklin Smith. As far as he was concerned, he had his mother back.

It was the only viewpoint he could bear.

NOVEMBER 3, 2081 — Ringling Brothers, Barnum and Bailey announces the closing of their all-machine circus, as the six-month experiment fails to attract sufficient attendance. "Our experience was similar to that of other entertainment organizations in dance, theater, and athletics," a spokesman explains. "Although it's impossible to discern the difference, even VR audiences insist on knowing that the performers are of the genuine flesh-and-blood variety." — The World Hedonism Conference sets a goal of ending all human (and if possible, all mammalian) suffering on earth by the middle of the third millennium. Conference Chairperson David Pearce explains, "exponential advances in nanotech, eugenics, genetic engineering, and clinical psychopharmacology should give us the power by the year 2500 to induce a permanent state of sublime happiness without impeding survival, progress, or creativity."

Dawn broke. Ben had survived 156 years to see this day, the biggest day of his life. It was as though every idea considered, every word spoken, every dream imagined, had led him to *now*. This exciting yet terrifying notion so energized him that he could barely force himself to remain in bed while the micromachines removed his whiskers and cleansed and dressed his body.

Slightly over six months had passed since Alice's reviv, and Gary remained her only direct descendant yet on ice. Ben had witnessed the revival of all three daughters and five grandchildren. My grandmother had achieved an especially satisfying outcome: Virginia had repaired Rebecca Crane's senility without memory loss by flawlessly executing a standard regimen of interpolation memory-reconstruction techniques.

But this would be Ben's most difficult reviv, and not only because his son's brain had undergone nearly two hours of ischemic damage. Even if Gary's memory remained intact, Ben wondered if he could ever build the loving relationship with his son that had eluded him longer than any other father in history. Indeed, reconciliation might be harder if Gary's immersion in Boston Harbor had *not* eradicated his memory.

All nine once-frozen Smiths now inhabited a 46,000 cubic foot space in the same Somerville, Massachusetts, residential complex where Ben had lived since 2073. As each new family member had been revived, AI-directed micromachines reconfigured the walls and floors, and arranged appropriate sound and odor shields for maximum privacy, but always at the expense of spaciousness. Each person now had a small room with private adjoining bathroom. They shared two kitchens, a foyer, and a medium-sized dining room/den.

Ben rose in a quick, fluid motion, as if propelled by a tightly wound coil spring. He took only a few steps before the wall separating his bedroom from the common rooms disappeared into the ceiling. He greeted most of the family at breakfast. Only Katie and Jan had yet to join them, and both would certainly arrive momentarily. Communal breakfast was a daily ritual upon which Ben insisted: a house rule.

Ben briefly considered another house rule he'd established: no more than one hour of VR per day.

"House rule!?" Maxine had shouted at him, just three weeks ago. "House rule? What did you do? Bring us all back so you could be *Daddy* again? Have a house full of girls to worship you?"

"Wait just a damn minute—" was as far as Ben got.

"No, Daddy dearest, *you* wait a damn minute. Or a hundred. Or a million. What difference does it make anyway?"

"Oh, come on—"

"No! You go on! Go on forever, if you want. I've already been around the big wheel once. What's the difference if I spend my second trip in a pod? I *like* it in there!" Maxine had begun to pant—hitching breath, but no sign of tears. "If you brought me back so you could tell me how long I can do VR, like you limited our TV time in the sixties or something, that's just plain sick. I'm not a child; I'm 129 years old, for chrissake, ninety-two of them conscious! Jesus. You are one sick asshole, you know that?" Then she started strutting; even kicked the wall. "You must've done all this just so you could finally get it right. This time. Being Daddy once wasn't enough, was it? You liked it so much you—"

"Shut up!" Ben bellowed. He hated it, but what choice did he have?

Now Maxine was frozen, suddenly crying, and there'd been something scary about it—like every ounce of moisture might drain from her body through those tear ducts.

Ben had stepped to his daughter's side and hugged her, burying his face in her hair.

"Let me guess," he whispered. "There's more to this than limited VR time, right?"

She was still crying, but the violence had melted. Now she seemed more hurt adult than angry child. He kissed the top of her head.

"Daddy," she'd said, warmth returning to her voice. "I'm sorry—sort of. But what have you done? What is there for me in a world like this? Everything I know is worthless here. I'm like a cavewoman in Paris."

He'd chuckled; hoped it would be contagious.

It wasn't.

"Honey," Ben tried, "I'm not the one to help you. I'm too close. Our emotions would swallow each other's. But I promise: Soon, being here will mean as much to you as it does to me."

She nodded ever so slightly.

Again Ben kissed her hair. "There are people who can help. We'll go see them together. Okay?"

Eventually she'd agreed. Although drug therapy had been required, she seemed okay now, even grateful that Ben had intervened. He prayed it wasn't an act. Thank God the drugs hadn't changed Max's personality, he now thought. Or cost her any crucial memory.

Of course, he'd run across far more difficult cases of VR addiction nearly every day in his practice. Sometimes entire brains had to be reformatted to keep them from atrophying! But Ben had always been able to separate himself from such tragedies; those cases were not his own flesh and blood.

After ordering breakfast from the microassembler, Ben announced, mostly to Katie and Jan, who were just then seating themselves at the table, "I was thinking Gary's three sisters should probably be there when he wakes up; and you, too, Katie, since he was there at your suspension."

"I wouldn't miss it for anything," Katie said.

"Don't know how much he'll want to see *me*," Jan said. "But I'd really like to go."

"Of course he'll want to see you," Rebecca said. "We were *all* ignorant back then. If Dad could forgive us, Gary certainly will . . ."

"Nothing to forgive," Ben said. "Back in the 1980s? Hell, I'm not even sure *I* believed biostasis would work. Besides, it was as much my fault as any of yours. I should've discussed it with you all before I set up that god-forsaken Trust in the first place."

"Oh, maybe not," Maxine said. "What if we'd talked you out of it? Some of us would no doubt be dead now. Cremated, embalmed, all that barbaric stuff. Anyway, we all made it, and that's what matters." She winked at Ben, who nodded back at her.

Alice grinned. "Amen."

"Do you want to come, Mom?" Ben asked her.

At first it had felt strange to Alice to be addressed as "Mom" by this young man who in most respects seemed older than she did. At times she had even found herself jealous of his memories, the measure of life. But she'd indulged him, and by now was used to it.

"Oh, no thank you," Alice answered. "I'll attend Toby Fiske's reviv if you want the company, but not Gary's. He'll have enough to deal with as it is. I think he'll need some preparation before he meets his amnesiac grandmother. Besides, I can use the time to study for my eugenics ethics exam."

Of course she didn't want to come, Ben realized. She didn't know her own grandson. Or *was* he her grandson? A wry smile hid Ben's uneasiness. "Always studying. If I didn't know better, I'd say you're in a hurry to move out of here."

Her expression changed to one of calm circumspection. "You're a wonderful son, Ben. But I need to be independent as soon as humanly possible. I'm sure we all do. I mean, a person can live without his or her own money these days, but, let's be honest, not nearly as well as those who have it. And envy is a great motivating force!"

Everyone laughed, but they all knew it was true.

"Besides," Alice added, "your daughters, much as they love you, would prefer to be living with their husbands. Once they can afford to revive them."

"Can't blame them for that," Ben said. Recently Jan had seemed especially heartsick.

A lawyer in her former life, Jan's skills were the least applicable to modern society. It would probably be three years before she would be able to revive Noah, which was still too soon for Ben. Never could stand that weasel, he thought.

These days, most of the Smith clan, Jan included, spent their time studying while holding low-paying apprentice positions, and would likely be forced to accept Ben's generosity for months or perhaps even years. Only two of his grandchildren, Sarah Banks (Alica's aunt) and Justin Swenson, having adapted their skills to today's world, had been able to resume their previous careers as a news service journalist and a real estate sales executive.

Sarah and Justin both planned on moving out today to make room for two new arrivals.

Ben had resolved to reintroduce Gary and Toby to consciousness on the same date. Toby's reanimation should be no problem, Ben thought. After all, his suspension had been predeath.

Therefore Toby was scheduled as today's lead-off reviv.

Yes, indeed, he thought, Toby ought to be there to joyously welcome Gary back—to a world infinitely more promising than the one he'd temporarily abandoned. But Toby might also have to help him reorient his son's mnemonically obliterated shell.

The moment I entered the room accompanied by both Wendy-girls, Ben knew Toby was fine. One of the golden retrievers ran up to Ben and began to lick his face.

"Textbook perfect biostasis!" I announced gleefully. "Those predeath suspensions are always the easiest."

Alice and Ben both beamed at the news. Ben hugged Wendy I, and rolled around with her on the carpet. It was now ten-fourteen A.M.

Less than an hour later, Toby was awake and grinning. "Ben! *Alice?* You two look terrific! Like generation X-ers, for goodness' sake. What year is it?"

"It's 2081. November third."

"Holy cow! We made it, pal." Then Dr. Tobias Fiske let loose a jubilant, "Whooooooooooopee!"

Of course! Ben thought. Toby had had himself frozen on a *schedule.* What a luxury! He'd been completely prepared for it. No stress. Just like going to sleep one night and waking up the next morning, in paradise.

My own perception about this morning's case, the easiest long-term reviv I'd seen, was almost identical to Ben's: It made sense. That was why short-term biostasis revivals tended to be so much less difficult than the long-term ones: not because of the time elapsed, but because the suspensions themselves had usually been performed under much less traumatic conditions.

"So where the heck's Gary?" Toby inquired.

"Funny you should ask," Ben said.

Gary's reviv was scheduled for one P.M., a fact that Toby was delighted to learn, until Ben explained that Gary had spent close to two hours at the bottom of Boston Harbor.

To pass the remaining, tense minutes, the two men borrowed my office to trade stories about the world and their lives; the years on each end of their suspensions when only one had been sentiment. It was a diverting celebration of their own victories over Death, and Ben contented himself by finally expressing appreciation to Toby for jettisoning a medical career to rescue him, first from brain damage and then from dissection.

Toby explained how instrumental Gary had been in preventing the autopsy. "And another guy who might deserve some credit for saving your life was Brandon Butters, the attorney who prosecuted me."

"Yeah? For blowing the case, you mean? Jan used to date Brandon in high school. Seemed like a helluva nice kid back then. I was pretty surprised, and a little disappointed, to see his name on those court documents."

"It wasn't like that," Toby said. "He was the man assigned to put me away, so I hated him, too, of course. But after it was over, I started thinking about it, and he was a real stand-up fellow."

"Oh? How so?"

"Well, I figure Noah must've been hounding him to accuse me of murdering you for the $200,000 you left me. Or maybe Banks just coerced Jan into suggesting it. I'm sure he knew the accusation wasn't true, but that wouldn't've stopped most assistant D.A.'s from making it, or at least using it as leverage. Career first, justice if convenient. And if Butters had made that argument, the judge would've had no choice; he'd have been required to uphold the autopsy writ."

"Really? I had no idea!"

"Good thing he was such an even-handed prosecutor, or you'd be worm food right now. He enforced, or attempted to enforce, the law, but he did *not* make sport of it."

"Luck enhanced by honor," Ben confirmed. "Today I feel damned lucky. Let's just hope our good fortune holds up for one more reviv." Wishful thinking, he feared, after those two hours Gary spent underwater.

Tabula rasa.

Ben fumed at himself for even thinking the words, but couldn't help it. Wasn't a "clean slate" between them exactly what he'd been hoping for since 1982? It was a dark thought which Ben knew had no place in his rational self; a gremlin, burrowed into his cerebellum.

Lord, no! He did not wish his son ever to forget what he'd done, he just needed Gary to reconcile with him for it. To make it clear and open again. In other words, they both needed a miracle.

Ben's three daughters and his granddaughter Katie entered my office.

Toby smiled at all four women. Only Jan had any difficulty mustering a sincere return greeting. There was no enmity in her now, only chagrin.

Toby's expression assured her that nine decades was far too long for either of them to bear a grudge.

"I'm so sorry," she whispered to Toby.

He responded with a grin. "No harm done."

"Thank you for saving my father," she said, ". . . from my ignorance." She'd spent the better part of a month composing those words in her mind.

Toby reflected for a moment. "Whatever happens today. Gary's gonna need us, and we're all gonna need each other."

I maintained some measure of hope. Granted, Gary had been submerged nearly two hours, while Alice's memories had been lost after twenty minutes of disruption. But the water temperature in Boston Harbor that morning had been only 37 degrees, and perhaps Gary did not drown right away. Every 18 degree drop (10 degrees Celsius) slowed ischemic brain damage by half. Gary's neurons should have deteriorated about one-twelfth as quickly as Alice's had. Furthermore, Gary was younger. So his two hours may have been less dangerous than Alice's twenty minutes. Theoretically.

Thus when Virginia's call came, I was pleased but not amazed. I told the six awaiting news in my office, "The early reports are encouraging."

The group was ushered to Gary's recovery room; the updates had been consistently positive. All damage and trauma had been repairable; his long-term memory was intact. Still, even with the latest mood-boosting medications, nobody expected this reviv to be easy.

Gary opened his eyes and looked at the very young, strangely familiar faces. "Where's Father Steve?"

"Don't you recognize any of us?" Toby asked.

"No. Who are you?"

"Listen to my voice, Gary."

Gary's head tilted forward as if staring at an oasis in the desert; making sure it was no mirage. "Toby? Toby Fiske? But you're a child!"

"So are you, now. Young and good as new. Even your leg is perfect."

Gary felt his left shin and knee. No pain at all.

"Perfectly healed," Ben announced. "You can run marathons on that leg if you want."

Gary stared at his own young, smooth, strong hands. "Where the hell am I?"

"You're almost home," Ben said. "Here in Boston, with your family. Welcome back."

"No. This can't be right. Father Steve and I were supposed to watch the sunrise in Boston Harbor. I have to finish *The Dawn of Life*. My painting. Six and a half years of my life, for chrissake. Where's my equipment?"

Katie stepped to the side of his bed. "Gary," she said, hugging him, "the important thing is that you're alive, with your memories intact. You have a thousand years to finish your painting if you need it. You're alive, Gary! Thank God."

"Katie? *You're* back!" He finally began to understand. "When?"

"About three months ago."

"Everyone made it? Alice, too? Where's Grandma Alice?"

"At home," Ben explained. "But her memories didn't survive that terrorist attack. She's young and healthy and smart. But she won't know you right away, son."

"Is she still . . . Alice?"

Ben considered the question. "To me she is."

"I see. What year is this?"

"It's 2081. November third."

"Lord. And Father Steve? Is he okay?"

"We don't know," I said. "He's frozen. At a facility in Wellesley. But you're fine, so there's a good chance he is, too."

"So what happened to me, Trip?"

"Boating accident on Boston Harbor."

"I don't even remember going out there."

"Short-term memory loss," Virginia Gonzalez explained. She was now the only person in the room whom Gary did not recognize. "But otherwise, you're completely sound. A miracle. You were underwater for two hours."

"Two hours? I thought brain damage was irrevocable after fifteen minutes."

"That was because passages in the brain begin to clog as soon as blood flow ceases. Blood coagulates in the vascular system, and medical science couldn't reverse that. Not true anymore. Nanomachines can clear all the plaque even before we restore blood flow. And information in human neurons usually lasts at least an hour even at room temperature. But the water that morning was much colder than that. You were lucky."

"I don't remember the water," Gary said. "We were just walking toward the harbor. Talking. Looking at the buildings and the stars. Then nothing. Then, what? Forty-eight years? Simply vanished. God. It all happened without me. Just like that."

"You have forever, Gary," Maxine said. "What's forty-eight years compared with a thousand?

"I'm not sure I want a thousand." He stared at Ben, his father, his suddenly young father, whose previous age and infirmity had for so long seemed his only vulnerability; Gary's advantage over him, his only revenge. And now the man was young again. Young and strong and healthy.

As was he.

Gary began to tremble and sob, and hard as he tried, he couldn't stop the tears. He cried for nearly an hour, not knowing whether he should feel joyous or miserable, grateful or angry, proud or ashamed.

FEBRUARY 28, 2083 — In the worst single irrevocable loss of human life on earth in nearly two decades, an antiquated Energia lifting platform explodes at the WASA research facility in Salisbury, Zimbabwe, incinerating 342 workers. A freak, clear-skies lightning strike is blamed for the accident. Zimbabwe is one of only seven states that have yet to accept the installation of weather-control throughout populated regions. AIs predict that today's accident will bolster weather-control's acceptance there enough to sway next month's referendum. — Zeppelins supplant ocean liners as the most popular sightseeing vacation option after Carnival offers a three-week around-the-world cruise aboard Aircity 50s, their 6,600-passenger luxury dirigibles, at half the price of comparable seafaring accommodations. Aircity 50s have recently been WAA-cleared for overland flights, now that the great airships automatically become sufficiently transparent over populated areas not to eclipse sunlight. — To foster species diversity and add fresh perspective to civilization, World President ·Montag Smits endorses World Referendum 62, allowing several dozen Neanderthals to be cloned from trace DNA in fossilized bone. The vote will take place next month.

It was early evening. Father and daughter sat alone in a booth at Marci's, a quiet restaurant on the 312th floor of their residential building. The room was empty of other patrons, but Ben activated their soundshield just in case.

"Jan, I know this conversation won't be easy. There are things I simply have to know."

"About the court case, right?"

"Yes, honey. About the court case."

"I was afraid of that."

"Don't be. I'm just trying to figure out something important."

"What, Dad?"

"Whether I owe my life to your friend, Brandon Butters. How well do you remember your conversations with him?"

"Too well. Sometimes Mnemex can be a curse, you know. I'm not proud of those conversations at all."

"Jan, you're my daughter. I don't condone or condemn you for any of it. It's a thing apart from blood. I'll always love you no matter what. You do know that, don't you?"

Jan noted the solid green Truth Machine light on her contact lens before she answered. She felt contrite for that, too, but had to be sure he really meant it before she could tell him what she'd done. "Yes. I do." *Now,* she did.

"Honey, did you ever suggest to Brandon that Toby Fiske might have murdered me just to get the money I left him?"

"Yes," she whispered.

"Did you really believe that? About Toby?"

"Dad, I don't know. Probably not. But Noah seemed so sure of it, and I wanted to believe it." She began to weep. Ben forced himself to sit still. "We thought we needed the money, and Noah told me that once they autopsied your body, it'd be much easier to challenge the Trust. You were dead. We were positive cryonics was a crock. But we were wrong. So wrong. Oh my God, we almost made them thaw you, kill you, over money."

"But they didn't, sweetheart."

"Only because Brandon didn't believe Toby had really murdered you. If he had, they would've performed that autopsy. And you'd be gone forever, because of me. And maybe I'd be gone forever, too."

"Weren't you surprised he never filed the first degree murder accusation?"

"Shocked."

"Why?"

Jan said nothing.

"Please tell me," Ben said evenly. "I have to know, It's important."

She began to tremble. "Because I knew Brandon was still in love with me. He never said it, but I always knew. So I tried to manipulate him. I was using his feelings for me as a way to get at that money. Your money. I knew exactly what I was doing. But he was too principled to fall for it."

Ben looked into his daughter's eyes and thought about how he'd survived in the freezer for nearly ninety years. Ninety years! He marveled that he was still alive and safe. An absolute miracle. The science had been the easy part. Of course it would be! It should have been obvious all along that they'd eventually learn how to reconstruct human cells. Only a matter of time. The hard part had been . . .

He pictured his frozen body, easy prey for predators like Noah Banks, or the three terrorists who'd destroyed the Phoenix suspendees. Those bastards had killed 508 people. Only luck and the family name had spared him. Luck and the family name. It didn't seem like much, arrayed against the forces of greed and ignorance. He shook his head, flooded with gratitude and something very much like wonder.

Then he stood and half circling the table, reached over to hug the child who had almost destroyed him.

In July 2029 Brandon Butters had taken early retirement from government service at age seventy-five. Within a few years after the Truth Machine's introduction in 2024, there'd been precious little for prosecutors to do anyway. But at least he'd retired with a clear conscience; he'd always done his best, clinging to his own idea of justice, no matter the temptation.

His one regret was that he'd never had children. He rued this lack from multiple perspectives: the love and meaning children would have brought to his life, the satisfaction of leaving a genetic legacy, the fulfillment of a biological imperative. And certainly not least: that only one's family would likely have reason to revive a person from biostasis.

But he'd never even been married. He'd been involved with different women, and had tried to make things work with each of them. Yet he just couldn't. After all those years, he was still in love with his high school sweetheart, his married high school sweetheart, whom he knew he could never have. He realized the obsession was foolish, and maybe even a little sick, but if this was illness, the primary symptom was poignancy. And in poignant memory lived everlasting romance.

A hopeless romantic, he thought. That's what I am.

When he retired, his medical AI had assured him of at least another twenty years of decent health. But he had no family, few friends, no career, very little money, nothing much left to live for. He'd disdained the notion of continuing his present lonely existence imprisoned in a rapidly decaying body. So he'd had himself frozen that same year.

He didn't believe in suicide, nor had he particularly wished to die, yet his rational side realized that without family to revive him, biostasis might amount to the same thing.

Brandon was surprised when he regained consciousness, and shocked to see a familiar face staring back at him. He couldn't place who that young man was, but realized he knew him from somewhere.

The young man spoke: "I'm Benjamin Smith, Jan's father. I'm also your sponsor. Welcome back, son."

Brandon stared at Ben. "Jan's father?"

Ben smiled. "Everyone's just a wee bit more youthful these days. Including you."

Brandon realized that he did feel vibrant and healthy; better than he ever had, even back in law school. "What year is this?"

"It's 2083."

Amazing. He didn't even feel stiff—after fifty-four years! "Why would you reanimate *me*? I'm the guy who tried to have you thawed for autopsy."

"Because you also saved my life."

"Huh?"

"By refusing to accuse Toby Fiske of first degree murder. Because most prosecutors in your position would've filed that charge just to try to work out a plea bargain. Because even though the twentieth century legal system was based mostly on leverage, you never ran your cases that way."

"I couldn't," Brandon said. "No justice in it that way."

"Same reason I decided to sponsor your reviv, Brandon. Because I, too, believe in justice."

JUNE 1, 2083 — Canadian sport-fisher Frank Trilby announces the capture of a 186-pound lobster, exceeding by 11 pounds the specimen washed ashore off Bar Harbor, Maine, six years ago. In the four decades since commercial fishing was replaced by cell culturing (then micro and nano food assemblers), many marine creatures have been found to grow to heretofore unknown size. Upon returning the lobster to the Atlantic Ocean, Trilby quips to news cameras: " 'Eah, in a few years I expect t'catch me a hot-danged ichthyosaur, eh?" — In an action termed by several newscasters as "curiously anachronistic," the World Tribunal declares all substance abuse laws in violation of the World Constitution. The Tribunal's declaration concludes: "The concept of substance abuse has no meaning in light of pharmacological advances over the past half century, and involves no appreciable physiological or ethical distinction from VR overuse, which is completely legal." There hasn't been a single conviction over violations of the laws since the founding of World Government in 2045, and the only two *arrests* occurred prior to 2050.

Brandon chose a seat at the breakfast table, across from Jan. Again. He'd lived with them for twelve weeks now, and had never sat down beside her at a meal.

Was he afraid of her? she wondered.

He always seemed friendly and sweet and solicitous, like a protective big brother. Maybe he was over her.

She would have thought that was just great several months ago, but living under the same roof, he seemed to be getting more attractive by the day. And when he sat across from her, she was forced to look at him, which was becoming quite a problem. Because now, whenever she saw him, she would get incredibly, well, aroused.

" 'I can't define it, but I'll know it when I see it,' " Gary Franklin Smith quoted to the class: forty-six students attending in person at Leslie Williams Auditorium on the Tufts University campus, and nearly three hundred seated elsewhere in real-time VR pods. "A United States jurist once made that remark about pornography. But it might apply equally well to artistic greatness in dance, sculpture, poetry, fiction, theater, painting—any form of aesthetic achievement. Sometimes you simply cannot define, except in vague generalities, what makes art pleasing, instructive, thought-provoking, memorable, compelling. Yet you know. You just know.

"Of course, some poor fools still depend upon that philosophy for their scientific worldview. And God help *them*."

The students laughed.

"But I do think subjective analysis might actually apply to art. At least the AIs aren't sophisticated enough to assimilate certain multidimensional art forms in objective terms, and thereby become better at it than humans. Not yet, anyway . . ."

After the lecture, Gary returned to his residence for a nap. He had a momentous afternoon planned, a duty he'd been anticipating and in some ways dreading. To handle the delicate task properly, he would need to be alert, well-rested.

Yet moments after climbing into bed next to his sleeping girlfriend, he suffered a change of heart.

Kimber Chevalier stirred gently, opened her dark eyes and gazed at him. "Come here, my sweet man."

About a year earlier, Gary had managed to strike out on his own despite having arrived at the era of nanorejuvenation without money. By the time he got his own place, he'd already spent seven comfortless months living in his father's dwelling, as if a still-dependent child. The tension between them, never inconsequential, had built upon itself. It had helped that Toby was there, and had Alice remembered who she was, the situation might have been bearable. But she didn't, and it wasn't.

By early June of 2082 Gary had figured out that he could cash in on his residual fame by becoming an art history and philosophy lecturer. Universities, he'd discovered, were willing to pay handsomely for familiar names. And his newfound autonomy was sweet. Now he could even tolerate his father—for an hour or two at a time.

Best of all was Kimber.

She attended his first lecture and had approached him afterward. He found her the most erotic-looking woman he'd seen in his lives—both of them. Something about the way she carried herself suggested that her extraordinary beauty was genetic, not artificially induced.

She told him that for nearly a decade she'd studied the great American landscape artists: Cole, Church, Bierstadt, Moran, and that he, Gary Franklin Smith, had always been her favorite. He knew it wasn't just flattery, because she could describe his paintings down to underlying nuances the critics had missed. Besides, his Truth Machine light had shone steady green as she spoke. Yes, he was really her favorite artist, seven decades after the worldwide craze for his work had faded. Amazing.

At first they'd become casual friends, meeting for lunch or dinner once or twice a week to talk art history. Unlike Gary, Kimber had never been frozen. She was born in Paris on June 15, 1997, almost fifty years after Gary's birth. Her father was French, her mother Japanese.

A few weeks after they'd met, Gary and Kimber made love one afternoon. All afternoon. It was delightful and satisfying, sumptuous yet comfortable, so they'd begun sleeping together regularly. Yet both balked at the prospect of committed involvement.

Slowly, they'd begun to share more intimate aspects of their lives. She told him of her first marriage, which had lasted only three years, when she was in her early twenties. Her husband had been violently jealous and abusive. She'd fled to her grandparents in Kyoto, divorced the creep, and on the rebound remarried a Japanese man.

Six years later, she'd been devastated when her second husband left her for a man.

She'd remained unwed for half a century.

Gary told Kimber about the harsh treatment he'd endured from his father, and how his mother's death had driven him to alcohol and drugs. He described his friendship with Tobias Fiske, his loneliness and VR gambling addiction after Toby's suspension, his recovery and obsession with his latest project, then the accident he could not remember, and his feelings of responsibility about Father Steve's (hopefully impermanent) death.

And, of course, the continuing strife with his father.

"When you get right down to it, my life's going okay. Everyone has problems, right? But why in heaven's name do I react to that sonofabitch the way I do?"

He soon realized he could talk to her about anything at all; he trusted her to respect and believe in him no matter what he revealed. As the love between them grew, Gary discovered his own self-confidence returning for a second springtime as well.

Perhaps he would even complete his masterpiece someday, if he could only capture the spirit missing from it. The perfect sunrise for *The Dawn of Life*. But then again, during all those years of painting, he'd never seen or been able to visualize the sunrise the work required. Why should he expect to find it now?

Gary sat in my office, holding Kimber's hand, feeling grateful that she'd allowed—no, encouraged—him to sponsor this reviv, even though it threatened to disrupt what little privacy they enjoyed.

"Do you think he'll be all right?" he asked me.

"Virginia?" I called to her through my two-way wallscreen. "Care to field that one?"

Observing us from the reviv lab on her own wallscreen, Virginia smiled in wry surrender. "Well, obviously *your* memory's okay, Gary. So chances are good that he'll be fine, too. But you never know. So if not, I hope you can handle it."

"We can," Kimber assured her. "We know what Alice is like, and she's delightful—"

Gary interrupted, "Yeah, maybe about ninety percent of the time."

"But imagine if you had no memory of your past life," Kimber chided. "In a way, she doesn't even know who she is. Under the circumstances, I think she's amazing."

"But if you'd known her before . . . if you'd known her back then . . ."

"Which brings up another point," Virginia offered. "Every amnesia reviv is different. The way memory loss is handled depends on the individual. Some adapt quickly, feel grateful to be alive at all. Like Alice. But others become depressed or even resentful. As I said, you never know."

"We'll be ready," Kimber said. "We have to be. Gary feels responsible for Father Steve. If he didn't feel that way, he wouldn't be Gary. I'm glad he wants to do this, because it's the right thing to do. No, we're ready to help him adjust; anything it takes, for however long it takes. Period."

"We should know in less than a minute," Virginia said.

"Whatever happens," Gary said, "thanks for being here, Gin, for helping us with this reviv even though we can't afford to pay you. However it comes out, if there's ever anything I can do for you—"

"Actually, there is."

"Just tell me. Anything."

Virginia answered, completely straight-faced: "Give me a lock of Kimber's hair. I'd like to have her cloned."

While all three of us in my office were laughing, Kimber somewhat nervously, Virginia looked down at her update screen. "His memory's still there. He'll be fine."

When Father Steven Jones first saw Gary, he didn't recognize him. On the day they'd first met, Gary was fifty-four years old. His frame had already become lopsided after decades of hobbling on a shortened left leg; very different from his present, perfectly proportioned, twenty-three-year-old physical aspect.

"Hey, stranger," Gary said. "Welcome to the year 2083."

"Gary?"

"Yep. It's me."

"It's 2083?"

Gary nodded.

"Holy Trinity! It really is you, isn't it?"

Soon their conversation veered toward the accident. "Gary, I tried to warn you about the wave, but it was too close and too bloody fast."

"I'm sure it was . . . Hey. You remember the accident?"

"Uh-huh. It being our last required early-morning excursion . . ."

"It was?"

"Of course. After that perfect sunrise, no reason to go back. Guess that's why the whole morning made such an impression on me. Where's the painting displayed, anyhow? I can't wait to see it."

Gary lowered his eyes in frustration, overcome by losing what he now understood had actually been in his grasp. "I never finished it."

"What? You're joking . . ."

"Steve, I lost my short-term memory. Nothing left of that morning at all."

"Oh, no," Father Steve said, shaking his head, intent, searching.

"It was really a perfect sunrise? One that would've completed the painting?"

"So you said. Even looked pretty good to my Philistine eyes, though I don't know how I could ever explain what was different about it."

"No, of course not. Damn!" Gary said, "But, hey, at least *you're* here. I imagine you've noticed you look like a twenty-three-year-old kid. Should feel like one, too."

"I do. How long will it last?"

"On average, oh, about 1,100 years." Gary smiled. "Sound okay to you?"

"Praise be to God!" Father Steve grinned. "By the way, seems to me I had my wristband set on 'Document' while we were out in the boat."

The implication of that revelation quickly dawned on Gary. "You mean the sunrise . . ."

Father Steve nodded. "Safely stored in my private archives. Unless it was erased in some monumental cataclysm. Anything like that you haven't mentioned yet?"

Gary laughed in unmistakable glee. "Nope."

"Then we can view it whenever you want."

NOVEMBER 16, 2083 — According to newly released data, average human intelligence rose by .93% last year, the highest annual increase since 2075, the year Mnemex was introduced. If every person on earth were tested today based on 1983 "IQ" standards, 143.4 would be the median score, a figure many specialists deem misleadingly low. "We can't employ today's standards when comparing modern intelligence to that of a century ago because we have no reliable statistical data on century-old human artistic, interpersonal, musical, kinesthetic, and emotional aptitudes. Intelligence tests were simply not as comprehensive then as they are today," notes Yale intelligence expert Dr. Howard Starmont, who ascribes this year's increase to eugenics, improved nutrition, advanced teaching AI systems, and various medical enhancements. — In a move considered by most citizens to be long overdue, polygamy is officially legalized worldwide. With several million de facto polygamous marriages formed over the last 17 years, when suspended spouses of remarried widows and widowers underwent revivification, the laws have long been deemed hypocritical. "Today's legislation finally halts a disgraceful injustice," explains Swiss Senator Alain Haberling. "Why must one spouse be temporarily and needlessly frozen, just so the other can legally take a second husband or wife?"

Jan sat in her pod facing Sigmund Freud. As always, she felt much better now than when her session had started, but her hour was nearly gone. Another half hour sure would have been nice.

Normally, she preferred Robert Steinberg. He was easier to relate to, especially since she and the renowned Dartmouth researcher had been born, frozen, and revived at roughly the same times. Besides, of all the shrinks from whom she could have chosen, Steinberg was by far the best looking.

Financial considerations had not induced her to opt for Freud. Even with the royalties that Virtual Analysis Ltd. paid the reliving Steinberg for the use of his likeness and proprietary methods, a session with him still cost less, in real terms, than a movie ticket had during the twentieth century. No, she chose Freud this time to enjoy a change of pace, and maybe also just to remind herself of what a fifty-year-old, never-rejuvenated human being looked like.

Jan felt a powerful seduction from the pod: the Covenant of Safety. No matter what she said to Steinberg or Freud or any of her other AI-spawned companions, her words could never come back. Outside, in the world of flesh-beyond-pixels, the most innocent statements, even those spoken in confidence, could set off a ricochet and boomerang; a nasty surprise with unintended consequences.

But that could not happen in the world of virtual humans. Within this barely reduced dimensional context, you could say or do anything without fear of its effect on others. How easy the self-seduction? Jan often wondered how VR addiction had managed to avoid becoming a genuine pandemic.

She was glad her father had instructed the AIs to limit each of them to an hour a day. But what about when she was independent, living on her own? Jan felt this tiny roundworm of uncertainty burrowing through her mind. What would happen when she and her sisters could buy their own VR pods and control their own AIs?

Freud interrupted her thoughts. "You're confusing love with sex, young woman."

"I know. Dr. Steinberg tells me the same thing."

"For a satisfying life, choose love over sex, my dear. It is far more permanent, and thus worthier."

"But doctor," she said, her confidence restored, at least temporarily, "I might not have to choose. I know what I need, and this time I intend to have both!"

Ben stood in the dining room and lifted his left wrist to his mouth. "The first reviews should come across our news service within the hour," he announced through his pager to all family members, whether at home or elsewhere. It was now ten-ten A.M. "I'll let you know what the critics say the minute they input it."

Gary Franklin Smith had unveiled *The Dawn of Life* on the Artnet forty minutes earlier. A few of the world's top art critics were no doubt already busy writing their analyses. Public opinion mattered more, but critical acclaim might give the work an early boost, speeding its conveyance to art screens worldwide, adding sorely needed royalty income to Gary's WCU account.

By now art was extraordinarily cheap to display digitally, and in quality indistinguishable from the actual composition, quite unlike viewing through VR, 3-D, or even an impeccably cleaned window; more akin to examining the picture visually and tactilely, in the flesh, as it were, at a museum or art gallery. Therefore, most homes maintained a dozen or more such screens. Even at three WCUs per artscreen viewing-year, a well-received work could provide its owner a comfortable income.

The copyrights on Gary's previous works had expired long ago, so all of his eggs were in one basket: *The Dawn of Life*.

The moment Father Steve obtained his archive record of their accident, Gary had set to work. While artists no longer applied paint by hand, the task of determining where every fleck of color should be placed by the micromachines had hardly been less demanding. Adding the sunrise to the programming datacube had required nearly 1,500 hours of concentration. Gary had to view and analyze every reasonable variation of color, shape, texture, and light on his design AI screen before he could be satisfied with the composition.

Like any commercial painter, writer of fiction, playwright, choreographer, journalist, or essayist, once Gary knew he'd given his best to the job, he simply released the work cybernetically and waited in purgatory for the world to respond.

While Gary sat apprehensively with Kimber in his home, Jan Smith invited Brandon Butters for a walk outside.

"I need your advice about something very private," she told him in words just barely true enough to pass a scip. "It'll only take a few minutes. Dad said we could get any news coming in on Gary from our wristbands."

The moment they were alone, Jan took his hand and waylaid him: "Brandon, are you still in love with me?" Once the words hung naked on the line, she felt relieved to have put them there.

Brandon's face froze, as though it might shatter if his expression were to change. "W-Why?" His lips moved little more than a ventriloquist's. "Why would you ask me a question like that?"

"Because I love you."

"You do?"

"Yeah."

He gaped at her. "Why? Why now?"

"I guess maybe I always did and just never let myself know it. But living in the same house with you, day after day, well, I can neither deny nor stand it. You're admirable, not to mention incredibly sexy. And I trust you. I could never trust Noah, which my shrinks tell me is what gave him such sexual power. Now that I understand, it no longer holds me. I'm ready for *you*, because I know you'll always do what's right. I was an idiot to give you up for him. A fool. But at least I know it now. So are you still in love with me?"

Brandon stood in reflection. "What does it matter? You're married to someone else."

Taking his answer as a yes, Jan grinned. "Actually, I'm not."

"What?"

"The law only upholds unions where both partners are either suspended or conscious. When one spouse is frozen, the animated partner decides if the marriage is valid. My choice. My marriage to Noah no longer exists, legally or in my heart."

"If that's true," Brandon said, starting to smile, "and if you don't revive your hus—I mean Noah, then who will?"

"Maybe no one. I'm not sure I care. Maybe he doesn't deserve to live again."

"That isn't for us to decide, Jan."

"Oh, Brandon. Of course we don't have the right to prevent others from reviving him. But it's damn well our decision whether or not we should sponsor his reviv, and I vote not."

"There doesn't seem to be much love lost on the part of your children, either."

"He wasn't much of a father."

"He's still a human being, Jan. You can't let him die. It's a different world now, one that enforces honesty and redemption. You and your children are his family, his only family. So if not you, who? And if not now, when? Each day he remains frozen lessens his chances."

"Don't be so sure. The technology's getting cheaper every year, and storage is becoming more expensive."

"Then what?"

"If they ever decide to abandon suspendees who don't have sponsors, we can always revive him."

"I suppose we'd have to," Brandon said. "I'm not sure I could live with myself if we didn't."

"I doubt it'll ever come to that. Besides, don't you think everyone will be revived? Maybe he'll wake up in about fifty years on some lovely space habitat in earth's orbit; find someone else to marry and have a nice comfortable life."

"I suppose," Brandon said, but he looked away.

Jan playfully arched her eyebrows. "Either that, or wind up on the out-colony of a lesser Jovian moon."

"But he's . . . he was your husband. And now he'll wake up alone, if at all."

"Don't feel sorry for him. That part's his fault, not mine. He almost killed my father, and got me to help him. But you saved Dad. I want to spend the rest of my life with you. I'll never forgive Noah, or stop loving you. Never."

"And what about Ben?" Brandon asked. "Your father revived me. Probably saved my life. I couldn't do anything behind his back."

Jan smiled. "Of course not," she said, then kissed his mouth. "God, I love you, Brandon! Let's go talk to him. Right now."

"Ben," Brandon entreated, "I've loved your daughter since we were teenagers, and apparently she's now in love with me. Fact is, we'd like to get married, sir, and I hope with your blessing."

Ben's response was unanticipated: "Now, let me get this straight. You're asking me whom I'd prefer as a husband to my daughter; you or some fellow who tried to have me thawed so he could get at the money in my trust fund? Quite a dilemma." He grinned. "Welcome to the family, son."

Ben Smith embraced Brandon Butters, just like the jubilant bear hug in which Toby Fiske had enveloped him on the day Marge gave birth to Gary. It reminded Ben that even in so joyful a moment, there yet remained in his life plenty of unresolved grief, all connected with his irrevocably deceased wife and estranged son.

The first of hundreds of media reviews that day was entered by Alec Auberty, art critic for the Dallas News Syndicate:

> *I happened to be born in the 1990s; the decade when the pitched battle between science and mysticism for the hearts and minds of the human race at last began to draw even. We hadn't the means to know it then, but after eons of domination by the malevolent forces of darkness and ignorance, civilization stood at the very threshold of our Millennium of Hope. I remember first being told, at the age of seven, that life began on planet Earth some three billion years ago.*
>
> *Like most of my generation, since childhood I have tried to imagine that miracle. Today, for the first time, I not only visualized the moment, I felt it.*
>
> *In creating what is perhaps this century's most important artistic accomplishment, a composition of unrivaled splendor, palpability, and eloquence, Gary Franklin Smith has single-handedly restored my faith that humans can achieve feats of which machines shall never be capable . . .*

By midnight, *The Dawn of Life* would tally over forty million viewer hours, a record-shattering statistic destined to be broken by the same work again and again over the coming weeks, months, and years.

As rave reviews mounted that day, Gary knew that his father would be proud and happy for him. Yet he was shocked to realize that his father's pride gave him no gratification. The fact that Ben would feel self-satisfaction tainted Gary's sense of accomplishment; damaged his own joy.

What the hell was wrong with him? Why couldn't he get past his father and just go on with his own life?

He would tell no one of this feeling, not even Kimber.

DECEMBER 31, 2083 — Chrysler Motors Corporation's recently revived DeSoto division unveils a fully operational prototype of its Sport-Explorer Hovermobile. The machine, which hovers on an air cushion at 16 inches above ground, includes one noteworthy new option, a manual override control. The vehicle will traverse almost any terrain without environmental consequences, and can scale up to a 60-degree grade with no loss of forward momentum. Chrysler's announced sales slogan is: "VR can't touch it!"—On the third day of his self-induced cold, medical historian Daniel Appel finally instructs his nanomachine immune system to banish the virus from his body. He explains, "Three days was about all I could stand, and I think I can now remember the feeling well enough to describe it in my next text. The last time I was sick was nearly half a century ago, and you forget what it's like. It's amazing to realize that people once lived with illness as a normal part of their lives. I'm glad I got to experience the disease one more time, but wouldn't want to go through it again." Since 2055, only 17 other humans have sustained any viral illnesses lasting more than a few minutes.

Gary Franklin Smith and Kimber Chevalier had been married two months. She hosted a New Year's Eve celebration at their luxurious new home, inviting only relatives, plus Toby and Father Steve. Almost every member of her family attended, and she'd insisted upon inviting Gary's entire family as well, especially Ben.

Kimber embraced her father-in-law at the door and escorted him inside.

"My dear girl," he said. "Of all my son's extraordinary successes, winning your heart was to me his most gratifying."

She giggled with unembarrassed delight. "Come. I want you to meet my parents and grandparents . . ."

While he chatted with his son's new in-laws, Ben Smith made up his mind about something he'd been mulling for a long time. It wasn't the perfect answer, but it was the best he could do.

Ben knew his daughter-in-law would be the perfect ally. Thus, later that evening, with Kimber present as a buffer, he told his son: "I've decided to clone your mother."

Gary ceased all motion and speech, as if disconnected from a power source.

"I have a lock of her hair," Ben added. "Trip tells me that's enough."

"But she won't be Mom," Gary finally said. "She'll be a stranger who looks like Mom."

"Not really," Ben explained. "Every person clones differently, and even every identical clone is raised in a unique way. She'll be an entirely different person, genetically the same as your mother, only without life-experience. She'll know us soon enough, though, and love us, just like Alice does."

"Who else have you told?" Gary asked.

"Your sisters, moments ago. And Brandon."

"What do *they* think?"

"Didn't ask for their opinions. I'm pretty sure Rebecca's for it. The others, well, I can't really tell yet."

"Do you propose to bring her back as an infant or an adult?" Gary's voice was now evenly modulated. But a tiny muscle danced at a corner of his mouth.

"Haven't decided yet. Either way, I need your support, because I have to do it."

"Dad, I'm not—"

"Ben," Kimber interrupted, pulling Gary's right arm, "will you excuse us for just a few minutes?"

"Of course."

When the couple returned six minutes later, Ben was chatting with Brandon, Jan, Katie, and me. Kimber spoke. "If you decide to bring your wife back as an infant, Gary and I would like to raise her."

Ben stared at her. Now it was his turn to feel profoundly disoriented. "That's a wonderful offer. But a mother raised from infancy by her own son?"

"Actually," Brandon volunteered, "it's quite common now for people to raise clones of their parents from infancy. There've been at least five million PCI parenting licenses issued over the last few years. In fact I've never heard of anyone being turned down—other than multiple requests, of course."

Ben marveled at how quickly the latest revivs seemed to assimilate. Barely ten months ago, Brandon had still been in suspension. Now he was talking about this stuff as though it had been common practice his entire life.

"That's quite an interesting statistic, honey," Jan said. "But what's your opinion about it?"

"I think it's normal for orphans to want to resurrect their parents," Brandon said. "I mean, if you've decided to have a child anyway, why not have one with the exact genetics of a lost loved one?"

"Are there many clones of currently living people?" Katie asked.

"Uncommon," Brandon said. "Not too many of us want exact duplicates of ourselves around, and of course nobody can clone a living person without any person's permission."

"Are you sure you want to do this, Kimber?" Ben asked. "It's much harder to raise someone from infancy . . ."

"And more satisfying, too," Kimber said. "In a way, it would be Gary's tribute to his mother. Besides, it should be less traumatic for the new Marge to be raised as a normal child than to become conscious as an adult with only generic, impersonal knowledge and no experiential memory. I'd imagine clones raised from infancy would be less likely to get lost in, or overuse, modern addictions."

"Not only that," Brandon said to Ben, "an infancy cloning would give you both more time to decide if you really want to spend the rest of your lives together."

"Oh. I just kind of assumed we would. But I guess . . ."

"It usually does work out that way, Ben," Brandon said, "simply because the same qualities that attracted the original couple to each other still exist, but not always. At least it hasn't always happened with adult clonings. Too soon to compile meaningful statistics on infants, though, since most clonings of deceased spouses have occurred within the last decade."

"Boy," Katie said, "this is real future-shock stuff. Back when I was suspended, I thought I was taking a risk donating my retinas. But now I know at least a dozen people who've been revived from just their frozen heads."

"I interviewed a married couple last week," Brandon said, "both revived from their brains alone. The amazing thing is that he had killed her, almost seventy-five years ago. Set her afire in a fit of rage, and received the death penalty for it."

"Then what happened?" Katie asked.

"I offered to have his brain frozen for revivification research, and he accepted. Six decades later, the state revives him by cloning his body to house his brain, and cures his mental illness. He starts a successful business, builds a new life, and revives his wife; his own murder victim! Now they're married again, happily, this time."

"Amazing," Jan said, "especially to anyone from our generation. During the twentieth century, if you'd predicted anything like that would happen, I'd've called for the men in the white coats!"

Kimber turned toward Gary. "Shows the healing power of time."

Gary must have understood her point, Ben decided. It wasn't subtle.

"When I viewed the AudioVid record soon after the crime itself," Brandon said, "I could never have foreseen this outcome. But I guess a lot of people reconcile after a divorce. Well, this was a divorce, albeit by the ultimate means. Plus, he did arrange for her reviv, and he's fixed in the sanity department. She loved him once, so maybe it's not that shocking."

"Sure it is," Gary said with a playful smile.

Brandon laughed. "Yeah, come to think of it . . ."

"But the fact that it could happen at all," Gary said, "shows that the information in your brain is what really matters. Too bad Mom's brain wasn't frozen."

Ben nodded sadly, as guilt over a 104-year-old lapse bubbled to his consciousness.

"Anyway, what do you say, Dad?" Gary asked. "You want us to raise her?"

"Bringing her back as an adult would be easier," Ben said. "And two decades is a long time to wait . . ."

"Nothing like it used to be," Katie said. "I once thought two decades would be my whole life, and now I hope to have at least a hundred more decades!"

Ben stood silently, distracted by thoughts of the real Margaret Callahan Smith. Forever lost. "Okay," he finally said. "For the next twenty years Marge's clone will be your daughter. Then I hope she'll become your mother. Or is it stepmother?"

Brandon shrugged.

Ben turned toward Gary. "Just don't go telling her I'm not good enough for her!"

Gary barked a laugh and wondered if it sounded as forced to the others as it did to him. "I'll try not to influence her either way."

SEPTEMBER 30, 2090 — AIs in Atlantis, the third largest underwater city, have cracked the language of Dolphins in the North

Atlantic, allowing humans to converse with the only species on earth possessing a comparable brain/body weight ratio. Zo-ologists predict a revolution of interspecies communication as a result of the software advances. Dolphins are expected to be among only a handful of species capable of expressing actual thoughts beyond emotional and instinctual responses. — The WASA board of trustees decides to go ahead with plans to complete within this century the Ceres XIV humaned space sta-tion, well outside of Pluto's orbit. "Even though we now have three similar stations that pass within 200 million miles of Ceres XIV's proposed course," WASA Chief Iruy Niragig ex-plains, "the new outpost will nonetheless be a technical mile-stone, the first ever positioned outside our solar system." — The last functional warship on Earth leaves service today with the decommissioning of the 2030s-era Typhoon III-class missile submarine ROSTOV-146. The "boomer" has spent its last 45 years of service as an event vessel for World Presidents on vacation cruises. Long vilified as a waste of taxpayer funds, the sub will now serve as a museum attraction, beginning with Dis-ney-St. Petersburg's grand opening.

On Margaret Callahan Smith's sixth birthday, the home of Gary Smith and Kimber Chevalier overflowed with three dozen children, most of their parents, and nine adult members of the Smith clan, not to mention seven holographic dinosaurs, six rented portable child-size VR machines, two mechanical spaceship simulators, hair and skin recoloring systems, and Margaret's enormous new android-doll undersea biosphere, her birthday gift from Ben.

"Sure glad nobody's spoiling her," Ben joked to Kimber.

She laughed. "Yes, I'm afraid Margaret's upbringing may be some-what different from that of the original."

"Times do change," he said. "I'll try to think of this as our own anec-dotal experiment on heredity versus environment."

Then Margaret leaped into his arms. "Hi, Ben. I love my new biosphere!"

She never called him Grampa, nor did she refer to Gary as Dad, even though Kimber was always Mom to her. All the guides on raising well-adjusted transgenerational clones suggested they be taught to use first names for double relations, or potential double relations.

"And I love seeing you smile, sweetheart," he said. Of course he did. It was the same smile he'd cherished since he was fifteen.

Gary felt a knot tighten in his stomach. Not that Ben had done any-thing wrong, or even indecorous, but what his unworthy father had in mind for their sweet little girl—that they would someday get married and have sex together—was unacceptable and not a little weird. Sure, he under-stood the original idea, but was no longer confident that he could handle it.

"Ben," Margaret asked, "I'm a clone, right?" It was a typical Margaret question, seemingly formed from the very ether.

"Right, honey," Ben answered, half hoping that would be the end of it, even though with her, it never was. Margaret was inquisitive, which Ben admired, but which also left him unstrung.

"What does that mean? A clone."

"It means you have only one biological parent; your genes came from one person, my wife, Gary's mother." Ben doubted she'd grasp the entire concept, but didn't know how else to express it. "You look just like her," he added.

"Is a clone as good as anybody else?"

"Sure. In some ways better. You were chosen to be like somebody spe-cial, somebody others loved. Your parent was so wonderful, we didn't think the world could do without you!"

"Where's the first me? Can she come today?"

"Oh, no, honey. She would've loved to; to be here with you, but she can't come."

"Why?"

"She died, sweetheart."

The child pouted. "Died? How?"

"Well, first she got very sick . . ."

"What's that?"

"You know how sometimes you stub your toe, or cut your knee, and the invisible little-girl-fixing-machines have to take care of it? And until they do, it kinda hurts?"

"Yes."

"Well, a long time ago, germs or viruses and things like that—sort of like those invisible machines, only bad ones—would hurt us. And some-times our bodies would fix themselves, or else doctors could help fix them. But we didn't have invisible machines back then, so sometimes we didn't get better at all."

"Never?" she asked. "Is that what happened to the other Margaret? The other me?"

"Uh-huh."

"Then what?"

"Then she went to sleep forever; never woke up."

"Forever? Like Brenda, my guppy?"

Ben nodded.

Margaret looked up in amazement. "But why?"

"Because back then, everybody grew old, and nearly everyone died. They died forever, because we didn't freeze people."

"Why?"

"Because hardly anyone had thought of it yet." Damn. Why hadn't he listened to Carl? "We just didn't know. Not really, anyway."

She thought about this for a moment. "You didn't die forever."

"No, I didn't. I was lucky."

"But you knew people who died forever, right?"

"Yes. I knew many people who died." He swallowed hard, fighting back his emotions. "Too many."

Margaret looked at Ben. Her expression was so lost-Marge, he had to look elsewhere. Little Margaret shone with the same sympathy his wife had radiated so easily to those in pain, most often to Gary. (And who had caused *that* pain?) Then she hugged him. "Oh, it must have been sad back then."

"Yes." He knew he should say more, but couldn't.

"But now it's better, right?"

"Yes. Much."

"I'm so happy you didn't die, Ben."

"Me, too, sweetheart. Very, very happy."

Alice, who'd overheard most of the conversation, put her arm around Ben's waist, whispering, "You handled that well."

"Did I?"

"It's not easy knowing what to say to a child. And knowing what to withhold."

"Especially when she's much more than just a child; when she's also my future wife, I hope."

Alice embraced him. "Yes. I'm sure."

"I get so angry sometimes, mostly at myself," Ben admitted. "Carl Epstein told me about cryonics back in 1971. I could easily have afforded it, too, but never even thought about it for Marge, or anyone."

"Guilt directed against yourself is a useless emotion," she said, her words sounding much like an Alice-of-old lecture.

His mother's memory was lost, but maybe not her essence. Why was it so hard to discern exactly what was still there and what was missing?

"Those who use it against others," she continued, "wield it as a weapon. And battles against self have only losers. Ben, you have to let go of it; it wasn't your fault; it's just the way things were. In the 1970s almost every cryobiologist was saying that cellular damage from freezing would never be reversible. Of course, cryobiologists were the wrong experts to ask, since they knew nothing about molecular technology. But hardly anyone had figured that out, just Feynman, Ettinger, Drexler, Merkle, and a very few others."

"Like Carl Epstein."

"Yes, like your friend Carl, and even he never understood how to teach without offending would-be pupils. He had to start teaching philosophy before he understood; now he counsels well. But you had to give him credit even then, because so few knew how to think. We still hadn't learned to use our logical minds, instead of following the mass hysteria of the times."

"Maybe we still haven't," Ben said.

"Maybe not. But I think we're improving."

"Mom . . ." He hesitated, then plunged ahead. "You suppose you'll ever want to clone Dad?" Alice must have been anticipating that question from him for years, yet she'd never broached the subject.

"Not yet," she answered. "Maybe someday, or maybe never. In a way, I'm still mourning Alice Smith."

"But to us, you *are* Alice Smith."

"No, Ben, I'm not. Maybe I've replaced her in your heart, and I'm very grateful to be here with you. And I'm thrilled to be alive. But she'll never know that. Whatever I do here, in this world, has no effect on her. The original Alice Smith is dead, forever without consciousness. Sometimes I feel remorse for that, even though I know full well there's nothing any of us could ever do to bring her back. I never met her, but I do know her, since I'm much like her. I mourn her death as if she were my twin. After all, I've usurped her place in the world. I rarely stop thinking about her."

"Maybe cloning Dad would help somehow," Ben suggested, unabashed by the self-serving potential of his words.

"Or maybe I'd feel guilt-ridden, seizing her life's last possession like that. I just don't know yet. They implanted a lot of knowledge in my brain, but as far as actual experience, I'm only nine years old, much too young to know what I want from life."

Ben gazed at this pretty young woman who was both his mother and yet not, and for once the hint of uneasiness he usually suppressed in her presence did not trouble him. The smile he offered contained only love and respect.

"To me, you seem wise; wise as the ages," he said, and meant it.

FEBRUARY 14, 2096 — Photographic evidence from the newly deployed Hubble-Sagan-IV telescope gathered in the apogee of its Jupiter/Neptune orbit strongly suggests the massive planet orbiting "solar twin" star 16 Cygni B in the Cygnus tri-star system supports wide grassland areas at the poles. The planet, informally named Cochran-A for its co-discover, travels an unusual orbit. However, its hyperseasonal conditions — approximately 170°F in summer; minus 140°F in winter — appear minimized in the polar regions, where green-colored areas of significant proportion expand and contract within parameters of established seasonal vegetation effects. WASA AIs rate intricate life forms as a 21.55% probability, the 83rd highest odds of any planet thus far discovered. — Separately, Hubble-Sagan IV AIs discover concrete evidence of a "pygmy" black hole crossing the Oort Cloud at the outer extremities of our own solar system. Tentatively dubbed *Nemesis*, the class-2 type-C singularity appears to track a hugely elliptical orbit around our sun, and passes through the Oort Cloud of comets every 60 to 70 million years. Because the singularity is tiny by celestial standards, possibly terrestrial-sized, and is by definition lightless, were it not passing through the Cloud, astronomers would consider its detection even by today's technologies a miracle of chance.

Margaret heard another beep emanate from her wristband. She glanced quickly at twelve-year-old Devon MacLane's elaborate 3-D Valentine's Day card as it appeared on the smaller of her two deskscreens, then resumed her studies on the larger one. It was flattering, as always, when boys in her school—so many of them—went to such trouble, and she resolved to acknowledge his attention in the nicest way possible without giving him the wrong idea. She did like him as a friend, but kept no room in her heart for more than friendship with any child from her own generation. Even at age eleven, Margaret knew.

Was it his voice? Or his smile? Or maybe just the way he regarded the world: with logic yet also with optimism. No matter the reason, someday soon enough, she would become Mrs. Benjamin Franklin Smith, just like the Margaret Callahan Smith she'd been cloned from. Only this time it would be forever.

That afternoon, as she walked from school toward the subway access, Margaret saw Ben waiting for her, holding a bouquet. She ran to hug him.

"Happy Valentine's Day," he said. "Cultured orchids. Should last till *next* Valentine's Day if you keep 'em in 3CLd solution. How was school today?"

"Good."

"Get a lot of love notes?"

"Sixty-two," she answered, "but who's counting?"

Ben laughed.

"I tell them I'm already spoken for, you know."

"You have plenty of time to decide about that," he said, wondering whether it was really such a good idea for Margaret to take herself off the market so young, then shuddering at the very language his mind used to grapple with the issue. Besides, he'd long ago sensed Gary's discomfort with their mutual expectation of marriage. It was the sort of discomfort that could easily flash into rage.

Not only that, he was starting to have second thoughts himself.

An image flashed through his mind of Humbert Humbert, the old lecher hanging around the schoolyard with flowers for his Lolita. No! God! It was nothing like that! But maybe such a marriage, even when she'd gained the maturity to make the choice, wasn't so wise, especially if Gary was against it. No sense adding more strain to uneasiness.

"There's a whole world out there," he added. "Years left to decide. Keep your options open." But it felt like he was lying.

"I don't want to," she said. "I'm saving myself."

Feeling inexplicably relieved, Ben kissed her cheek. "I won't hold you to that."

Margaret wondered when Ben would *really* start kissing her, but decided she'd better not suggest it. Not directly, anyway. "Ben," she said as they boarded the pneumatic commuter car, "tell me about your wife. Why did you love her?"

"Hard to know. Many different reasons. She was beautiful, of course . . ."

"Like me?" Margaret asked, batting her eyelashes.

Ben laughed. "Just like you. And not only intelligent, but also wise and compassionate and dependable . . ."

"Also like me." This time she batted her eyelashes furiously.

Ben wouldn't bite. "Yes."

"So, how am I different from her?"

"Well, she grew up in a different time, with different realities and concerns."

"So did you."

"Sure. Marge and I shared a period of history together. We lived through the Second World War, the nuclear age, the assassination of President Kennedy, the first time men set foot on the moon, and the Needless Extinction—"

Time! Time! Time! Ben thought. Margaret looked and acted so much like Marge, he sometimes let himself forget there was no shared history. How could they be right for each other without it? What had he been thinking?

"The Needless Extinction?" Margaret interrupted. "What's that?"

"It's what historians call those last decades from 1975 to 2015, when hardly any of us were suspended even though we knew how to do it."

Margaret said nothing, just patted his hand.

"Nothing sadder. A hundred times worse than any war. Virtually everyone died before reaching a hundred years. And it didn't have to happen. Absolutely pointless . . ." He ran out of words but let himself bask in the child's touch.

"My history AI calls it the Lemming Generation," Margaret said.

"Not a very flattering label for us, but it fits, I guess."

"What happened to people when they died back then?"

"Usually we were embalmed and buried in the ground. Or sometimes cremated, burned until there was nothing left but ashes."

She shook her head. "Even people whose brains could have been saved. I know it's true, but it's so hard to believe. How could it have happened?"

"It's complicated," Ben explained. "For one thing, after a while the aging process itself made life less pleasant; made you less able to resist disease, drained some of your energy."

·"And shriveled everyone's skin, too. I've seen pictures." She wrinkled her nose.

"Not to mention what happened to eyesight and hearing, digestion, and joints. Nobody liked to think about aging and death, yet almost all of us considered it inevitable. So young people would wait till they were older before they'd think about it. And old people didn't have the strength to go against the grain, to fight the hysteria of the times."

"What hysteria?"

"Superstition, I suppose. Nothing else I can think of to call it. Oh, it's possible some people would've been frozen if it were less expensive. But if more had signed up, and if the government had passed laws to make it easier and safer, freezing wouldn't've cost a whole lot more than being buried. Maybe even about the same. The real reason it didn't happen that way was superstition and inertia. Hear something often enough, you tend to believe it; believe in something long enough, and it becomes reality. The tradition of most religions back then was that the dead must either be buried or cremated for their souls to be reincarnated, or go to heaven."

"Heaven? I know that's a good thing, but what does it mean exactly?"

"Paradise. An eternal reward for your good deeds in life. Back then, most people believed in resurrection—an afterlife."

"You mean somewhere else other than this solar system?"

"Yes. An altogether different universe."

"How would they get there?"

Ben shrugged. "The theory always was that God had somehow arranged it, magically. It was pure speculation of course, since no one could ever prove they'd been there. Faith, they called it. But blind faith was more like it, because it was only humans, purporting to act as God's emissaries, who'd described the nature of this place called heaven."

"Why don't people believe in heaven anymore?"

Ben groped for a simple way to describe what had happened. "Before the early twenty-first century, afterlife was at least a useful idea. Anticipation of heaven or paradise or nirvana made the idea of death more bearable, and caused people to be more cooperative with each other. But after the scip was invented, more of us started choosing our own belief systems, since it became more obvious that nobody knew the truth for certain. And around 2035, a couple decades after most people first started to realize they might never die, the AIs calculated that belief in afterlife actually encouraged reckless behavior, even a subtle form of suicide sometimes. I suppose that believing death was coming scared many people; made them think: Why not now?"

"Weird."

"Not really. Everyone becomes unhappy, temporarily unhappy, or scared for various reasons. And if they believed in heaven, they'd tend to care less about sticking it out; waiting until things improved, or struggling to change them."

"But it still could be true, couldn't it? There might be an afterlife, like heaven."

"Sure, it's possible. Afterlife's a reality about which the living can never know. The point is, there's no real proof of it. And worse, you'd have to die to find out. When I was 'dead,' if there was an afterlife, I sure don't remember it."

"But we do know we're living now," Margaret said, "here on Earth. Today. We absolutely know that!"

"That we do."

"We also know that life is better than death, don't we?"

"Of course it is. Without life, the universe has no meaning."

"And accidents and suicide are the only reasons people die now. But if you're careful enough, if you don't take silly chances, you could live long enough to be around when scientists figure out how to end all death."

"It seems possible," Ben said. "Even likely."

"So in today's world, who cares if there's an afterlife?" asked Margaret.

"Precisely!"

Just then, my image appeared on Ben's corneal-implant screen. "How soon can you get here?" I asked. "It's an emergency."

He answered through his dental PC: "What do you mean by emergency, Trip? Margaret's with me."

"Oh," I said, feeling like an idiot. "Maybe I'm a little too excited. By all means, take her home."

"Twenty minutes," he advised.

The moment Ben stepped into my living quarters, two great, furry, sixty-five-pound balls of dog stood upon hind leg and, pressing paws against his chest, licked widely at either side of his face. Both Wendys were ecstatic to see him, of course. How could they know?

I was not so fortunate.

The unfolding story of our neighborhood singularity, so provocatively named Nemesis, had begun to consume my every thought. All my instincts told me that today's discovery would radically transform the very paradigm of our new immortalist society. Unless my calculations were in error, the singularity now passing through the Oort Cloud of comets, about a light-year distant from us, had already pulled huge clusters away, hurling many toward our sun and its orbiting planets. Every sixty-five million years or so, the Earth had experienced major extinctions, the most recent of which being that of the dinosaurs—roughly sixty-five million years ago. This phenomenon now seemed the most logical explanation for it.

The notion terrified me. Here we'd all but conquered human death, only to discover that our huge new expanses of time might not be so infinite after all.

I'd called my great-grandfather because I needed the input of someone who had a perspective of glued-to the-television events such as the assassination of a President, the moon landing, the fall of Saigon, the Falkland Islands War, and the like. While my own life span had witnessed hyper-accelerated changes, those life-redefining events, above the personal-tragedy level, had been incremental and almost universally for the better. Suddenly I felt this potential world-shatterer squeezing me like the hand of an angry giant. I hoped Ben could help.

He listened to my story and summation, and though he said nothing particularly derogatory or dismissive, as we talked, Ben's facial expressions became increasingly skeptical. His was the sort of countenance one might expect to encounter on the face of a modern scientist watching sixteenth century religious scholars debate, in all seriousness, how many angels could dance on the head of a pin.

Ben just didn't understand.

"Can't you see it?" I asked.

He smiled and offered a nonchalant shrug of his shoulders. Neither his expression nor his gestures held any trace of commiseration. "I understand it's more real for you than for me," he said. "Sure, the world may be due or even overdue for a cosmic event. But Jesus, Trip, how can you expect me, a man reborn into a world free of want or pain, to dwell on—"

"Hold it!" On my wall screen a simulated onslaught of comets had appeared, while the primary-secondary window showed the strained face of an overanimated human announcer. I punched up the volume.

"... AIs running continuous forecast scenarios have reached a shocking conclusion. With a 96.4 percent probability, this planet can expect the next swarm of comets to arrive in the range of 98 to 604 years. The calculations have been substantiated through carbon dating of iridium samples from the comet impacts in the Chad Basin and Antarctica, and comparing their ages to the 64,977,551-year-old Yucatan crater. More definitive calculations should be forthcoming over the next few days.

"While it is scientifically possible, theoretically, to deflect or destroy a colli-sion-course comet of limited size, there is no assurance of success in such a prob-lematic endeavor. In the face of multiple strikes, chances of such a success become remote indeed.

"We've all seen the spectacular pictures of comet fragments smashing earth-sized holes in Jupiter's atmosphere in August of 1994. Imagine such an incident..."

"I told you!" I wasn't even aware that I was screaming. "I told you, Ben! Maybe it's all been for nothing! All the advances, all the science, and for what? To be wiped out in less than a hundred years?"

Ben exploded into laughter.

It was awful. My great-grandfather didn't comprehend; didn't even seem to *want* to comprehend the nature of the problem. He only laughed and laughed, tears quickly streaming down his cheeks.

"Have you gone crazy?" I demanded. "Is everyone from yester-world nuts?" Maybe there was something fundamentally wrong with our revivtech. Maybe people came back missing some component we'd never properly understood. "What the hell are you laughing at?"

One of the Wendys was at my feet now, her hackles raised, her rump bunched against my shins. I knew if I didn't calm down, there was a very real chance she might nip Ben, so I decided to humor him. "Ben, I think this has been a bigger shock than you're ready to admit to yourself. Having come back not all that long ago, the prospect of environmental catastrophe is just too much for you. Let me get you a sedative."

He raised his head, looked at my face with an expression that almost seemed like one of relief, and burst into laughter again. It wasn't until both Wendys actually growled that he stopped.

"Look," he finally said through tittering hiccups, "I'm sorry, Trip. I really may not be the right person to talk to you about this. Even if I knew for an absolute fact that this planet would be destroyed in a hundred years—and I think nothing of the sort—I might not be as upset as you are now. I can see your perspective, sort of, but I think you'll do better talking to Gary. He knows more about this stuff than I do. Mind if I call him?"

"Sure," I said. What difference would another yesterworlder make? Still, a few minutes ago I'd assumed theirs was the perspective I wanted. Perhaps from the right yesterworlder, it still was.

When Gary arrived, the old guys looked at each other warily. I knew there had been, probably still was, a major rift between them, although I had no idea what. Another component exempli-fied our strange new age: By the most objective standard, Ben's son was older than he was; had thirteen years more experience in the world than his dad.

"Trip's got a problem," Ben said. "I thought you could help."

The strain on my great-uncle's face vanished when great-grandfather told him that. Gary said to him: "Oh . . . so this isn't about you."

I didn't much care for the way Gary had said *you*; I looked into Ben's face, finding a hurt grimace. I intervened: "So, uh, thank you for coming over."

"No problem, Trip. What's on your mind?" When he looked at me instead of his father, there was only kindness in Gary's eyes.

"Ben says you have a big-picture understanding of cosmology. I guess you know about Nemesis and its effect on the Oort Cloud ... and the potential for coming disaster."

"Yeah, I've been having a hard time tearing myself away from the viewscreens."

I felt better already. Gary would understand. "You know what it means, then?" I asked. "The cycle of mass extinctions and all. Half the people I know are wondering what it's all been for. Here we've achieved near-immortality, only to find out there's a swarm of comets coming and that there are almost certainly uncountable baby black holes swallowing up the universe. It steals the meaning out of everything!"

Gary began to smile. At first I thought he was about to let loose with some horsecrap bromides about how I was being a pessimist. I looked at Ben, but he didn't return my gaze. He had locked-on, fascinated eyes only for his son. Then, damn, if Gary didn't explode into laughter.

I wanted to kick him. "What are you gonna do? Tell me this isn't real? That it doesn't effect me? That I shouldn't worry about something so far away?"

"Nope."

"Wrong."

I couldn't tell which had said what. "Then why is it so funny?"

"It's not funny, exactly," Ben said, though I could see from his face that he was searching his head for a real explanation. "More of an exhilarating release, like that moment when you first figure out the solution to a puzzle you've been struggling over."

"Exactly!" Gary took a forward step, then not so lightly cuffed my shoulder. My Wendys didn't even growl. The traitors. "Trip, you gotta understand, when Dad and I were young—and that's what matters from our standpoint—we grew up knowing that everyone would die. No exceptions. Then we wake up to all this."

"To *what*?" I demanded. "You don't think this is better than what you had before?"

"Of course it is, but I knew there was something missing, too. And today's discovery helped clarify it in my mind."

"Maybe you'd better explain."

Gary's face reflected the patient love of a parent, which I suppose in some ways he still was to me. "Trip, you're worried about a catastrophe that might or might not happen, that humankind might or might not know how to prevent, but will certainly figure out how to mitigate, one to six hundred years from now. What troubles you today would have seemed absurd to us. Kinda the same thing as a guy in 2000, terrified of being late with a mortgage payment, might seem to a feudal serf in eighteenth century Russia. You get the idea?"

Grudgingly, I did, so I nodded. But understanding the analogy did nothing to address the problem. "It still means immortality may be unattainable. And missing a mortgage payment isn't quite the same thing as having half the life on Earth obliterated."

Gary didn't even hesitate. "No, it's not," he admitted. "And I'll tell you something. Given enough time, if we don't do anything about it, I think the Earth *will* eventually be hit by a giant comet or an asteroid, or maybe even ripped out of its orbit by the tidal influence of a black hole."

"But so what?" Ben said.

"Yeah. So what?" Gary continued. "We *will* do something about it. We have at least a hundred years of life; at least hundred years to get ready for this thing, whatever it is, even if it means the end for some of us. And if we beat this problem, as I'm sure we will, more problems will come. In life, there can no permanent security, Trip, no ultimate safety except in here." He touched my forehead. "Cults, druggies, and VR addicts are all symptoms of empty lives, of fear that there's no ultimate meaning. We had them when I grew up, and we still have them today. So let me tell you something, Trip: Security isn't the goal. Striving for it is. It's in the action and passion that we find the joy."

That was the first time I'd ever wished I'd been born sooner, and the first time I really understood what a treasure our yesterworlders were. We who had seemingly rid ourselves of death now had too much, and it had come too fast. How could we have known?

I spread my hands so Gary could appreciate his sobering effect on his grandnephew. "I suppose the machines, the AIs, given all the time we have, will devise a way to save us."

Gary gave me a funny look. Ben slapped his hand against his forehead. Wendy II chuffed.

"What?" I demanded. It was crazy, completely disconcerting. Here, I was the acknowledged scientist, yet it seemed every other mammal in the room was looking at me as if I were a three-year-old who'd just wet his pants.

"Trip," Ben said, his tone kind but indulgent, almost patronizing, "that's what's wrong with your whole overview on this."

Gary nodded his head avidly.

Ben went on: "Whether the problem winds up a tempest in a teacup or Armageddon from the sky, the strategic solution will result from intuition and imagination, properties of human emotion. Properties no machine has."

"Yes," Gary said. Now the way he was looking at his father made me feel good, like they were allies not only of the mind but the spirit. "Machines, artificial intelligences, may offer priceless tactical advice, but they won't know how to feel about it."

"What's that got to do with anything? It's a scientific problem." No sooner were the words were out of my mouth than I felt like a moron. Had my emotional response been scientific? Were we forgetting so much of our basic nature so quickly?

Ben stood, then walked to stand directly in front of my body-sculpt chair. Worse, Wendy I padded over and hunkered against his leg. I guess dogs have an instinct for who the rightful pack leader is.

Shaking his head slowly while a strangely grandpalike smile spread over his face, he began a speech I'll remember all my life. A hundred years, a million, a billion, or until the universe goes cold, I will never forget.

"We could implant intelligent machines in physical bodies like ours, or some other higher life-form's. Hell, before you know it, we'll be advanced enough to create a whole new species. Sure, we could do that, but why would we? Then we'd have created a hyperintelligent competitive life-form. Such an act would be insane; would have a wholly unpredictable out-come. It would be as mad as a full-scale nuclear exchange in the 1980s, so I don't expect it, even in light of today's crisis.

"Therefore what we have is artificial intelligence without emotions. I'm sure I don't need to explain to you that your emotions are manifest in your body's physical response to your five senses, in concert with the rea-soning capacity of your brain. Loud music can make you cry if you're an infant, or give you joy if you're an adult listening to Mozart . . ."

No, he hadn't needed to explain it, but I somehow understood things better because he had.

"Now we're faced with something unknown and to some degree unknowable, so our initial reaction is fear. How could it be otherwise? Right now, you find the fear paralyzing. But not for long, I predict. In fact, it's that very fear that will save us."

I sat there, thinking I'd understood. I almost rushed to him then. Almost told him how wonderful he was. I'm glad I waited.

"A husband and wife walk into a home furnishings show," he mused. "We'll say the year is 2010, because it's a transitional time all of us can relate to, whether we lived it firsthand or not.

"Anyway, our couple presents their ticket stubs at the door. As they stroll inside the hall, someone marks the back of one of their hands with a small red dot, so they can gain readmittance without having to pay a second time.

"Husband and wife had a tiny spat that morning, so there's a little wall of distance between them. Nothing serious, but it's there. They stroll about for a little, then hubby spies a concession stand. Tells the wife he's thirsty. They buy two cups of cola and sit down at tables provided for snackers. On their table is a vase of faux flowers, pretty but bland. Hubby's still feeling bad about the morning's tiff and wants to make the cloud go away. After all, he started it by whining that he didn't want to go to the show in the first place. But he also can't quite bring himself to admit all that.

"He looks at the red dot on his hand, then smiles. Says to wifey: 'They can find us now.' 'Who?' she asks. 'The Bosnian secret agents,' he replies; points to the dot. 'There's a homing device in the ink.' Wifey's expression doesn't change, but she bends to one of the plastic flowers, whispering into it: 'He's on to us, Marvik.' Both break into laughter, then reaching out, they find one another's fingers."

I looked at Gary; he was smiling. So was I, ear-to-ear, but didn't understand why. I only knew I suddenly felt better, and glad to be a member of the human race. Still, I wondered, What was his point?

"Trip, could a machine have written that?" Ben asked.

"No," I allowed, replaying Ben's story in my head: action, sensation, emotion, humor, a goal, and success; all interwoven into a simple object-lesson on the nature of the human thinking process. "Any machine, no matter its computational or inductive-reasoning capacity, would have no frame of reference for it."

"Exactly," Ben said. "The answers will come from our uniquely human combination of physical emotion and objective reasoning capacity, and our physical need to survive. Hell, even our tendency to disagree with each other at times, and our occasional bouts of irrationality," he laughed, "might be indispensable to the creativity of civilization.

"We might construct great orbiting lasers. We might take shelter deep in the Earth's crust. We might colonize new star systems. Whatever we do, *humans* will decide what and how. Sure, our machines could help us do any or all of these things, or help solve problems not yet conceived. But they can function only as our servants, not our saviors. And sometimes it takes a crisis to remind us of that."

Wendy licked Ben's hands as Gary began to clap his own.

After leaving me, Ben and Gary walked through the Japanese rock garden in front of my building. Their stroll hadn't been planned, but when they'd left the place, their common gravity attracted; held them together.

Ben stopped at a crossroads in the perfect pathways, listening to the music of water dancing over pebbles. The small, rounded sandstones had been carefully placed, he knew, each angled to create perfect dulcet tones. This was a symphony of natural materials, finely tuned under the fingers of thoughtful human beings. Like himself.

Like his son.

"They're going to need us, Gary. I used to worry about that all the time, you know." Ben hunkered down on his knees and stared into the water. "Used to worry I had nothing to offer."

Gary sighed and nodded.

Ben dipped a finger into the cool water. It felt wonderful. "I think it's a genetic reversion, son. I think, like all events that bring forth disproportional responses in humans, we have a species memory, much akin to instinct. I think at times in the dim human past, comets and meteors must have struck the earth with devastating consequences. Nothing like the comets that killed the dinosaurs, of course, but terrible just the same. And millions of our ancestors must have witnessed such events. I guess the basic fear of objects falling from the sky never burned out of our genes."

Again Gary nodded.

"I think it's like our fear of spiders. Even infants seem scared of them. I think spiders used to bite us in the darkness—in the caves."

Gary tipped him a smile.

"That's why this Nemesis thing is going to become a nightmare. Or could. We'll need to be allies in this, son. For once, we have the better perspective."

Gary offered a broad grin.

It wasn't until he was halfway home that Ben realized how much he'd enjoyed talking to his son, and also, that Gary had never uttered a single word.

JULY 25, 2096 — In the midst of the so-called "Comet Panic," former United States President David West and his wife Dr. Diana Hsu West joyously announce the impending rebirth of their son, Justin, who died from a genetic disorder in March 2013 at the age of 10 months. Justin West was cloned from repaired DNA in February, immediately after World Government AIs determined that the comet shower from the Nemesis/Oort intersection would begin to reach Earth during mid-2308. In a Worldscreen interview, David West states,

"Diana and I made this decision based on our love of life, and our unshaken confidence in the capacity of the human spirit to overcome all obstacles." — In Tulum, near the ancient Mayan ruins on the Yucatan Peninsula of the state of Mexico, 470 people are discovered dead from an apparent mass suicide. The site is thought to have attracted the so-called Judgment Day cult because of its proximity to the impact point of one of the dinosaur-killer comets, and because the cult professed that this area possessed holy connection to Mayan astronomers. All victims stabbed themselves in the heart with ceremonial daggers, each bearing a stylized likeness of a comet on its haft. All 41 who did not strike themselves mortal blows have received emergency restoration and cerebral repatterning, and will survive with memories intact. Unfortunately, because the historical area closes from 5:00 P.M. to 9:00 A.M., the fatal victims are beyond the help of nanotech.

A familiar face filled Ben's VR pod. This one was young, the real McCoy.

It wasn't much of a trick to tell the twenty-something faces from those merely appearing to be twentyish. Their eyes told him. Something about their color—their sheen—advertised real youth, middle age, or the deep glowing depth that came only with wisdom. The difference wasn't something Ben could put into words, though he figured an artist like Gary could.

Ben had also found he could differentiate yesterworlders like himself from the main body of humanity. He could tell them by their facial expressions; by their responses to dubious ideation or outright silliness. His fellow survivors from the bygone days were quicker to display cynical reactions. And they were more easily infuriated on those occasions when he screwed up and became patronizing or preachy. Ben supposed folks who'd been steeped in the poison of Watergate, the O.J. Simpson mess, and the Nobine mouse fraud, were by definition apt to be less trusting, and less susceptible to suggestion.

Raised in a world virtually free of what these people called greed-lies—as opposed to leave-me-alone lies or politeness-lies—new-timers had built up little resistance to fantasy or speculation cults, clubs, and parties. Offering one's particular spin on what might have happened, why something happened, or what could conceivably occur in the future, had nothing to do with lying per se. Unfortunately, the results could be as bad as any lie, and the potential for damage, when such illusions were foisted on the genuine innocents of these new times, was tremendous.

The voice of Ronald Berry invaded Ben's aural canals. Ron was barely twenty-two years old, handsome and marginally intelligent for a new-timer, but in no epoch was he anybody's genius.

"There's all this evidence, dontya see?" the boy was saying. "Life on Earth came from outer space. Water came from comets and they had these microbes in 'em and that's where everything came from. After the comets start hittin' in 2308, then people from Nemesis'll come down again and redo everything, dontya see? Change everything in the whole world. So what's the point anyway? Everything'll just change no matter what we do. They're coming and that'll be that. Dontya see?"

What a weird world this had become, Ben thought. Infinitely better in so many ways, infinitely safer and more intelligent. Yet the same people who scored off-the-charts on twelve-dimensional intelligence tests could turn into imbeciles when faced with intellectual voodoo.

Ron needed help Ben decided he couldn't give him. Perhaps psychiatric drug therapy, and maybe even a prolonged stay in a so-called safe environment. Ben's fingers signaled out a call-back message to Ron's mother. Since Ron was age-of-consent, he hoped she cared enough to intervene with a flash-petition to her local magistrate.

"Those people down in Yucatan had it right, but they were stupid, too, dontya know? Killed themselves for no reason."

"Oh?" Ben took heart, until the boy continued:

"Yeah, those aliens, the ones who live around Nemesis, only come to Egypt, dontya know? That's the place they'll find us; we're the disciples, dontya know? Lottie Crayton, she's the one who's had the visions. Says we can all go live with them . . . forever. None of us, none of the disciples, ever have to die. Not really, anyway. She's gonna wait for 'em in Egypt. I'm gonna go, too." Ron took a breath.

Ben decided he'd better not waste any time with this one. Young Ron didn't seem far from core meltdown, from going cuckoo, as they used to say when Ben was a kid. He would give the boy a quick verbal shock treatment, then try to do what he could for him.

"Ron," Ben said, his voice ten decibels too loud. The boy's eyes looked distant, glazed, nonresponsive. "Ron!" he yelled.

Ron's eyes flew open. Ben had his attention. "That's stupid, Ron. Stupid! You listen to crap like that, you'll ruin your life."

"Huh?" Ron flinched, as though no one had ever spoken to him that way before. And perhaps no one ever had. But there wasn't time for gentle words or subtle philosophy with this kid. Wake him up, then get him some heavy duty help: That was the only way that ever worked with this sort of problem.

"B-But Lottie Clayton . . . We all scipped her," Ron complained. "Lottie's telling the *truth*!"

"That's right, Ron. Lottie is not lying. She's not delusional or clinically pathological, either. Back a hundred, hundred fifty years ago, Lottie is what we would've called a ditz. She is so, hmmm, intellectually challenged, she believes her own vivid dreams represent truth.

"Look, Ron. I'm not going to pull any punches with you. Lottie Crayton is an articulate, charismatic idiot. Do not listen to her. Having been raised in such an innocent world, you're susceptible to stuff like this. And being human, you resist the notion that your soul is anything less than eternal, even though there is absolutely no evidence either way. Listen to me, Ron: This life might well be all you get. Nobody knows. Nobody *can* know. Don't gamble everything you have on some entity or being that no living person has ever seen outside of their dreams and visions and fantasies. Cherish what you *know* you have: your life. Here. Now. On Earth. I've got friends who can help you understand this better, Ron. But they'll need to visit you in person instead of by VR. Is that okay?"

Amazingly, the kid didn't hesitate even a second. "Why sure, Mr. Smith. That'd be great. I've never known anyone who talks like you, dontya see? You're like from somewhere else, real old-movie-like. Like old, old movies. Dontya see?"

That was when my message showed up on Ben's corneal screen, informing him that I had to see him right away. He clicked his tongue once, our signal that he would arrive here in about an hour.

"Okay, Trip," my great-grandfather said. "What's so damn momentous you could only tell me about it in person?"

Virginia, Ben, and I headed toward the main conference room at our new headquarters of Neural Nanoscience Laboratories, the business partnership Virginia and I had formed back in 2084.

"They've discovered a way to replicate human beings," I said as we seated ourselves at a sound-preclusion console near the door.

"Is this another one of your jokes?" Ben asked me, probably remembering the time I'd programmed micromachines to reposition furniture in his office whenever he glanced at his deskscreen. "Y'know, some Frenchman already beat them to it," Ben added. "About sixty-two years ago."

"No," Virginia explained, "not just biological cloning; we're talking about entire adult human beings, including memory and environmentally induced personality."

"You've got to be kidding."

"No, we're not."

"And right now we're the only facility on the northeast coast of America with the necessary equipment and training," I added. "We should have a monopoly for several months."

Ben stared at us. "But how?"

"Ever since the Nemesis discovery, human scientists have been feeding all sorts of crazy projects to the AI banks," Virginia explained. "Of course, some of them were bound to bear fruit. And last week, at the suggestion of about thirty nanoscientists, including Trip, the entire World AI Network spent four days calculating a safe way to upload data from human brains using nano-disassembler/assemblers. To put it in layman's terms, we survey the position of every molecule in the brain, with some shortcuts, then store the information digitally in datacubes. That way we can transport it. Maybe transmit it all by radio, microwaves, or even infrared. Duplicating the body is simple, of course; all we have to do is replicate a single strand of DNA and clone it. But not until the memories are attached would you have the entire person."

"And probably," I said, "after a few thousand people have gone through the process, AIs can learn how to analyze what every neuron molecule *means*; the way each molecule's position and makeup translates into information."

"A radical leap in technology," Virginia said, "with, if you'll pardon the pun, mind-boggling implications."

"Such as?"

"We think we'll be able to implant specific knowledge without disrupting memory. It could eventually lead to AIs being incorporated inside our brains, maybe linking our thoughts to the minds of others via transducers and radio signals, a sort of artificial telepathy. Someday, people might even choose to give up their bodies entirely in favor of nearly unlimited, machine-enhanced intelligence and physicality; to live their lives in ways we can barely imagine."

"Maybe even safe from cosmic disasters," I gushed.

Ben ignored me. "Why would anyone want a duplicate of themselves, though?" he asked Virginia. "Would such replicas be human? And more to the point, would they still be the same individuals?"

"Those are interesting questions," she said, "but maybe more about semantics than science. For example, are you the same person you were ten years ago? Or the same person at age sixty that you were at ten? Arthur Clarke, the science fiction writer, once said the reason he decided not to be frozen was that he became a different person every ten or fifteen years anyway. Do you agree with that?"

"Well, you've taken his statement out of context, but in what you're saying, absolutely not. It's ridiculous. Even in context, he was wrong, but explaining it would take a four-hour dissertation."

Virginia smiled concurrence.

Ben went on: "If you subscribe to that theory verbatim, why study in high school or go to college? Why learn anything you can't use right away? Why invest your money for the long term just so 'some other person' can spend it? No, I believe I'm essentially the same human being I always was."

"Good. I do, too, Okay, then what if you had partial amnesia? Or total amnesia?"

"Now I'm not so sure. Of course, I'd still have the same fingerprints, maybe the same personality . . ."

"Yes," she said, "but so do clones, and we agree that they're not the same, right?"

"I see what you mean."

"Now let's say we transplant your brain into my skull and vice versa. You inhabit my body and I inhabit yours. Which one am I?"

"You'd be the one in my body," Ben said.

"Yes, I agree," Virginia said. "It might even be fun to try someday, but I digress. Now here's an interesting riddle: Suppose we learned how to duplicate parts of the brain mechanically, and begin to replace your brain at the rate of, let's say, one percent per year. You don't actually notice it happening, and your function and memory remains unchanged. After a hundred years, your brain becomes entirely mechanical, yet your personality and recall are the same as they were before. Are you still the same person?"

"I say: yes," Ben declared.

"Okay then, what if you did it in a hundred seconds instead of a hundred years?"

"I'm not sure it would matter, would it?"

"Depends on your perspective. But so far, it seems you agree that information constitutes identity."

"Maybe, maybe not. Okay, Virginia, I have one for you. Let's say we construct your perfectly analogous mechanical brain, but keep the old biological one intact, too. I think most people would agree that the biological brain is the one that holds that person's identity. Yet the only real difference between my example and yours is the continued existence of the biological brain. So why should the mere existence of the original brain affect the identity status of the mechanical one? And do you think it would matter whether or not one brain were aware of the existence of the other?"

"Interesting supposition. Reminds me of one of Robert Ettinger's identity 'experiments.' "

"What's that?"

"Well, back in the 1960s, Ettinger proposed that we imagine a syn-thetic brain that could not only replicate the exact function of a particular human brain, but also maintain a total, radio-controlled interconnection with it. Now assume we can use various parts of each, the synthetic and the original, and the corresponding part of the other brain simply lies dormant. You could decide to use, say, the artificial medulla oblongata, hypothala-mus, and brain stem, along with all the other parts of your original brain. You with me so far?"

"Sure."

"Okay. Now we start the experiment with a normal, fully conscious woman, and the machine brain switched off. But slowly we start dis-connecting various parts of her brain and simultaneously activating the corresponding parts of the machine. She never notices any of it, yet when we finish, the machine controls her body. Does she really become the machine?"

"I don't know. It's pretty confusing."

"Wait. It gets worse. Now assume the machine has its own sensory apparatus. And whenever we want to, we can also cut off the woman's senses, simultaneously activating the machine's. In other words, we can cause her senses to switch from one body to another, woman's to machine's."

"Wow. Okay, I still think she's the same person."

"So do I. But there's more! Now her original brain and body are both fully dormant, and to an observer, she appears to be an unconscious woman, alongside a functioning machine that thinks it's a woman directing a machine."

"Uh, okay."

"So now we reactivate her brain. She notices no difference. Then we switch her back to her normal human senses so that the machine is dor-mant. And we keep switching her back and forth, until she becomes accus-tomed to it, maybe even preferring to occupy the machine. Eventually she might decide it was irrelevant to her which vessel she occupied; perhaps if her original body were destroyed, she wouldn't care one way or the other."

"Fascinating idea," Ben said, "but a little too weird for me. Obviously we can't really do any of that stuff, right?"

"No, of course not. Not yet anyway," Virginia said. "I was just trying to give you another way to look at the nature of identity. But applications of this technology even weirder than Ettinger's experiment are going to emerge. You just wait. In fact one astounding application is ready right now. Have you figured out what it is, yet?"

Ben considered her question. "I can't visualize the details yet, but this discussion seems to suggest that your process could make a person effectively, uh, immortal . . ."

"Bingo!" I said.

"Okay, now tell me how."

"Well, consider how people die," I said.

Ben's eyes narrowed. "Never from disease or old age anymore. Only from freak accidents, or at their own hand."

"Exactly. So wouldn't you want your DNA pattern and memories stored off-site, on a satellite or space station somewhere, maybe even outside our solar system, just in case you, or even the whole planet, happened to get destroyed in an accident? As long as the accident didn't destroy every last human, or the medical and scientific knowledge we've accumulated, then any information needed to reconstruct you would be saved."

"You mean like a backup disc used in a twentieth century computer?"

Virginia nodded. "Except that now we could simply send the information to the storage facility. Even if it's light-years away. Do that two or three times, and the chance of simultaneously losing all stored 'yous' becomes incalculably small."

"Amazing," Ben said. Then he grinned. "Take your singularity and shove it."

Virginia's mouth fell open.

"We think there ought to be quite a market for it," I said coyly. "Especially since the complete brain-survey process takes only ninety minutes."

"How much would it cost?" Ben asked.

"Oh, we'll probably charge two week's earnings for it," I said, "at least until competition from other companies drives down the price. Our first buyers will be those most able to pay; we'll recover our costs quickly. In a negligible amount of time, anyone will be able to afford it."

"Incredible." Ben folded his arms, nodded and smiled. "Everyone except the cult-crazies should love this. But you didn't have me come down here just to tell me about it, did you?"

"Not quite. Virginia and I decided that since you're the oldest person in our family whose memories are still intact, we want you to be our inaugural Cache."

"Cache?"

"That's what we named the process," Virginia said. "It means hidden reserves; like savings for a rainy day. But in this case, we're preserving something much more valuable than money. Of all the great treasures in the universe, the most precious by far is information. Because information is the essence of every human being, and of life itself."

She paused, so I turned a big grin on Ben and asked, "Well, what do you say? How'd you like to become the first immortal?"

OCTOBER 20, 2098 — Seven members of the Canadian karate team are temporarily killed during a morning match against Japan. After molecular reconstruction, team captain Montgomery Paul describes his own death at the hands of world champion Akio Narato as "intensely painful, yet indescribably exciting. And no doubt it'll be great preparation for the big one in 2308." A spokeswoman for the Tokyo Humanism Council described today's match as "unconscionable and borderline insane. This sort of nihilistic behavior has increased exponentially since the Nemesis discovery. The reasons, I think, are obvious." — World presidential candidate Sven Langervist proposes doubling income tax rates from 9.5 to 19% of gross income to finance a particle collider encircling the sun between the orbits of Jupiter and Saturn. "The potential benefit to humankind of such a research contrivance is unknowable, but it may lead to discoveries that will help thwart disasters from outer space," declares the candidate, to whom AIs assign a "statistically insignificant" chance of winning next month's election. — The World Addiction Bureau releases September's statistics which show a 7% drop in VR addiction over the previous month. Addiction Czar Bennett Williams declares, "This represents barely a twentyfold increase over the pre–Comet Panic rates, and nearly a 15% decline overall since July's peak. Suicides are down by 11% as well. Obviously our programs have succeeded brilliantly." Separately, Williams announces his intention to retire from his post early next year to lecture and write about personal motivation.

"I'm real glad I did it, Gary. Gives me a comforting feeling, almost like signing up for cryonics did in the 1980s." Ben tried to express the ideas in terms of his own experience; a thoughtful assessment of the advantages of our Cache service, rather than a plea to his only son. Ben figured that if he asked his son to do it because he'd hate to ever lose him, Gary might feel pressured. Lord knows, Ben made him feel uncomfortable enough just talking about day-to-day stuff. "In some ways, it was even more soothing."

"How so?" Gary asked, grinding his teeth. It seemed the only way to keep his father's voice from disintegrating into white noise. Hard as it was, Gary found he wanted to listen.

"Cryonics was like insurance," Ben explained nervously. "You knew you'd eventually need it. Did you know that after the invention of life insurance, almost a hundred years passed before it caught on?"

"Yes, I've read about that." With Mnemex now added to all commercial drinking water, both men understood that reading had become the same as knowing.

"Hell, it took almost fifty years for cryonics to gain general acceptance. And today, though actuarial tables suggest the average person should have a brain-eradicating accident every 11.3 centuries, people refuse to think it can happen to *them*. At least not before the comets arrive. I wonder how long before Caches become the norm? Probably ten years or more. You realize how many lives it could save just in those ten years? Almost 160 million worldwide, counting suicides."

Gary stared back at Ben's image on the screen and said nothing.

"Of course, back in the 1980s when I was frozen, few people were confident cryonics would work. Even I harbored doubts; herd mentality, I guess. But now if I'm ever killed, I know they can restore me. I'll lose whatever occurred since my last upload, of course, but I should even recover most of those memories from the archives. It really is de facto immortality, and well worth the price of admission."

"Pretty convincing." While Gary agreed with the concept, his father's verbal style assaulted his ears and nerves like chalk on a blackboard. Why did the man have to put everything in terms of his own experience?

Gary thought: Would it kill him to say that he'd feel better if I got it done because he actually cares whether I live or die? "Okay, Dad," he said. "I'll arrange it."

"For Kimber and Margaret, too?"

"Of course." Jesus. What did he think I meant? Gary thought.

"Good."

Without saying goodbye, Gary pressed the off-button of his two-way imager; Ben's face disappeared from the screen like a wayward intruder falling through a remote-controlled trapdoor.

A tad impolite of me, Gary thought, but better than letting him see my face right now. "Shit. The guy's fucking insufferable!"

"Ben is?" Kimber said. "You're the one who hung up on him!"

"Huh? You overheard us?"

"I was standing right here, honey, in case you didn't realize . . ."

"Sorry," Gary said. "Guess I'm not myself where he's involved."

"I noticed."

"He's just the most egocentric, selfish man, Kimber. He mostly ignored me throughout my childhood, and when he didn't, it was usually to harp at me about something. What that's done is to turn his voice into an instrument of torture. Now he's become my tormentor. It's bad enough he's my father; if he has his way, he'll soon be my fucking son-in-law!"

Kimber massaged Gary's shoulders. "He's trying, Gary."

"I know. *Very* trying."

Kimber swiveled Gary's chair around until they faced each other. "I've watched you two go at it for fifteen years, sweetheart." Her voice still bore its customary affection, but Gary detected a new resolve in her eyes. "I'm on your side. You know that, don't you?"

"Yes."

"Well, this time you're wrong about your father. Stone cold wrong."

He looked back at her in bewildered silence.

"I understand your resentment. I do. You've explained how he treated you, and it must've hurt you terribly. But that was more than a century ago in real-time, when he was recovering from injuries of his own. You've never been to war. Neither have I. But I've heard plenty of family stories about my great-grandfather. He died in Tokyo ten years before I was born. World War Two must have been appalling, worse, I'm sure, than anything your father and my great-grandfather could even describe."

"I know that," Gary cried. "But he injured me, Kimber. He doted on my sisters and spurned me, which killed my self-esteem; he left me defenseless! Maybe even crippled me, literally. He's probably the reason I couldn't stop drinking when my mother died, why I got hooked on VR gambling when Toby left. He cost me decades of my life."

"He also gave you your life. Twice! Things were different back then. You know that. Death was inevitable and life finite. Now you have time—all the time you need! Plenty of time to do whatever you want, to make the most of all your potential. And plenty of time to let your injuries heal. He's your father. He's changed, you've changed ..." She paused and smiled. "... and you're both going to be around for a very long time; possibly even forever. It's time to let the hostility go."

"I don't know," Gary growled, his body quivering with tension and anger. "I've bottled this resentment inside so long; how can the mere fact that I came from his sperm ever inspire that kind of forgiveness?"

"Then do it for Margaret. She loves Ben and she loves you. So did your mother; *she* never stopped trying to bring you two back together." Kimber kissed Gary's lower lip. "And if that's not enough, do it for me. For the sake of my love for both of you, and more significantly, my ... well, sanity!"

Gary fought the impulse, but soon heard his own quiet laughter. "A powerful incentive, indeed. Especially when my own mental health is so intertwined with yours."

She scowled. "A couple years ago, after you and Ben talked Trip down from his comet-silly attack, you spoke of your father in glowing terms. At least for a few months. You were happy, Gary. At peace. Have you forgotten?"

"No," he conceded. "And I want to let this go. I really do. But how?"

"Talk to him. Face-to-face. Today. Tell him how you feel, and why you think you feel that way. Then listen calmly, openly; give him an opportunity to express himself. And remember, he's not the Ben Smith who mistreated you. You're blind to whom he's become. And you're not the same, either. You no longer have to prove yourself like some adolescent. So stop acting like his hurt little boy. Every living person changes. Every would heals, given time, and life. And don't forget who gave you yours."

"C'mon in, son," an obviously startled Ben Smith said, welcoming him at the door. "I must say, you just showing up like is something of a surprise, a pleasant surprise . . ."

"Got time for a private talk?"

"Always." Repressing a swell of panic, Ben escorted his son into the study and activated its soundshield. "What's up?"

"I know I owe I owe you my existence twice-over—" Gary began, reciting his rehearsed speech.

"I might owe you mine, too." I'm gushing, Ben thought. Gotta stop.

"Please. Just let me finish."

"Of course."

"I also know you've never been a malicious person. I realize you did the best you could at the time, and how hard you've tried to atone for ignoring me during those first thirty-five years." My thirty-five most formative years, Gary thought. "I understand you were suffering from a trauma that took decades to heal, maybe still hasn't healed completely, and that your attitude erupted from an ordeal you had no control over."

"All true." Ben braced himself. "I assume there's more."

"There is. For the past few hours I've been thinking about that court battle after you were frozen. If I hadn't been there myself, it would be impossible to imagine how skeptical everyone was about cryonics. And in hindsight, you still remain blind to your own ignorance, even if you never forget it. My sisters gave you up for dead, which was a rational view of things at the time. But I couldn't. You know why?"

"I figured it was because there's so much of Alice in you—in us. You're more of a scientist than most, including your sisters, I guess. You were always a thinker rather than a follower."

"I agree, and I'd like to believe it was logic that put me on Toby's side of the court battle. But today I started reexamining my motivations. My career was soaring. I was on the way to becoming one of the most famous artists in the world. And you know what the key to achieving great success in any field is?"

"Talent? Intelligence?"

Gary shook his head. "Perseverance; the ability to stay motivated, and the inability to satisfy an unquenchable obsession. That was always my secret, Dad, and it came from you."

"It did?" Ben asked, daring to believe that his son might indeed have come to make up with him. "How?"

Gary deflated these hopes like a laser spear puncturing a beach ball. "I fought side by side with Toby for only one reason: the chance to show you I wasn't the boy you thought I was, not some carbon copy of you, but my own person with aptitudes that did not spring from you. I wanted to prove you had nothing to do with my success; that my success came not because of you, but in spite of you. And I could never have done that if you were irrevocably dead. I wanted to save your life, Dad, to make sure you finally knew I didn't need you."

For a moment Ben could only stare. "I get it," he said finally. Something inside him was falling away, but he refused to let go. "That was over a century ago, Gary. What about today?"

"I need it to heal." Gary paused. "But I don't see how that can happen. Frankly, I'm scared to death there's going to be this wall between us forever."

"I see."

"I see? That's all you have to say about it?"

"Hell no, Gary, I wanted to make sure you were finished. Are you?"

"For now."

"Okay, then I'll start by thanking you for finally telling me how you feel, for not faking."

Gary said nothing.

"I know I haven't been open with you, but I didn't want to seem cloying; didn't want to rush you, or make you more nervous. But you should know that we have something in common. You've just described the greatest terror of my life: the fear that I've irreconcilably lost you."

"I'm supposed to believe that?"

"You're my only son."

"Big fucking deal. I was your only son from the day I was born," Gary fumed, again turning away from Ben. "You never appreciated anything I did. Nothing was ever good enough."

"I know." Ben strained to fight back his panic. "I was unhealthy; damaged. Hell, I couldn't even look at you back then, the same way you can't seem to look at me today. It's almost as if what I had was contagious, and you caught it." Ben instantly knew: the wrong words.

Gary's body twitched. "It was, and I did," he said. "That's how it works with parenthood, you know. Your children might not do what you tell them, but they always do what you *do*," He slammed a balled fist into an open hand. "Christ. And now you want to infect Margaret. Well, I won't let that happen!"

Ben kept silent, but his hands shook. Gary saw it.

They avoided each other's eyes, sweating and stewing, both men wanting to speak. But both also understood that without a time-out, words would be spoken in haste, more hurtful words that could never be withdrawn.

So they sat together in silence.

Several times Gary looked toward Ben, and invariably caught him staring back, but, as always, he could not discern the feeling behind his father's eyes.

Calculation or self-examination? Gary wondered.

B e n   c o n s i d e r e d   h i s future with Margaret, a future he'd counted on for some fifteen years. In his mind's eye he saw, God help him, her ripening fourteen-year-old body, almost identical to the one that had driven him crazy in their—*their?*—first spring together in 1940. He imagined her without clothes, imagined holding her naked body in his arms, feeling her perfect skin against his.

He hadn't even kissed Margaret, not *that* way, but the idea of never caressing her, never making love to her, seemed too much for his mind to integrate.

He would sooner die.

Then he considered Gary, his own flesh and blood, and tried to recreate within himself the ambiguity of his feelings over the six decades when both were conscious: six decades that had brought them to the present. An image flashed through Ben's mind of a proud antelope, temporarily distracted, suddenly forced to watch his own fawn being carried off by a jaguar, a beast he knows he is too slow to catch and too weak to stop.

But still, he would have to *try*!

Both men continued to stew.

Your children may not do what you tell them, Ben recited to himself, but they will always do what you do. Well, I forgave Jan, he thought, and Gary should forgive *me*.

Ben's eyes avoided his son's. He looked at the floor, the ceiling, his own hands; then realized that he hadn't quite forgiven everyone, had he?

Ben finally broke the silence. "Gary, I'd never marry Margaret without your blessing. Don't misunderstand: I'd want to. But I wouldn't, because I could never live with that much conflict in my life. Not happily—"

"Isn't my decision." Gary interrupted, "It's for her to decide, and you. I'm sorry I said that, Dad, truly. I shouldn't have come."

"I'm glad you did." The words seemed dredged from the pit of his stomach. "This may have been the most honest conversation we've ever had. I only wish we'd had it about fourteen decades ago."

Gary just stared at him.

"Like it or not, Gary, we're family. Granted you hate me, maybe forever, and that hurts like hell. But you're still blood from my blood, bone from my bone, mind from my mind. I have a stake in your happiness and your success.

"You and Kimber chose to love each other. I have no choice. I'll love you and pray for only good things to happen to you for all the centuries of my life, whether you return the feeling or not."

And in that instant, Ben Smith realized he would somehow have to make himself absolve a man he thought he could never forgive: the now-frozen father of three of his grandchildren.

At the very moment Ben revoked his own burden of anger toward Noah Banks, Gary gazed at his father's young face and felt a similar transformation within himself. He's right, Gary decided: It's family! It's not about me submitting to him, or who owes what to whom. It's beyond that. He can't shake me, and he never will.

He suddenly saw his father now not as his tormentor, but as his ally. An *annoying* ally, but someone who had no choice but to be on his side. Ben was like any highly evolved animal, driven by instinct to protect its young, its love overpowering, even mindless.

But he knew Ben was human, too, and unlike other animals, compelled to examine and identify his own feelings. What a wonderful, terrible thing! He also knew that other than with each other, their perspectives and emotional responses to outside forces tended to be identical. The tragic silliness of the comet-crazies had made that all too clear.

Gary remembered something that happened to him in high school in 1962 during a science lab. He'd extinguished his Bunsen burner, but neglected to turn off the gas jet. Before rekindling it, he'd turned the jet off briefly. Too briefly. To his horror, a giant arc of fire had appeared in front of him. Then, just as suddenly, the fire was gone. *Gone!*

The gas had simply burned off and disappeared.

That had been exactly like this moment, seconds ago, when his anger and pain over his father's treatment of him, during another lifetime, vanished in a flash of brilliant heat, leaving only the memory of itself behind.

SEPTEMBER 30, 2103 — The World Government sets a population target of 26 billion humans living throughout the solar system by the middle of this century. President Sims declares, "With death all but defeated, at least for now, population is expanding much more slowly than even our most conservative projections. Ironically, a large, intelligent, and highly motivated population improves our chances of surviving external threats like the early 24th century Oort/Nemesis comets — the very reason fewer of our citizens are choosing to raise children." — The Dian Fosse University in Kigali, Rwanda, reports on its successful implantation of a larynx, tongue, and nanosynthesized speech patterning in the left medulla oblongata of Boku, a mountain gorilla. While some public disapproval has dogged the project, researchers suspect that a previously untapped well of understanding and shared insights between species can be opened. Boku's first spoken word is "doughnut." — The World Health Department issues a recommendation that all citizens who have not already done so, receive permanent ocular implants at once. All implants adjust upon cerebral command to render telescopic and microscopic vision, infrared and ultraviolet detection, and off-site digital documentation, as well as the standard media-screen reception, but the newest versions also self-repair and therefore never wear out. Nearly 75 million citizens worldwide still maintain temporary implants, some of which may expire before the end of the decade.

He felt her neck against his mouth, and inhaled her perfume.

Margaret moaned and Ben's pulse quickened. Her voice, features, and scent exploded inside his head; her touch was becoming more skillful every day. They'd nearly reached the point of no return; he was getting close, and could tell that she was, too.

Then she stopped.

Why?

"Make love to me, Ben," she demanded.

"I thought we were going to wait," Ben said, chest heaving, heart pounding.

"Please. I can't wait any longer."

"You might regret it."

"I'm not a child," she said, her face flushed as though painted in red shades of resolve. "I'm nineteen years old. I love you, you love me."

"We'll be married in six weeks. Just six more weeks."

"I don't want to wait six weeks, or six minutes. I want you now."

"What about our appointment this afternoon?"

"*Because* of that."

Now Ben understood.

He kissed her and she kissed back with such urgency, such passion, it almost felt like the other Marge was kissing him—the real Marge. But only for a moment.

"Oh, my darling," he said. "If that's what you want . . ."

Part of him relieved to have it over with Margaret had saved herself for him all those years, just as she'd always promised, just as he'd been waiting for her. Sure, they'd each found release by the other's touch, and in the VR and other sensual devices they'd shared. But nineteen was too old to remain a virgin in today's world, so *that* tension had finally been lifted. Real sex felt wonderful, too; more tangible than what they'd been doing, and not nearly as uncomfortable as he'd dreaded it might be.

Yet something hadn't been right. Did he feel he'd been cheating on Marge somehow? No, that wasn't it.

Thank God Margaret hadn't inquired how he felt afterward. She must have known better than to ask.

Although they'd traveled separately, Ben, Gary, and Margaret each arrived at Neural Nanoscience Labs within a minute or two of their one-twenty P.M. appointment. Virginia and I were waiting.

"How many times have you actually performed this procedure?"

Gary asked Virginia. He knew specific-memory implantation was a brand new discipline, and didn't envision his beloved Margaret as the ideal guinea pig for it.

"Six," Virginia said, "and the last one worked, we think."

Before Gary had time to pull Margaret out the door, Ben and I laughed in unison, "She's kidding, Gary."

"Oh, you think that's funny?"

"Sorry, I can't help myself," Virginia said. "Fact is, we've done almost 1,600 of these without the slightest hitch. That doesn't mean the procedure shows identical efficacy with every subject. Just means we haven't had anyone who wasn't glad they did it."

"Explain how it works again," Gary said.

I began: "For three and a half decades we've known how to implant generic memories into human brains—as long as we were willing to lose any unique memories. Sort of like erasing a twentieth century computer's floppy disc to add new information. You could always replace an entire file on a floppy, but until around 2010 there was no way to add and subtract specific data from a file without going back inside the computer."

"Okay. I remember that."

"When we started Caching people, Virginia and I figured: Since we have to store all this information anyway, why not program our AIs to analyze each component of it? After all, the AIs from last month's line are at least a hundred times more complex than human brains."

"That way," she explained, "we'd learn how to dissect individual memories piece by piece. We could take any specific memories from one person, and implant them into another person without disrupting any of their existing memories."

I nodded. "So, after about the one thousand one hundredth Cache—"

"One thousand one hundred seventh," Virginia interruped.

I pretended to glare at her; she grinned, of course. "Okay," I said. "After 1,107 of 'em, the AIs had cataloged every molecular pattern, effectively cracking the human memory code. Big breakthrough! Obviously there's an astounding number of applications for stored memory. We hope to retrieve forgotten memories with absolute certainty, erase selected traumatic events from someone's life, even produce crude home VR movies from a person's past experiences. We can also sort a person's memories by any category we choose, and implant those memories into any other person, with whatever degree of vividness we want. That's what we plan to do today, with Margaret."

"I tried to get Alice to undergo the procedure, too," Ben explained, "but the original Alice's memories began long before I was born. Besides, she felt that without my father to share those memories—and she doesn't plan to clone him for another fifty years or so—what would be the point? She considers herself an entirely new person anyway."

"Not me." Margaret smiled lovingly at Ben. "But then, I have considerably more incentive."

"I'd marry you anyway," Ben said, "and love you forever, whether you do this or not."

"I know, but I want those memories." Margaret turned toward Virginia. "So after you implant Ben's common memories with Marge into my brain, will I recall those events as Marge or as Ben?"

"It doesn't matter," Virginia answered. "Within a week your brain will reviewpoint everything. A split second after they're imprinted, your brain will subsume them the same way it integrates any new knowledge. Human memory has always done that, which is why you can only remember certain things about each experience. Otherwise, memory would be as vivid as life itself, and you'd never be able to retain as much information as you do."

"Fantastic!" Margaret said. "Now all we have to so is figure out how to deflect the comets. After that, what could possibly be left to invent?" This was a rhetorical question, asked amidst the wrong crowd.

I couldn't resist. "Oh, we'd still be so far from finished," I said, "I barely know where to begin. But for starters, we'd need to find places for our ever-expanding populace. With nanoprocessors creating food and other necessities, we can live anywhere. Soon, we'll honeycomb the earth, and build habitats along Earth's orbit using raw materials from the asteroid belt."

"I've been studying that proposal," Gary asked. "Micromachines could create space cylinders miles long, and AIs could rotate them just fast enough to replicate Earth's gravity."

"Absolutely right," I said. "With the proper materials, landscaping, and technology, space cylinders would be virtually indistinguishable from this planet. There's enough matter in the asteroid belt alone to build habitats for half a trillion people. And we've barely begun to colonize the outer portions of this solar system. No human has ever been a light-year from Earth. Within a century, we might routinely send peopled spacecraft to other stars, and sometime this millennium, colonize their planets."

"What about energy?" Margaret asked. "Won't we run out?"

"No time soon," I assured her. "Only a billionth of the energy cast by the sun reaches Earth. And atomic energy is for all practical purposes limitless."

"Then what?" Gary asked.

"There's plenty to do," I said. "Subatomic particle manipulation might allow us to form any element from any other: true alchemy. We might even discover the unified theory of physics to help us prevent our universe's projected Big Crunch. But time is short." He laughed. "We only have a couple quintillion years left!"

"Are there any limits to what scientists can accomplish?" Gary asked.

"Of course," I answered. "The hardiest flexible materials nature permits might only be about twenty times stronger than steel. I doubt we'll ever travel or transport solids—maybe never even communicate—faster than light-speed. Under singularity conditions, nothing's predictable, and might never be. No organization, no intelligence, no imagination can conquer even a single law of physics. We'll push the very limits of those laws, but eventually, whether it's a thousand, a million, or ten billion years from now, all physical advances may cease, and not just for a year or a millennium. They'll stop forever."

"And when progress ends, what's the purpose of humanity?" Gary asked.

"Same as it's always been," Ben said. "We exist for our own joy, and to bring that joy to those we love." He gently kissed Margaret Callahan Smith, step-granddaughter, clone of his past, embodiment of his future. Then he asked Gary, "You sure you're okay with this, son?"

"If Margaret's certain, then so am I."

"I am," she said. "I intend to love and cherish your father forever."

Gary turned to Ben. "Gives the expression 'She was made for you' an almost literal meaning." He paused, wondering if his sentiment had come out as intended. "And I couldn't be happier for you both."

To Gary, the most amazing aspect of his statement was that he meant it.

NOVEMBER 1, 2104 — All of the oldest Neanderthals announce their intention to vote in this month's World Government elections. Of 612 Neanderthals currently living on Earth, only 17 have yet attained voting age. Nine say they would cast their ballots for Vice President Andreopolus were the election held today; six intend to vote for Councilor Parrino; two remain undecided. — The names Johannes Brahms, Victor Hugo, Stephen King, Christopher Reeve, Gary Franklin Smith, and John Wayne are added to the Honor Roll for the Ages Monument in Hamilton, Bermuda. The monument, designed by Lillian Upton, now bears the names of 297 artists judged by the Monument Advisory Committee to have "inspired humanity throughout history." Not counting clones, Reeve and Smith are only the 18th and 19th living persons to be so honored.

As the day began, Margaret kissed Ben the same way Marge always had: same suction, same moistness, same pressure. She gently pulled herself back, disentangling her supple, sweat-glistened body from his. "That was wonderful, Benny!" she said, and cheerfully inserted another old coin into the piggy bank by the side of their bed.

Just like Marge, Ben thought.

They'd been married forty-seven weeks, and had made love 584 times. About on schedule.

"Only thirty-six more days before we start removing them," she said.

"And how long you think it'll take us to *empty* old Porky?" Ben asked, stroking her back the way Marge had always liked to be cuddled. She sighed; he knew exactly what she wanted, as always.

"It took almost twenty months the first time we were married," she said, "but when Gary was born, it slowed us down a little. This time, we'll do it in fifteen."

"You always were up to a challenge."

She was Marge. At least in *their* minds. What a miracle!

That afternoon, Ben and Gary stood thumbing through the folios of old maps at Ashley's Antique and Knickknack Emporium in Falls Church, Virginia. The place was a bit seedy, but fascinating, offering almost-nice-wicker furniture circa 1880, precybernetic toys from the early twenty-first century, and everything in between. Prices ran the gamut, too: near-bargains to the absurdly overpriced.

Both men loved shops like this. Every time they ran across a new one, they felt as if they'd stepped through a worm hole in interstellar space, falling backward into unpredictable epochs.

Pulling out a beautifully watercolored, freehand map of 1890 Cape Cod, Gary nudged his father. "This one seems too cheap. And even better, I like it."

Ben ran his molecular scanner over Gary's selection. "Kind of amazing in a joint like this. Hasn't even been microrepaired. If you don't buy it, I will."

Gary offered a wolfish grin. "Don't hold your breath. It's already mine."

Herb Ashley ambled over. The owner was one of those very peculiar people who'd let his body age to about thirty-five before having his nanos programmed to maintain that physical aspect. Ben and Gary had seen others like Ashley, all involved in the antique collectibles business. Apparently this was done to add an aura of authenticity to their trade.

Ashley nodded his head. "Good choice, my friends." He said that to everyone.

"I'll take it," Gary said, then resumed thumbing. Ashley's register AI had already debited Gary's account and transferred ownership.

"You two check ScienceNews today?" Ashley asked, seemingly out of nowhere.

Ben shook his head.

"Bad news," Ashley declared. "Really bad. In less than 120,000 years, apparently, half the atoms in your brain and body break down. Shoot. I guess by then we'll only be halfway the same people we are today."

"Actually," Ben said, "that would be 120 *million* years."

Ashley's face brightened and his posture straightened noticeably. "Oh, thank goodness. I've been depressed all afternoon."

Ben and Gary traded glances. Both bit their tongues. This man wasn't kidding with them; he was utterly serious.

After about a minute Gary asked, "How old are you, Herb?"

"A hundred sixteen."

Ben cleared his throat. He wasn't delicate about it. "Let's see, Herb. In your lifetime, you've gone from an at-birth life expectancy of maybe seventy-nine years to a lifetime that's arguably infinite, right?"

"Well, yeah. Assuming the comets don't get me." He chuckled.

Ben immediately recognized these words as a throwaway line, almost a joke. Ten years ago, everyone had still been terrified of the comets, but these days people seemed a lot more confident that astrophysicists could eventually come up with a foolproof plan. Or if not, the nanoscientists could probably put every casualty back together.

It was amazing how easily human thinking adapted over time, Ben mused. Few could stand to shift their core views all at once. Shock led to confusion, most often temporary; then it usually rectified itself.

"So," Ben asked—he couldn't help it—"you were worried that in a thousand times as long as you've already lived, there wouldn't be any quantum breakthroughs?"

Ashley glowered. "What's your point?"

Herb Ashley's two customers laughed so long and so hard that he finally asked them to leave.

JANUARY 14, 2125 — All life signs from the nine mammalian and six avian subjects on Orion II continue to register in the normal range after 16 days in space. The lightsail-powered spaceship has already achieved a velocity of .39 light-speed. Orion's grand tour of our solar system will last five more months and reach a maximum speed of .84 L.S. WASA officials anticipate full recovery of all 15 subjects, clearing the way for humaned flights late next year and journeys to other solar systems within the next few decades. — ATI Co-Chairpersons Randall Petersen Armstrong and his wife, Maya Gale, appear close to perfecting a brain circuitry regimen that will replace nerve impulses with electrical energy, allowing humans to think at computer speed. The WFDA announces it stand ready to rule on the efficacy of the Armstrong-Gale Process immediately upon consummation, perhaps as early as next month. It seems likely that almost every human in the solar system will purchase the product once it becomes available. AIs project that this innovation will greatly improve odds for indefinite human survival against the forces of nature.

I've long enjoyed collecting and toying with old computer programs, ancient floppies, and old CDs. In data of the past, I often find inspired nuggets to help place the here and now and my visions of the future into proper perspective. What I like best is to dump the encoded material into my AIs, especially the new mind-reading Random Image Organizers. What emerges always comes as a surprise. The thing might tell me a story, draw out visuals, create a VR movie, even spin an essay.

I knew tonight would be extraordinary, a night that for 99.9967 percent of human history would have been unimaginable, an absurd dream of only the most ambitious (or overmedicated) science fiction writer. And yet this was no dream, no result of magic or wishful thinking. Tonight we would celebrate the result of tenacious will and teamwork throughout human civilization, combined with luck and the inevitable consequence of fortunate coincidence.

The occasion put me in mind of my long-lost parents, of course, the times they'd missed and the ultimate vindication of nearly all they'd believed. I'd been obsessing about them even more than usual recently and, with Stephanie's help, had just reached a watershed decision. Impelled by the choice we'd made, I began digging through a small box containing a multitude of George Crane Jr.'s recorded thoughts and experiences from days prior to the university of the central archives. The old storage units varied widely in size, of course, from clunky twentieth century floppy discs right through the hundred-gig, half-inch-diameter datacoins of the early teens.

I came upon an old CD ROM inscribed with the date July 1998 and penned on its faded label a single word: "Coincidence."

Dad had been a writer of essays, great and small, even from childhood days. Dad—childhood? I smiled, a million scattered thoughts racing through my head. Picking up my antique Digital Language Universal Translator, I dumped Dad's old disc into it, then swept the cerebral image scanner across my brow, thinking of all that once had been and of all that might soon come.

I looked at my primary display screen and read words my own father had composed 127 years ago, long before I was born:

> *Coincidence is the inadvertent ally of mysticism. If enough potatoes grow in the world, some of them are bound to look like Jesus Christ or Elvis Presley.*
>
> *Chances are that every person you see in public is somehow connected with a person related to someone you know. Such discoveries, while amusing, do not mean fate intends the two of you to become interwoven in a great enterprise.*
>
> *If every human being on Earth tosses a unique marble into the ocean, some will eventually find their way back to their original owners. With every breath you take, you inhale molecules once part of nearly every other person who has ever lived; a new fragment of Benjamin Franklin enters your lungs every five seconds. Put fifty random people in a room, and invariably at least two will have the same birthday. Think about enough friends you haven't seen in years, and one of them is bound to call you—or die that day. Wait long enough, and you'll see a solar eclipse. Give enough people mango juice, and some of them will win the lottery, experience spontaneous cancer remissions, or earn a gold medal in the Olympics. If a million baseball players alternate between red and green underwear, some of them will lose very red-underwear game and always win wearing green.*
>
> *Even coincidences themselves are not so amazing when one considers how many trillions of different kinds are possible. Coincidences occur as simple numerical probability; it would be far more amazing if they did not occur. Yet through the ages, human beings have used the ubiquity of coincidence to sell their snake oil or invoke the illusion of divine intent.*

Gary had insisted on entering the room first. Now Ben understood why. In mild shock, he flashed a bemused smile, then occupied the seat of honor, nestling snugly between Alice and Margaret.

Over the past months the two women had been planning tonight's surprise two-hundredth-birthday banquet.

One gigantic table, microconstructed moments earlier to permit all thirty-six human guests a clear view of each other, filled the restaurant's private dining room. Food and tonic nanoassemblers built into the table were programmed to serve each guest instantly from an astounding six terabyte menu, while tranquil outdoor scenery illumined the wallscreens, and quiet custom-synthesized music lifted through the flawlessly blended atmosphere.

Already seated were Ben's wife, his mother, four children, six grandchildren, nine great-grandchildren (including Alica and me), two great-great grandchildren, eight spouses or former spouses of his offspring (including Brandon, Virginia, Caleb, Noah, Kimber, and Stephanie Van Winkle, my former assistant—who three years earlier had become my wife), Epstein, Toby, Father Steve, and of course our dogs: both Wendy-girls.

Ben had been the last to arrive.

How long have you known about tonight's ambush? Ben telepathed Gary.

His Cerebral Implant Nanotransceiver system, ideal for such gatherings, permitted private conversation even in noisy crowds. This biological upgrade, partially based on Cache research at our Neuro Nano-Science Labs, consisted of approximately seventeen billion nanomachines swallowed in a small pill, then self-deployed throughout the brain. Royalties from this invention had allowed Virginia and me to expand our business to forty-six employees, and at the same time reduce our own working hours— a fact that had played a role in the decision I intended to announce next. Although our royalty percentage was infinitesimal, nearly every human throughout the solar system had purchased the product.

Ben was so used to the eleven-month-old innovation that he barely had to think about the destination of his transmitted thoughts.

About a month, Gary confessed.

Ben declared out loud. "We must've seen each other two dozen times in the last month, and not even a hint about it!"

"So now you know I can keep a secret. Happy birthday, Dad."

"Thanks, son. Without you, I wouldn't be here at all. In more ways than one."

Gary smiled, without effort.

I was nervous as hell, so when I rose to speak, I put my hands on my wife's shoulders. "I have an announcement, something I've been saving for tonight's celebration." Everyone stopped talking. I grinned at my great-grandfather. "Stephanie and I are going to clone my parents."

Ben's knees seemed to buckle. "But how?" he demanded.

"How? I'll bring them back as infants." I laughed, then answered his real question: "I commissioned a search of my parents' medical records, and found a usable skin sample of my mother from 2011. The AIs interpolated Dad's genetic code from Mom's and mine. Chance of error's less than one in four million."

Ben collapsed into his chair, his face radiant.

Stephanie kissed me, then added, "We figure it's about time Trip nurtured something more than his wounds . . ." Wendy II snatched a canapé from my hand and swallowed it in a single gulp. ". . . and our dogs."

Everyone laughed. Rebecca and Katie embraced. Ben rewarded me with a wide smile. Then Gary hugged me and whispered a simple, "Thanks."

This moment had to be bittersweet for everyone there; it certainly was for me. An injury would finally be diminished, though never healed. "What a perfect gift," Ben finally managed. "You'll make a wonderful father, Trip."

I felt my face redden, more from fear than embarrassment. No turning back now "I'll sure do my best."

Gary stood and lifted his wineglass. "I propose a toast to the man who taught me through example the two most valuable qualities a parent can demonstrate to a child: logic and perseverance. The key components of a successful life."

"Thank you," Ben said. "But I have to disagree, Gary. Two even more valuable qualities are those which I was pleased to discover in *you*: compassion and forgiveness. Toby, do you remember what I used to say, back when we were teenagers, about every act of kindness?"

"Of course. That any act of kindness, or spite, is like a stone pitched into the sea." Toby explained: "Both throw off ever widening waves."

"You said that, Dad?" Gary asked.

"Yep. But I managed to let myself forget it for about thirty-five years."

"Well, thirty-five years isn't such a long time anymore. Kimber taught me that. I've been thinking a lot about human kindness, and I agree with you." Gary looked first toward Father Steve, then at Epstein. "Which is why Jesus Christ was such an important philosopher. Whether or not you believe he was really the son of God, his teachings might well have saved the human race. I suspect forgiveness may be our most life-preserving characteristic."

Alica wrapped an arm around the shoulder of her grandfather, Noah Banks. Noah smiled, then nodded at the man whose chance at life he'd tried to eliminate; the man who, despite that, had revived him twenty-five years ago. Ben returned the nod.

Father Steve grinned. *Yes,* he transmitted to the entire room, *whether or not Jesus was the son of God is irrelevant. His philosophy is what mattered.*

"Probably true at that," Epstein agreed aloud. "Without Christ's doctrine of forgiveness, we might've self-destructed a century ago. Philosophy's a powerful preserver of our species."

Ben's mouth flew open in amazement. *Sure, you've mellowed over the years, Carl. Yet who would have ever expected you to endorse the value of religion? I must be dreaming.*

Many laughed.

Epstein nodded. "Like your widening waves, Ben. That which leaves you is that which finds you."

"Yes," Ben said. "Everything influences everything else, given enough time. Everything is intertwined, from human history to the trajectories of celestial objects."

Ben detected a few titters from the group, but assumed they came more from habit than anxiety. Hardly anyone worried about comets anymore; confidence in science and human ingenuity seemed to have permeated world culture, at least for now.

"I know that's true," Kimber said. "My family's proof of it. Ever since I was a little girl, growing up in the very early twenty-first century, I knew I wanted to live in America. You know why, Ben?"

"Tell me."

"It started with my grandfather, my father's father, who was just a child himself when the Nazis occupied France. He was seven when the war ended, and nine when the Marshall Plan was adopted. Half a century later he still remembered the packages of food that tasted a hundred times better because everyone who got them had been so hungry. He told me how he felt about the Americans who sent those packages, such kind people who'd liberated France at great sacrifice, then after returning home from that victory, in the midst of their own daily troubles and concerns, made sure the children of their allies were sustained until their economy could recover. What loyalty! he'd thought.

"But years later he was amazed to learn that Americans had also fed and helped rebuild the economies of Germany and Italy; the same countries whose armies had sent so many of your sons home in coffins."

"And that's why you decided to move here?" Ben said. "I can thank George Marshall for the daughter-in-law who sent my son back to me?"

"There's more," Kimber said. "When I moved to Japan after my first divorce, I heard other stories. We Japanese compartmentalize our views well. Sure, we remember the Americans firebombed Tokyo, and dropped the atomic bomb on Hiroshima and Nagasaki—our own comets from the blue. But we also know these allied occupiers, especially the Americans, were fair with us once the war actually ended. My great-grandmother described how American soldiers would receive care packages from the Red Cross. Yet she's rarely seen Americans themselves consuming anything from those packages. They'd give it all away to the street children and starving women, the loved ones of their enemies. In the face of crisis, these men acted so that all might survive."

"Yes," Ben said, remembering the words of Colonel Rand, his commanding officer at Purgatory, on the day they had learned of Japan's surrender: *Grudges just ain't part of the American way. So remember that, and do us proud.*

"But the most impressive story of all," Kimber continued, "was about my great-grandfather, a man I never knew. He died in 1987, ten years before I was born. When the war ended, most men of his rank committed suicide. He was the commandant of a prisoner-of-war camp, and had brutally interrogated an American sailor to get information about their ship movements."

Ben froze.

"Following the orders of his general," Kimber went on, "he'd tortured and permanently maimed many of that sailor's friends and shipmates. Yet that same American convinced my great-grandfather that his own life was too precious to destroy. An American's forgiveness is responsible for the fact that I exist at all. That's why I decided to live here, and why forgiveness is a concept I value so highly."

"Oh? Tell me, where did your great-grandfather serve? What camp?" Ben asked, his voice flat, the best acting job of his life.

"He was *taisa* Hiro Yamatsuo, stationed at Futtsu. Why? Did you know him?"

"Know him? Not really," Ben said. The Truth Machines all stayed green. "But I know his great-granddaughter, and that's enough to know he was worthy."

Kimber smiled. So did Ben. Then he looked at Epstein, who wore an expression proclaiming that maybe he'd just seen God.

Ben glanced toward Toby and winked.

Dear Toby, he transmitted, *you fought off all those superstitions you were raised to believe; fought them off through sheer force of will. But when I asked you to gamble on what must have struck you as quack science, you never thought twice about it. You accepted a sketchy premise that helping me die was the only way to save my life.*

Toby smiled, giving his head a single nod.

Then Ben considered the fates of Sam and Mack, and the original Marge and Alice, each of whom had also given him the gift of life yet did not survive their own incarceration in decaying bodies.

But at least he had the new Alice and Marge: children of a new era, yet familiar, too, each a bewitching composite of two identities, almost like another kind of being.

He looked across the table toward his granddaughter Katie, noble and wise, once imprisoned by the same disease that had destroyed Marge; but Katie had survived by assuming rational influence over her life while she still could.

He contrasted Katie's fate with that of her brother, his grandson George, my father, whom history now regarded as a warrior for humanism and logic, incinerated as a collateral casualty in a lesser war he'd neither waged nor understood.

Now Ben gazed toward me, and the thoughts he transmitted nearly brought me to tears: *Even in Final Death, George granted an incalculable gift to our family and to the world: a son, injured by his parents' murders, but also inspired to achievement. A legacy far beyond mere DNA.*

As he mourned lost loved ones, Ben also relished the celebration, here among so many of his offspring and their loving partners in marriage. He found a special joy and justice in welcoming Brandon Butters into his family, and in reconciling with Noah Banks, father of Sarah, David, and Michael, grandfather of Alica, great-grandfather of Lysa and Devon.

Then he gave thanks to a God he would never deny or fathom for the far easier pleasure of forgiving his three daughters, who, although they'd never stopped loving him, had once foolishly abandoned him for dead. Indeed, Ben felt an astonished gratitude that all four of his children were with him tonight, especially Gary.

Finally here, if only in spirit, was Hiro Yamatsuo, whose code of *bushido*, his blind loyalty to a deified emperor, had cost all semblance of rationality, taking him to the brink of a suicide that even Ben, the colonel's tormented prisoner, had regarded as too evil a punishment for crimes committed in search of doubtful honor. And now, somehow, through an accidental sequence spanning one and a half centuries, Colonel Yamatsuo had returned the kindness through progeny, when his great-granddaughter Kimber restored to Ben his only son.

Yes, he thought. All of us who arrived too soon upon this earth have suffered the senseless bondage of Purgatory.

Ben stood, eyes sweeping the room. The legion of his extended family began to rise, and those he loved as blood stood with them. Generation upon generation of Smiths, all alive, all together tonight. Soon many more would join their number. And somehow he knew he would live to greet them all.

"I stand here before you in celebration of my two hundredth birthday, a thing quite impossible even a few decades ago. Though now the rarest of events, I hope this bicentennial marking of a human birth will soon become noteworthy only in its commonness. And it will, unless we lose sight of who and what we are: human beings, uniquely able to examine the nature of our own existence."

Ben raised a champagne glass, first to his eyes and then to the full extension of his arm, and spoke words that were his alone to speak:

"This battle for life is nearly won. All that stands between us and eternal life is fear and gullibility: Dread of the unknown forges faith in the unknowable. Confronted by lost security, we overreact, and too often we self-destruct. But not you, dear ones. Not anymore.

"So what shall we do with our hard-won prize? Consume or build? Slumber or advance? Withdraw into pods or soar through the universe? I cannot speak for the world, but for you gathered here, yes, I would dare."

Ben Smith tipped his glass toward the assemblage, and each of us felt his salute. "The treasure is yours," he said. "Now go and live it."

Would You Want to Live Forever?

Most of us wonder what will become of the human race. Advances in technology could result in our self-destruction, our spiritual and intellectual stagnation, or even a fantastic heaven on earth. Here I have presented an optimistic view of the future, but perhaps not as optimistic as it might seem. Human life has been steadily improving, on average, for centuries.

It does seem clear that any twenty-second-century world that you and I could actually reach would have to possess the spirit, though not the specifics, of the world I've drawn. For human beings to be revived on a wholesale basis, the ultimate value of human life as a philosophical axiom is prerequisite. Any society with such science at its command could have no other reason to revive humans from the ice. And if the human race self-destructs, those in suspension will never know the difference.

But would those of us accustomed to twentieth century life enjoy even a utopian future?

All change takes getting used to, yet we may have good reason to adapt. Just imagine how today's civilization would seem to those who had lived five centuries ago. After the initial trauma wore off, former citizens of the 1500s would come to appreciate modern life as itself a form of utopia. Despite its many problems, our world is an astounding improvement over theirs.

What would it be worth to you to glimpse, and perhaps inhabit, our world of a century or more from now?

I suspect we walk among the last few generations of mortal humans. Perhaps our great-great-grandchildren, grandchildren, or even our children will stave off death long enough to see the final defeat of aging. Most likely, however, we will not. Worse yet, once we die it is only a matter of time, and generally not much of it, before we, and nearly everything we value, are forgotten. Yet hope endures for those of us born too soon, now that a bridge might well extend across the chasm of time to whatever curative marvels await humanity on the other side.

Over the past two years, while researching this novel, I immersed myself in the culture of the cryonicists. I subscribed to their newsletters and e-mail lists, monitored their news groups, joined various organizations, and devoured countless books and Web sites on cryonics and nanotech. I've corresponded and spoken with pioneers of cryonics, always trying to keep an open mind. I've also listened to and read the often well-reasoned arguments of detractors, skeptics, and cynics.

Will Cryonics Work?

This is not an easy question, but there is reason for hope. Indeed, the answer may well be contained in a second question: *Is repair at the molecular level possible?* The answer is yes. Nature herself proves it.

And when will molecular technology become available? That is unknowable, of course, but time is on our side. Liquid nitrogen temperature will hold cells in near-perfect stasis for thousands of years.

Half a century ago, most scientists deemed space travel unfeasible, and some contented that the sound barrier would never be broken. Many doctors, forty years ago, considered heart transplants scientifically impossible. Who, even thirty years ago, could have imagined today's laptop computers, omnipresent cellular phone systems, or the Internet? And when I wrote this story in 1996, many biologists believed it scientifically impossible to clone an adult mammal.

Is it imaginable, even likely, that within the next few centuries we will learn to repair damaged cell structures molecule by molecule, either through nanotechnology or any other scientific discipline from an infinite array of possibilities? What do you think?

At first I was skeptical. But to paraphrase a line from this novel, the cannons of science thunder from the side of the cryonicists. I considered the immortalist's metaphor (or is it just metaphor?) that we all suffer from a terminal disease. Cryonic suspension is the only experimental treatment available. The question to ask ourselves is simply this: *Would I rather be part of the experimental group, or the control group?*

The alternative being death, whatever that may mean, only cryonics offers genuine hope, a realistic chance for revival and rejuvenation; perhaps even immortality. Such a prize, however likely or improbable one might deem its attainment, ought to be worthy of substantial investment in money and time. It seems the height of arrogance to insist that cryonics cannot work simply because science does not yet possess the ability to revive frozen mammals. By the time medical science possesses the technology to repair freezing damage, we will most likely know how to reverse aging as well, and thus no longer need cryonics. Eventually, I signed up.

In case *the hopeful ice* is an option you would consider for yourself and those you love, this section offers advice which, of course, you should accept or reject as your own common sense dictates.

INVESTIGATE: Here is a list of recommended books, Web sites, newsletters, magazines, news groups, and other sources of information. I adapted many of the concepts in this novel from ideas encountered in these fascinating publications:

BOOKS: *The Prospect of Immortality,* by Robert C.W. Ettinger. Published by Doubleday in the early 1960s, this is the book that started it all. Although the time frame has not progressed as rapidly as predicted, the concepts are presented with accessibility, humor, and great intelligence. (Note: This book is hard to find, but generally available from Alcor and the Cryonics Institute, both listed below. Also recommended for adventurous readers, Ettinger's sequel: *Man into Superman.*)

Engines of Creation, by Eric Drexler. (Also available free on the World Wide Web at: http://www.asiapac.com/EnginesOfCreation/) First published during the mid-1980s, EOC is an amazing book on nanotechnology. Clear, concise, easy to understand, and brilliant. I consider *Engines of Creation* one of the best books ever written on any field of science. Trade paperback published by Anchor Books, 1987.

The Demon-Haunted World, by Carl Sagan. A logical treatise on the differences between science and superstition. Random House, 1995.

Virus of the Mind, by Richard Brodie. An accessible and entertaining book about memetics, the science that attempts to explain how people become enslaved by advertising, religion, cults, mysticism, and other "memes." Integral Press, 1996.

OTHER SOURCES: *CryoNet:* A free electronic forum on cryonics. To sub-scribe, send an e-mail to: majordomo@cryonet.org with the following mes-sage in the body (not the subject line) of your e-mail: "subscribe cryonet"

Cryonics, Alcor's excellent quarterly magazine. Subscriptions, $15 per year U.S., $20 Canada and Mexico, $25 overseas. Subscribers might also wish to receive *The Alcor Phoenix,* which comes out eight times per year, for an additional $20 U.S., $25 all other countries. Alcor, 7895 E. Acoma Dr., Suite 110, Scottsdale AZ 85260

sci.cryonics: The cryonics news group on Usenet.

www.alcor.org: Alcor's Web site, with links to many other cryonics and nanotechnology sites on the World Wide Web.

Extropy, a fascinating quarterly magazine about advanced and future technologies and their uses in overcoming human limits. Subscription rate: $18 per year. Extropy Institute, 13428 Maxella Avenue #273, Marina Del Rey, CA 90232. e-mail: maxmore@primenet.com

www.firstimmortal.com: Explore *The First Immortal* Web site, and post your comments on the discussion forum. I intend to visit this site myself from time to time, and respond to many of the messages.

CHOOSE AN ORGANIZATION: The following six cryonics organiza-tions all appear to be operated by reputable, competent, and conscientious individuals:

Alcor Life Extension Foundation. Nonprofit, tax exempt. The largest cryonics facility in the world. Founded 1972. Current rates: $120,000 whole body or $50,000 neurosuspension. May be funded with a life insurance policy. See "quickquote" listing below. Address: 7895 E. Acoma Dr., Suite 110, Scottsdale AZ 85260-6916. Phone (602) 922-9013 (800) 367-2228 Fax (602) 922-9027. e-mail: info@alcor.org for general requests. Web site: http://www.alcor.org

American Cryonics Society. P. O. Box 1509, Cupertino, CA 95105 For information on joining, and on services they provide, telephone (415) 254-2001, (800) 523-2001, or e-mail: cryonics@earthlink.net Web site: http://home.earthlink.net/I~cryonics

Cryocare. Nonprofit, hires some for-profit companies to perform sus-pensions and storage. Not tax exempt. Current rates, under most circum-stances: $125,000 full body; $58,500 neuro. May be funded with life insurance. For more information, call toll-free 1-800-TOP-CARE (1-800-867-2273). For inquiries via U.S. mail: CryoCare Foundation, Suite 3410

Northeast Plaza, 1313 N. Market St., Wilmington, DE 19801-1151. e-mail: cryocare@cryocare.org Web site: http://www.cryocare.org/cryocare/

Cryonics Institute. Nonprofit. Incorporated 1976. Probably your best bet if your finances are limited. Current suspension fee: only $28,000 whole body. May be funded with life insurance. Address: 24355 Sorrentino Court, Clinton Township, MI 48035. Telephone (810) 791-5961, phone/fax (810) 792-7062, e-mail: ettinger@aol.com or cryonics@msn.com

International Cryonics Foundation. Address: 1430 North El Dorado Street, Stockton, CA 95202. For information, write or telephone (800) 524-4456 or (209) 463-0429.

Trans Time, Inc. (for-profit) Address: 3029 Teagarden Street, San Leandro, CA 94577. For more information, telephone (510) 297-5577 or e-mail: quaife@math.berkeley.edu

DON'T PROCRASTINATE: If you decide to sing up for cryonics, the process is not easy. Yet neither is it particularly difficult once you make up your mind to confront each roadblock with determination. We humans are barnacled with traditions; rigged with a genetic propensity to accept and succumb to cultural norms, one of which is the acceptance of death's inevitability. Furthermore, most people do not enjoy thinking about death or any of its aspects, and dealing with a cryonics organization's paperwork—obtaining all the necessary signatures, obscure information, and documentation—forces us to do just that.

Begin your investigation of cryonics immediately. Call two or more cryonics organizations to get their information packets. When they arrive, read them carefully and promptly. Don't be discouraged. Keep reminding yourself of the astounding potential payoff versus the nominal cost in time and money. Make your decision in a rational and timely manner, and if you decide in favor of cryonics, grit your teeth and get it done.

PROTECT YOUR MONEY: Every major study ever conducted on the connection between the two confirms that increased wealth improves one's chances of survival. If you are willing to work hard, live below your means, and invest the difference wisely, you will likely live longer, maintain sufficient means to afford suspension for yourself and your family, and perhaps even have funds left over to place in trust for your eventual revival.

Often it is most frugal to purchase a life insurance policy, naming your cryonics organization as beneficial owner. If you are on the Internet, you can get competitive quotes from numerous competing companies through Quickquote, at: http://www.quickquote.com For example: A forty-four-year-old male in perfect health can purchase a $125,000 term policy for as little as $277.50 per year, although most cryonicists prefer to buy a whole-life policy, which is more expensive upfront, but often more economical in the long run.

If you are financially strapped, you now have new incentive to cure your self-destructive ways. Make up your mind to reform immediately! I recommend *The Only Investment Guide You'll Ever Need* (Harcourt Brace, 1996) by Andrew Tobias, available at most bookstores, or from www.amazon.com Fun to read, easily understandable, this book offers sage guidance about all aspects of money management. You can also catch Tobias's daily financial advice column free on the Internet, at www.ceres.com

STAY HEALTHY: Every day you survive with mind and memory intact increases your odds of immortality. Cryonic preservation techniques will no doubt continue to improve, so the longer you live before being frozen (assuming your mind and memory remain sound), the more likely you are to be revived with your identity intact. Thus the importance of maintaining your health takes on a new dimension.

Beware of quackery, mysticism, and sloppy science. You can't believe everything you read, even in the *New York Times*, but the odds of finding accuracy there are considerably better than in the supermarket tabloids. The same rules apply to all other health publications. I generally recommend mainstream magazines, books, and newsletters about health and nutrition, because information found in most "new age" and fringe publications tends to be less reliable.

Health and *Prevention* magazines are excellent sources of health-related information. *Consumer Reports* publishes an outstanding health newsletter. My favorite book on health, exercise, and nutrition is *Living Lean* (Simon and Schuster, 1997) by Larry North.

A few more suggestions: Practice moderation in your diet and other health habits. Learn to work with your doctor(s), prepare for each visit, and keep a list of intelligent questions to ask. Proactive patients receive a much greater benefit from the doctor-patient relationship than do passive patients. Exercise regularly but try not to overexert. People who walk three to five miles a day live as long, on average, as marathon runners. Do not succumb to fad diets and other health-related frauds, which are omnipresent.

And don't forget to exercise your mind, too!

YOU DON'T LIVE IN A VACUUM: If you can afford to, support cryonics and biotech research. Join a local cryonics chapter if you can find one near you. Otherwise, start one.

Perhaps most important of all, subvert mysticism by tactfully debunking it whenever you can. We denizens of the twentieth century are drowning in new-age pronouncements "proving" the existence of life beyond the physical. But life's countless coincidences in no way prove (or disprove) the existence of an afterlife. In fact, the only thing coincidences prove is the law of probabilities.

The next time someone mentions some mystical or new-age book, belief system, or organization, try to get them to read *The First Immortal*, or any of the books listed earlier in this section.

All humans are entitled to their own opinions, but you can help undermine mysticism by encouraging others to learn to think for themselves. Immortalists will have to change the world's view of death, one person at a time.

Never be afraid to tell your friends and loved ones about cryonics, but expect some skepticism. It's not necessary to convince them, yet how much better are your own chances if your loved ones truly understand that cryonics is what you want? And how much improved are all of our odds when the cultural attitude about death has changed throughout the world from one of resignation and despair to optimism and hope?

Perhaps you and I will meet a century or more from now.

Best wishes and long life.

—Jim Halperin